HOUSE OF CARAVANS

HOUSE OF CARAVANS

~ a novel ~

SHILPI SUNEJA

MILKWEED EDITIONS

Published in 2023 by Milkweed Editions
Printed in Canada
Cover design by Mary Austin Speaker
Cover photo provided by the Philadelphia Museum of Art
Author photo by Matt Eames
23 24 25 26 27   5 4 3 2 1

Library of Congress Cataloging-in-Publication Data

Names: Suneja, Shilpi, author.
Title: House of caravans / Shilpi Suneja.
Description: Minneapolis : Milkweed Editions, 2023. | Includes
  bibliographical references. | Summary: "Moving back and forth from the
  tumultuous years surrounding Partition to the era of renewed global
  sectarianism following 9/11, this extraordinary historical novel
  portrays a family and nations divided by the living legacy of
  colonialism"-- Provided by publisher.
Identifiers: LCCN 2022052518 (print) | LCCN 2022052519 (ebook) | ISBN
  9781639550142 (hardcover) | ISBN 9781639550159 (ebook)
Subjects: LCGFT: Historical fiction. | Novels.
Classification: LCC PS3619.U5634 H68 2023 (print) | LCC PS3619.U5634
  (ebook) | DDC 813/.6--dc23/eng/20230206
LC record available at https://lccn.loc.gov/2022052518
LC ebook record available at https://lccn.loc.gov/2022052519

Milkweed Editions is committed to ecological stewardship. We strive to align our book production practices with this principle, and to reduce the impact of our operations in the environment. We are a member of the Green Press Initiative, a nonprofit coalition of publishers, manufacturers, and authors working to protect the world's endangered forests and conserve natural resources. *House of Caravans* was printed on acid-free 100% postconsumer-waste paper by Friesens Corporation.

To my mother, Neena Wahi
and
to the memory of my grandfather,
Ram Saran Das Wahi

CONTENTS

Prologue | August 1947 ✦ 1

August 2002 ✦ 6
April 1943 ✦ 24
August 2002 ✦ 53
September 1943 ✦ 56
August 2002 ✦ 78
September 1943 ✦ 84
August 2002 ✦ 95
January 1944 ✦ 102
August 2002 ✦ 113
September 1944 ✦ 128
August 2002 ✦ 162
June 1945 ✦ 175
February 1946 ✦ 180
August 2002 ✦ 193
August 1946 ✦ 207
August 2002 ✦ 231
March 1947 ✦ 236
August 2002 ✦ 271
September 1947 ✦ 274
August 2002 ✦ 302

Bibliography ✦ 307
Acknowledgments ✦ 309

If only somehow you could have been mine, what wouldn't
        have happened in the world?

I'm everything you lost. You won't forgive me.

My memory keeps getting in the way of your history.

There is nothing to forgive. You won't forgive me.

. . . .

If only somehow you could have been mine,

what would not have been possible in the world?

—AGHA SHAHID ALI, "FAREWELL"

HOUSE OF

CARAVANS

Prologue | August 1947

Two days after the birth of the nation, Chhote Nanu races toward the Lahore-Amritsar-Lahore Express. But before he can shove his way inside, the cargo staring back from the benches stops him dead in his tracks. He won't be taking the train to free India. For once he is glad for his lateness. Not glad, no. For the most part, Chhote Nanu is numb. But in a small chamber of his heart, he is pleading with a fate that has spared him once to spare him one more time.

He brackets the golden-haired boy against his body, covers the boy's eyes. But it's too late. They have both seen a sight they will never forget: mothers and fathers, wives and husbands, grandparents and children, especially the children, even the ones in the wombs, all undone. No one stirs. No one is left alive. The train is no longer a train, but a tidal wave of blood. In Punjab, the land of five rivers, a sixth is born.

The boy's green-blue-green eyes demand an answer. But Chhote Nanu has no words to speak, his throat closed as though over a chicken bone.

The boy's skin burns with fever, his body shivers like a telegraph needle poised on a piece of bad news. *My little boy.* Chhote Nanu buries the child's nose in his neck. A cricket trapper, all knees, and sprightly on most occasions, the boy feels like deadweight, his bones dense with fear. Chhote Nanu feels he could crumble under the weight of a child. His own short legs, bulked from jail labor, won't stop wobbling.

On the second night of their escape, he runs once again, abandoning the man-made routes of railway lines and roads, toward the lavender and honey predawn sky. In the distance, there are fields of wheat, corn, millet, mustard. No limbs, no cut-off noses, no wide-open eyes.

But to leave the city, they must traverse it again. The old Mall Road, the civil station, the hundred windows of Nedous Hotel. One rainy afternoon, under the blue awnings, the boy had heard Judy Garland on the gramophone. He presses Chhote Nanu's finger. *Do you remember?* Chhote Nanu, who remembers, presses back. The city is no longer theirs—new things swallow old ones—stone colonnades disappear behind posters of the national army, which disappear behind banners of the new party that has birthed the new nation. It is best to say goodbye and move on.

A while later, they reach the refugee camp.

"We are safe now," Chhote Nanu tells the boy. "We are among people of our sort, waiting to cross the border to the other side." There is comfort in numbers, he tells himself, there is comfort in the thousand canvas tents pegged in an orderly fashion, as far as the eye can see. This is what the mountains look like up close, he tells the child. A euphemism, a lie. Rich men in cravats await their caravans of cars, haggle over jeeps for hire; the poor haggle over mules. They hear cattle wailing, utensils clanging, people everywhere.

The refugees stare at the golden-haired boy with interest. Chhote Nanu pulls up his shirt, wraps the child around his frame, hides the boy under the shirt. He fears the living more than the dead.

In the distance, he sees army trucks, six in all, each vehicle surrounded by crowds clamoring to get on. The fittest push through, the men haul themselves on roofs, the women press inside. On the roof of one of the vehicles, like a star in the night sky, Chhote Nanu spots two pale hands waving, his big brother's.

"Praji!" Chhote Nanu shouts, beating through the crowds toward the trucks. "Wait for me! Don't leave me behind."

✦

From across the field, Barre Nanu sees his brother, all of him intact, his wild hair, his jaunty shuffle, his rumpled oversized shirt. The sound that escapes Barre Nanu is an infinite laugh. His body laughs with the joy of an insomniac waking from a deep sleep. The little fool with his wayward ways and poetic disposition is alive, and Barre Nanu aches to hold him and tell him all that is trivial and treacherous and vital in the world.

✦

Chhote Nanu pushes through the crowd. The caravan of peasant men and women, city dwellers and merchants, heckles and shouts; but Barre Nanu's yell shuts them up.

"Let him through, that is my brother come back from the dead, went to prison for the country while the whole lot of you slept."

Chhote Nanu elbows his way forward, both arms wrapped around the child clinging to his body.

Barre Nanu's hungry hands reach for his brother. "I thought the English woman swallowed you whole."

Chhote Nanu covers the child's ears, the only surviving memory of the woman he loved. Loves.

"Who is that?" Barre Nanu points to the boy's golden hair poking through Chhote Nanu's shirt.

"No one." Chhote Nanu climbs onto the truck. He pleads with the passengers to make room.

The caravan curses even as it squeezes and coils like a boa constrictor.

Chhote Nanu lifts his shirt to reveal a boy clinging to his chest. "*Hari Om,*" an old man says, both in shock and as a benediction to guard their journey. Chhote Nanu settles the child between his legs, puts his hands over his golden hair. There is nothing to see here, his eyes say to the men around him. There is nothing to see, he wants to tell his brother.

But Barre Nanu isn't easily deterred. "Whose child have you stolen?"

The question causes the boy to dig his head into his protector's chest.

Chhote Nanu pats his head. "In times of worry, we pray."

"La Ilaha," the boy mutters, "Muhammad ur Rasul Allah."

A young man with a nascent unibrow spits onto the ground. "*Eh*

Bhai, this truck is headed to India," he tells Chhote Nanu, as if he doesn't know. "You want to get off at the next stop."

Some of the men nod in agreement. Best if Chhote Nanu and the boy and their prayers remain on this side of the border. More men chime their displeasure. Only fair for Muslim prayers to stay back in Pakistan, and Hindu ones to migrate to India. They roll up their sleeves in indignation, ready to chuck Chhote Nanu and the boy off the truck.

Below them, the driver, oblivious to the quarrel on the roof, shifts the engine to a higher gear.

Barre Nanu grabs his brother's wrist. "Who is this boy? Who are you throwing your life away for?" The boy has a nose like the nib of a pen, eyes that are blue and green, a faint, carefree brow; he bears no physical resemblance to the wide-nosed, big-lipped Chhote, his brow perpetually knotted like he's withholding a grievance. Why, at such a time when empathy costs more than diamonds, Barre Nanu wonders, would his brother give it away to the first English child he found on the streets? "Little boy, who is your father? Where is your mother?"

The questions bring the boy to tears. In as calm a voice as he can manage, Chhote Nanu tells his brother: "This is my son. Do what you like."

The caravan grows restless. "Are we dropping off the *musalmans* back in Pakistan?"

Barre Nanu's blood curdles. He doesn't approve of men using religion as a spear. But neither does he approve of kidnapping. "Nobody lays a finger on him," he warns the fanatics. He yanks his brother's ear. "Don't lie to me. Whose child have you stolen. Tell me, or I will toss you off myself."

Chhote Nanu blows air through his mouth to feel less afraid. "Never," he shouts back.

"Well then. See if I care what they do to you."

Their truck hurtles toward the new country. Yellow fields of mustard stretch as far as the eye can see. Food is days away, shelter and roof another five hundred miles southeast, and for Barre Nanu, my grandfather, empathy for my granduncle will take many years to manifest. At that moment, as he makes his way out of a new Pakistan and into a new India, all he can see is the golden-haired boy—he has propelled the brothers to the brink of war and stands in-between their undoubtedly mottled future and their quickly evaporating past.

August 2002

I came home to Kanpur because Barre Nanu had died. I kept thinking of his last days throughout the journey, the shouting in my head getting louder as the train pulled into the station.

In the chaos of the platform, the handcarts piled high with grain, tea stalls selling hot breakfasts of fried bread, travelers elbowing each other to hop on, I sought a moment of clarity. By the station master's office, near the city's edge, the sunshine spread clean like a river—the abundant Kanpur light could turn winters into summers. It was as though I'd arrived into mid-June, into a time instead of a place on a map.

"*Zara khisakiye*, step aside, please, brother." A fellow passenger, who'd combed his hair for the past hour, waved to his wife waiting for him on the platform with a garland in hand. I stepped back to let him pass.

I almost missed her standing beside a poster advertising umbrellas—Ila, in a monochrome blue sari. She'd thinned, acquired cheekbones and collarbones and shadows. Her eyes hid behind a pair of sunglasses, the ridge secured with blue tape. She looked agitated, as though she'd been robbed or slapped or both. She wrapped the folds of a blue cotton bag around her arms. A braid snaked over her shoulder. My baby sister. She could do anything, such as packing away our grandfather's life, wiping away every trace of him so that there remained nothing for me to do but take her word for it. One of her harried emails shouted inside my head: "Dear brother Karan, Barre Nanu died. You intend to come back ever or what?"

For the past several months, I'd hauled copious guilt, wondering how she must have handled Barre Nanu's last days with no one to help her. My sister had stepped up, and I'd proved myself unnecessary, once again. "It's all taken care of," Ila replied once I'd finally surfaced. In-between the lines, I could hear her taunting me: *Where was my big brother when I needed him? As usual, not around.*

I receded into the vestibule, while she consulted her wristwatch, folded her judgmental arms. I contemplated taking the train back to where I'd come from, but the ticket collector hopped on and began clicking his ticket puncher.

Head bowed, heart brimming with guilt, I stepped off the train and approached my sister like a pilgrim. Ila let me reach for her chin, kiss her forehead. How easily her small body disappeared into mine. It has always been this way. But she pulled away too quickly, leaving a faint black line of *kajal* on my collar, leaving me feeling incomplete. She was upset I'd stayed away for so long, that I hadn't come right when Barre Nanu's heart had started to give trouble. For six years I hadn't returned.

She walked ahead, swinging my backpack on her shoulder, leaving me to juggle the two suitcases heavy with the books I'd packed in a fit of optimism. She found a rickshaw, the most decrepit looking of the lot, the seat broken, the driver in rags. She sat sideways, her burdened back a C-shaped accusation. A sudden *azaan*, a caustic call to prayer from a nearby mosque. My sister, a grievous Auden poem I longed to understand.

If Barre Nanu were alive, he'd have come to collect me, held us both like two pearls inside his benediction. Ila wouldn't have marched ahead, and everyone would have known we belonged to each other and to him, everyone would see we were family.

Our rickshaw passed the old English dance hall, its colonnades dark from age, the interior taken over by Kashi and Sons. "For All Your Sporting Needs." Wooden tennis rackets and a faded photo of Boris Becker still adorned the glass display. Indoors, in the dim light, the grandfather and grandson played cards. God only knew the last time they'd made a sale.

"He didn't ask about you," Ila said sharply. "In the last month he was alive. He didn't ask about you. He didn't leave you anything."

I deserved her rage. I hadn't shared her burden. Did Barre Nanu have much to leave? The house, yes. The bare bones of his old business, the old looms, a few woodblocks. But all that was far from my mind—

"He wasn't coherent near the end. He wasn't completely sane."

The ticket stub flew out of my hand. Barre Nanu. Our Noah, no, our ark that carried us out of the floods. Had he suffered near the end? Ila was telling me this to break my heart all over again.

"But what does it matter to you?" She turned to face me until our knees knocked. "It took you six months to book a ticket."

"Tell me everything," I murmured. "Tell me how it happened."

"Very well. I suppose you should know."

This is what Ila said:

Sometime last year, Barre Nanu complained of chest pains, and Ila took a midnight train from Delhi to Kanpur to take Barre Nanu to the doctors. She administered his pills, made sure he convalesced for the prescribed two months. But with nothing to do and his workshop folded, no workers to entertain him with gossip, his mind began to falter. He began obsessing over his teeth. Every few hours, he would grin into a mirror, bare his frightful yellowing teeth, and complain he hadn't eaten well in a decade, had forgotten the taste of raw mangoes and meat. He wanted a new set of dentures so he'd have something to look forward to for the rest of his days. The heart surgeon gave him the go-ahead, and all of Ila's objections were shot down.

On the morning of the appointment, Barre Nanu put on trousers over pajamas to keep out the morning chill (white hem showing) and smiled at the photo of his ex-wife. Ila followed him out the door, but he wouldn't let her come with. Still, she trailed behind in a rickshaw.

In the dentist's office, she watched him lie on a plastic-covered recliner and name treats he'd enjoy—unripe guavas, peanut brittle, roasted corn. The dentist administered anesthesia, and Barre Nanu's eyelids fluttered shut. When he came to, his old teeth removed, he re-assured the nurse he felt well enough to travel home. But by the time he emerged into the waiting room, he was completely changed. He looked straight past Ila, and walked out into the street.

Ila caught him staring at the grand yellow-bricked Life Insurance Corporation building with the ochre colonnades. Barre Nanu looked lost, as though all his memory had seeped out of him like tea through a sieve. He crept toward an electronics store, stared at the poster of the Murphy Radio Baby (the baby's index finger poised by his lip as though he were advertising porridge and not radios). Barre Nanu regarded the landmark that had guided him home for half his life as though he were seeing it for the first time. He pounded his fist into his jaw, as if to pummel pain away.

Ila caught up with him, touched him lightly on the elbow.

His eyes widened with surprise, and he smiled, revealing a mouth devoid of teeth. "Child, you are very pretty," he slurred, flirting with his granddaughter a little and pinching her cheek. Then, as though recalling something, he turned to the park.

Ila watched him cross the street toward the gregarious mynah birds and the swaying red gulmohr trees, light and airy and full of joy. She found him staring at the yellow domes of the museum, dirty and aging. They must have reminded him of his old teeth, because Barre Nanu doubled over with pain. After a minute, he clutched his jaw with both hands and approached an old plaque on the building. He read the history of the town's founding, sounding out the names of the British generals and causing the morning joggers to stare. Once again, he left Ila pleading, and circled back to the park gates. There he ordered a butter sandwich, the butter soft and white, the rock salt purple and pungent, breakfast he'd treated us to countless times.

"We should go home," Ila insisted. Without a word, he handed her the sandwich, remembering he had no teeth with which to chew. The sun rose higher and cars and scooters crowded the street. Barre Nanu hired a rickshaw, and when Ila climbed into the seat next to him, he did not object, only stared at the beautiful, uneaten sandwich until Ila tore out for him the softest center piece.

He was telling her a story of the British origins of the town, most of his words slurring, when he clutched his chest and crumpled onto Ila's lap, his body heavy and warm.

"Hey Ram!" escaped his lips.

She tried to sit him straight, but failed. "*Bhaiya*! Ursula Housman!" she shouted at the rickshaw wallah, urging him to rush to the nearest hospital. But just then a bus disgorged its passengers, who began to cross the street, and even as she shouted, cursed, begged them to make way, they paid her no mind. An old man collapsed on a rickshaw presented no cause for alarm, a hysterical woman elicited no one's response.

Barre Nanu began to die. Ila knew the end was near because his memory came back in jumbled bits. He pointed to things, mumbling about their significance in his life—the long road home, the trees, the buildings, the paths in the park. Ila saw his soul flying out gram by gram, rationed to the city, recognizing its beloved bits: five grams to the temple where he'd married our grandmother, two to the mosque the newlyweds visited next, two to the custodian of refugee housing, five to the telegraph office, whose truculence in locating our grandmother's family in Pakistan had brought our grandparents together in the first place. He pointed delightedly to these, his words flowing, his memory also, even as pain split him into pieces.

But then his narrative stopped. His finger paused at Gandhi's statue. The mahatma's message of passive noncooperation had never appealed to Barre Nanu. His hero was Bhagat Singh, the famous revolutionary of Punjab.

"Where am I?" he cried. With the last remaining strength in his dissipating body, he reached for the rickshaw wallah's shoulder and commanded him to drive to Shahalmi.

"Sahib?"

"Go past Charing Cross and turn left."

"Charing what?"

"La . . ." the syllable fell from Barre Nanu's numb mouth. "La . . ." it fell again, "La," once more until it became a song in the wind, hitting Ila's ear like a chorus she ought to know. But Barre Nanu's tongue never curled upon the last syllable, and it was only later that Ila understood he was trying in his last moments to return to Lahore, the city he had left behind in Pakistan more than sixty years earlier.

◆

I couldn't hold back tears. I took her fingers in mine. "How did you arrange for everything afterward? Where did you take him?"

"Home," Ila said simply.

"How did you take him inside?"

"With Bebe's help. And the neighbors'."

My stomach turned. Our mother had witnessed her father's passing. I hadn't been there to ease her sorrow. "How did she react?"

"Like a daughter who's lost her only parent.

"She saw him from the balcony, lying on the rickshaw, and came slipper-slapping down. You know, heavy-footed in her white rubber slippers. 'Is he asleep from the anesthesia?' she asked. She was shuddering a little. Her gray-white hair was wet from the bath. It stuck to her back like streaks of mountain snow. She held Barre Nanu's limp hand in hers. She witnessed his eyes open to all the indiscriminate light in the street, and she couldn't hold back her tears. I linked arms with her to keep her from collapsing in the lane."

Ila's arm. Not mine. I wasn't there.

"She tried to help the rickshaw wallah and me to carry his body inside. But even the three of us couldn't manage, so I ran to the mosque down the lane. The morning prayers had just ended."

I could picture the holy hour—rows of white shirts and white skullcaps dotting the mosque courtyard, all the men full of piety, looking to do a kind deed.

"Three Muslims and two Hindus carried Barre Nanu inside. But the atmosphere at home was far from pious. Chhote Nanu had heard the commotion. He'd had to have heard it. Three times I banged on his door to tell him what had happened. Twice, Bebe begged him to come out. And yet Granduncle did not budge. He began his bell ringing and conch-shell blowing, singing his own prayers. But he did not attend to Barre Nanu's death."

I couldn't believe it. Chhote Nanu couldn't have turned so cruel.

"An hour later, Barre Nanu's Muslim weavers and Hindu printers came to pay their respects. They carried his body to the Ganges. I went with the men. I didn't listen when they said women aren't allowed near the pyres. 'I'm his granddaughter and his grandson,' I told them. 'Hold me back if you can.' There, by the river's edge, I watched a weaver light fire to our grandfather, watched his brown-green-gray atlas eyes, his anger-tipped nose, his Lahore loss, all go up in flames. Afterward I paid the pundit to perform the prayers and schedule the thirteen days of mourning and food for the priests."

She *had* arranged for everything without me.

"When I came home later that evening, Bebe handed me a note:

> You have fifteen days to leave my house.
> —Chhote Nanu

"Bebe had already packed bags, tossed clothes, books, shoes into suitcases. She cried as she looked about the room that had been hers since childhood, where she'd raised us.

"'How can we leave our house all of a sudden?' I asked her, trying to talk sense into her. I opened the suitcases and reversed our mother's packing, flung the saris back into the cupboards, tossed the shoes at the door.

"But Bebe had already given up. 'This is my house before it is yours,' she declared, reversing my unpacking. 'I don't want to keep fighting with your granduncle. My father is dead, but this stupid war won't end.'"

Even in the torpid Kanpur heat, I felt a chill. Ila had done too much. I didn't know what to say to her, whether to thank her or praise her or apologize, or tell her she wouldn't have to face things alone again. I didn't know if I could promise her that. I sat in the rickshaw feeling useless, feeling afraid. "I'm glad I got a break from 'the war,'" I said carelessly.

Ila looked at me quizzically. "That's not the reason you stayed away." A wild light played in her eyes. Since I'd seen her last, she'd gained the ability to bear considerable pain, and the ability to reduce me to smithereens. All she demanded was a smidgen of truth, me shouldering my share of the burden. I was failing at both.

Our rickshaw passed the park and the bronze Gandhi on the pedestal where Barre Nanu had realized he was dying in the wrong city. What an old fool the mahatma had been. Chhote Nanu used to say that in trying to prevent the Partition of 1947, Gandhi had precipitated it, exacerbated the violence. The mahatma had a thing for unity. He'd spent half his life trying to unite a people divided every which way. How violent this idea of unity could be, binding Dalits with Brahmins, Punjabis with Tamils, Muslims with Hindus. Maybe that was what had happened to Ila and me. Once again the ghost of Barre Nanu peeped from the dust-laden leaves, and I looked at Ila, her resolute, small mouth, her angry chin.

"You're right," I conceded. "*You're* the reason I stayed away." There. I'd said it. I half-feared she'd leap off the rickshaw, overturn it with her rage.

She held her breath. A minute passed. I feared she might scream so loud, she'd frighten the birds off the trees. "It's not me you're angry at. It's Bebe."

So this was how she arrived at truth. Without blinking.

"What Bebe said that day changed things for you."

This was true. I hadn't recovered from the wound Bebe had inflicted on me—on the both of us—that afternoon. I wondered if Ila thought about it as often as I did.

It'd happened six summers ago. I'd just begun my first year of college at IIT Bombay. I was nineteen. A few months into my freshman year, our mother's kidney gave out. It could be bacteria or it could be something worse, the doctors hypothesized, so I hopped on the first train out.

In the east wing of the ICU at Ursula Housman, with a nasogastric tube running up her nose, golden nose ring in place, Bebe's cheeks hollowed as she took a breath. Certain she was dying, she summoned both her children to her bed. I had my upcoming trig paper in mind, and Ila, sixteen, had the dreaded phase of college applications to worry about. Still, we both gave Bebe our hands, held her in the hospital bed, trying to make her feel less lonely. In between jagged breaths, Bebe told us she'd loved two men, one Hindu, one Muslim. This much we knew. Ila was the result of her marriage with the Hindu man, and I, the result of her romance with the Muslim. My father had died in the '84 riots, trying to save a Sikh family. Ila's father, an engineer with a weakness for the bottle, had died of a poisoned liver when she was one. Beyond these details, we knew nothing else about our fathers.

"I lied," Bebe said, taking our hands and holding tight. "Both your fathers are alive." She dug her bones into our flesh. Her breathing steadied. She turned to the side, trying to hide from our gazes.

My father was alive. Alive and not dead as Bebe had made me believe the nineteen years of my life. I felt as though someone had just alerted me to the fact that I had a javelin sticking out my back.

"Who is he?" I asked uncertainly. "Are you finally going to tell me more? What is his name? Why haven't I met him all this time if he isn't dead?" This was a new javelin, its sting unfamiliar. I became aware that I'd been yelling at my hospitalized mother.

Bebe avoided our questioning eyes. "Both your fathers are alive. That is all I can tell you. Don't ask me for more, please."

"Are you hearing this?" I asked Ila.

Bebe shut her eyes. Her fingers fumbled for mine, but I pulled away my hand; I couldn't offer her the reassurance she sought. Not even when I thought she was dying.

"Why hasn't my father inquired after me all this time?"

Bebe's head flipped side to side like a windshield wiper. "I don't know why. Don't ask me, please."

I shook her by the shoulders, forgetting the tube snaking up her nose.

Ila boxed my ear. "Why can't you be a little more understanding? Can't you see Bebe is upset. You have to face facts. Your father wants nothing to do with you. Learn to live with the truth like the rest of us."

I couldn't believe my sister. Wasn't she furious at Bebe? Curious to discover her father? I didn't know whom I resented more—our lying mother or little bossy Ila. I didn't want to be in the same room as them. I didn't wish my mother a speedy recovery, didn't bid Ila goodbye. I turned around and left. Bebe's infection healed, but I didn't come home that summer, didn't write, and, halfway into my senior year, I applied for graduate school in New York, all the while unsure of what to do with the revelation Bebe had shared with me, or the wound Ila had inflicted on me with her unkind words.

◆

Our rickshaw pedaled in silence. Ila sat stoic, as though she could face any plight unblinking.

"That day didn't change anything for you?"

"What would it change? Bebe is still Bebe. You're still my brother. Our fathers were never a part of our lives." She said it so simply, and yet, I knew she was lying. She'd changed. She had a new curiosity in her life. She'd use her inexhaustible energies to track down her father, track down mine as well. She was intrepid like that. Me, on the other hand, I was slow. I'd stay the same, unsure of how to change my life. Bebe still hadn't told me anything more about my father. I didn't know how to ask.

Perhaps the bad Kanpur air was to blame. Betrayal bred like fungus in our city. Mothers betrayed their children, brothers betrayed one another, half-siblings could never be trusted. What else could you expect from a town that'd begun as a garrison? Back in the late 1700s, when the East India Company began to morph from a group of tea-and-spice traders to a colonial power, it stationed an army here in Kanpur to spy on a nearby prince. Eventually, the prince was ousted like countless others, his kingdom usurped. Then, in 1857, Indian sepoys mutinied. They couldn't believe that after generations of loyalty, the British would force them to use Enfield rifles that required their cartridges—greased with cow and pig fat, offensive to both Hindus and Muslims—to be chewed open. In Kanpur a chieftain riled up the local soldiers, seized the treasury, freed prisoners, burned public offices, gave the British army hell for three weeks. But the company called in reinforcements, and the rebellion was squashed. The traitors were hung from trees, and just to be sure this sort of thing never happened again, the British army imprisoned the last Mughal emperor in Rangoon, and dragged India under the direct rule of the Crown. What came later—cotton and wool mills and a thriving war economy that supported a well-fed middle class—owed their existence to the British army men who resettled Kanpur. But each time the town appeared in the history books, her penchant for betrayal was remembered. The sentinel buildings along Mall Road—the English chemists, the museum, the police station, the cemetery—recalled her checkered history. In the shadow of that history, the divisions continued. The saffron propaganda signs of the ruling party advertised their candidates outside the park, and, across the street, the green-and-white signs in indecipherable Urdu, the opposition party advertised their candidates in turn. Saffron on one side, green on the other, and in the middle, the hot, white street with our rickshaw wallah's labored wheel—a veritable flag of India.

Ila and I were two warring parts of the same town. We'd inherited our town's discontent. We'd inherited our grandfather and granduncle's war.

We reached the lane that led to our house. The rickshaw wallah refused to go any farther. He stopped beside the telegraph office, now renamed the telecommunications center (you could still make out the ghost "graph" on the wall where the paint had been chipped). Behind the whitewashed building, the minarets of the neighborhood mosque rose sharply. But they did nothing to comfort the driver, who tugged at the *taveez* tied around his neck. We saw his hesitation as he kissed the paper prayer three times. I pulled out a fifty-rupee note, but Ila shoved it away.

"Don't force him. He doesn't want to enter a Hindu *mohalla*." She hauled a suitcase off the footrest, nearly tripping on her sari as she stumbled ahead.

The three stories of Tilat Villa rose abrupt like a wayward tooth, the rest of the houses around only one or two floors high. The top windows looked angry, boarded with black wood, as though charred from a recent fire. Dark vines consumed its bare brick facade. Time had treated our house savagely, the steps to the front door punctured, the walls abused with bills posted, torn, reposted over signs that said "Post no bills."

The door was shut. My hand paused midair. It is awkward to ring the bell of your childhood home.

"Don't you have a key?" I asked Ila.

"Like Chhote Nanu would give me a key."

We heard the latch open, but the door stayed shut. Someone asked us who we were, and Ila announced herself from behind me. Any minute I'd see my granduncle. Or Bebe. Despite our disagreement, I hoped it would be Bebe. The hibiscus tree in the lane swayed in a sudden gust. The milkman next door poked his head out of the window and called: "Karan *beta*, is that you?" More neighbors, aunties and uncles, stopped on their way to the shops and waved. But I stared at the fingers that held the door, willing it to open.

This had been my house once. The memories came. Ila and I running in the courtyard, slipping at every turn. Barre Nanu behind a newspaper, shouting at us to stop. Bebe on the third-floor balcony combing her hair. Once, I caught a few stray strands in my hands, the ones that had turned gray. In my eagerness to document the passage of time, I lost my balance and fell. Chhote Nanu swept me up before I could cry. The sweet smell of his hair oil, his mischievous chipped front tooth, his soft flesh, his hard bones. We'd continue on like that, I'd always thought, Barre Nanu behind his papers, Bebe on the balcony, and Chhote Nanu anticipating our tears. But of course, it hadn't happened that way. Barre Nanu had died, Chhote Nanu had hardened his heart and kicked us out, and Bebe and Ila and I had long scattered like seeds in the wind.

The door finally opened, but the woman at the threshold wasn't familiar. She was short, her hair shorn and white under her scarf. I had never seen her before in my life. The courtyard was overrun by men with their heads shaved and women with their heads covered.

The pilgrims wore dhotis that reached their knees and the women wore old saris. They came in and out of the rooms arranged around the periphery and crowded by the kitchen. At the foot of the old peepul tree in the center grew a pile of rubbish—green plates of banana leaves, rice, yellow lentils. Our swing, which had hung in the branches for as long as I could remember had been dismantled and put away.

"Who are all these people?" I recognized none of them.

A meal was in progress. Two bald men carried buckets of potato curry and fried bread into the rooms, where two dozen people sat and ate. The house swelled with smells. Cumin, asafetida, ginger, and here, close to the front door, piss. From another room came the scent of incense and fire. I looked at Ila for an explanation, but she marched to the stairs, carrying my bag.

"Is Bebe here?" I asked her.

She did not confirm with a yes or a no, but said simply, "Upstairs."

Before I could follow her, I heard a bus's brakes screeching outside. The front door opened and more pilgrims with shaved heads entered the courtyard. In a minute, they slipped off their old leather sandals and queued for the bathroom and the kitchen. An old man with an opulent beard, thinking me part of a reception party, handed me his jute holdall to carry. It reeked of mustard oil and small-town congruity. "Lunch is ready?" he demanded perfunctorily. "And baths? I paid good price for full bed."

Trying to hold back several choice curses, I marched out of the house and dropped his bag by the door. That's when I saw the sign, painted on a piece of metal: "Khatri Rest House. Vishram Sthal. 100% Full Veg. Om Jai Jagdeesh. Hari Om." I couldn't believe it. Chhote Nanu had turned our home into a hostel for pilgrims.

The old man retrieved his holdall, pushed me into the wall. On his way to the kitchen, he spat red betel juice all over the door that had once enclosed Barre Nanu's sari workshop.

"What do you think you are doing?" I shouted, unable to contain myself. "You can't spit wherever you like." Even rest houses had rules.

The man glared at me. I was mistaken. He wasn't old, but devoutly dressed in a white loincloth and an ochre shirt that I considered old-fashioned. Something bold and alive and modern lurked in his eyes that made it clear he wasn't lost in devotion but alert in his belief that, as a paying guest and a pilgrim belonging to the dominant religion, he had rights. His eyes darted around the courtyard, as though to warn me that I was outnumbered.

"Why are you standing here?" Ila interrupted, slipping down the stairs. She must have seen our exchange, because she linked her arm with mine and led me away. "Good thing I came to your rescue."

I don't need you to rescue me, I wanted to say, but I was no longer sure of this.

From the old drawing room, I heard chanting and the clanging of cymbals. Curious, I pulled Ila close and entered. A crowd swayed before an effigy of a goddess. The one-foot-tall idol sat perched on a high table swathed in shiny fabrics. A priest wove in and out of the pilgrims, thrusting a plate of flames under palms extended to receive the blessing. He shouted chants in Sanskrit. The women near Ila threw a cover over her head. They sucked their teeth, eyeing her vacant hair parting that ought to glow red with vermillion. What was she doing unmarried at her age? As for me, the women spared me, but not the men. As soon as the plate of flames went away, a dirty water bottle filled with a neon-green liquid was brought to my lips.

"Drink this, *mata's prasaad*," a man demanded. His eyes looked small and determined. I stared at the bottle, fearing all kinds of diseases and bacteria swimming in it.

"He just got off a plane, he should only drink boiled water," Ila interjected.

"Pray, then, pray, sing."

"I don't know the words," I said. "I didn't grow up singing these songs."

"These *bhrasht* children," someone said, criticizing our lack of faith.

But then I did pray. I concentrated on the eyes of the goddess, shut my own, and tried to conjure up the image of my mother. Where was she? Where was Chhote Nanu? When would I see them? When could we get our house back to its former self?

I could fly back to New York, I told myself. My room in Jackson Heights awaited me, as did the assistantship with my professor. But no, this time I wasn't going to run away.

After the prayer, Ila dragged me upstairs. She unlocked the door to our childhood room. Smart of her to sequester a small corner of the house to herself. The light inside looked morose and unanimated. Two children's beds flanked opposite walls, two desks by the beds. A red cotton sari covered Ila's mattress, another hung over the balcony door, sieving the daylight. Our mother's scroll paintings haunted the walls. Saint Meerabai's ochre devotion fingers plucked a coffee sitar, her eyes closed in despair; a fictional pair of violet mynahs mated in the corner.

There was no Bebe.

"I thought you said she was upstairs?" I asked Ila.

"No, I didn't."

"Where is she?"

Ila closed her face like a door. She didn't wish to be probed on the matter. She sank into a chair before her pile of books, a child facing a mountain.

Ila's desk displayed her sociology books—an omnibus on Delhi, several of Mark Tully's novels, the *Baburnama* from precolonial India. Heavy, important books that required heavier books to parse them.

Last I'd seen Ila, she was a girl of sixteen. Her pastimes had included pasting cutouts from fashion magazines in a scrapbook, and making furious, castigating lists of her least favorite people and how they'd wronged her. In six years, she'd turned away from herself and toward social studies (but what's sociology if not a long list of complaints, as a classmate once joked). She'd grown out her bangs and chosen a single braid, a severely simple style. She'd forgotten to have fun. This too was my fault. Her face had acquired new shadows, and a Bebe-like caustic air. She'd developed a new habit of turning away, imposing her profile on me. I'd never won any arguments against her, never wanted to. She was the fighter, I was the chronicler. At least, I'd always felt like the chronicler of our family, the taker of notes. I hoped that she needed me. I hoped she turned to me to fight our fight with Chhote Nanu. Ila didn't have the knack to soften people, only to rile them up.

I turned to my desk, but it suffered no books, only a brass lamp with its wire coiled around the base. Gone, my childhood comics and my collection of *National Geographic*. The countless times I'd imagined this room, I never imagined my things gone. It seemed Chhote Nanu had plans of repurposing it. Or was it Ila who'd tossed my books away?

I left Ila in our childhood room and went up to Chhote Nanu's quarters, taking the dark set of stairs outside the kitchen. The partition of steel trunks deterred egress, and I had to maneuver around them. With Barre Nanu gone, our granduncle would likely replace the trunks with walls. The three floors would finally become disconnected, cease to belong to one another as they once did. A stranger visiting might think entirely separate families lived in the same house.

The stairs opened into a balcony that jutted over the courtyard. Among the potted plants of *champa* and the night-blooming jasmine, I caught a familiar sight—a blue tricycle with a rusted bell that Ila and I would ride through the house, terrorizing our elders. The streamers I'd tied on the handles had now frayed, their original color (blue? gold?) faded over twenty monsoons. Chhote Nanu had neglected to throw it away, out of laziness or sentiment or both.

He wasn't inside his room. It still bore its monastic aspect—simple and clean, with a bed and a cupboard on one side, a large table covered with a white sheet on the other. The cupboard was ajar; I nudged it open. The scent of naphthalene leaked out. A row of laundered clothes, white kurtas and black achkans hung in the center. No one wore these outdated knee-length jackets anymore, and I doubted Chhote Nanu did. I touched a sleeve. The fabric felt sturdy and dignified. What was I looking for? A trace of my grandfather, perhaps. Silly of me to think that I would find it in his bitter brother's quarters.

Someone switched on the light.

I turned, my heart in my mouth. Ila stood at the edge of Chhote Nanu's bed.

"Look at this," she pointed to the floor beside the bed.

Gold-plated idols—Rama bearing a bow; Sita, his wife; Hanuman, the monkey god; Saraswati, the goddess of wisdom, playing a sitar—crowded inside a small wooden shrine. An incense stick burned at their feet.

Ila looked at me expectantly, waiting for me to comment.

"He's always been spiritual," I said.

"But he's never turned the house into a temple before!"

"Rest house."

"Ashram," Ila insisted.

"Semantics."

"It's our grandfather's house too. He would have hated to see it defaced like this."

"Defaced with gods and pilgrims?"

"Defaced with religion."

"Someone's turned Marxist," I said, in mock horror, but I saw Ila's point. In his youth, Chhote Nanu had run away with a half-English woman who'd embraced Islam. He'd hung her portrait in his room in a secret place. Ila and I had discovered it as children. I gestured to Ila, and together she and I pushed the bookshelf forward.

There she was—the great Nigar Jaan. Her dark hair framed her face with soft curls that caught the light. She had a resolute face, her delicate lips set and unsmiling, like someone who couldn't be outwitted or persuaded against her will. But her eyes bore a liquid fragility, betrayed a kinder heart. She looked like she believed in compassion. She was beautiful, plainly so. She held a baby in her lap, white as milk, the sparse hair on its head golden brown. I felt a tinge of bitterness looking at their faces. They'd become a reminder of all that Chhote Nanu had lost. Nigar Jaan and her baby were the cause of all the fighting between our grandfather and granduncle, and in many ways, the reason our lives had turned out the way they had.

I pushed the bookshelf back in its place and sank into the bed, taking in the transformation of the room. The walls that were once covered with drawings we'd done at school were now bare. The English books in the bookshelf were gone. The *Brer Rabbit* series, *The Five Find-Outers*, all the Enid Blyton, gone. There, by the door, I would throw my school bag and leap onto Granduncle's bed, re-read the books I'd read countless times. I lay back now, and I felt Ila's body sink next to mine.

"Why did you come back?" I asked Ila. "You could have left after Barre Nanu died. You missed six months of college."

She folded her arms under her head. A teardrop slipped out of an eye and disappeared in the forest of her hair. She didn't say it, but I knew her answer. Everything that mattered to us belonged to this house. Barre Nanu's ghost, Bebe's memories, and the ghost of the former pre-religion Chhote Nanu, all were here.

Where was he now and why had he turned our house into a pilgrim guesthouse? Why hadn't he cared that his brother had died? Why had he turned Bebe out? This time Chhote Nanu had veered too far. But then, he'd always fashioned his own waywardness.

April 1943

1

A few months after he turned seventeen, Chhote Nanu became infatuated with a half-English girl from Heera Mandi. From across the tent at the wrestling arena, he saw the frills on a white dress fluttering like flower petals in the wind, saw the twinkle of her tight English smile. He guessed she was English and off-limits, but this detail didn't deter him from growing curious. He fixated on her lush black hair done up in curls, her skin the same color as his, and his heart leapt off and away as swiftly as pigeons taking flight.

The tent was beastly hot. In the field before them, two hefty men, one Indian and one English, rammed into each other like oxen, trying to take the other down. Dust rolled in giant swirls straight into their mouths, crunching under their teeth. Chhote Nanu's own wild hair blew about, and he wrapped his *gamchha* around his face, no doubt looking like a peasant in his white shirt and pajamas. It was hard enough to keep his eyes open. But when he spotted her, he couldn't look away.

He'd never seen anyone so beautiful. The rest of the women in the audience squatted on the mud floor with their faces covered. But she, she was different. She sat on a raised dais wearing what looked like a man's hat (a fedora? a panama?) with a black band. Her small brown hands played with the lace on her dress, which glowed so white she seemed composed of light, competing with the sun and winning. Her face was a striking shade of sunned wheat. Even the way she sat, one foot crossed over the other, her skirt ending just below the knees, her calves shiny, he thought, how bold, how unabashed. A maid brought her a child, a boy of no more than two, and she smothered the toddler with kisses. How perfectly divine she looked parading in English dress. From across the tent, she gave the whiff of Trafalgar Square and the real Charing Cross, places Chhote Nanu had only read about.

Who was she? What was her name? What was she doing in the vile, dusty block of men? Granted, she sat several paces away from the general audience, with a group of women who could only have been her attendants. She wasn't accompanied by a man. She couldn't be an Englishman's wife. All the wives had left for Simla to summer in cooler climes. He ran his hands over his young arms, hopeful for the muscles that would one day burst with potential.

Right then, the match picked up. In the field, against the backdrop of the mulberry trees, Uddham Singh lifted the English challenger into the air. The referee, also English, in wide khaki shorts and a sola topee, buzzed like a bee around the mud-caked contenders. Why had the British adopted the dirty Indian sport? Just so they could have their faces shoved in the dirt? Why couldn't they keep content with cricket or billiards or cards? Still, Chhote Nanu had to admit he derived a distinct pleasure watching the British lose. He wasn't alone. The audience roared every time the Indian *pehlwan* won a point. Now too, Uddham Singh brought the lightweight Mr. Briggs crashing to the ground, and the men in the tent leapt off their haunches. The khaki contingent booed, but no one expected them to defy the Crown while it kept them in service.

"Crush the *gora*, Uddham," someone shouted. "Beat the sahib to a pulp."

Chhote Nanu watched Mr. Briggs's sad, mud-covered face, and he could not help but feel a note of sympathy. The Englishman looked older, less experienced than Uddham, the way he panted, stood stock-still while his opponent meandered and stomped around him. If the rumors about the British leaving India came true, would Mr. Briggs stay or leave? Maybe he had gone so native, he'd choose to stay back. Chhote Nanu looked to see whom the mysterious lady with the shiny calves cheered for—the reigning champion or the English contender. She was busy with the little boy in her lap. The child covered her face with his little palms, and she happily kissed him, while adjusting his European sailor's outfit of shorts and a jumper with a matching blue cap. The way she fussed over him and coddled him, Chhote Nanu wondered if the child belonged to her. Where was her husband? Did she have a husband?

Uddham Singh delivered his opponent a final, decisive gut punch, and won the fight. The audience went mad. People poured into the field from all sides, clamoring to hug the winner. But the lady with the exposed calves made her way to the exit, the little boy's wrist in her hand, followed by her attendants.

He spotted her easily in the crowd. There she went, her bare legs striding confidently, her dress highlighting her shapely calves. Wherever she went, the lackeys followed her, eager for a closer look. Her admirers, even the respectable college students with a stack of books under their arms, could not stop staring. She walked swiftly, dodging catcalls and whistles and declarations of love.

Chhote Nanu kept pace, admired her from a few steps away. He didn't dare come as close as the other onlookers, who trailed her and by doing so frightened her little boy. The child, golden-haired and curious, kept turning back to stare at the men with his big eyes, seeking a friendly face in a sea of lechers catcalling his mother. Chhote Nanu felt sorry for him, wished he could shield the little man, lift him up and away. The boy bumbled along, bumping into the lady's legs and the maid's, clutching a raggedy brown bear close to his heart, while the ladies pulled him along. The bear fell, and the child looked back forlornly, his eyes tearing, fingers outstretched, but out of fear of the onlookers, he didn't utter a sound.

"*Arré, arré*, please!" Chhote Nanu tore through the file of men, suffering elbows and knees. In a daredevil act, he leapt onto the stuffed animal before its button eyes could be crushed. He then held the dusty bear to the grateful child, smoothed its red satin bow, which was frayed at the end. The boy blinked, tucked his toy under his little chin. Before they could exchange words, the lady in white pulled him along.

As the white dress drifted away into the crowd, Chhote Nanu realized he'd been too stunned to ask anyone for her name.

2

A black Ford jeep forced its way through the crowd, the only one of its kind in the whole district, with headlights the size of a horse's face. The superintendent of police sprung out of the driver's seat, knocked a student off his bicycle, and held the door open for the lady and her legs. Chhote Nanu guessed that she must be familiar with the officer. Familiar but not married, because they hadn't sat together during the match. The prospect of competition did not discourage him—he'd just turned seventeen and felt at once naive and full of hope. But the policeman familiar with the lady—and there could be no mistaking his identity—was none other than Mr. Mutton, a tawny-skinned Englishman with red slits for eyes and barely enough blond hair to cover his head. The fellow who had orchestrated the massacre at Jallianwala. The man Chhote Nanu had vowed to assassinate.

It was easy to dislike the policeman. The poets still composed mournful verses about what he had done at Jallianwala and published them in underground literary journals. It was hard to forget the suffering he'd unleashed on that fateful afternoon.

It'd been springtime. Great blooms of laburnum hung thick like shimmering gold earrings. Families gathered at the park to celebrate the spring, decked out in sunrise shirts and sunset *salwars*. Children flew yellow kites. Mothers chased old lovers to shove cream sweets into their mouths. To a passing cloud, the gathering must've resembled a field of mustard in full bloom, swaying yellow, all teeth and notorious singing, not a flag or a soapbox or a frown in sight. But Mutton interpreted the peaceful gathering as an act of civil disobedience. His jeep crept toward the park. Their rifles aimed, Mutton ordered his subordinates to block the foot-wide gates and open fire, fire until the brick walls of the garden were splattered with Punjabi blood, fire until not a soul was spared and not a bird stirred.

Even the British newspapers called the incident a slaughter. Mutton's superiors set up an inquiry committee, chastised him officially, but didn't fire him. He continued to serve as policeman, rose through the ranks.

Rumor had it, as soon as his Indian subordinates had exhausted their bullets, Mutton leaned over and said: "Just like shooting fish in a barrel."

This very same Mutton, Chhote Nanu had vowed to assassinate.

Before he'd set his eyes on Superintendent Mutton, Chhote Nanu had bumbled along without much success as the planner-in-chief of his and Samrat's nascent two-person outfit, collecting intelligence on officers with Indian blood on their hands. By 1943, a lot of Indian blood had been spilled in the famines and the wars and as a result of bad economic policies and mismanagement by a foreign power. The British had been in India since forever—or, well, since the early 1600s—and their crimes were adding up.

But it was more complicated than that, as Babuji explained. Chhote Nanu's father liked to compare Great Britain's colonial mission to the hunting ritual between a predator and its prey, a whirling and twirling before the dominant race gobbled up the subjugated one. All the buildings they'd erected, the churches, the dance halls ("Indians and Dogs Not Allowed"), the schools, were gestures meant to lure the prey closer, quell any suspicion. Part of the complication was, neither Chhote Nanu nor Babuji could remember an India without the British, a Lahore without their beeping jeeps and ham sandwiches and Tom Collinses.

For this reason, Chhote Nanu first petitioned the queen and Mr. Churchill with letters written in the proper English he'd learned at Central School, his admission to the school a matter of great pride for his mother. She didn't know, of course, that he'd sat in one corner of the classroom most of the time, punished for not being able to pronounce the words to the satisfaction of Master Willis. In language borrowed from textbooks

("Your humble subjects would like to humbly point out the un-British rule of the British by one police officer named Mutton etc. etc. He open-fired on innocent babies and ladies etc. etc. on the Thirteenth day of April in 1919"), the letters conveyed the failure of the British justice, which not only had not punished the man who'd killed five hundred innocent people, but continued to employ his services. When Chhote Nanu didn't hear back from Buckingham Palace or 10 Downing Street, Samrat's brother, back without his legs from the big war in Italy, advised that they escalate actions, use violence to right the wrongs.

Samrat fashioned a bomb out of firecrackers and laid it en route of the police jeep. The thin strips of saltpeter stretched across the dirt road connecting the native part of town with the British civil station. The boys hid behind the wall guarding Anarkali's tomb. As soon as they spotted the superintendent's jeep bumbling up the road, Chhote Nanu ran to light the strip. "Bang! bang! bang!" went the explosions, like guns firing. "*Inqalaab!*" the boys exclaimed privately, patting each other on the back. But they'd celebrated in vain. The nitrate didn't react, and although the air smarted with smoke and the scent of sulphur, the fire wasn't even big enough to frighten the band of dogs playing in the opposite corner, let alone blow up the target.

Still, the jeep stopped, and a native constable leapt out to inspect the disturbance. He held the measly paper strips in his hands, sniffed the gunpowder.

"Sahib," he addressed the superintendent sitting in the jeep. "Leftover firecrackers! Boys playing games."

Superintendent Mutton nearly choked with rage. "I want you to produce these hooligans right now," he ordered the constable, but the chap just stood there scratching his ear. Mutton turned to his subordinate. "Gordon! See to it!"

Warden Gordon, a Balliol man two decades his junior, was less surprised than Mutton by the anti-British air circulating in the bazars. Men like Mutton, guard dogs of the British Empire, would never in a million years have predicted that their Indian subjects would hate them so. The jewel hated the crown. How could it be? But it was so, it was just so.

Rallies erupted all over the country despite the thousands they'd locked in jail. India had chosen her moment well. Just when the British Empire had leapt into a very important war against Hitler, India'd begun clamoring for self-rule.

"India for Indians, sir," said Gordon, keeping his tone as emotionless as possible, which was easy to achieve in a country full of people who felt too many emotions. "I suppose the Indians were bound to think for themselves eventually." He stepped out of the jeep, cast a perfunctory glance around, tilted his face to the blighted sun.

"India for Indians indeed," said Mutton through his abundant, white teeth. He leapt out, inspected the site of the blast, looked about, and returned to the jeep. "What a grand disaster that would be," he continued, pounding the wheel with his fist. Gordon joined him in the jeep. "It's that damned two-faced Gandhi's fault. Begging the Japanese to help rid India of the British! Does he think the Japanese will serve as better masters than the British? Hasn't he heard of their cruelty in Burma? In the Andaman Islands?"

The trouble with Gandhi, which Mutton hated to admit, was that the old fool wielded too much power over his people. His "Quit India" call was birthing vicious crops of young rebels. The Indian National Army, the new chaps called themselves. Did they really think they could take on the greatest empire in the world and liberate India? Sure, they'd set off bombs in Burma, fired at their own brothers and fathers. Rumor had it, the INA leader, this so-called Bose, had met Hitler and was conspiring to perpetrate more violence on their troops overseas. But Mutton didn't think they'd succeed. Their penchant for betrayal confirmed to Mutton that the Indians were an abominable race. The British army would squash these rebels like flies.

Mutton shouted at the constable: "See if these boys belong to the INA. Every boy over fifteen ought to be locked up. If you pardon one, twenty more will flourish."

The ear-scratching constable wiped his hands on his uniform. "Sahib, so many hooligans about. How to catch every single one?

Every day we are putting so many behind bars as it is. These fire-cracker boys seem like novices. Not INA quality."

Mutton moved his small mouth in a chewing motion. Was the chap praising the INA? It was imperative to punish any and all misdemeanor to the highest degree. "If I find out you are protecting them, I will have you skinned."

"Saheeeeb! Never! Death to Bose, death to the INA, death to Gandhi also! Long live the British Raj," he added for good measure. He climbed inside the jeep just as Mutton slammed his foot on the accelerator. The constable had to hold on for dear life.

To Chhote Nanu and Samrat, hiding behind the tomb wall, the sight of the departing jeep was deeply insulting. Samrat threw his army cap to the ground and cursed the Raj.

"Their queen plops her fat bum on our peacock throne, wears our koh-i-noor diamond on her ugly head, while our beautiful poet king died in exile. Mutton is going to get a bomb next time." He smacked Chhote Nanu on the shoulder. "Start planning."

3

Chhote Nanu found it difficult to plan an assassination while a certain lady colonized his mind. In love, he could imagine a new nation, more peaceful than Gandhi's, more patriotic than the rebel INA's. Its anthem began with a meditation on her skin, moved on to the sturdiness of her legs. His body and his bicycle continued to follow the superintendent, trail his jeep as it drove from the jail to Nedous Hotel for lunch and into the native part of town for shopping, but now he hoped his search would lead him to the liberated lady with the man's hat and mysterious native skin. He had yet to hear her speak, yet to observe her eat, laugh, cry.

One Friday evening, Chhote Nanu followed the superintendent into Heera Mandi. The policeman parked under a chai wallah's blue awning and flew up a dark set of stairs. He'd come alone. Chhote Nanu's heart drummed as he contemplated whether to return home or wait. He had never been to the red-light district. The market of sin and sordidness sat alive with raunchy delights and griefs. He couldn't look, he couldn't keep his eyes shut. The houses were an assemblage of mismatched thin and tall and squat and long *havelis* trapped inside a narrow lane. Black, red, and blue balustrades jutted from the top floors and cast a morbid shadow on the passersby, who ranged from well-dressed old nawabs in elegant long black jackets to young Englishmen in bulbous dusty khakis. Ruckus poured from the windows—whistles, claps, classical music, jazz. A man leaned out from one of the dingier balconies in the back and puked. A drunk tommy nearly knocked Chhote Nanu off his bicycle, and crashed into a horse's drinking pail.

If his neighbors saw him here, he'd become the laughing stock of the mohalla. His father would likely twist his ear off. His mother would blame herself for rearing him so ill.

He mounted his bicycle and turned in the direction of home, but just then he heard a familiar tune from the English pictures—"Für Elise." What a beautiful melody! Chhote Nanu began to hum despite himself. He drew closer to the house from where the music came. On the neem tree that grew in the middle of the lane, he read a faded sign: "Defeat the Axis, use prophylaxis." On the door behind which Mutton had disappeared, a plaque read: "The house of Nigar Khan," followed by something that looked like a license issued by the imperial police. Is this where she lived?

A boy slipped past him and limped up the stairs bearing a plate-ful of rose-scented *paan*. The fat doorman with eyes like a bullfrog's nodded at the boy. But when Chhote Nanu tried to follow him, the doorman pulled him back and pointed him to the street.

"I have a message for superintendent sahib," Chhote Nanu lied.

The doorman paid him no mind. "Go home before I break your legs."

He saw her again. Early one morning, on his way back from the shops in the civil station to fetch the morning paper for his father (who'd abandoned doing business with the British but not their intellectuals), he took a detour through Lawrence Gardens. Usually, he avoided the park for fear of running into British ladies, who regarded him as though he were a rabid dog and told him to get out of their way, or British soldiers playing their awful military tunes, as if Lahoris didn't know who ruled India.

As he rode up the garden path on his bicycle, he saw her stand-ing under a mulberry tree, her panama hat with the black band pulled low over her eyes. She wore a simple green house skirt and a yellow blouse with puffed sleeves, as if trying to blend in with the shrubbery. Her cuffs looked damp from the dew. Her gaze darted left and right, as if, like him, she feared being caught out. Chhote Nanu got off his bicycle but didn't stop, didn't dare look at her so as not to prolong her discomfort. But as soon as he passed her, he heard a child's delighted laughter. He stopped and looked back. The golden-haired boy sat sequestered on the grass, ensconced behind a spray of papaya trees. The boy saw him and clapped his hands with delight.

"Mama! That man saved Colonel Bob from going to he-ven!" The child had remembered Chhote Nanu from the wrestling match.

The lady's beautiful mouth spread into a silver smile. "Did he really, pet?" She took the boy's face in her hands and brushed some dirt clinging to his cheek. Her eyes came to settle on Chhote Nanu.

Chhote Nanu felt warmth spreading over his body. He dug foolishly into his pockets, found a tamarind pod lurking there, and offered it to the lad. This allowed him to stand quite close to the lady, barely a foot away. She smelled of books, of woody ink, something musty but also alive and green like fresh grass. Her collarbones dipped like two bows of a boat.

"Thank you, but he's too young for *imli*," she said to him, snatching the pod from the child's hands. "He might choke." Her voice was like the melodious mid-notes of a sitar, like water trickling over stones.

She cracked the rind between her teeth, scraped the flesh with her index finger, and stuck the finger in the boy's mouth. The boy's mouth puckered instantly, causing her to break into giggles.

His hand trembled as he rooted in his pockets for another tamarind pod. Finally he found it and presented it to her, a new boldness taking over his body. "How come you are fond of wrestling? So few women are—" Chhote Nanu heard himself ask. He hadn't been able to shake the vision of her at the match, bathed in sunlight in her white clothes. Only peasant women ever watched wrestling. She'd elevated the sport to something spectacular with her attendance, like polo or cricket.

She wiped her mouth with the back of her hand, evading his eyes, and immediately he regretted his question.

To mask their mutual discomfort, he said hurriedly: "It's something to do on a Sunday, isn't it?"

The child spotted a squirrel and dragged the lady away.

Chhote Nanu thought it was time for him to depart. But then, the lady's maid—a woman in a plain white kurta pajama, head covered with a pink *dupatta*—emerged from the shadows. In the crook of her arm, she carried a picnic hamper containing a flask, an apple, and finger sandwiches. She plopped herself on the grass, didn't tell him to bugger off.

He took this as an invitation to sit beside her. There was so much he wanted to know about the lady. But all he managed to blurt out was a question about her dark skin.

The maid suppressed a yawn. "Nigar Jaan's an Anglo. British mother, Indian father." She suppressed another yawn. A few feet away, the toddler was encouraging the squirrel to emerge from its hiding place.

"Is that her child? I just want to know. I've never seen anyone so beautiful."

"You and all of Lahore!" The maid raised a sharp eyebrow. "Don't get any funny ideas about my Baby Jaan. She is not allowed to see your sort." She produced a *paan* from the folds of her *dupatta*, tucked the beetle leaf in the corner of her mouth. She puckered her lips to spit, remembered the English garden, and stopped. She softened a little. "She's off-limits to everyone—Indian, American, French. Why do you think we've come to this park before the break of dawn?"

He knew the answer—to avoid the rude English *mems* as much as the men, the ones who wouldn't accept Nigar Jaan because of her station. "Is it because she is seeing the superintendent?"

The maid sat up straight. "Don't speak of the superintendent . . . sahib . . ." she twirled the end of her shawl around a finger, didn't say more. The "sahib" was an afterthought. Did she feel the same dislike for Mutton that Chhote Nanu did?

In the distance, under a yew tree, the lady collected lantana flowers. There was something private in the way she held herself, not wanting to join them. What was this moral code of the English that caused her to feel unsafe in her own country? He wished so much to shield her from the nastiness. Chhote Nanu hugged his knees, feeling hopeless, lost in her beauty. "I'm sorry for my questions. She is the first English lady who hasn't ordered me to fetch her a tonga."

The maid's sleepy eyes opened like two oysters. "That's because she knows what it's like to be snubbed."

They heard the gentle clop of a horse. The sun had emerged, coloring the burnished-plaster balustrades of Lawrence Hall golden white. The maid shot up. "Baby Jaan, time to go."

Chhote Nanu rose too. But the child had just discovered the spokes of Chhote Nanu's bicycle and didn't wish to part from it.

"Pet, it's time to go," the lady said. "Pop-Pop is coming by later."

"But what if he doesn't come, like yesterday?" the child protested. His face crumpled, eyes brimmed. In a fit of enthusiasm, Chhote Nanu swung the boy onto his bicycle, held him on the frame, rang the bell for his delight.

"You're very kind," the lady said to Chhote Nanu, retrieving her child. For the sake of the boy, because why else would she care for a fool like Chhote Nanu, she said meaningfully, "We will have this pleasure again, won't we? We will see you tomorrow?"

Chhote Nanu felt as though he'd been granted a boon from the gods. "Tomorrow!" He tucked the information deep inside his heart.

From then on, he made a habit of appearing at the park. He put the little child on his bicycle and took circles around the garden paths. Some mornings, he took them saffron *jalebis* soaked in sweet syrup and milk, savory pancakes with onions and fried bread. The boy anticipated his arrival, surprised him by leaping out from behind trees. But the lady sat tucked away behind trees, privately picking flowers, leaned out but rarely to make sure her child breathed unscathed. Chhote Nanu felt neither surprised nor completely disheartened. She was discovering something new, that strangers could be trusted, and the discovery took some getting used to. One day she might let him in a bit more.

Soon, he got what he wanted. The maid extended an invite to their house in Heera Mandi. A coterie of poets would gather there for an Urdu festival. Wouldn't he come?

4

Chhote Nanu cycloned home. The bazaars, the hawkers, the river, the mosques, the temples, the cows, the dogs, everything was a mad rush of sound and color that, like a tunnel, linked him to her. He collapsed in his bed, calling out her magical name. "Nigar Jaan! Nigar the beloved!" He opened a book of Ghalib's romantic ghazals, buried his face in the rosebud preserved between the pages. He attempted to transform her into a metaphor. "Eyes like a peril of locusts."

A rude knock on the door interrupted him. Samrat stood inside his room. He carried a handsome pile of books.

"You've made new friends and forgotten all about the old ones."

Chhote Nanu stared at the books, then at the young nawab. He recognized his error. The nawab hadn't heard from Chhote Nanu in weeks. He wanted a report on the bomb planning. Chhote Nanu wondered if the books were for him. They looked like freshly published volumes on Russian social theory.

Samrat placed the pile in the center of Chhote Nanu's desk, already a mess of newspapers and volumes of poetry. The gift given, Samrat turned his uncompromising eyes on Chhote Nanu. His neatly pressed kurta sleeves billowed angrily in the hot winds that blew into Chhote Nanu's room. "What have we been studying lately?" the young nawab asked, leafing through the collection of Mir Taqi Mir's poetry open on Chhote Nanu's desk. "*Patta patta buta buta*," he read. "Who is this flower bud oblivious to your pining, hmm?" Samrat sucked his teeth in dismay.

Chhote Nanu's heart sank. He had the same feeling of shame when Barre Nanu entered his room and found him smoking.

"Oh, how the mighty have fallen." Samrat linked his arm with Chhote Nanu's and marched him out of the house.

Their bicycles trembled over the hot cobblestones as they rode through the market, Chhote Nanu's heart collapsing under the weight of Samrat's expectations.

Samrat knew the power he wielded over Chhote Nanu. For the past year, Samrat had provided vision, petty cash, and unimpeachable knowledge of chemicals to their outfit of two, and for much of that time, Chhote Nanu had admired him quietly, followed his lead without protest. He'd taught Chhote Nanu to feel angry about Jallianwala. Their twinned rage had felt empowering. Chhote Nanu had been only too eager to make maps of the superintendent's movements. It'd involved bunking classes at college, shirking duties at home, thrusting importantly past hawkers and layabouts in the native part of town and toward the British part. He'd feasted his eyes on English pastimes such as dances at Montgomery Hall, drinks at sunset, even a game of polo. It'd allowed him to pledge allegiance to a higher cause. The chief of police was powerful, yes, but also plainly visible and past his prime. Chhote Nanu had made a map of his goings-about, and Samrat would take care of the rest.

"Who's the *gora* boy and English *mem* you've been hanging about with in the park?"

Chhote Nanu's heartbeat dulled. Samrat had been following him secretly. What if he fired him for good? "Oh, her?" he said disinterestedly. "She's no one special. She's Mutton's lady friend." A part of his head singed to introduce Nigar Jaan as the superintendent's associate.

Samrat pulled on his brakes, causing Chhote Nanu to crash into him. He dragged Chhote Nanu under a sweetshop's awning.

"That's brilliant. Mutton has a lady friend." Samrat's eyes lit up as he extended three annas at the sweetmeat wallah sitting on a raised dais and pointed to the milk sandwiches. "Her house might be the perfect place," he said meaningfully as he stuffed a milk sandwich into his mouth. He tossed the leaf dish under the sweetmeat wallah's cauldron, where a goat promptly appeared to lick it.

Sweat dripped down Chhote Nanu's back. He took a small bite of the airy sponge extended toward him. The sweet released a new fear into his mouth. "Perfect place for what?"

Samrat led Chhote Nanu's quaking heart toward his haveli. The mansion towered behind Lohari Gate in the inner walled city, rising like a white tide with high walls overlooking the Ravi River, its terrace surpassing the width of several neighboring houses. They no longer built havelis like Samrat's. Chhote Nanu felt as though he were entering a time of kings and queens as he climbed the high stairs filled with shadows and intrigue. Inside Samrat's bedroom, a set of white pigeons roosted on a white windowsill. Except for a bookshelf, a clock, and a bed, the room was bare; gone were the chandeliers and the carpets that Samrat had grown up with. Within his own lifetime, the British had annexed more than half his father's estate. The old nawab had his pension curtailed and remained a nawab only in title. The ramparts of the haveli were emptied, gone the elephants and camels that once sauntered here.

Samrat slipped off his leather shoes with his toes and sank onto the four-poster bed, legs folded, one elbow propping his head, eyes trained on Chhote Nanu. "So Mutton's lady friend." Chhote Nanu didn't like the tone of his voice. "Where does she live?"

Chhote Nanu swung the jute seat to face the wall. An old newspaper cutout of Bhagat Singh stared back from the wall. The revolutionary with the jaunty trilby. Fired at an English policeman and hanged for the crime. Keeping him company was a newspaper cutout of the moon-faced and dreamy-eyed Bose, the founder of the Indian National Army. Bose was going to liberate India from the British, Samrat was certain of it. The rebels presided over a whole shelf of pirated books on the Bolsheviks. Could Chhote Nanu hide Nigar Jaan from well-read, resourceful Samrat? Sooner or later, the young nawab would follow him and find out, if he hadn't already. "Heera Mandi," he mumbled, eyes low, his toes scraping a stain on the stone floor.

"Heera Mandi? That's the perfect place for the onion!" Samrat hopped off the bed, retrieved something from the alcove behind the bookshelf, and placed it on the bed. It was small tin box, the kind stu-dents carried to school. "Open it."

Despite his heart telling him not to, Chhote Nanu crept toward the bed. Inside the box sat "the onion," a harmless-looking ball of black yarn. Even without being told, he knew its composition—a giant firecracker packed tightly with saltpeter and an explosive tail that he would have to light to create a blast. Chhote Nanu picked up the bomb. It easily weighed as much as a cricket ball; his rough guess: a quarter kilo. Samrat's biggest firecracker yet. From the outside it looked innocuous enough, but as soon as he let it fall, its thump, its cruel maligned heart sent shivers all over Chhote Nanu's body.

He couldn't. He wouldn't. Bring this near Nigar Jaan? No. Her lit-tle boy? Never. Sweat dripped down Chhote Nanu's body. He wanted to run away and never set foot in Samrat's haveli ever again.

"What's the matter? Have you taken a fancy to the lady? Let me tell you, there's no permanence in romance. Four days' heaven, as the poets say, until she finds someone new."

Chhote Nanu swallowed hard. "I haven't taken a fancy." He felt two-faced saying it, as though his mouth had come unhinged. "What if . . . what if someone got hurt? Or I couldn't do it?"

Samrat fell into the bed as if Chhote Nanu had pushed him. The craters on his face filled with shadows as he shifted into the darkness.

The world went deadly quiet, the sullen quiet of a Lahore after-noon. An ironsmith's steady beat of *tan-tan-tan* rose from the market. Chhote Nanu sweated quietly in the airless room. The *tan-tan-tan* continued, kept beat with the grandfather clock mournfully ticking in one corner. He couldn't help but hear the ironsmith's deliberate vengeance as a metaphor. His father didn't speak to him, didn't even look at him these days. Barre Nanu called him lazy, never once in-vited him to the shop. Not that Chhote Nanu found their half-dead cloth business interesting. Only Samrat. He'd seen a promising clean space in Chhote Nanu's mind that could be put to use for something worthwhile. Such as producing maps of a cruel superintendent's day for revolutionary purposes. Chhote Nanu regarded his friend. Samrat lay spread-eagled, a tear quietly streaking down the side of his face.

"You've heard about my cousin Ullhas, haven't you?" His voice came out splintered. "His friends took him to Jallianwala that afternoon. Poor boy thought he was going to picnic with friends. He got a bullet in his head instead. A boy like me, younger even. He wiped the corners of his eyes. "If Mutton hadn't given the orders to shoot . . ."

Chhote Nanu's legs gave in, and he sank into the bed. Jallianwala. The name caused an incessant ringing in his ears, a desperate feeling of drowning. His father too had lost a family member at the bloodied park. Grief had sealed everyone's lips on the topic, but the dead aunt cropped up in conversations like silverfish in books. ("Remember how we danced at Nimmi's wedding? Poor Nimmi. Only twenty-one springs in her kismet.")

"This thing we are doing, it may mean nothing to you. But believe me, it will bring Mutton to justice. The colonial apparatus will have to take notice. We might go to jail for what? A month? Three months? Are you afraid of going to jail? Is that it?"

Strangely enough, the jail didn't frighten Chhote Nanu. Gandhi and Nehru practically lived behind bars and wrote books. Stories of their well-lit and comfortably furnished cells complete with a desk and two chairs floated in the underground newspapers. But Chhote Nanu feared the damage to his reputation with his parents, and with Nigar Jaan, once he was imprisoned.

Samrat turned to his side, his lips dry, his voice croaking but hopeful. "All you have to do is light the fuse. I'll take care of everything else."

Chhote Nanu sank beside his mentor. "But my father—"

"People will stop your father in the street," Samrat nearly sang. "They will stop him and touch his feet. They will ask your mother about you, 'What did he read? What did he eat? What is the diet of a revolutionary, tell us!'"

How Chhote Nanu wished he had Samrat's vision.

Samrat rested his hand on Chhote Nanu's chest, their nerves as though uniting to one beat. "Light the onion in the police car as soon as he leaves her place. He'll be inebriated and out of sorts. He won't know what hit him. He turned his head to the light filtering through the window. The craters on his face dissolved. "May the god of good blasts go with you."

Where to plant the bomb for maximum damage? Chhote Nanu spent the next week thinking and overthinking. Following the superintendent was one thing. Blowing him into pieces was quite another. Would he blow up into pieces? Could Samrat's bomb achieve such a blast? In the past, the worst his firecrackers had done was take out his maid's eye. With any luck, the bomb would rip off a small patch of the policeman's skin. Then the brute would know he was hated. Chhote Nanu would get thrown in jail. He could compose a collection of verses. Surely the jails didn't skimp on paper and pencils. How else did the prisoners pass their time?

How to catch the policeman alone? He couldn't gain access to the superintendent's house. Two constables always stood guard outside the bungalow, flaunting the hateful Enfield rifles. If he hid in the bushes, the gardener would discover him. Intercepting his jeep between the British part of town and the Indian had led to the earlier fiasco. With its constant distractions, Heera Mandi, where the superintendent could be found on a regular basis, inebriated and off his guard, as Samrat had argued, was his best option. But how could Chhote Nanu catch the man alone? A bomb took several seconds to fire off. And, how could he bring a weapon into Nigar Jaan's neighborhood? What if she got hurt, or her son? He'd have to make sure the two were no-where near the superintendent when he lit the fuse. But what if she hated him for the act of violence? How would he beg for her forgiveness from behind bars?

5

On the day of Nigar Jaan's poetry gathering, Chhote Nanu didn't look at the bomb. In the evening, he brushed his long hair, buttoned up a black achkan borrowed from his brother, tucked a rose in its top pocket, fastened his watch on his wrist. The jacket reached his calves, and the smart fabric imparted him with a striking profile. He looked tall for once, older and respectable like a teacher. He emphasized his eyes with black soot from the kerosene lamp. He felt grateful for his big nose that made him look modest and trustworthy. Bomb in the tin box, box handle dangling from his index finger like the leash of a beast of burden he detested, he put his right hand upon the divan of Daagh Dehlavi. The book seemed appropriate for the occasion. Back in the day, before the mutiny, Dehlavi's father was hanged for killing a British civil servant. If Chhote Nanu's nerves failed him, which they no doubt would, and nothing came of the bomb, which he fervently hoped, he could recite a Daagh verse and redeem himself. The poets would applaud, recognize his hidden revolutionary intent. He opened the box and put the collection under the bomb. He shuddered even just touching the vile object.

On his way to Heera Mandi, he ran into Samrat. The young nawab slid open Chhote Nanu's box to make sure the onion sat inside.

"Stand tall, *shaheed*! All the dead of Jallianwala are going with you."

Dear God, I hope not, thought Chhote Nanu. He didn't have it in him to become a martyr, seal his own death. His shoulders drooped. He swung the tin box limply as he marched down the lane.

Heera Mandi bubbled with excitement. Even before he reached Nigar Jaan's doorstep, Chhote Nanu spotted a crowd of well-dressed men waiting to gain entry. They looked like a parliament of penguins in their black achkans and freshly laundered silk kurtas. Chhote Nanu patted his own achkan, grateful for having borrowed it. Maybe Nigar Jaan would give him the gift of a glance, a bouquet of whole sentences. But then he felt the weight of the tin box, and he began to sweat. What if the doorman didn't let him through?

The line began to move. The doorman flicked a silver *ittardan* on the guests, showering them with rosewater incense. The guests chatted energetically about the famed poets in attendance.

The doorman frowned at Chhote Nanu's box and held him back.

"It's just some poetry," Chhote Nanu blurted, wishing he'd dropped the box in the river.

They went up the stairs. The plain walls opened into a vast room with big windows. Seats were arranged all around the periphery, chairs for Europeans, carpet for Indians. The men made a mad dash for the front seats, scattering over the floor.

A few poets, the uninvited ones who'd barged in with the crowd, sat discussing Nigar Jaan's family history like it were a sordid piece of gossip. Her grandmother, a destitute Englishwoman, had landed in India before the Mutiny of 1857 and moved into the army bar-racks in Cownpore for the pleasure of the soldiers. One day, Prince Nana Saheb saw her, fell head over heels in love with her, and rescued her from the barracks. He brought her to his *bibighar* in Bithoor and married her. When the mutiny was squashed and Nana Saheb disap-peared, well, the memsahib fell on hard times. For a while she passed herself off as a maid in English houses, first in Delhi, then Lahore. But her old reputation caught up with her (these English housewives, so cruel!), and she had to return to the houses. Years later, her daughter, Nigar Jaan's mother, suffered a similar fate: she too caught the eye of an aging nawab. He didn't marry her, but he provided for his unac-knowledged daughter, even sent her a tutor from France, made sure she had all the comforts, even if he couldn't give her his name. "So grandmother, mother, daughter, all have been in the trade for generations, huh?" The poets made rude faces. Chhote Nanu wanted to punch them.

Outside, a pink sun set between the golden domes of the Badshahi Mosque. Pigeons came to roost on the golden domes, then, as if chased by a call in the wind, they all flew south in unison. Chhote Nanu couldn't take his eyes off the view. It pleased him to think that Nigar Jaan awoke to it each morning. If proximity to a mosque could make one Muslim or Indian, she was certainly both.

By and by, the musicians filed in, short men in kurtas and pajamas and elaborate headgears, and took their places on the dais. The famed poets paraded in, followed by more local boys, admirers of Nigar Jaan; the thrill of gaining entry colored their faces red. The room was finally fully packed.

There couldn't have been a worse setup for the bomb. The room was brightly lit, a chandelier hung from a center hook, an oil lamp burned in every corner. The audience sat on tenterhooks. What was he supposed to do? Light the bomb and toss it in the center, so that the public, the musicians, Chhote Nanu himself, were all blasted together? It occurred to him that he would recreate Jallianwala, not protest the massacre. He prayed to God that the ladies would sit separately, Hindustani style and not English style, so the bomb would only harm the men. If by any luck the bomb went kaput, Chhote Nanu could shout a weak *"inqalaab!"* and surrender himself to the police.

The lights in the eastern corridor dimmed, and a memsahib glided into the room. She wore a cream dress of English embroidery, but her gray-black hair and wheat skin confirmed her Indian roots. She possessed charm enough to cause an old nawab to forgo his scruples. She took a chair to the east of the musicians. Nothing in her demeanor betrayed her unfortunate profession, except the nervous way she withheld her smile. Chhote Nanu marveled at her self-regard, the way she held herself proudly and sat frankly back. She may have lived in India a long time, but in that moment she looked contentedly English.

A moment later, her daughter walked into the room. Every head turned to look at her. Nigar Jaan wore a black sari with silver embroidery, an elaborate gold pendant around her delicate neck. She took a chair next to her mother, and Chhote Nanu saw the resemblance— the straight English nose and yellow-green eyes. She'd inherited her mother's best features, and enhanced them with more Indian coloring. He'd seen her many mornings for the past two weeks, but her face was always mottled by the shadows of trees, shaded by her panama hat. Here in her house, all the lights aglow, he saw her more clearly. He wondered if she noticed him. But there were far too many faces for her to focus on his.

The matron gave the signal, and the musicians began. They played an evening raga, a soft *yaman kalyan*. Nigar Jaan joined them, her voice strong, scaling the low registers beautifully. Chhote Nanu couldn't take his eyes off her. A painting had come to life.

The poetry recital began. A servant placed a candle before the senior-most poet, who recited couplets in the traditional style, repeating the first line until the audience had savored every word, and when they could take the suspense no longer, the poet delivered the second line. The hall resounded with "*wah wah*" and "well done" and "encore." More poets shared their compositions. But more than the poetry, the audience craved Nigar Jaan's reaction. Often, she tossed her smile liberally. But occasionally, she withheld her praise, and the poet crumbled, not sure whether to wait for a nod or to pass the flame. The candle made Chhote Nanu nervous. He clutched his box to his chest.

His side of the room reeked with eager amateurs. The boy beside him flipped the pages of a book, leaned back as though in a trance.

"What time is it?" the boy asked, snapping out of his trance. Chhote Nanu unclasped his watch to tap the thing back to life.

He looked like one of those Mori Gate boys from the crammed neighborhood behind the wool mills who switched allegiances for two annas, Gandhi one day, the Indian National Army the next, British one day, independence the next. There was something dismally upbraiding about his unpressed shirt, his devotion and nervousness at a mere poetry gathering.

"Good crowd she's gathered," said the nervous poet, following Chhote Nanu's gaze. "She has good taste for a market woman. Chiragh," he said, extending a hand.

Chhote Nanu's ears burned. He wanted to slap the chap, beat him until his mouth bled.

An hour later, Mutton marched into the room in khaki trousers and a sola topee, followed by three constables. The gathering came to a hush. The poets, the musicians, the audience rose respectfully, everyone except the two Anglo-Indian women. Chhote Nanu felt compelled to rise too. Samrat's voice began to shout in his head: "Light the fuse, find the superintendent alone."

Steel-faced, chastised but little for Jallianwala, in a room full of Indians, Mutton looked at ease, sweating not a bit, his face powdered dry. His red slit eyes scanned the room as though the house belonged to him and they'd all been trespassing.

The superintendent went to Nigar Jaan, and as though as a challenge to all, put a hand on her knee. Chhote Nanu's heart sank. Then it broke into a thousand pieces.

The great Jigar Moradabadi, finishing the main lineup of poets, wondered if they might hear from the youth in the room. The senior poets nodded in agreement. The great Jigar looked about for a suitable candidate in Chhote Nanu's section of the room.

"Anyone brave enough to charm the charming Nigar Jaan?"

A whole balcony of men raised their hands.

"You!" Jigar sahib's finger pointed straight at Chhote Nanu. "That is a very dignified black achkan. We might not get into too much trouble with you."

Chhote Nanu stood up. Everyone was looking at him, including the superintendent, and, to his surprise, Nigar Jaan. A smile of recognition played on her lips. The night turned into day.

"What is your *takhallus*?" Jigar sahib asked. Nigar Jaan scanned him from head to toe, and Chhote Nanu felt a wave of love for his brother, whose jacket he'd borrowed.

He looked around. Jigar sahib expected a truly brilliant pen name. Nothing sloppy or cheesy or clichéd would do. Aatish? Zikr? Haalat? All those pen names had already been uttered in the room. "Chiragh," he said suddenly, "Chiragh Dehlavi."

"A lamp from Delhi?" Jigar sahib raised his eyebrows.

The real Chiragh, whose name Chhote Nanu had stolen, slammed his book shut.

"Do you have an original verse for us, Chiragh? You can read from your book if you are nervous, young man."

He could read some Daagh, that much he could do. Chhote Nanu clutched the box close to his heart, fumbling for its clasp, trying to open it gently, afraid all its contents would come tumbling out. His hands sweated; he wiped them on his jacket.

At that moment, Nigar Jaan's son crept into the room. The ayah rushed in after him to scoop him into her arms. But the lad had seen his mother, and wouldn't give up his demand of going close to her. Nigar Jaan rose to take him away, excusing herself from the gathering. Soon after, her mother followed.

The ladies gone, Mutton's face took on a new pallor; he withdrew his eyes from Chhote Nanu as though he were a bug. The superintendent surveyed the party with disgust. How quickly they all became his inferiors—Chhote Nanu could see it in his eyes. A senior poet dressed in a faded Harris Tweed jacket and bearing a glass of drink tripped on Mutton's extended foot, spilled the liquid on the policeman's shoes.

"You stupid blind wog," the superintendent cursed him openly. "What are you staring at, you nincompoop," he shouted at the poet.

The gathering took in a collective breath. Even their most esteemed weren't immune to the white man's abuse.

A handful of poets rose to take reluctant leave, anxious to escape the abuses that awaited on the superintendent's tongue. This wasn't the gathering they'd been invited to. A sensation like an uncontrollable itch took hold of Chhote Nanu. *Light the fuse! Bring the bastard to justice!* He snapped open the tin box. He grasped the onion. Mutton had hidden behind his British hierarchy for far too long. Without a second thought, Chhote Nanu marched toward the candle.

"Everyone leave," he shouted in Hindustani for the benefit of the Indians in the room. "*In-kill-aaaaab! Down with the Raj!*" He pushed a poet toward the door, and the poet stared back, more in awe than shock, as though condoning his rebellion.

"It's a bomb!" shouted the superintendent. He made a mad dash toward the eastern corridor, but, finding the door locked, ran toward the stairs, chockablock with poets. The younger poets, as though in solidarity with the bomb, as though they'd anticipated the stunt all along, shut the door on the superintendent, leaving him and Chhote Nanu alone in the main hall.

This was his moment. It was now or never. Chhote Nanu thrust the wick of the bomb into the flame of the candle. "*In-kill-aaaaab!*" he shouted again as he tossed the lit bomb in the direction of Mutton.

The propulsion that thundered through his ears was nothing like Chhote Nanu had heard before. It felt as though a wild animal had descended in the room. From behind a fortress of cushions, Chhote Nanu watched the bright orange flash like a tiger's skin. A window burst, a lamp crashed to the floor, several glasses lay smashed.

The room shimmered under a blanket of firecracker residue. Chhote Nanu's own body was unharmed. More shaken than hurt, he pulled himself up blinking, waiting for the dust to settle.

A moment later, the superintendent's head emerged from behind the English sofa. A fine dust of debris settled on his gray hair, betraying his true age. He extricated himself from under cushions, his body whole, looked about the room as though waking up from a dream. He picked his way through the debris, batting the cloud of soot. Had he suffered any injuries? Chhote Nanu couldn't be sure. The policeman's eyes came to rest on him.

It occurred to Chhote Nanu that he ought to make a run for it. But the door to the stairwell remained shut, the stairs clogged with poets, many of whom awaited the outcome of the bomb.

Mutton marched over the wreckage toward Chhote Nanu. He didn't seem to be limping or bleeding. The policeman caught Chhote Nanu by the elbow and raised him, the gesture almost more helpful than accusatory. He escorted Chhote Nanu to the door, ordered the doorman to unlock it that instant or find his whole family in jail.

A minute later, the Indian constables pushed through the crowd. Chhote Nanu's hands were tied behind his back with ropes; he was dragged down the stairs.

The poets regarded him not with disdain or reprimand, but with something Chhote Nanu could only describe as surprised admiration. He saw a strange soft light in Jigar sahib's eyes, and understood it as approbation. Chhote Nanu hadn't produced revolutionary poetry; he'd produced a revolution. He felt vain, but also, for the first time, quizzically unafraid.

The gathering was herded out by the police. At the bottom of the stairs, Mutton turned to them. "All these years you have blamed me for Jallianwala. I am the monster. Today you see the British don't have monopoly on violence."

Chhote Nanu couldn't let the superintendent get away with assuaging his guilt in this manner. The senior poets' defiance guiding the muscles in his face, he shut his eyes and said in the most unhurried voice he could muster: "The bomb was for you alone, Mr. Mutton. For Jallianwala."

The constable behind him slammed a baton into Chhote Nanu's back. He fell headlong over someone's feet. Still, at that moment, he felt vindicated. In a twisted way, he'd succeeded in the mission. Who knew if his parents, Barre Nanu, and Nigar Jaan would forgive him. He craned his neck up the stairs to steal a look, even as the constable tried to turn him away.

For a minute, all he could see were the poets clogging the stairway, all swaying in various shades of pride, and this vision of their grateful eyes calmed him. But then, the magnanimous crowds parted. There she stood, in the middle of the chaos of the room. She took a step toward the stairwell, and Chhote Nanu saw. She had cut her hand, and a drop of blood glistened on her wrist. She must have cut herself on a piece of glass. This, and also this: her shouting eyes were upon him. And this time he wasn't mistaken. She saw him in a way she couldn't have seen him before. Her irises dark with shock, registering the altered aspect of her house. Something had come alive in her body, and she was almost leaning toward him, as though stopping herself from rushing down the stairs to slap him or shake him or both. Unlike in the park, she didn't look away but directly at him. Her profession, the superintendent, all had suddenly ceased to matter. Something told him she would defy the policeman for him. Something urged him to hope against hope.

August 2002

Someone kept shouting. I opened my eyes to find a determined old man waving a brass lota. A pilgrim from downstairs. He wore only a flimsy loincloth, and yet, the way he stared at me as I lay sleeping, I felt more exposed. Their prayers were starting, could I fetch more milk? What kind of a Hindu household did not keep a private cow?

I told him we were a house in mourning. We'd lost our grandfather only eight months ago. We couldn't purchase a cow so soon. To my surprise, he accepted the explanation and went away.

I looked about the room. Ila's bed was made, her slippers gone. Bright white light invaded from the balcony facing the lane, uniting with the light from the courtyard. Ila's books lay scattered on the desk by the window, each one uncovering some aspect of the social history of Delhi, each one open, pages tucked in-between other pages. In the last three years, she'd switched her major three times, flitted from one department at Jawaharlal Nehru University to another. She'd begun with English then switched to anthropology, given that up for political science, then given that up for sociology, last I heard. I felt partly responsible for her indecision. I hadn't shared her burdens. I'd let her bear all the disruptions, left her to care for Barre Nanu, sort through Chhote Nanu's madness. She organized protests in college, climbed monuments and held up posters, demanding higher wages for the cleaning staff and better safety protocols for the all-girls dorms. Once, she and her collective spent a few hours in jail for blocking a politician's car on its way to the parliament. She emailed me about her incarceration only because she feared the papers might carry the news, and she didn't want Barre Nanu to find out. She lived on the edge in a way that I hadn't, likely couldn't.

If Barre Nanu hadn't died, I'd have stayed away for six more years. Ila's condescending words had turned my heart cold, broken our already dysfunctional family. I could still hear her taunting me—"You have to face facts. Your father wants nothing to do with you."

It came back to me again, my freshman year at IIT Bombay, Bebe's kidney failing, her white face in the hospital, her black lie, the darkness after. No one told me not to go to CUNY, not Ila, not Bebe, not Barre Nanu, not Chhote Nanu. No one told me to come home. Barre Nanu wrote once, on his coarse Rehman Saris stationery, telling me the following in his clipped, precise prose: "Enclosed please find one kilo of almonds and two kilos of dried figs. Your mother wants you to take them with milk. Don't be angry with her. I spoiled her. If you want to blame someone, blame me." He didn't understand. I needed someone to be angry for me. At one time, that job had been Chhote Nanu's. I needed my granduncle to shout at Bebe, to send me some Urdu verses and bandage my wound with poetry. But ever since he turned to religion, he'd distanced himself from our wing of the family.

Bebe and I hadn't talked in six years. She'd written once, describing the weather, the season's mangoes, and her improved health. I wrote back, demanding she divulge the details about my father. But she didn't respond. She stopped writing altogether. And so did Ila, the one person I'd hoped would plead my case. Ila didn't write once. That is, not until Barre Nanu's heart began to fail.

"Ila," I called needlessly in the empty room, put on my slippers, and went downstairs. My sister stirred a pot of tea in the kitchen. She twisted open a small plastic bag of milk and emptied the contents into the pot on the stove. The concoction came to a boil. She poured it into two cups.

"I went and got some groceries. I figured I should shelter you from all these Hindus. Considering you're half Muslim." She dipped her thumb into a pot of sugar and sucked it.

"I don't know for sure if I am Muslim."

"Your father is. Means you are too."

"I don't know if he is a practicing Muslim or not. Or where he lives. Or what he does." I'd just turned twenty-five and I didn't even know my father's name.

Ila tilted her head toward the living room. "To some people, knowing a person's religion is more important than knowing their profession or name." She began washing the cups. "Anyway, it's only a matter of time before you know everything."

"Why? Have you talked to Bebe? Did you ask her about my father?"

"No, *rey*, I know nothing, just like you."

"I don't believe that." Ila couldn't have lost her knack for manipulation, for protesting and shouting until administrative bodies gave into her demands. She looked smug as she rinsed the teacups. She'd met my father. She'd met hers too. They'd become pen pals, talked on the phone every week. She'd convinced him to fund her education.

"I know nothing. Same as you."

I didn't believe her. Just then the pilgrims in the living room started chanting.

"Bebe has a lot of explaining to do. Has she called?"

Ila shook her head.

I tried not to let self-pity engulf me. What was keeping our mother? Why didn't she feel the need to see us?

September 1943

1

Near the steps of the Badshahi Mosque, Barre Nanu heard a commotion passing through the night market: the police were dragging a handcuffed man. Barre Nanu returned his gaze to the potatoes, more pebbles than potatoes, under the dim lights of the vegetable stall. The faint kerosene lamp imparted a funereal glow to the otherwise cheerful Lahore market. But the lights had to be kept low for fear of air raids. The Japanese air force might bomb them anytime, but the rations had to be bought and the looms kept running. Barre Nanu nestled a lemon in his palm to judge its juiciness, promoted it to his basket. A half-moon of discounted jackfruit enticed him, and he asked the vegetable wallah to put it on the scale. The man complied and even tossed a bunch of green chilies into Barre Nanu's basket.

The grocer couldn't help but be kind to him. He saw Barre Nanu most weeks, and knew that he came from a good family, a family with some means even in these difficult times of war and black marketing; there was not a crease on his fine black achkan that finished smartly below his knees, just above the ample attractive folds of his white *churidar* pajamas. Barre Nanu's frank, deep-set eyes afforded him the look of a man whose trust you wanted to earn. He wasn't a man of many words. He never haggled. What was his opinion on the war, the grocer with the perpetually green fingers wondered. Whatever it was, Barre Nanu looked like a smart gray raincloud rising above these times of hardship. Even the ruckus didn't shake him.

The commotion passed right behind Barre Nanu. A constable bumped past him, carried on. The policemen were escorting a prisoner in a black achkan, equally as dignified as Barre Nanu's. The prisoner kept his hair long. As they stuffed him inside the jeep, the policemen shone a torch at him, and Barre Nanu saw his face.

Chhote wore a noose around his neck. A streak of blood ran down his forehead. Barre Nanu dropped his basket of potatoes and elbowed his way through the crowd, trying to reach the convoy. "Sahib, this is my brother. There must be some mistake." But the superintendent swung his baton at Barre Nanu, hopped into the driver's seat, and drove off, leaving behind a cloud of dust.

Barre Nanu tried to run after the jeep, but the lane teemed with shoppers. He asked the vegetable sellers the quickest route to the police station. Apart from directions, they didn't offer any words of wisdom. They witnessed young men being dragged to jail on a regular basis, beaten for petty crimes or for no reason at all. Barre Nanu looked mournfully at his potatoes and the newspaper parcel of jackfruit clogging the drain—the war in Europe had been going on for four years, and the intense rationing and the black marketing had hiked the prices of everything. He wiped a handful of vegetables under the hem of his achkan and pocketed them before mounting his bicycle and riding to the police station.

At the station, he pleaded with the police to see his brother, but the constables did not relent. Behind them, the superintendent wrote furiously at the big desk. The sahib looked old, in his fifties, pugnacious, the way he sat leaning forward and frowning. His mouth looked scrubbed raw, as though he'd swallowed a handful of chilies.

"*Huzoor*," Barre Nanu addressed the superintendent. "You have my brother. He is only seventeen. What has he done? If you've caught him for loitering, I promise you I will break his legs as soon as you release him." Chhote liked to push his luck, go where Indians were expressly frowned upon, like Lawrence Gardens. He'd been forbidden to take that shortcut.

The superintendent trained his small, cold eyes on Barre Nanu, eyes so pale they saw straight through him. Even in this heat, he wore a collar and a tie. His lip curled. What he saw was a smartly dressed Indian man, who even in this difficult time looked well nourished, most of his wits about him. Handsome in the Indian way, with a plain, straight nose. He spoke perfect English. Exactly the kind of wog Mutton hated, the kind who might look down upon Mutton, like all the upper-class English. The policeman's blood rose to boiling temperature. "This isn't your mother's place of business," he barked. "Get lost."

Barre Nanu swallowed the insult and left the station. The guard at the gate told him to wait an hour until the English sahib went home for the night.

Barre Nanu returned to the police station after an hour. This time the head constable blinked at him furiously, but did not tell him to leave.

"What has my brother done? I am going to tie him to the court-yard tree. He won't set foot outside the house ever again."

The younger constables debated whether to answer Barre Nanu's question or throw him out. They didn't care how dignified Barre Nanu looked. They might have been all Indians in the room without the *gora* sahib, but the colonial enterprise divided them—the British law permitted the khakied men all kinds of meanness. The older constable finally relented. The case was hopeless. Telling Barre Nanu wasn't going to change a thing.

"Your brother tried to assassinate the superintendent of police. He set off a bomb the size of a cricket ball at a gathering at Heera Mandi."

The world went still. For a long moment, Barre Nanu wondered if he'd gone deaf and mute. When he found his voice, he asked: "Was anyone hurt?"

The policemen were unmoved by his state of shock. "No one was hurt. But this is treason of the highest order. Trying to blow up the chief of police! What guts!"

"Technically, he carried a firecracker," the older constable tried.

The younger constables scoffed. "The superintendent isn't going to consider technicalities."

Barre Nanu felt as though he'd been shot in the heart. How could Chhote get his hands on firecrackers? Where on earth could he . . . It had to have been Samrat. That ne'er-do-well nawab's son was a bad influence. One night, Barre Nanu had seen him loitering outside Montgomery Hall with a set of older boys dressed in army fatigues. The next morning, posters had appeared on the theater's outer walls. "Twenty English dogs for every INA soldier." The INA had brought out the devil in civilized young boys. Did they really think their ragtag outfit could liberate India from the British?

It took all of Barre Nanu's strength not to collapse. "If you let me see my brother, I will drag the name of the real culprit out of him."

"Your brother confessed to his crime. Besides, he is not permitted visitors. Don't you know how serious this is? Don't you know what can happen to him? Transportation to Andaman. *Umar qaid.* Life sentence. That or the gallows." The younger constable raised his voice as a challenge.

Barre Nanu felt weak in the knees. The gallows. The Andaman Islands. Transportation, the most lenient of punishments on the list, was likely the cruelest. The islands lay hundreds of kilometers away, in the Bay of Bengal. No one ever came back from Andaman alive. Prisoners were sent there to spend the rest of their days in misery, a fate worse than death.

"He's a boy of seventeen. If there is anything I can offer . . ." Barre Nanu's hand flew to his pocket.

The older constable colored. His eyes lingered, and Barre Nanu didn't pull his hand away. The war had left everyone hungry. So many families had gone without food, some hadn't eaten rice in as many as three years.

"There's nothing to be done. Superintendent sahib will make sure your brother gets the strictest punishment. He won't even get a trial. Under the Government of India Act, the superintendent can punish whomever he likes however he likes. Now please." The constable pointed to the door.

Barre Nanu left the station dejected. His brother wielded bombs and frequented prostitutes. How had this come about? Barre Nanu had been caught up with his own affairs, ignored Chhote all this year. Samrat had swooped in and misled the boy, made him dream dreams of revolution. Equally, he could blame Gandhi, who'd escalated his demand to the British to quit India in a matter of months. Dear God, what would happen if the British left? For one, those upstart constables and the whole colonial apparatus would fold. But what if the British held on to India? They'd need her to fight their wars, keep their mills running. He wouldn't believe the British were leaving until he witnessed the Queen Victoria statue on Mall Road razed, the English menus at Nedous Hotel replaced with Urdu ones. Besides, unlike Chhote, he wasn't completely sure that the British quitting India was such a good idea.

Because he'd seen lawyer Baksh's photos in the newspapers alongside Gandhi's, Barre Nanu pedaled to Lawrence Gardens. The lawyer had a reputation for representing Indians in difficult cases, sometimes even getting their sentences reduced. If anyone could save Chhote, it was him.

The bungalows on Lawrence Road were grand and freestanding, not like the havelis packed cheek-by-jowl in the native part of town. Each was exclusively built for British residents, although, since the turn of the century, wealthy Indians had moved into the smaller houses. Barre Nanu rode past the public gardens. A handful of English gentlemen roamed the winding paths, no Indians in sight. Ironic, because the gardens, like most of the bungalows, were funded by native landowners.

The gate to lawyer Baksh's bungalow on Lawrence Road stood open. Barre Nanu took the liberty of riding up the circular drive. Wicker chairs sat expectantly on the front veranda, and on the flat roof, behind a decorated balustrade, a gardener was watering a row of marigolds. A servant in a white uniform appeared at the door and pointed to the private garden. Baksh sahib's son was tending to the rose bushes.

Ali Baksh looked in his mid-twenties, two or three years older than Barre Nanu, with a long nose that gave him a handsome profile. He introduced himself as a reader of law at King's College. Barre Nanu couldn't help but feel a bout of envy for the chap's good fortune of being able to study abroad. But then again, Ali had descended from a nawab loyal to the Crown. The British had practically manufactured these families after the 1857 mutiny, surrounding themselves with loyal locals, rewarding good behavior with titles and land and money.

"I'm surprised you haven't heard. My father is in jail. All the papers carried the news." Ali plucked a yellowing leaf from the rose bush. The flowers were of a foreign variety—small and pink. "After Gandhiji refused to cooperate with the war effort, the British arrested the Congress Working Committee."

Ali Baksh and the rest of the world tilted, as though on an axis. Barre Nanu grabbed onto his bicycle. The lawyer who could get Chhote out himself languished in prison. How could it be? Gandhi had poisoned everyone's minds. "My brother, sahib. He tried to . . ." Barre Nanu couldn't say the words. "The police say he took a bomb to Heera Mandi. For the superintendent."

Ali's eyes widened with surprise. "Your brother tried to assassinate Mutton?"

Barre Nanu pulled off his pagri in shame. "I can swear on my mother's life Chhote cannot make bombs. It must have been a small firecracker." *Arrest that Samrat*, he wanted to shout. *Arrest that no-good nawab's son.* "We are a law-abiding family. Not one Khatri has ever broken a British law."

Ali nodded with concern. "I'm sure you abide by British laws. But under the Defense of India Act, the British can do whatever they like. If they can arrest Gandhi, then what chance does your brother have?" He clipped a dead stem. "You speak well, clearly you've finished college. Government College, am I right? Your trouble is, you see the British from the inside, not from the outside, like your brother does. You're too optimistic."

Barre Nanu didn't think there could be such a thing as too much optimism. Had he put too much faith in the Raj? He couldn't bring himself to feel the same anger for the British that Chhote felt. How had his brother manufactured his rage? There was so much he wanted to ask his brother. "Is there nothing I can do?"

The young lawyer dropped the scissors, brushed his hands on his kurta. "You could try to bribe someone so you could see him. Take him some food and books."

"A bribe? There is a chance I can see my brother?"

"A very small chance. But you should forget about getting him released."

Barre Nanu dropped his head. "What about your father?" he dared to ask. "Will he get released? Have you seen him?"

Ali's brow clouded with worry. "I haven't seen my father in over a year. I have no idea how they are treating him. The British can do anything they like." He squatted and thrust the scissors into the ground. "Only the INA can save us now. You know they're responsible for the Japanese taking Burma? Tasting more defeat overseas might make the British see sense. When a great empire falls, a new regime takes its place. I hope it's our boys who taste victory."

Since when had everyone begun to hate the British so openly? Since Gandhi had come to the fore. Him and the rest of the Congress Party. Until then, the nawabs and the rich supported the Raj. The nizam of Hyderabad, the richest man in the world, had donated lakhs of rupees to the war fund. But a sudden gust of revolutionary winds had changed everything. "Do you really think the INA can drive out the British?" Barre Nanu asked. The lawyer was right. He'd been educated by the British, taught to trust their justice, their competence. "Every war the British have fought they've won."

"All the more reason for them to lose their hold on India. The sun is going to set on their precious empire."

Barre Nanu didn't understand the first thing about statecraft. He understood cloth. Cotton, silk, muslin, khadi, Harris Tweed, how long each took to weave, and what looked good on a fat *sahukar* on his way to his jewelry store or on a young bride first setting foot inside her in-laws'. He conveyed his hopes for the lawyer's father's release. His eyes brimmed as he maneuvered his bicycle up the garden path. Who knew if he would ever see his Chhote again. Who knew if the bribe would work, and how much money he would have to gather for it.

He cycled into the inner walled city, the native part of town, built and destroyed several times as regimes changed. The mighty gates, several feet tall, stood salient through time, bearing their endearing names with equanimity—Kashmiri, Dilli, Shahalmi, Lohari, Bhati. He admired Shahalmi Gate's royal aura, felt pride as he passed through the tall arches.

The air in the house felt thick with the orange shock of vermillion. Their mother's troop of hymn singers must have departed a few minutes ago. In the room adjacent to the kitchen, Chaiji's sewing machine sat laden with wedding trousseaus she altered for the wealthy neighbors. People didn't know just how hard the times had been for their family, and everything they had to do to make ends meet.

In the kitchen, oblivious to the news, Chaiji slapped rotis on the hot *tava*. Her thick glasses fogged from the steam, and she kept wiping them on her sleeves.

"Are you home, Barre?" she asked without turning around. Her arms traveled deftly between her arsenal of spices. "Wash your hands and come eat. Tell your brother also. It's only you two for dinner. I am fasting. I am asking God to give you both some wisdom."

Barre Nanu's heart hurt for her. How could he tell her about Chhote? Chaiji was insatiably hardworking and acrimonious. She could cook for a hundred in a matter of hours, sew a complex design with ten different threads within minutes. But he couldn't remember the last time he'd seen her laugh or cry. She was a piece of land someone had forgotten to water. "I'm a broomstick you men keep in the house," she liked to complain. "Clean this, sew that, keep the stove hot. No one ever tells me anything." His heart hurt to keep her in the dark, but he was determined not to tell her about Chhote's recent misdemeanor. It surprised him a little how easily he could manipulate her.

He came and sat on the floor next to her.

"Where is Chhote? Is he eating at Samrat's?"

"No," Barre Nanu said, disturbed by the mention of Samrat's name.

Chaiji put Chhote's share of rotis on his plate, then retreated into her sewing room. Time and again she'd berated him to learn sewing. The more skill one possessed in one's hands, the richer one was, she liked to say. Chaiji hadn't read Marx. More skills would make you more of a worker. Ought he to listen to her now? They'd likely need to sew trousseaus from here until Kashmir if they wanted to see Chhote. Barre Nanu folded his brother's share of rotis and placed them carefully into a cloth napkin. Better to offer them to a needier person on the street.

He couldn't comprehend the magnitude of what his brother had done. What kind of a man was he becoming, frequenting prostitutes in the red-light district, setting off bombs? But then came the memory of the chilly mornings he'd walked Chhote to school, their fingers linked in the predawn light. For a number of years, Barre Nanu had watched over his brother with an almost paternal longing.

Chaiji called him again, shaking Barre Nanu out of his reverie. What kind of bribe would make the constable bend his scruples, and how long would it take Barre Nanu to earn it? Mending trousseaus wouldn't do it. He had to get the family business going, even if it meant betraying his father. He ran down the stairs, flung a leg over his bicycle, and rode into town.

2

The remnants of Khatri Fabrics lay tucked in a corner of Shahalmi Market, a cluster of lanes thin as a hairpin. The grand red-brick apartments were built in the times of the Mughals and the Sikhs. Once, they'd housed prominent courtiers and nawabs. Now they had been repurposed into shops. Cloth merchants, jewelers, furniture wallahs, and shoemakers shared tight quarters. Tea stalls nestled like flowers in a head of hair, sending aromas of ginger and cloves in giant coils at all hours. The war had renewed many businesses. Steel mills and cotton gins had erupted on the outskirts of the city to supply the army with uniforms and kit bags. Smart boutiques advertised European-style clothing. Many new shops glittered with electricity. But here, in the corner of the last lane, their family boutique lay shrouded in darkness.

Barre Nanu fumbled for the kerosene lamp as soon as he set foot inside. The workbenches sat empty, the yardstick expectant, glistening like a sword. Columns of dusty fabric arranged like soldiers in the shelves waited to be measured and sheared and sold. The shop hadn't had a decent order for either wedding trousseaus or daily wear since the beginning of the war. The two tailors they'd employed back when orders trickled in with some regularity had quit. He sank on a bench and studied the pattern of an army uniform drawn on brown paper that he'd stolen from his uncle's shop.

Across the street, the showrooms of Tijori Fabrics simmered with activity. Each month, Babuji's own brother supplied one thousand uniforms to the Government of India Defense Department. Countless sergeants and captains strode in and out of Tijori Uncle's shop, followed by native boys carrying brown parcels of tailored suits and trousers, while the cash register overflowed with new money. Despite the war, or because of it, Tijori Uncle had done well.

There could be only one explanation for Tijori Uncle's success—the portly, pragmatic man with a penchant for silk cravats had refused to take a hit for the nationalist cause. His competitors who'd joined the independence movement had shut down their shops and ceased doing business with the British. But Tijori Uncle had chosen the winning, unrepentant side of history. His house brimmed with light, laughter, and rice.

Babuji hadn't followed his younger brother's footsteps. He'd chosen to swim against the forward march of history. In 1922, Gandhi had visited Amritsar for a public meeting to share his message of noncooperation with the British government. Babuji, in attendance, had felt himself shedding a skin. He'd bought the four-anna Congress Party membership, subscribed to *Young India*, read a banned copy of Gandhi's *Hind Swaraj* that evening. That same month, at a gathering, he'd tossed his beloved Harris Tweed jacket, his only piece of foreign clothing, into a bonfire. Then, a year later, when the Congress volunteers came to enlist support for the independence movement, he discarded all the Manchester cloth sitting inside his shop and vowed to work exclusively with handloom cloth, even if that meant reducing their operations to a handful of orders a month. Their customers dwindled. One by one, he fired the weavers who'd been in the family's employ for generations. Their shop hollowed out, bereft of most of its contents. Babuji did nothing all day except scour the newspapers for news on Gandhi. He didn't bat an eye when Chaiji took in sewing to make ends meet. For this last reason, Barre Nanu resented his father a little.

Tijori Uncle had an explanation for Babuji's madness. He believed Babuji had turned defeatist. Not wanting to work with the British was as good as giving up. But in truth, more than anything, his father wanted to restore the family business to its former glory.

As a child, Barre Nanu had heard Babuji tell stories of the illustrious Khatri Fabrics. Back in their heyday, about a hundred and fifty years ago, their family shipped cloth as far west as West Africa and as far east as Japan. They'd employed almost a hundred weavers and another hundred spinners, willowers, bleachers, dyers, spoolers, a vast network of workers. But then the East India Company gained an appetite for India, and began gobbling up territories and monopolizing all trade. One fine day, the power loom came into existence, and almost overnight all the ancient cities that had clothed the world—Calicut, Dhaka, Surat, Madras—turned into consumers of the "fast" machine-made British cloth. Babuji's grandfather was forced to trade English cloth, same as his father. Babuji himself, when he inherited the business, tried investing in ginning and failed, applied for loans and failed, hired an English engineer (before the independence movement) and failed.

Firing most all of his Muslim weavers weighed on Babuji's conscience. He'd had to let them go because it was no longer profitable to buy and sell Indian cloth. But after Gandhi appeared on the national scene, spinning-wheel in hand, Babuji began to hope for the return of the golden days of Khatri Fabrics. The mahatma would revive the old weaving traditions; he would make handloom cloth popular again (all the nationalist leaders were already wearing handmade khadi); he would see them through toward independence and self-reliance.

But Barre Nanu could see the error in his father's thinking. Handloom cloth would never make a resurgence, not at the scale that would help their business, and not at wartime. As his uncle said, the time of the Mughals was over. The time of the Sikhs was over. You could no longer wait around for a God-ordained monarch to come around and grant you a royal charter. You had to take risks, move with the times. If you wanted to stay afloat, you had to work with the British.

Now, inside in the shuttered shop, Barre Nanu knew he had to disregard his father's nationalist sentiments and join his uncle. If he wanted to ever see Chhote again, he had to swallow the guilt of breaking his father's heart.

Barre Nanu heard the shuffling of feet at the door. He hastened to gather the earthen tea cups, kicked the biri stubs under the carpet. A customer at this hour?

It was his father. Chaiji must have told him he was here. Babuji had thinned in recent years. The white pagri on his head looked too grand for him, failed to grant him the prestige it once did. His eyes lingered on the proprietor's raised platform in the semidarkness. Barre Nanu could see the disappointment on his father's caustic face with its un-pomaded mustache. It would be better if he yelled, cursed the British. But Babuji wouldn't utter a word. He'd taken a vow of silence since the previous year.

Babuji regarded the earthen water jug on the stool. His father wanted a drink of water. But the jug was empty: no one had been by the shop in over a week.

"Babuji," Barre Nanu said. He could no longer keep the bad news to himself. "Something has happened to Chhote." He told his father about the bomb, about Chhote frequenting the red-light district, about his arrest. He couldn't bring himself to mention Chhote's likely punishment—transportation over the black oceans to Andaman.

Babuji's eyes blinked like a metronome, trying to grasp the details of Chhote's crime. Babuji raised his hand and tapped a finger on his forehead. *Chaiji must not be told.* He pointed toward the door, put a finger to his lips. *No one must know.* His watery eyes looked to heaven, fell back. *It's destiny, what can be done?* He'd already begun to despair. Tijori Uncle was right. Babuji was a terrible fatalist.

"The police might take a bribe," Barre Nanu said slowly, paying no mind to his father's histrionics. "You don't approve. But if we could gather funds . . ."

Babuji cupped his hands over his ears. Both his sons had disappointed him in one night. He shuffled to the table, ripped a piece of paper from the ledger and scribbled something.

Barre Nanu read the note: "Bribery is ugly. Gandhiji says: The means determine the end. We take everyone with us, or there is no true independence. You can't fight fate." Barre Nanu wanted to shout. His father would rather they sit and do nothing. He read the next line: "Don't go running to your uncle. His morals are corrupt."

Barre Nanu couldn't understand his father's cold heart. Babuji had never paid his sons any mind, never taken interest in the matter of their schooling. Chaiji had done everything, paid their fees, stitched their uniforms, covered their textbooks. When the time came for Barre Nanu to choose a college, he'd turned to Tijori Uncle for advice. "Are we going to let our Chhote languish in jail?" Barre Nanu protested.

Babuji's face took on a faraway look, his eyes monk-like in their resolve to disregard all earthly entanglements. He scratched his arm indulgently, sat leaning forward. At any moment he might abandon their family and set off with the sadhus to meditate in the Himalayas. He adjusted his pagri over his head, then with uncharacteristic violence, he tossed it to the floor. He left the store, not asking if Barre Nanu wanted to come along.

Barre Nanu slammed the door behind his father. "What's going to happen to us after the English have gone?" he shouted to the empty shop. "Does the Congress have a plan? Why must we talk only of revolution?" He took the portrait of Gandhi that'd been hanging on the wall since Babuji's conversion and smashed it against the floor.

Barre Nanu couldn't rely on Babuji for anything. He'd have to pay his uncle a visit, first thing the next morning.

Uncle Tijori's new house in Gowal Mandi stood past the British civil station. The English town with its whitewashed colleges, hospitals, and the Masonic Lodge looked clean and orderly. Khaki-clad officers dashed about in their jeeps, beeping at his bicycle even though Barre Nanu didn't stand in their way. As he rode past Montgomery Hall, he noticed the remnants of anti-British posters, the same ones Samrat and the INA rebels had posted. Barre Nanu's hands shook and he rode on farther past Nedous Hotel. On the lawns, the gentry, both Indian and British, mingled, ate cake, sipped tea under the mid-morning sun, oblivious to the war. Barre Nanu envied them their simple pleasures. How fine their clothes looked—the smart knee-length frocks on the English ladies, the black jackets on the men, the white trousers. The simple idea of making European clothes had launched Tijori Uncle's business. His morals might have been corrupt, but he'd made more money in thirty years than Khatri Fabrics had made in two hundred. If Babuji was the dull, grumpy tortoise, Tijori Uncle was the unrelenting hare, steps ahead, winning the short-term race; but the way the British were rewriting their future and their old parables, Tijori Uncle might win the long-term race as well.

Tijori Uncle's haveli boasted five floors, the top two unfinished. Here, in the native part of town, the houses grew vertically, as though afraid to take up space. Each floor inside the house was the size of two, the ceilings as high as a Mughal tomb's. In the study, a portable electric fan whirred in a corner. Uncle sat bent before a small table, hands clasped, beaming at a chessboard, as though the game would reveal its methodology if he simply stared at the pieces. At his uncle's house, Barre Nanu became aware of a modern idea of prosperity, one that incorporated Mughal excesses with English impatience. He took a breath, told himself to weigh his words. But the thought of profiting off his uncle made him nervous. Chaiji (and in a way Babuji too) had raised him to be proud, to offer help rather than to ask for it.

Tijori Uncle waved Barre Nanu to a chair. A bemused look played on his face as he practiced incorrect moves on the chessboard. He looked two decades younger than Babuji. Barre Nanu credited this to his good fortune.

"Finally, I can stop looking like a fool. Come join me," his uncle said indulgently. "Be patient with a novice!"

Barre Nanu's sweating hand closed upon a pawn. "Chhote is in jail," he said softly. He'd failed to weigh his words. He swallowed his shame and told his uncle about the bomb and the superintendent. "They didn't even let me see him."

Tijori Uncle's features, clean and handsome like Babuji's, scrunched into a despairing "Oh." He retrieved a bottle of scotch and a crystal glass from the glass cabinet and took a swig.

A swell of hope bubbled in Barre Nanu's heart. Why couldn't Babuji have mustered such a reaction?

Tijori Uncle rested the glass against his forehead, his eyes shut, as though trying to conjure some magic. "What can we do? I can write to the magistrate. No, better to go see him. Have you considered bribing the police? Good, then you must do all you can. Don't listen to your father." A nervous energy animated his uncle.

Barre Nanu wiped his face. Where his father saw the impossible hand of fate, Tijori Uncle saw a world of possibilities. There was no way out of this chasm except clinging to the ropes Tijori Uncle tossed. In return, he would do anything his uncle asked, short of selling his soul. "I want to join your shop. I have to make money for Chhote." There. He'd offered his uncle his body *and* soul.

His uncle's face spread into a broad smile. "How long have I waited to hear you say this?" He offered Barre Nanu his glass of scotch, daring him to drink.

Barre Nanu held the glass with both hands, unsure of what to do with it. He'd never taken a drink in his life. "I can learn to sew, or anything else you want me to do—"

"No need for that," Tijori Uncle said smartly. "I can set you up with sewing machines in your father's shop. The army wants to double my orders. Let's see how you do with a hundred uniforms."

Barre Nanu brought the glass to his lips. The drink tasted like betrayal, but he swallowed nonetheless. His father would never agree to repurpose the shop for Tijori Uncle's business. Barre Nanu would have to defy him openly. What was the worst that could happen? Babuji would throw him out. It wouldn't be the first time. Once, Babuji had found a ticket to the English talkies in Barre Nanu's pocket. Chhote had wanted to go to the movies. Babuji dragged both his sons out of the house, and locked the door. The disagreement lasted a whole day, after which time Chaiji fetched her boys from the corner shop where they'd slept, and advised them to pretend like nothing happened. Babuji protested mildly: refused a meal, returned to his routine the next day. But pride told Barre Nanu not to use his father's shop. "Can I rent a small corner at yours?" he asked his uncle.

"Not possible. We are completely full. I thought of setting up machines here. But I can't bring workers where my wife and my daughters live. The neighbors will ridicule me."

He'd have to use his father's shop. "Babuji said something about including everyone. He means the handloom weavers, doesn't he?" All his father cared about was reviving handloom cloth. "He feels bad about firing his weavers."

Tijori Uncle stiffened with envy. Over the years, it felt as though he kept a tally of the times he'd drawn Barre Nanu out from Babuji's care, as if he wanted to prove that he deserved his nephew's adoration more. "Don't listen to your father," he warned, his eyes unblinking for the first time. "This isn't the time to do charity. Focus on Chhote. The weavers are doing fine. They are working the mills. Who do you think is keeping the British army clothed?"

"Babuji feels guilty they aren't earning a living wage."

Tijori Uncle shut his eyes. Barre Nanu feared he'd angered his uncle for good. But then his uncle said: "Why don't you employ the weavers? Offer them a higher salary than the British. Have them make the army uniforms. They can weave, how hard can it be for them to learn to sew?"

Could it really work? He could ask Babuji's old weavers to join the business. Babuji wouldn't have any objections then. Perhaps he'd even bless the enterprise.

"People want to be happy," Tijori Uncle said. "If it profits the weavers to work with you, they will."

Barre Nanu reached for the scotch, but Tijori Uncle put it out of his reach. His uncle hadn't the devil in him, he had wisdom, and a new way of looking at things. He had modern eyes. What if the weavers agreed to work with him? What could they not achieve together? They might reconcile Tijori Uncle's laissez-faire capitalism with Babuji's Gandhian moral code. They might even be able to rescue Chhote.

Later that day, Barre Nanu went to pay Moin Ansari a visit. He hadn't seen the weaver since the Khatris stopped employing Moin's father.

Moin lived in a dilapidated mohalla of weavers. The mismatched brick houses resembled slums. Shacks of wood protruded from crumbling facades, sprouting like ugly outgrowths. Crude metal signs advertised bicycle repair and handloom fabric for cheap. Rickshaw limbs lay haphazardly on doorsteps, tires hung from trees. The men here had achieved a kind of two-dimensionality possible only in cubist paintings, their tight lungis and loosely hanging kurtas revealing the meagerness of their meals. The children running errands had hair the color of hay from malnutrition.

When did the weavers last earn a living wage? In the old, prewar, pre-British days, a wedding sari might bring in two, even five hundred rupees apiece. The money lasted months. Now, according to a newspaper report, the weavers earned barely an anna a day. What did that buy? Two rotis and a *sabzi*, barely enough to feed a person, let alone a family.

What if Moin Ansari still blamed Babuji for his family's downfall? Moin Bhai, Barre Nanu corrected himself. The endearment that had come so naturally sounded odd after two decades of disuse. Barre Nanu tugged the threads that fastened the parcel of sweetmeats he'd bought. He hoped the tribute would soften the weaver enough to want to work with him.

Once Babuji had dispensed of Moin's father's services, Barre Nanu hadn't seen Moin Bhai, hadn't given much thought to how the family had fared. He'd lived his life, learned English, gone off to college. But what of the weaver's son, who had no other fallback, his only education the knotting of threads, his only tool his father's squeaky wooden loom? Barre Nanu hadn't wondered once.

Moin Bhai's house had thinned like the thinning weavers, sliced into divisions and subdivisions. The courtyard had been repurposed into a storage area and housed bales of unsold cloth. The rooms that went all the way around the periphery had been reduced to two; the left section of the house ended in a wall. A strong scent of correction fluid lingered in the air. In the darkness of the rooms, Barre Nanu discerned a loom, a sheet of cotton cloth under production. Once, the same machine had woven silks. A girl slipped past him carrying a basket full of bobbins and ran back upstairs. Barre Nanu waited for someone to appear, and when no one did, he had to shout, hoping his voice would bring his friend out.

The man who came down the stairs was as thin as the ones Barre Nanu had passed on the street. The bones of his face were chiseled and sharp like the ridges on a mountain. Emaciation had preserved his youth. Moin Bhai glided into the courtyard with the same alacrity he'd possessed as a child. But up close, Barre Nanu could see the prematurely thinning hair that gave his friend the subdued aura of an elder. His beard was neatly trimmed, white skull cap in place. Moin Bhai vigilantly followed his faith despite the disarray around him.

Barre Nanu extended his arms. "It's me, *bhaijaan*, the Khatri from Shahalmi. Your father's old employer's son."

The shock on Moin Bhai's face was palpable. Barre Nanu nearly fell as the weaver threw himself onto Barre Nanu, greeting him like he were a long-lost friend.

Moin Bhai dragged Barre Nanu into the workroom, shouted for someone to fetch a chair, fetch tea, fetch a bamboo fan. The room brimmed with things—a massive handloom that took up most of the space, baskets and baskets of bobbins, stacks of yarn. Moin Bhai fussed, but Barre Nanu insisted on sitting beside him on the floor.

Barre Nanu had a speech prepared. But Moin Bhai had the focused eyes of a jeweler, his brow perpetually frowned from concentrating on threads of cloth. His gaze made Barre Nanu nervous. He couldn't keep himself from disintegrating.

"My brother is in jail, *bhaijaan*. We will never see him if I don't arrange for a bribe."

"Has he turned into a freedom fighter?"

"It's nothing like that," Barre Nanu said shamefully, providing details about the red-light district and the bomb. "I have to make money fast. I need tailors. You have to help me, *bhaijaan*! You can learn the work in no time."

Moin Bhai shifted away. He wrung his hands and regarded his loom. He hadn't been in the best mental state. Lately he had taken up building roads for the municipality. The work earned him five annas a day, barely enough to purchase a hundred grams of rice, barely enough to feed his family of four. But what kept him going was the hope that his old trade would pick up again. Like Babuji, he awaited the day handloom cloth would return into fashion.

Moin Bhai pulled his knees into his chest. He was all bones. "I am sorry to hear about your brother. I wish I could help. But tailoring is below me. Only the Chhimbas are tailors. They are house servants. I am not a servant." He swung forward on his haunches and held the beams of his looms. "If I take up tailoring, I bring shame upon the name of Ansaris." He was all bones and meanness.

As off-putting as Moin Bhai's words were, they confirmed one thing—Muslims clung just as tightly to their castes as the Hindus. This had to be the surest sign they belonged to one race, Moin Bhai and Barre Nanu, one stock. They were one people, no matter what the political parties were saying, trying to divide them up on the basis of religion.

"The times are changing, Moin Bhai," Barre Nanu insisted. "We all have to take up different types of work. You are paving roads."

But Moin Bhai didn't agree. "Khatri sahib," he said, pulling the beam on his handloom forward. The formality of his address made Barre Nanu's throat feel parched. "I too am waiting for the times to change. One day people will favor Gandhiji's handwoven khadi cloth, and weavers can earn a living wage. I am paving roads while I wait for this awful time to pass."

"But, *bhaijaan,* Gandhi can't change fashion. Everyone is wearing European dress. My uncle's European bespoke gets so much business!"

"What happens when the British leave?" Moin Bhai countered.

"If they leave."

"If they leave."

"They won't take their clothes with them."

"You don't know that. Gandhiji will make sure every last sign of Englishness is gone."

"Gandhi is an old fool," Barre Nanu said. "He must be eighty years old now."

Moin Bhai pulled the beams on his loom. The room squeaked with the shedding of the warp threads. How complicated the machine looked, with many moving parts and threads hanging everywhere, requiring much coordinated action. Moin Bhai worked it expertly, his naked feet pressing the treadles, hands pushing the beam back and forth. How easy it would be for him to master the Singer. "If you could come and see the shop, *bhaijaan*. You can make your own hours, come and go as you please."

Moin Bhai's feet slowed, but didn't stop. He harbored the old grudge.

"You resent me because Babuji fired your father. You will never trust me again."

"You are wrong, *bhaijaan*. This is about being loyal to my loom."

Since when had Moin Bhai turned so proud? "Tell me, *bhaijaan*," Barre Nanu said, fingering the finished cloth. "What good is your loom if it can't even feed your family?"

Moin Bhai stomped on the treadle, and the machine paused. He leaned on the beam, the light from the window forming a halo about him. "Your brother deserves the punishment he is getting for consorting with prostitutes. The British see us as an expendable race. All you can do is make sure his last days are peaceful."

Barre Nanu couldn't believe Moin Bhai's words. "Chhote is not expendable, not to his family," Barre Nanu said, fuming. "As for your loom, take my advice: sell it to the *doms* for burning with the dead. At least you will earn five annas for your children. Your pride has made you completely inhumane."

Moin Bhai's face appeared from behind the cloud of the threads, full of rage. He swung his legs out of the frame and leapt toward Barre Nanu. The gesture recalled an earlier memory—him, a boy, rushing to greet Barre Nanu, who'd come over with his father. Briefly, as children, they'd been equals—eating on the same plate, sleeping on the same floor. Now Barre Nanu had got himself a fancy English education, dreamed dreams of making English clothes. How dare he expect

Moin Bhai to pick up a needle when he could maneuver a loom? Moin Bhai's hand closed upon the scissors on the shed. He threw them at Barre Nanu with all his force.

Because he couldn't believe Moin Bhai would do such a thing, it took Barre Nanu a second to leap out of the way. Panting, afraid another blow remained in the weaver, he scuttled out the door.

Barre Nanu didn't look back. He had poor expendable Chhote to worry about. What were they feeding him? Had the superintendent decided on the matter of his transportation? Barre Nanu crept out of the weaver's house as soundlessly as he'd entered it.

August 2002

The house was still devoid of Bebe. At all hours, the chanting rose from the ground floor and swallowed us. We lived inside the throat of a whale, perhaps Matsya, the first avatar of Vishnu. What was Bebe up to? What was so important in Delhi that she couldn't come to see her children?

Only Ila knew about her recent life in Delhi.

Per Ila, our mother had moved to the capital after Barre Nanu's death, after Chhote Nanu asked her to vacate his house. Since her dismissal from her father's house, she managed a small pop-up art gallery in Connaught Place. In the back of a long, airless room, she sold skirts and palazzo pants and Rajasthani jackets featuring prints done by local artists with humanities degrees. She sat behind a pile of dusty books, taking the money. When the gallery slowed, she opened a notebook and sketched the faces she'd seen that day.

Once, she'd presided over Barre Nanu's sari business. After he retired from his job at the bank around the age of fifty, Barre Nanu spent all his life savings on six handlooms and installed them inside the rooms around the courtyard. He hired Muslim weavers from Colonelganj, and because Bebe had won medals for her paintings in college, appointed her chief designer. She threw herself wholeheartedly into the work, consulted books on Byzantine, Moroccan, and Persian art that she borrowed from the college library. The patterns she created became so popular in the 1990s, almost every middle-class woman in town owned one of her saris. Big mosaic faces of Roman warriors stared from the backsides of Kanpur women, Arabic calligraphy (words that Chhote Nanu taught us to read—*maqsood, mausam, libaas*) danced down their arms, tile patterns from Fez and Isfahan bedecked their bodies, all thanks to Bebe, who launched new trends in textile design. She dedicated twenty years of her life to these patterns. All of her twenties and thirties. She took a two-year hiatus to marry Ila's father, and when the marriage ended, she returned home and recommenced her work. Relatives speculated why her marriage had ended so abruptly. To shut them up, she told a lie—her husband had died, she'd been widowed. Had she poisoned him? Nagged him until he committed suicide? Did she want to marry again? Bebe turned a deaf ear to all the rumors and unhelpful advice. She found contentment in surrounding herself with her father's team of weavers and printers, the big woodblocks of patterns she created, and all her prints.

Now, she lived by herself in a rented *barsati* on a terrace in Paharganj in Old Delhi. Ila had visited her once. The room contained a bed, a desk, an electric sewing machine, and a stack of trunks that reached the ceiling, some empty, others full of blank pieces of cloth she used to copy palazzo pants and other styles of clothing on, hoping a new business venture might take off, trying half-heartedly to revive the earlier glory of Barre Nanu's business. She preferred her solitude. When Ila suggested she move in to save on rent, seeing that they lived in the same city, Bebe refused, cited her insomnia as an excuse "I'll keep you awake all night with my stitching," she said. "Best to stay separate."

I tried to picture Bebe, how she sat with a slight slouch, all alone in one corner of her room, refusing Ila's companionship, her head turning this way and that at the slightest sound—the phone buzzing, the neighbor's TV, a cricket ball smashing through her window and missing her glasses by an inch. Did she cook for herself? Did she have a hot plate? A kettle for tea? Two cups or just one? She had to have a tin box full of jaggery. She had a sweet tooth. Or, did she keep no food in her room and survive on chai and samosas?

Unlike most mothers I knew, Bebe never enjoyed cooking; she believed that the kitchen was a cell where men imprisoned women, prevented them from participating in things like sports (she'd won awards at school for long jumping) and fine arts. It didn't help that our kitchen resembled a dungeon, with its high dark brick walls, its windows facing the outer walls of other houses. Still, she forced herself into the prison every morning to warm the water for our bath. On her way upstairs to wake us, she paused by the patterns the designers had carved on the woodblocks, proceeded to correct their errors, forgetting all about us. Ila and I awoke to the whistle of a neighbor's pressure cooker, with no more than five minutes to drag the lukewarm water upstairs, bathe, comb, and put on our uniforms. As we ran out the door, Bebe realized she hadn't packed us any lunch. She scrambled for leftovers, tossed some stale rotis and leathery parathas into polythene bags. Ila incorporated her lunch into papier-mâché projects. Her neon-green and pink trays bolstered with Bebe's parathas graced the pottery studio's glass displays for years. As for me, I offered my lunch to the school cow that grazed behind the campus walls. My classmates avoided me during recess; their mothers had packed them crisp potato fingers with ketchup pouches, lentil curries garnished with fresh sprigs of coriander and a golden layer of butter, cucumber yogurt dips, lotus-stem pickles, buttery breads still soft and warm. I learned about the vast acreage of Indian cuisine from the dregs of my classmates' lunch boxes. "My mother works," I bragged to my classmates at the taps, filling my stomach with water. "She is a designer in a sari factory." They laughed. "So bring a sari for lunch," they taunted.

We tried not to hold her cooking against Bebe, but we'd been hungry for decades.

Once, to make up for all the bad cooking, she took an afternoon off and appeared at school with a bag of fruits and baked treats. Our teachers must've understood our dire need for nourishment from our hungry faces, because they excused us from class right away. Ila and I sat under the banyan tree in the school courtyard, and Bebe sliced apples for us with a Swiss Army knife she always kept in her purse. She held the slices in her palms. She pinched the white tissue off oranges. She pulled apart a puff-pastry shell into two equal halves. We ate the fruits, licked the flakes off our lips, the spiced potato filling hot against our palates. We felt our bellies distending against our legs. We felt satiated; for the first time, we forgot we'd been hungry, forgot what we'd been hungry for. The snack finished, she snuck us out of school (we had only an hour left) and took us to the market. We shared a *kulfi* and a vanilla cone.

"Your granduncle kicked me out of the house," she told us, our mouths slathered with ice cream. "What should we do? Museum? Picture? Shopping? Manchurian for dinner?" Secretly, I wished Chhote Nanu would kick her out more often.

But when we returned home, I regretted my wish, because Chhote Nanu had locked the door from the inside. Bebe shouted at the windows until she was hoarse, but our granduncle didn't let us in. Ila and I had to bother a neighbor to use the bathroom. Unsure of what to do, Bebe sat on the stone steps of the house next door and waited.

The windows to our room flew open. Chhote Nanu's bulbous, cloudy face appeared in all its pent-up fury. His gray hair was in disarray. He let loose a string of Punjabi curses, condemned us for being ungrateful to him, telling us we'd amount to no good if we continued smooching off Barre Nanu and if Bebe didn't strike out on her own. "There's nothing for you here," he told Bebe. "Go to Bombay, go to Delhi." Then he began tossing us our things—my *David Copperfield,* my abridged Shakespeares, *The Hardy Boys,* Ila's *Nancy Drews*; our mother's clothes, her blue VIP suitcase packed with clothes but not shut, so that her saris poured out in a stream of fabric with patterns of racing horses, solid silks and cottons and organzas, rapid-fall streaks of blues and pinks and lilacs; her blouses and bras and panties, some of which got shamefully stuck on electric wires for the whole world to see; Bebe's solid-metal sewing machine; Ila's frocks that Bebe had stitched. The books landed spine down on other people's doorsteps and on patches of buffalo dung.

Because I could think of nothing else to do, I packed. I gathered and folded our clothes and lined them in the suitcase. I told Ila to dust off the books, stuff them into bags. We gathered until the lane was cleared of our things, and no sign of Chhote Nanu's rage remained.

While her children packed, Bebe sat stone-faced, a thousand-yard stare in her eyes. She looked terrified and small, her arms gathered about her knees. "Where can I go?" she asked no one in particular. "Where should I take my little ones?"

"Why is Chhote Nanu doing this?" Ila asked. "Why does he love us less than before?"

Bebe gave no answer, so I stepped in: "He's losing his mind."

"Why should he suddenly lose his mind?"

"It happens to people when they get old."

Our things packed, we sat next to Bebe, stared at our house, and waited. For Chhote Nanu's anger to cool, for Barre Nanu to come home and let us back in.

Our grandfather returned in a few hours and sorted things out, gave Chhote Nanu an earful, warned he'd send him to a mental institution if this sort of thing ever happened again. He coaxed Bebe back inside, but she sulked anyway.

"Maybe Chhote Nanu is right," she said to her father. "Maybe I ought to take my little ones and start someplace new. Somewhere I'm wanted."

"This is your home," Barre Nanu retaliated. "You are my daughter, and you are wanted. Who's going to help me sort out my weavers and printers?"

✦

Back in our old room, I lay in bed, an arm covering my eyes. The afternoon light from the balcony flooded the room. A hot August breeze blew through the doors. I felt stifled. "I hope someone's cooking for her in Delhi. Why couldn't she have stayed here with you and fought for our house?"

"Because," Ila explained, as she marked her course packet with a pencil. "Bebe thinks her rightful place was in her father's heart. Now that Barre Nanu is dead, she doesn't think she has any claim on this house."

"She is avoiding me. She knows I won't spare her this time."

"Of course she is avoiding you."

I turned to face the wall. On the streets of Delhi, our mother hailed autos, eyes dilated from the exhaust, mouth covered to avoid the pollution in the air.

"Here!" Ila handed me a business card. The white matte paper displayed the name of a gallery in a smart font; its back carried a phone number.

"What do you want me to do with this? I can't talk to her."

"You won't rest until you do."

I sat up, punched the number on my cellphone. It took me a minute to hit the green button.

"Akansha Art Gallery." It was really her, her thin voice unmistakable, unchanged. The way her tone went up at the end, like she was asking a question or making a request, the noose around my throat tightened. I stood up, completely still.

"It's me."

"I'm sorry?"

"It's me, Karan."

There was a long silence. Ila turned to watch. *What's going on?* she mouthed.

"I don't know if Ila has told you," I began. "But I am back at the house. In Kanpur." I wondered what to say next, how to beseech her. "Here!" I handed the phone to Ila. "You talk to her."

She pushed the phone back. "Talk to her. Tell her you want to see her."

"Please come home," I blurted. "Or should I come see you?" The address was in front of me.

But before I could ask, the line went dead.

"What do you mean she hung up on you?"

"She didn't say two words to me. She said 'yes,' and, 'I'm sorry.'"

"Well that's three words."

"Does she hate me because I didn't keep in touch? Because I didn't make it in time for Barre Nanu?" A worry came to sit inside my throat like a lump. What if I'd ruined us forever?

September 1943

1

Chhote Nanu had been misinformed about British jails. Unlike the rumors he'd heard, the Indian jailers didn't treat him like a hero, didn't provide him with papers and pens so he could compose poetry or prose in the style of Nehru and Gandhi. As a political prisoner, the most dangerous and hated kind of criminal, he was thrown into a dark cell with only a small slit of a window, high up. During the day, he heard the mynah birds chattering vigorously outside. At night, he heard the prisoners begging for food and water.

On the second day of his internment, he was kicked awake, yanked out of his cell, and forced to join a queue of prisoners, disheveled, hungry, and terrified like him. Together, they marched to the basement. Inside a cavernous room, they were ordered to work an oil press. When Chhote Nanu's turn came, the jailer dragged him to the center of the room and forced a wooden yoke weighing fifteen kilos on his shoulders, fastened it to his back with a rope that cut through his skin. Thus tethered to the oil press, he had to walk in a circle around a large wooden mortar filled with coconut husks. The husks rustled but little, and only tiny drops of oil dripped into a vat despite his best efforts. Three turns around the mortar, and he began to feel dizzy. When he raised his arm to wipe his brow, the warden thrust the butt of his rifle into his side and shouted: "Keep moving! Who is going to finish your quota? Your father?"

The warden believed the INA rebels had put Chhote Nanu up to assassinating the superintendent. As part of the rogue Indian National

Army, he'd foiled the holy British mission, fought brave British soldiers (most of them Indian) alongside the Japanese and the Germans, set off bombs in Imphal. Chhote Nanu implored, insisted he didn't belong to the INA. He'd never been to Burma. Samrat might have conspired with the INA, but he'd sheltered Chhote from all that. But the warden considered this a matter of mere technicality. In the grand scheme of things, he'd committed a crime as bad as the INA rebels. Nobody wanted to hear the story of how he'd been tricked by an older boy, and oughtn't they catch the real culprit before he set off more bombs?

That Samrat! He hadn't been by, hadn't sent missives, not even in secret. No one had been by to see him. His family hadn't wreathed him in garlands, their arms trying to reach him through the jail doors. They hadn't sent sweetmeats. Milk rimmed with golden ghee. Parathas slathered with butter. Lassi thick with globs of cream. Skewers of kababs. *Keema* scented with rosewater. Tea straight from the flask, the mouth of the flask steaming. The outside world had ceased to exist.

Two months into his internment, Chhote Nanu heard his sentence. The warden announced it through the jail bars one morning: Chhote Nanu would be piled into a boat with other INA rebels and shipped off to the Andaman Islands, hundreds of miles away from India, a thousand miles from Punjab. The warden advised Chhote Nanu to believe the rumors he'd heard about the island prison—the worst jail in the history of jails, which the British reserved for political prisoners. No one returned from the islands alive. Many tried, all failed. Some scaled the high prison walls, only to fall into traps laid by local fishermen and be returned to the jailers for a ransom. Others escaped the fishermen, only to drown in the black waters or get ripped into pieces by sharks.

The other prisoners offered little solidarity or comfort. Even at the oil press, nobody talked, nobody hummed, nobody offered palliatives or little hopes for erasure or escape. His quota never changed. As soon as they clamped the yoke on his sore shoulders, he crumbled under its weight. The jailers kicked his sides and threatened to serve him *lapsy* of watery rice creeping with maggots if he didn't rise. He tried but fell again and was dragged to the side of the room and chained to the wall. Another prisoner took his place under the yoke, but he fell too, was dragged away and chained.

Chhote Nanu experienced a brief moment of elation—here was another human similarly tortured. He slid sideways, twisted and propped his head to a painful position to offer his compatriot an upside-down smile, two moments of his breath laced with poetic zeal. But as soon as the boy felt Chhote Nanu's hair brushing against his thigh, he screamed. The jilted poet from the gathering, his neighbor who'd spoken ill of Nigar Jaan and whose pen name Chhote Nanu had stolen, headbutted Chhote Nanu. "You! I am going to kill you!" He pummeled Chhote Nanu with his feet. "You are the reason," he spat into his face. "I have three sisters. Who is going to marry them?"

The jailers rushed to separate them, pounding them with batons. The boys were dragged into a different room, hung over a frame like towels, their hands and feet tied, their backs caned fifty times. Chhote Nanu cried out in pain. He'd confessed to his crime. Why did they jail Chiragh? "Let him go, I'm the real bomb carrier! I'm the fire-cracker boy! Just kill me and be done with it. My family wants me dead. Mutton wants me dead. Nigar Jaan wants me dead. Just kill me and be done with it." He shouted until he passed out.

◆

Contrary to Chhote Nanu's assumption, Nigar Jaan didn't want him dead. She hadn't stopped thinking about him since the night of the gathering. How could she forget the boy who'd warmed up to her son and then set off a firecracker inside her house? His face never left her—the strong nose, the stronger jaw, the big eyes full of guilt, aghast at his own blunder.

She should hate him, she told herself, but no urge to poke out his eyes consumed her. Instead, surprisingly, she wanted to see him. She wanted to ask him one question: Why did he use her house to harm the superintendent? She wondered if more bombs would arrive at her place encased in innocent parcels. Ought she to break off ties with the policeman to keep her son safe?

"Tell me I am stupid not to want the earth to swallow that firecracker boy," she said to her maid one day. "Tell me it is stupid to want to see him."

The girl moved soundlessly about the room with a cloth duster, her anklets so tight, they didn't tinkle. "You are not stupid, Baby Jaan, but you are too trusting. Every year you let anyone walk into your gatherings."

Nigar Jaan expected Shehnaz to say that. The girl's social cachet depended on her mistress's exclusivity. "How can I help it if I am popular?"

The girl raised an eyebrow. "You are certainly popular now."

This was true. The firecracker boy had made her the talk of the town. The newspapers had reported the blast. All the uninvited poets had sent condolences. Women from the neighborhood, men from as far away as Amritsar had come around, expressing interest. The threat of air raids, the weekly protests, nothing kept her admirers away. The doorman had been turning away people, gifts, jewelry, books, calling cards, letters for days. If she were being honest, she felt a little thankful to the firecracker boy.

But she couldn't let herself forget that he'd nearly put a stop to her gatherings. What would she do with herself if that happened? She would turn into her own worst nightmare—just a *kanjari*. Mutton's mistress. The mother of his child. The gatherings allowed her to hear contemporary poets and quietly defy Mutton's mandate that she entertain no one else. They made her feel she had her own life, separate from him; they made her feel she understood something subtle and vital about her place of birth.

So many men attended the recitals. Most came with disdain. Still, she looked forward to playing hostess. She enjoyed the planning, the hustle and bustle about the house, the cleaning and the dusting, the ordering of new dresses and jewelry, the prospect of putting on a public face before her private one. And then the prospect of the new poetry. All year she looked through the journals, mining them for verses that spoke to her. She cut out pieces she loved and put them in her notebook to read them over and over, until another piece came along that moved her. She had an ongoing correspondence with the editors, who gladly put her in touch with the poets. The poets weren't averse to writing to her. If anything, they welcomed attention. If they responded to her letters, which they almost always did, she invited them to her residence. The gatherings began this way, small at first, with only two or three poets in attendance, then they grew as poets began to bring their own audience. Soon, writers from far and wide, published and unpublished, began to stop by. "Why an English lady is interested in Urdu poetry, we don't know," was the refrain. Then Josh Muradabadi pointed out she wasn't English. "She is Hindustani, through and through." The others had to concur. They all had opinions about her background and welcomed the audience she gave them. It didn't hurt that she dolled up. But it could all have gone in a flash if the bomb had succeeded. Which begged the question: Why did he do it?

Nigar Jaan uncoiled her hair. "We must find out why the firecracker boy hates me."

"You heard him say it, Baby Jaan. The bomb was intended for Mutton sahib."

But Nigar Jaan found it difficult to take the firecracker boy for an assassin. "I don't think we know the whole truth. He seems too naive to plant a bomb."

"You say that about every boy who falls in love with you." Shehnaz slapped her arm.

Nigar Jaan felt her face grow hot. "He is not in love with me." She sat up to look in the mirror beside her bed. She gave her reflection a bewitching smile. Had she made another conquest? "Did he say anything to you at the park?"

"Nothing out of the ordinary."

She dropped her head on her pillow. What were the reluctant

assassin's true feelings about her? She had to know. She shot up and grabbed Shehnaz by the arm. "You have to go talk to him."

"Me? No, Baby Jaan, don't send me on this mission."

She pulled Shehnaz close to her and hugged her. "Do this for me, *janum*! Don't you want to know the truth?"

"What do you want to know, Baby Jaan? That he wanted to kill superintendent sahib or that he is in love with you?"

Nigar Jaan bit her tongue. Could her maid be spying on her for Mutton? It couldn't be. If she couldn't trust Shehnaz, she couldn't trust anyone.

"The firecracker boy is certainly the opposite of superintendent sahib. Young. Impressionable. Maybe even malleable."

Nigar Jaan didn't think the boy was malleable. He had a wild streak. He'd been calculating—earning her trust and an invite to her home, then putting her in harm's way. "Go talk to him, *jaan*." She held Shehnaz's wrist. "Or better still, take a letter."

Nigar Jaan picked up a notebook and scribbled a letter, a thoroughly incoherent letter that she crossed out several times and rewrote. She folded the letter into Shehnaz's hands and asked her to deliver it the next time the superintendent took a day off.

◆

The next week, the Indian jailer snuck into Chhote Nanu's cell to tell him he had a visitor. Both the superintendent and the warden were out. Gangadhar escorted Chhote Nanu to a room in the basement, where a girl waited for him.

It was the ayah from Nigar Jaan's. She sat in one of the two chairs in the room, casting furtive glances at the door. She was the first person Chhote Nanu had seen from the outside world. He took her in, her small body in the black burka that covered most of her except her face, her furtive, kohled eyes that filled with anger as soon as she saw him. She looked less friendly than the last time he'd seen her at the park. He had so many things to ask her, but didn't know where to start. Thankfully, she spoke first:

"Some nerve you have, acting friendly with my Baby Jaan and her baba and then lighting a firecracker at her house."

Chhote Nanu hung his head. "No one was hurt."

The girl tossed her head dismissively. "You didn't have to clean up after. Look, I didn't come here to chitchat. Baby Jaan sent me. With this." She extended a piece of paper toward him.

His heart came to sit inside his mouth as he opened it.

My son asks about you and your bicycle often. I know the bomb was intended for Mr. Mutton. Did you have to light it inside my home? Do you belong to the INA? Have they told you if they are transporting you to Andaman? Mutton hates the INA. He fears the army might succeed in liberating India from the British. At least you have public support: everyone in the market is grateful to the brave army lads.

Please do not tell anyone of Shehnaz's visit. Gangadhar can be trusted, but no one else.

Chhote Nanu didn't know what to make of the letter, or why Nigar Jaan had written at all. The feeling of elation he'd experienced near the end of that evening at her house, her eyes solely on him when the poets called on him to speak, returned for a brief moment. And then he remembered he was in prison for high treason.

"It's time to leave," the watchman interrupted. "The warden is due back any minute."

"Is Nigar Jaan going to visit?" he asked the girl. But she turned away and slipped out.

2

Warden Gordon saw the girl flying out of the police station as his jeep pulled up. He recognized her instantly as the superintendent's mistress's servant girl. Gordon had been in India long enough to know to look the other way when superiors engaged in dalliances with local women. They had all had dalliances. What else was there to do after the blighted work and the dreadfully dull do's at the club? But the superintendent had taken it too far, fathering a child with the nautch girl. So what if she had European blood? This sort of thing just didn't happen anymore. Not since the Mutiny of 1857—when loyal Indian sepoys turned on their British commanders and drowned British housewives inside a well—had etched clear racial lines one simply did not cross. He didn't care how much of an eccentric Mutton was. First the awful business about Jallianwala, and now this.

What did Mutton see in Nigar Jaan? It couldn't simply be her beauty. No, what he saw in her, Gordon believed, was history, the historical fact of her birth, the two races cohabiting in one body. She'd descended from a notorious nawab. The same who'd orchestrated the Cownpore leg of the mutiny. Nana Saheb, his name was. That too must have fascinated Mutton, Nigar Jaan's own notoriety, her racial impropriety. It matched Mutton's own.

Now that Gordon thought about it, the two were well suited, Mutton and Nigar Jaan. Mutton, an outcast at the club, coming from a family of no consequence. A grammar-school boy. He wasn't the right sort of English. But that didn't seem to matter so much in the bazaars. Oh, but it all felt too unwholesome. Not that Gordon cared for all that nonsense about class, that felt unwholesome too. Gordon himself hoped to break with it all and make his way to America. He'd been talking with the GIs visiting from Bombay. He knew they made fun of the Raj behind his back. Their fat salaries made the British mission in India look like a child's foolish play. The new world was full of opportunities, and Gordon hoped he might find some work in America. Perhaps he could teach at an American university once the war was over.

But this business of Mutton and Nigar Jaan. He considered letting it go. But what if it morphed into something awful? Besides, it would be far more entertaining to see the look on Mutton's face when he told his superior about the servant girl's visit to the prison. Maybe the mistress had taken a liking to a local fellow. How the old fool would suffer!

Gordon summoned Gangadhar and questioned him. "You'd better tell me before I find out on my own," he said firmly.

Gangadhar, nearly fifty, a seasoned employee of the British jail, was aware of his own precarious position. He knew being on the fence meant he had to weigh each side carefully before deciding where to offer his allegiance. In this instance, he thought it best to convey the information.

That same night, Chhote Nanu's room was searched, the straw mattress punctured, the pillow ripped open. The letter was discovered inside the pillow cover. Before it could be read, Chhote Nanu ripped it into pieces in the tussle.

Gordon presented the pieces of the letter to the superintendent. Mutton's face turned all shades of red as he tried to parse the meaning of the furtive message.

"The maid brought it, sir." Gordon wanted Mutton to know he'd been to the red-light district. He'd seen Mutton and judged him.

◆

The thrashing Chhote Nanu received as a consequence was worse than the first. This time the blows were meant only for him, and they were counted. His face was splashed with water so he stayed awake and aware he was being beaten. All he could see bent over in that uncomfortable position, his hands and feet tied, were boots, English boots made in India with sturdy Indian leather, bearing the East India leather emblem containing the royal crest shining in the dim light.

◆

After his shift, Gordon drove home to the civil station. Habibullah had laid out a change of clothes in the bedroom. A new bar of soap awaited him, rose scented. After he'd washed and changed, Habibullah brought him a gin fizz and told him dinner would be ready in a half hour. He ought to eat in tonight because at the club they were serving meatloaf. How well Habibullah knew him. He could give the best English butler a run for his money. Sometimes Gordon considered taking the man back to England. But that would not be in order. If only all Indians could be like Habibullah. It struck him as strange that out of a whole country, he'd only warmed up to one man. But stranger still the realization that trusting one Indian didn't make it any easier to deal with the rest.

After dinner, he decided to stay in. He wrote a letter to Geraldine.

"I've realized something," he wrote. "We shouldn't be here in India, should never have been here. Not for a single year out of the three hundred. We understand nothing and will continue not to understand. What was it all for? Spices? Cloth? Jewels? Or was it for that elusive and more permanent kind of wealth, that feeling of superiority, that we had collectively got something right, showed the world the way to live. All bloody nonsense, as far as I am concerned. There is only personal gain, personal freedoms, personal evils, personal good. Don't you think so, my darling?"

He thought for a minute. Had the realization made India seem less awful? No. If anything, it exacerbated his desire to leave. He lifted his eyes to the photo hanging on the wall. The summer of '38, the last time he'd been in Somerset. Geraldine with her basset hound. He missed the winters the most.

He continued to write: "But then I realize, if I hadn't taken this post, they'd send me to Burma or Bechuanaland." He paused once again. It was the age of empire and the empire needed men like him.

"It is midnight and I must end this letter. Two kisses for you, my lovely. Yours, Freddy."

He folded the letter. Then he tore it up. He let the bits drop into the drawer. He picked up the note he'd received from Geraldine three years ago. She didn't think he would be back from India anytime soon. She'd met a law student in London. They'd decided to get married. Gordon opened the invitation card, reread it for the hundredth time, gulped down his gin fizz, and fell asleep.

◆

Back inside the jail, Chhote Nanu lay collapsed on the floor of the torture chamber. He'd been to the room twice in the same week. Hungry, delirious, his body throbbing, he thought of Nigar Jaan's letter. He wished he had swallowed it. He wished she had never written. He wished he'd never cast eyes on her. What Chiragh said about her was true. She was a Muslim *kanjari*. He had dared to love the superintendent's woman, and now he must suffer. Where was his big brother and when would he get him out of here?

August 2002

A shadow hung over the house. Dark clouds had gathered overnight and swallowed the moon. I could hear Chhote Nanu tapping his cane on the stone steps. A light tap-tap-tap and a quiet sigh as he pulled his body along. Once inside his room, he blew on a conch shell, a bellow so loud, it filled the whole house. Next, he began to chant a mantra from the *Gita*. How long would he continue to pray? Ila had already fallen asleep, so I couldn't ask her. I lay in bed listening, and each time I awoke, he was still singing.

I went up to his quarters to see him. His door was open to the night breeze.

He sat on his bed, eyes shut. He looked deep in thought, his lips parsing a verse of scripture. A small book of Sanskrit verses, a cheap edition from the railway station bookshop, sat open before him. In my early childhood, that book would've been a collection of Urdu poetry. How Chhote Nanu had changed. The years had been unkind to him. His face had shrunk, narrowing his eyes, turning his smile upside down. A tree of worry grew over his brow. Even though he was submerged in meditation, he couldn't have looked more disappointed with the world.

I knocked on the door, hoping he'd invite me to collapse beside his big white shirt, his soft flesh, his still-hard bones. It had been six years since we'd spoken. I felt my throat burn. But even though Chhote Nanu opened his eyes to look at me, he did not spread an arm wide for an embrace.

He kept his gaze on me for a moment, then reached for the light switch and turned off the light, submerging us both into darkness. I heard him lie down, turn his face the other way.

The next morning, I passed by him in the courtyard as he sat with his legs up on the bamboo chair, chin resting on a knee, rubbing Vaseline on his cracked feet. The tub was nearly empty. I offered to bring him a new batch. He peered at me as though I'd said something offensive, then he gave a little nod. "Get some more Nivea too. From the English chemist on Mall Road."

I took the back roads out of the mohalla and walked along the Parade. At one time, Indians weren't allowed on this wide avenue, so called because of the marching soldiers on horseback parading for the queen. Back then, everything was designed with the queen in mind. She could appear anytime to make sure everything was shipshape— soldiers clomping down tree-lined avenues, Indians and dogs kept out of the British clubs, doilies on trays. Queen Victoria, however, never once came to India.

Now, open-air markets selling everything from children's clothes to bathroom supplies to stationery dominated the Parade sidewalk.

I entered a tighter, older lane dotted with gun shops. Countless rows of rifles and batteries lined their shelves. My muscles tensed as I walked past. In 1857, local sepoys wielding rifles had run rioting in the streets, their bodies festooned with batteries of bullets. Their ghosts still haunted the city.

When I reached the Machhli Mosque, my feet stopped. The old house of worship had shrunk since the last time I saw it. The municipality had bitten off its courtyard to expand the street. The temple right across, however, hadn't had to compromise its space, had in fact gained fresh silver paint on its dancing idols that studded its stupa tower, and, judging by the pile of shoes on its steps, many more followers.

I turned away from the temple and toward the mosque, took my shoes off, washed my feet under a tap outside. But I hesitated to enter. I didn't think I had the permission. It'd barely been a month since I'd been disallowed from returning to the Flushing mosque.

◆

The soot from the Twin Towers might have lifted from lower Manhattan, but its memory continued to weigh down Jackson Heights. Shops on Seventy-Fourth Street that once glittered with gold and rang with synthesized Bollywood music kept their shutters closed. On more than one morning, people awoke to read cruel words like "TERRORIST" and "SAND N*****" spray-painted on shop windows. The shop owners, old uncles with bad knees, climbed ladders and smashed their own windowpanes. Mothers pulled along their children, shielding their eyes from the offensive words. Several Sikh uncles gave up wearing turbans, broke their faith's fundamental rule and cut their hair short.

South Asians became the most hated ethnicity in America. This ought to have brought the people of Jackson Heights together. But most hid behind old grievances, behind boundaries that made them Indian versus Pakistani versus Bangladeshi. The community made no concerted efforts to unite; no rallies, no meetings were organized to discuss a way out of our American predicament. South Asians sulked; we'd been sulking for so long. The pen that had sliced India from Pakistan, the war that'd separated Bangladesh from Pakistan, had done a poor job of the surgery. Siamese twins and triplets would have been cleaner to separate, and, like Siamese twins and triplets, the countries stayed connected, sharing a contemptuous heart.

Kabul Kababs (run by Bombay Parsis, their dry kababs ruining the reputation of Afghan food) and Delhi Durbar (run by a Karachi family, their oily dals giving Delhi cuisine a bad rep), had both closed their doors. I'd begun to frequent the Krishna Temple in Jackson Heights. Behind the prayer hall, inside a small canteen, conscientious men served four-dollar three-foot-long papery dosas and thick lychee milkshakes that satiated a need for home cooking I didn't know I had. My roommate Meelad and I went every Sunday to empty our wallets and fill our stomachs.

We lingered at the temple canteen for hours, downing Styrofoam cups of milkshakes and filter coffees. Often, we watched the staff clean up the five-table canteen and take their meals with the priests in their white striped shirts and dhotis.

One evening, the head priest pointed to Meelad's beard and the hair he'd neglected to cut. "Bold choice, *ciruvan*, to keep a beard these days. You are from where? Iran? Oman? Pakistan?"

"Bangladesh."

"Muslim?" he asked, his bald head shining.

"Don't answer him," I told Meelad, loud enough for the priest to hear.

"Don't get angry," the priest consoled. "Ey, Raman! Get these boys some more *kapi*," he told the cook. "*Ciruvan*," he turned to me. "It might not be wise to bring your friend here. Or for you to keep a friend like him. Their mullahs preach jihad, while innocent Hindus are getting attacked in the street. How is that fair? That is all I am saying."

Meeld and I rose abruptly, upsetting our cups of coffee over the flimsy folding table. I told the priest he would never see us again at the temple.

That night, Meelad suggested we take our appetites to his mosque.

But the Islamic Center of Flushing felt spooked. The old Victorian house Meelad took me to hummed cold like a freezer. The congregation prayed in a large hall in hushed tones, the imam's voice cracking over the microphone that conveyed more static than wisdom from the Qur'an.

At least the food was generous. The meals were served buffet-style in the kitchen, and featured cuisines from all over the world—*fufu*-and-okra stew, *sukuma wiki*, *machboos*, *kofta*, and biryani of every variety. In difficult times, people took comfort in food.

Meelad introduced me to the people he knew—a young programmer from Nigeria who'd lost his wife in the attacks, and a law student from Lahore.

"Where in Lahore does your family live?" I asked Omar. I was eager to tell him about Barre Nanu's connections to Lahore, about Chhote Nanu's history there.

The imam interrupted us.

"Karan? Khatri? Is that a Muslim name?" His accent betrayed his Arab roots.

"Karan's father is Muslim," Meelad said, throwing a protective arm over my shoulder, his studious eyes behind his glasses glowing with simplified indignation. "A Muslim from India."

The young imam tucked a finger inside his shirt collar and pulled it as though he was choking. "You are welcome to eat here, Karan. But it would be best if you don't participate in the worship."

Later that night, while Meelad and Omar chatted in the living room, I shut myself in my bedroom. Ought I to return to the Krishna Temple? The thought made me sick. I browsed their website for pictures of food, already missing their dosas.

On a page titled "Important Resources for Jackson Heights Hindus," I saw a link to a site called "Satan's Verses." I clicked on the link. Page after page, in black text over a bloodred background, the author explained why the Qur'an was the most violent piece of literature in human history. Verses from the holy book danced on the screen in their English translation, each page ending in an animated gif of a bleeding heart. At the end of the twenty-page screed was a list of names, all Hindus who'd shamed the religion by speaking in favor of Islam and who the writer suggested should be wiped off the face of the earth. Several prominent authors, academics, journalists, and a few Bollywood veterans had made the hit list. I checked the website's "About" page and learned that it was operated by a group of Hindus who called themselves the Saffron Rage. Formed inside a Queens basement in October 2001, the group had as their mission to awaken the world to the bloodthirst of Islam.

The imam had good reason to keep me at a distance.

The next time Meelad invited me to his mosque, I declined. I understood the need for this segregation, but couldn't help feel a tinge of disappointment.

"Maybe if you kept a beard?" Meelad suggested.

"You mean as a decoy?"

"You said you were Muslim."

"I am. I mean, I don't know." Hurt over Bebe's betrayal opened like a cut. My mother hadn't responded to my numerous letters, hadn't divulged any more details about my father, not even his name.

The next week, we learned on the local news that Meelad's mosque had been firebombed. The bombers had targeted the Sunday school, where kindergarteners had baked a batch of snickerdoodle cookies the day before.

We took the 7 train to Flushing, wanting to witness what felt like an important moment in our lives. I felt agitated, eager to help and prove my good will to the imam. By the time we reached, the firemen had finished dousing the fire. The white facade of the Victorian house had turned so black, I couldn't distinguish the windows from the doors. We waited with the small crowd that had gathered across the street and watched. A few minutes later, the imam extricated himself from the group and ducked under the yellow police tape. But the police refused him access. The damage had been significant. They pushed him into the street, where we'd been waiting.

The young imam saw me. His beard, more scruff than hair, looked uncombed, morose.

"If there is anything I could do to help . . ." I tried in my awkward way.

But the imam refused to look at me. He watched the firefighters as they entered the charred house, his hands in his trouser pockets nervously jangling keys.

I felt responsible, implicated in some way in the mosque's burning. A week later, when I opened the Saffron Rage's website, I saw the imam's name on a second hit list, along with other leaders of the Muslim community.

I didn't return to the mosque after that, not when Meelad invited me to witness the renovations, not even when he asked me to lend a hand.

◆

Now, outside the Machhli Mosque, I put my shoes back on. I couldn't muster the courage to enter the sacred space. It didn't belong to me. I didn't know who I was, Hindu or Muslim or both or neither. I needed my mother to help me decide, to fill in the fundamental gaps in my knowledge. After a quick stop at the English chemist for Chhote Nanu, I came back home.

Ila sat by her desk, typing furiously on her laptop. I flopped on my bed.

"Who is Omar?" She had her back to me. "His name kept flashing on your phone last night. He sent you an SMS." She turned to face me. "He said he is going to Pakistan in the winter and he wants to host you."

I pulled a pillow over my head.

"Are you going to Pakistan?" Ila pulled the pillow away, bore her eyes into mine, her breath hitting the top of my head.

"None of your business." I pushed her away. I wasn't ready to tell her about Omar, and if indeed I would go to Pakistan. The revelation of Omar's last name, his relation to our family would birth a new catastrophe, upset Chhote Nanu even more.

"If you want to help, call Bebe. Tell her to come home," I told Ila and shut my eyes.

January 1944

1

It had been four months since his weaver friend had refused the offer of a job at Barre Nanu's bespoke. They'd received two orders of children's pajamas, which Barre Nanu had completed in a day. Still, early each morning, Barre Nanu cycled to the market, unlatched the door, and waited for someone to appear in response to the ads he'd placed in the newspaper. But no one came. Not even those impoverished by the war stopped by looking for work. Three times he'd been to the jail, and three times he'd been turned away. Visions of Chhote Nanu floating away on a boat, his face full of accusations and broken, lost in the fog, haunted Barre Nanu, but he couldn't win over the constables without cash.

Chaiji had retreated into her sewing room. Gossiping busybodies at the market had told her about Chhote's arrest, advised her about the potentials of bribe. She'd dragged her wedding trousseau to all the tailoring shops in Shahalmi Market as advertisement of her services. She'd received a dozen contracts for alterations. Now she sat behind her Singer, body a C-shaped curve, her feet perpetually pedaling, her hands dragging an endless measure of silk and brocade under the needle. Her helpers—two weaver wives, both pregnant—sat at her feet, sewing sequins on the hems of skirts while Chaiji tucked borders and installed buckram. She emerged from the room once a day to make rotis, which Barre Nanu and Babuji ate with a curry Barre Nanu bought from a corner shop. Chaiji's eyesight was failing. Sometimes she burned the rotis and her fingertips. Other times, like today, the rotis were raw. Quietly, Barre Nanu wished his mother didn't have to see this day. Only one thing could relieve her burdens: the cloth shop. But Barre Nanu simply couldn't find trained tailors to work for him.

His lunch finished, Babuji burped indulgently. He moved his hands forward and back, pulling on the beams of an imaginary loom. *What did the weavers say?* He pointed in the direction of the lane. *Will they work with you in the shop?*

Barre Nanu shook his head. Moin Bhai, that skeleton of a weaver, had as good as stabbed him in the heart.

His father yanked the army rucksack lying beside Barre Nanu's feet, pulled out the sample army uniform, bit into it, flung it on the floor, and stomped on it. This is what Babuji thought of Tijori Uncle's enterprise. He was glad Moin Bhai had refused to work with Barre Nanu to make army uniforms. He washed his hands at the tap in the courtyard, grabbed his cane, and left the house for his afternoon jaunt.

His father's gestures of madness terrified Barre Nanu. Would he deteriorate like this one day? He closed his eyes and thought of the times Babuji had been sane, agreeable, loving. He thought of the rainy afternoon Babuji had bought an oak desk for him. Their lane had flooded, and the tonga wallah's horse had refused to go the last hundred steps. Babuji had carried the heavy piece of furniture on his own back. Barre Nanu ached to do something as gallant as that. But he couldn't even take a box of sweetmeats to their Chhote.

Barre Nanu cycled to Tijori Uncle's, to see if there'd been any word from the magistrate.

His wealthy uncle was fuming. The magistrate was taking his time to write a letter of reference. The government wanted a contribution to the war fund in exchange.

"In 1941 alone we gave them fifty million rupees," said Tijori Uncle. He was drinking early in the day again. He gestured wildly about the room, a glass in hand, the silk belt of his smoking jacket trailing behind him like a leash. "That's more than we gave for the previous war. The magistrate isn't even here. He's off golfing in the mountains. What has he done for the men dying in the trenches? Nothing more than picking up a pen and asking for money. I've done more for this war than him! I must've clothed at least a hundred thousand soldiers." He paused to look out the window, as though he could see the magistrate's bungalow, but all he could see were other havelis like his, homes of other affluent Punjabi men.

He continued his tirade: "I took him my finest bottle of American rum. But his butler refused to let me see him. Who does the magistrate think he is? The king of England?"

Barre Nanu felt responsible for the snub his uncle had suffered.

"What makes them so much better than us? Money? Power? We had money. The Mughals had no parallel. What do they pride themselves on? Language? Literature? What do they have that we don't?"

Barre Nanu didn't like to hear his uncle talk ill of the British. He was beginning to sound like Babuji (if Babuji were talking). Would he stop doing business with the army? Barre Nanu tried to picture Tijori Uncle turning Gandhian, sitting in his cavernous haveli surrounded by all kinds of modern luxuries (even Gandhi couldn't convince him to give up the electric fan, the imported furniture), trying to meditate. He wouldn't last a day. He'd still try to acquire more and more luxuries in secret.

Tijori Uncle sank into the yellow couch, pulled his knees up. "I wish you were my son." His eyes on Barre Nanu were full of feeling. "What we could have accomplished together. Any word from the weavers?"

Barre Nanu hung his head. If only Moin Bhai had joined the business. What they couldn't accomplish together.

"Offer them more money."

Tijori Uncle regarded his topaz ring, as if contemplating offering it to Barre Nanu for the bribe. How much money would it fetch? Five hundred? A thousand? But Barre Nanu wouldn't ask for it, wouldn't accept it if offered. It wasn't a question of money. His pride was at stake. Same with Moin Bhai. Barre Nanu had hurt the weaver's pride by asking him to work as a tailor.

Tijori Uncle burped. "What do the weavers want, then? They love working for the British, don't they? Offer them that."

Barre Nanu didn't think Moin Bhai loved the British. "He has too much pride."

"Don't be so naive, my dear nephew, everyone wants something. My own Muslim tailors didn't like to learn from a Hindu master. I had to find a German chap. Very accomplished fellow. Used to work on Savile Row before the war. Entice the weavers with lessons from a *gora*. They will come running."

The diversity of his uncle's contacts never ceased to amaze Barre Nanu. He thanked his uncle for the offer, but he didn't wish to degrade himself once more before Moin Bhai. That skeletal weaver had nearly stabbed him with a pair of scissors. He too had pride. "At this point I am ready to learn the work myself. Please send the tailor master to the shop."

Tijori Uncle kept his promise. The next week, a European man appeared at the boutique, fully suited. Barre Nanu hadn't seen a better-dressed gentleman: the knot of his tie impeccably snug inside his white collar, a folded handkerchief in his top pocket. If it weren't for his trilby just beginning to fray at the brim (a detail he was most conscious to hide), Barre Nanu would have taken the European for a diplomat. The half-English, half-German tailor, a Mr. Miller, turned out to be a genius. He worked swiftly, his nervous energy filling the shop as he stretched over and across the worktable despite his short torso, his movements sharp with military precision. Within two hours, he'd cut nearly ten pairs of trousers. His fingers were tinged blue from the chalk he carried in his pocket, knuckles shiny from maneuvering the yardstick. He talked the whole time. He wanted Barre Nanu to know what he was doing. "Now, the collar is the most crucial aspect of a shirt, very tricky to get right. For the trousers to fit, we need the exact inside leg. A man seldom notices his wife, ja, but he will notice his sleeves if they constantly ride up. A snug fit for a jacket is best fit. We don't want our customer swimming inside his jacket."

Mr. Miller came again the next day, and in just four hours he'd sewn a pair of trousers, a shirt, and a vest. He offered to work twice a week, more often if necessary. He consulted at plenty of bespokes. His sojourn in India had proved worthwhile. He didn't want to leave the subcontinent. How long could Barre Nanu afford to employ Mr. Miller? He wasn't sure. Barre Nanu wished he had a partner to help him make decisions like this. He'd studied accounting in college. And yet, he hesitated to put his book knowledge into practice. Working with British cloth felt unnatural, immoral. Army uniforms required precision, a different set of hands, a different set of values. Even if he finished a hundred uniforms by some miracle, the army would reject them all.

2

Moin Bhai had been thinking about Barre Nanu and his offer since the visit. That afternoon, long after Barre Nanu left, scissors in his hands, regretful of his outburst, the weaver thought about his childhood days. Once, Barre Nanu had invited him for a swim in the Ravi, Barre Nanu deft with his strokes, urging the young Moin to keep up. Moin Bhai recalled his own wide-eyedness, his belief in the goodness inherent in all things. What a light-headed feeling it was to think well of everyone. Even of Barre Nanu's father and all other Hindu bosses.

His son came to fetch him for lunch. On their way upstairs, they discovered the box of sweets. Barre Nanu's peace offering.

"Abboo, what's this?" Jamal sniffed the rose-scented syrup, his eyes seeking permission to open it, and he ran with it up the stairs, chanting "Abboo brought a treat, Abboo brought a treat," leaving a trail of sweet rose fragrance lingering behind. Moin Bhai sat before the spread his wife had prepared—*keema*, roti, *sabzi*. To this the child added the prized possession, golden swirls of fried dough bursting with syrup.

"What's the *jalebi* for?" his wife asked. "Did you get some good news?"

Moin Bhai thought for a while. What should he call his father's old employer's son who'd come with a proposal and a box of sweets? Despite the bruise in his heart, Moin Bhai felt a glow of kindness. "Better than good news, wife. I saw an old friend."

Why hadn't he wanted to join Barre Nanu's business? Doubtless, he'd make more money with Barre Nanu. But there was the matter of trust. Even though Hindus and Muslims had been working together for generations without trouble, even though the social separation and caste laws that prevented them from eating together hardly mattered when commerce went on smoothly, there had been betrayals. On both sides people had partnered with the British. On both sides people had betrayed and backstabbed to hold on to positions and land and jagirs and contracts. The British had complicated the picture. And what with their mills running the show and their war dictating the market, it was hard to know if Barre Nanu's proposal might be a viable enterprise. What if Britain lost the war and left India and took the fashion of English clothes with her? What would be the point of learning a trade no one needed? But what if Barre Nanu was right? What if the demand for English cloth grew and grew? Ought he to trust him? Was he a fool to do hard labor to keep solvent? Moin Bhai kept pacing the kitchen long after lunch, weighing the pros and cons of Barre Nanu's offer. But even after countless sleepless nights, he couldn't make a decision one way or the other.

Four months later, one cold January morning, Moin Bhai prepared to go to the job site. He kissed his wife, their baby girl, and their son, who lay in his own bed in the second room. The boy's body was warm with sleep; it barely made a dent in the stuffed cotton *gadda* under the sheet. But as soon as Jamal heard his father taking a bath, and later descending the stone staircase, he insisted on coming along. It was Sunday, the madrasa was shut, and the boy had made friends with other children at the job site.

"Take him, *naa*," his wife insisted. "He is going to ask me a thousand times, 'When is Abba coming back, when is Abba coming back.'" She practically pushed little Jamal down the stairs.

At the construction site, a Sikh house of worship in the new Model Town, where the Lahore elite had bought apartments (Tijori Uncle included), Moin Bhai poured rocks into the concrete mixer. The country was in a state of war, but the rich were building more houses. The residential colony rose tall and complex behind him like a forest. Long rows of identical bungalows radiated from a central garden, which buzzed with birds of every variety.

The work was slow and tiring. Moin Bhai had to shovel rocks from a quarry. He hoisted the load over his head, carried it up a mound, and shoved the rocks into the concrete mixer. While he worked, Jamal played games of chase with the other children. The youngsters ran wild, weaving in and out of their parents, who moved about the job site in a queue. The winter morning felt warm; the sun beat down on their heads and made their shirts cling to their backs. The heat put the foreman in a foul mood. The Hindu Munshi shouted at everyone to hurry: the project had gone on for too long, were they trying to cheat him? They had to work twice as fast today, no breaks or chatting.

Moin Bhai called to his son as he ran in circles, chased by an older girl. He paused to admire the boy. Jamal would turn out tall; his thin limbs were fine and strong, a more perfect copy of his own. They would find him a good girl. It was too early to dream of his marriage, but Moin Bhai couldn't help himself. He wouldn't spare a single expense for his son's wedding; there'd be feasting for days.

"*Beta*, don't let the foreman catch you. He's angry today," he told his son.

The boy obediently came to a stop, along with the rest of the children. They regarded the foreman, busy with his accounting book. A slump spread over their bodies, and they ambled up the mound to the mixer, where they sat waiting for their parents to finish work.

"Another two hours and we can go home," Moin Bhai told his son.

Jamal played with rocks, stared fascinated inside the cement mixer, a monstrous rakshasa's mouth wide enough to swallow two grown men. It tilted and turned, grinding stones into cement paste. He stared at a lump as it circled about, falling flatly from one arm of the mixer onto the next. The blades moved like a mad dancing ascetic's arms, round and round and round. The inside of the mixer smelled sweet and wet and cool, like the earth when it rained.

Moin Bhai worked as fast as he could, hoping the foreman would notice and reward him with an early exit. The shovel felt heavy as he swung it on his shoulders, the wooden handle warm, and he staggered a little under its weight. Another two hours, he told himself, two more hours, and he could take Jamal home.

Moin Bhai was bent over the rocks, facing the other way, when the foreman came running. Jamal had had an accident. The boy was tossing rocks into the mixer and leaned too far inside trying to dislodge a big piece of rock stuck between the blades. If it hadn't been for a coworker who'd latched onto the boy and yanked him out, they might have lost him. It had been too late to save the boy's hand.

Moin Bhai ran to his son like a madman. The boy lay on a hand-cart, awake still, his eyes wide and wet and afraid. Moin Bhai took hold of Jamal's mangled arm. The little fingers were lifeless and bloody. Deep gashes on his palm and wrist and forearm revealed bones, tendons, muscles, flesh, dripping blood. Moin Bhai swatted at the flies. He had to save as much of his son as possible. The foreman looked aghast. He shoved a full week's wages into Moin's pocket, ordered two other workers to run him to Ganga Ram Hospital.

Moin Bhai pushed the handcart along the road with all his might. His coworkers shouted at the traffic of bicycles and cars to get out of the way.

"It's all my fault," Moin Bhai cried. "I shouldn't have brought him to work."

At the hospital, they couldn't save Jamal's hand, nor the arm, which had to be amputated from the elbow down. Four hours later, an English nurse patted the gauzed half arm and said that he could resume normal activities in a month's time.

Moin Bhai's wife accused him of breaking their son. "Why couldn't you keep an eye on him?" she asked, shaking as she cried. She'd brought Jamal's toys wrapped inside a piece of cloth—a clay stove and clay kitchen utensils. "Why can't you take up a safer job? This is all because of your pride."

"You said to take him with me."

"You could have worked at the mill, or accepted your friend's offer. If you were sewing clothes, my son wouldn't have lost an arm."

Moin Bhai sat beside his son on the hospital bed. His breath came out heavy as he watched the ghost of his son's right arm. His wife was right. A sewing machine wouldn't have sliced off his son's arm. Pride had clouded his judgment, and Jamal had to pay the consequences. Moin Bhai wiped away hot tears. Enough, they'd suffered enough.

◆

Barre Nanu couldn't believe that Moin Bhai stood before him at his doorstep. Four months had passed since their fight. After all the un- kind words, he'd expected never to see the weaver again. Moin Bhai looked somber, his earlier resolve gone, his eyes wet and hollowed of feeling, like wells. His pressed white kurta trembled in the wind, and the skeleton inside trembled with it. The weaver took off his shoes and stepped into the shop, hands folded.

"You were right, *bhaijaan*. Our loved ones aren't expendable. Neither their fingers nor their hair is expendable."

"*Bhaijaan*, what has happened?"

Moin Bhai told his friend about Jamal's accident. How wrong he had been to ignore Barre Nanu's advice. "Please, *bhaijaan*, give me the job. Tell me what needs to be done, and I will do it. I won't utter another word in protest."

Barre Nanu pointed to Mr. Miller pedaling away on the sewing machine in the corner. He introduced the apprentice to the expert. Moin Bhai took up the second pair of scissors, his shoulders slumped in surrender, and began following his teacher's instructions, Barre Nanu interpreting in the middle.

Looking at the weaver, no one would think he'd suffered a terrible shock. He maintained his composure, immersed himself in the work. Barre Nanu wondered if he ought to give the poor man all the cash in hand, tell him to take a week off. But no. Moin Bhai had too much pride. Steady work was the only cure. All Barre Nanu could do was to provide a structure to the days and a pace at which to exhaust his energies. The rest would take care of itself. They might even build back the trust they had lost in one another.

◆

Moin Bhai listened patiently to all the instructions. The newness of the work engaged his mind. No one was expendable, not his Jamal, and not Chhote. How wrong he had been, how lucky that Barre Nanu had given him a second chance. Moin Bhai shut his eyes and prayed for the success of the enterprise. All the bad thoughts he'd thought earlier—Hindus couldn't be trusted, Hindus had handed the subcontinent to the British—he'd been naive to think them.

August 2002

The train from Delhi would arrive in the late afternoon. Bebe had booked a seat on the Shatabdi Express. She called Ila last night to tell her so.

"How did you convince her to come?" I asked.

"I told her I'm pregnant."

"What?" I held my stomach, contemplating murder.

She slapped a cold hand on my arm. "Chill, *rey*! I told her Chhote Nanu isn't keeping well. Which isn't far from the truth, is it?"

My pulse relaxed, then quickened. I would finally have the chance to question Bebe. I wouldn't let her shirk away this time. I'd ask her about my father, and what'd caused him to keep away all my life, why he'd never tried to get to know me. I grabbed Ila's hand as she tried to type. "Are we agreed? We are going to grill Bebe together? You will take my side?"

"Uh-huh."

I couldn't be sure. My little sister might throw me under the bus the first chance she got.

Because a right-wing political rally had shut down Mall Road and Ila wished to avoid them at all costs or risk going in jail a second time, our rickshaw took a longer route to the railway station, past the Parade and the Machhli Mosque and the gun shops. But before we rounded the corner past the mosque, Ila told the rickshaw wallah to pull over. She dangled a foot off the footrest; her white keds scraped against the road.

"You have to go to the railway station alone," she told me. "Don't let Bebe get back on that train."

"But where are you going?" I asked in annoyance.

"Home."

She'd already begun her march, swinging her reed arms like an angry schoolteacher.

I doubted very much that I could fetch Bebe on my own. She'd make up some silly excuse such as having forgotten to turn off a burner, or simply because she felt it wasn't the right time to see her children. "Too soon, too soon, it's best we don't see each other right now," I could hear her say, her voice uneven like a recalcitrant radio unable to catch a signal. Only Ila could manipulate her.

"I need you," I told my sister, grabbing her quarter-sized wrist.

"You expect me to go past Lal Imli," she barked, freeing herself with surprising alacrity. "Have you forgotten?"

Her words felt like a slap. "Yes, I suppose I forgot for a minute—"

I stood rooted on the side of the street, in a busy market, with people trying to get past. Behind me, a scooter, an apple peddler, and a peddler of silver-foiled neon-green sweets demanded passage. Without question, I couldn't face our mother without Ila. "Are you going to avoid Lal Imli all your life?" I called slowly.

Ila whipped around, her eyes wide with hurt and disbelief.

I hung my head. "Forget it," I said, joining her. "Bebe can come on her own. If she wants to go back, so be it."

We'd walked as far as the gun shops when Ila paused. She rested a hand on a wooden crate of apples. The apple wallah picked out the reddest and shiniest fruit and held it to her. She accepted it without the usual gratitude in her eyes. Under the Kanpur sun, in her lime-green sari, she glistened like a gecko, not a dull, depressing Indian gecko, but a pretty, tropical gecko with rubies buried in its skin. I wanted to hug my sister and never let anything bad happen to her ever again.

"Bebe isn't going to face you or Chhote Nanu unless I force her," Ila said. "Why are you men such a pain in the butt?" She slipped a rupee into the apple wallah's hand and turned back toward Lal Imli. In another minute, she hailed a rickshaw.

I hopped onto the seat next to her. "You can hold my hand. Or punch me or kick me if you feel the need."

Ila stared at the road with a thousand-yard stare. She tucked a finger into her shoe. "My feet are sweaty. Do you mind giving me your *chappals?*"

My feet felt squished inside Ila's sweaty keds. But this was the least I could do.

◆

Lal Imli throbbed green, a world of wild creepers and vines and perpetual monsoons. Vines of morning glory snaked up and across brick walls and electric poles; a flaming-red creeper attacked signage, reduced "SHEILING HOUSE" to "SHE LING HO E." Here the British had put up mills and factories, attempted to force a modern London order on a tropical, Munshi Premchand farmland country. We passed a red-brick mill that erased a chunk of an ancient forest, occupied a whole block, the sun on its windows reminding me of Mott Street in New York. But likely it was Mott Street that reminded me of Lal Imli.

Ila sat stone-faced, unmoved by the shrubbery. She knew Lal Imli's dead, gray heart. She pushed her glasses (still held together with tape) up the bridge of her nose. I pulled them off, put them in my front pocket, made a mental note to get her a new pair.

Our rickshaw traveled past the lane with the bungalow, its vast acreage expectant. Ila's arm next to mine turned goose-pimply. Her eyes shut and her mouth released a breath.

◆

Fifteen years ago, a week after Chhote Nanu threw our books and clothes out the window, Bebe left for Delhi to look for jobs. We woke up one morning and found a note pinned to Ila's uniform: "Gone to Delhi. Ask Barre Nanu for snack money, but only when he isn't busy." A week passed. She hadn't returned. At school, Guitar Bobby, a humorless boy with a humorous name, invited us to his bungalow that Sunday for an afternoon of TV watching.

Ila was eight, I eleven. Together we aimed for the shadows inside Guitar Bobby's house, ran past the green-uniformed guard with a gun at the gate. "We want to see Guitar Bobby!" Our shouts lingered. "Guitar Bobby! Tell your guard not to shoot us."

We ran through a thicket of eucalyptus, mango, papaya, and palms. The main house sat squat and low to the ground like a sumo wrestler, its veranda washed and glistening, its white columns bright. We crept past a lonely field loud with sunshine. From behind distant trees, the flash of a white river. We could hear its onward rush, its ecosystem of rocks and birds, its rapid, murderous heart. Ages ago, mutinying Indian sepoys had drowned a boatload of English housewives here in an attempt to overthrow colonial rule. Our child hearts drummed at the sight of the ferocious river.

Too bad Barre Nanu still loved only Lahore. He didn't sit us down and tell us stories about Kanpur, didn't take us to the river for picnics or prayers, didn't tell us to forgive the Ganges (the drowned Englishwomen weren't the river's fault), forgive the sepoys (they only wanted to free the land of the colonizers), didn't tell us about the Ganges' mythical mountainous beginnings, its fanfare Bay of Bengal ending. All this I learned at school.

"We could live here," Ila suggested, her straw arms outstretched, twirling in the sunlit field. "Guitar Bobby won't mind."

"You need a roof over your head, silly," I advised my sister. "You can't live under trees."

"What do you know?" Ila taunted me, hands on hips.

"I'm in fifth standard, stupid. I know a lot more than you."

We sauntered to the edge of the field and happened upon a cowshed.

A beautiful auburn cow (she looked imported) grazed in a far manger. Sunlight filtered straight into her trough from the barred window. Ila giggled. "Let's live here, in Guitar Bobby's cowshed. It has a roof."

We could sleep by the troughs, eat sunshine, wear hay, drink from the river. It wasn't a bad idea. If only Guitar Bobby would let us.

We heard music in the far garden. The eucalypti were singing.

The music drew us to a yellow concrete hut tucked behind the mango trees. Guitar Bobby was playing a popular *filmi* tune on his guitar. Instantly, Ila began to sing along, "dinga dong, o baby singer song." Her braids flopped back and forth as she shook her head side to side. One of her red ribbons came undone—without Bebe, she couldn't braid her hair tightly enough. She picked it up and danced with it, twirling her skirt like a film star.

"Shhh!" I warned, but Ila couldn't stop.

"The chorus is coming on!" She wanted to demonstrate she could hit the high notes.

Despite his music, Guitar Bobby didn't have many friends at school. At lunch he sat alone under the canteen tree with an imported video game. Some of the boys in my class said that he'd been suspended from a posher private school for doing drugs, that he was really fifteen years old, pretending to be twelve. Unlike the others, I couldn't decide on the matter of Guitar Bobby's goodness. Once, I'd accepted his offer of five rupees so I could buy a bottle of Goldspot soda at the canteen. That's how we met, with him offering me money. I didn't see a reason to refuse his friendship.

"You are going to behave in front of Guitar Bobby," I told Ila, dragging her toward the yellow hut. "None of this singing and dancing. Sit with your legs crossed."

"Why is he called Guitar Bobby? What kind of a silly name is that?"

"I don't know. Maybe because he has a guitar."

I tapped the windowpane. Guitar Bobby peeped out, his brows knitted in suspicion.

"It's me, Karan, from school," I said unnecessarily. So far as I knew, I was the only person who talked to him at school.

He nodded us in. We stepped inside the grandest room we'd ever seen. A wide, polished, four-poster bed draped with mosquito netting sat smugly in the afternoon light. An enormous entertainment center dominated the opposite wall. Tall glass vases boasted ferns, the orphaned limbs of trees.

Guitar Bobby returned to the entertainment center, opening

drawers at random, browsing videotapes and cassettes. For someone so rich, he was dressed poorly in a white tank top and shorts despite the December chill. His limbs looked fairer than ours; a red mole on his neck sprouted a single hair. I didn't like the look of the mole. Perhaps he was paler because of the dense darkness around his house and the fact that he didn't play any sports.

"This is my sister, Ila. You've probably seen her at school."

He nodded absently. "It's Sunday and I can't decide which picture to watch."

"How about *Hero?*" Ila said with excitement, remembering the song he was playing on his guitar.

She flipped through the cassettes greedily until they slid tap-tap-tap on each other. "Can we watch this? Or this?" She pulled out one tape after another, pulled out the liner notes to admire the pictures and the lyrics.

Guitar Bobby snatched his tapes from Ila. But she moved on to the next drawer and the next, flipping through the VHSs.

"Your sister has no manners." Guitar Bobby shut the drawers Ila left open. At that point, I had no control over her. I too was lost in the endless catalog of films and film songs displayed before me. The only cassette tapes Bebe owned were from the 1970s, when she was young. We had to wait for our favorite songs to play on the radio. Guitar Bobby could listen to any song anytime he wanted. Grumpily, he sank into a vast white couch and picked up his guitar, his eyes scanning Ila's body.

She wasn't much to look at. Her arms were dark and reedlike from being Punjabi and spending too much time in the sun. She had thick hair; her braids had come completely undone. Another reason why Bebe shouldn't have left. But her legs were strong; her ankles weren't absurdly thin like some other girls', and her eyes were big and frank and demanded attention. Under her dress, she had mosquito bites for nipples, same as me, and I knew this because in the mornings we bathed from the same bucket to save time. My sister wasn't cranky like other girls, but talkative and friendly. All the girls and even some boys wanted to talk to her at school because she wasn't shy.

I wondered if Guitar Bobby had noticed her in school. He seemed to be getting over his annoyance, because he went up to her and stood by, taking an interest in the cassette in her hand.

"Can we watch this picture?" She held up a videotape.

Guitar Bobby nodded.

"You have a VCR?" she asked, surprised.

He pointed to a cabinet in the entertainment center.

"I can make you a copy of any tape you want." He opened a cabinet to reveal a large audio system with not one but two cassette players.

Ila handed Guitar Bobby the tape and he dutifully pressed it into his VCR. A television enthroned in the center of the cabinet came to life. The lion capital of Ashoka with the four lions followed, promising a delicious Hindi picture filled with jokes and music and dancing and car chases.

Guitar Bobby sank into his couch, and Ila and I followed. "Something to eat? I'm hungry! What do you want?"

Ila the shameless: "Potato fingers and chips and *frooti* and *kulfi*."

"Ila!" I warned.

Guitar Bobby turned to me. "Why don't you get us some snacks from the main house? If I go, my father will keep me there for one reason or another."

"Okay," I said, taking Ila's hand, but she pulled away, her eyes glued to the television set.

Guitar Bobby threw an arm over Ila's shoulder. How quickly he'd warmed up to her. "Your sister loves the pictures too much. You go. Only, don't get lost in the house. Tell the cook to fry samosas. And to make lassi. And you only bring it. If he comes here, he will want to clean the room. And don't get frightened of the tiger in the sitting room. And the deer."

"Heads or whole animals?"

"A whole tiger, man! Some English colonel shot it."

I couldn't contain my excitement. Barre Nanu had come to Kanpur with only a suitcase. He had nothing to show from the times of the British, except a tattered military jacket. Chhote Nanu had only his Urdu and Farsi poetry books. I wanted to see something of colonial India. I skipped off.

I didn't care a bit about leaving Ila alone with Guitar Bobby, a boy I barely knew.

It happened to Ila in my absence. I remember it, even though I wasn't there to witness. Some memories, especially the ones in which you don't feature, haunt you the hardest.

Guitar Bobby and Ila snuggled on the couch, the two engrossed in the picture on the screen. A familiar song came on, and Guitar Bobby picked up his guitar. "Dinga dong, o baby singer song," he sang. Ila joined, coming in with the "la la la la la la la la la la."

"What's your favorite song?" he asked Ila.

She had too many to name. He paused the picture and played another famous number for her.

"Play the song from the picture. The song about marriage. When they are running away to get married. Play that song. *Jaanu . . . jaanu . . .* That one."

He laughed. "They aren't running away to get married. They are running away to do something else."

"That is marriage only."

"It is not."

"Then what is it?"

"You want me to show you?"

It was Ila's turn to grow sullen. "No. That's all right. My brother will be back soon, then we will leave."

"Where will you go? He told me you want to run away from home."

"We can live in the railway station. Or your cowshed."

"You are a funny girl. You want to live in my cowshed? It'll cost you to live there. You'll have to pay me rent. One lakh rupees. How much money do you have?" He invited himself to sit even closer to her, dug into her frock pockets without permission, then inserted his fingers under her thighs and pinched them. "Phew, you smell of cow."

"I said hello to your cow on my way here."

He pushed her in the direction of the bathroom. "Go wash your hands."

She complied.

He followed her inside the bathroom and didn't leave.

"I have to do *soo-soo* also."

"So, do it then."

He stayed put, and Ila had to go with him watching. She pulled down her white school bloomers and climbed on the commode. Her feet dangled. She waited. Guitar Bobby waited. Her *soo-soo* came, a bold gush that slowed to a self-conscious trickle. She pulled up her bloomers, the elastic slapping on her tummy with a twang. Guitar Bobby took her arm and dragged her to the wash basin. He washed her hands with an expensive soap that held the afternoon inside its heart.

"Do you have this soap at home?"

"No," she said meekly. "My grandfather buys Lifebuoy for everyone."

"That's a very rough soap for someone with such soft hands. Take this." He produced a new packet of Pears from the cupboard under the sink and slipped it in her pocket.

He wiped her hands on the towel, then, taking them to his nose, he sniffed deeply. "Such a nice smell! Smell it!" He pushed her hands against her face, dragged her into the room. She resisted. He pulled her harder.

It was December. Ila complained of the cold, but still Guitar Bobby turned the ceiling fan on high. It made a loud rattling sound. He dragged her to his bed. "Let me show you what marriage is. It seems you're very interested in those sorts of things."

"I'm not. I don't want to know. My brother will be back any minute," she protested.

Guitar Bobby lifted the phone receiver and banged her knee with it. "You come into my room and touch my things. All I have to do is call my guard on the intercom. I will tell him there is a trespasser on the premises. They will catch your brother and put him in jail. They will shoot him in the leg first so that he doesn't run. You want that to happen to him?"

"N—no."

"Then stop complaining."

Ila didn't say another word. Thoughts of her brother limping with a wounded leg, turning into a pitiful Hindi film character, crossed her mind and she bit her tongue. She let him toss her on his bed. He straddled her so she couldn't move, sniffed her up and down like a dog. He unpaused the film, so that the shouting began again.

"Sing if you like, while I marry you," he suggested.

Guitar Bobby pushed up her frock with the red poppies, pulled down her white bloomers, sniffed the faint hair on her thighs, and in-between her legs. He spat inside her belly button and she felt a chill so urgent she thrashed her legs. His hands clamped down on her feet, pressed them until her bones hurt. With his two fingers, he began prodding her like a doctor.

"Is there anything here?" He pressed her nipples, two eyes shut. He pressed them like they were doorbells. He squeezed her belly.

"Is there a baby in here? Or maybe a chicken? Or a goat?"

Before she could shut her legs, he rammed his fingers up inside the space between them. Pain shot up, her eyes smarted, she opened her mouth but no sound came.

"Why aren't you singing?" he shouted, and forced the same two fingers inside her mouth.

She tasted herself—her salty, buttery, musty, suffocating scents. The tasting felt extremely rude, not at all like the time she explored herself, the milkiness of her arm, the red-appleness of her thigh. She was shouting now: "Little Bo Peep . . . she lost her sheep . . . Bo Peep . . . lost her . . ." He buried his face between her legs and bit her there. Her screams came, loud and uninterrupted, and maybe they joined the screaming in the film, maybe they didn't, but no one except Guitar Bobby and a sleepy cow were near enough to hear.

Guitar Bobby emerged from under her dress, lips wet.

"There. That is how. Now we are married."

He went to the bathroom to wash up. Ila alone pulled her legs together. She alone put on her bloomers, pressed the place that throbbed, pulsated, screamed with pain and shame and shock.

Guitar Bobby returned to the room, took up his guitar, played a furious, fast number. On the TV, the picture continued, the heroine tromped around the trees, mourning her lover, who'd left her for someone wealthier. "Your brother is taking his time, isn't he?" He strummed some more. "Well, I have to take my bath. So you will have to wait outside. Let me know when you have one lakh rupees to rent my cowshed. Make that two lakh. You shout too much."

With that, he put her out. He didn't look at her again.

After what felt like hours but was likely twenty minutes, I returned from the main house, carrying a tray heaped with samosas and mango drinks. I had so much to tell Ila. I'd seen a whole tiger's hide plastered on the wall, a whole stuffed deer standing alert and lifelike, the antlers of several wild beasts. We could return to Guitar Bobbys's from time to time, learn more about the time of the British, make up for Barre Nanu's lack of stories.

She waited for me under a tree.

"What are you doing here? Why aren't you in the annex? Where's Guitar Bobby? Come, let's go." I nodded for her to go inside, but she stepped back and sneezed. "Have you caught a cold?"

She pulled out her handkerchief embroidered with her initials, IK, and wiped her nose. A bar of Pears soap fell out of her pocket. She picked it up and tossed it in the direction of the field.

"What's that? Why are you throwing away a perfectly new slab of soap? It's your favorite too."

"It's not my favorite," she shouted at the top of the lungs and ran toward the field.

"What is the matter with you?"

She threw herself on the grass. "He married me."

"Who?"

She didn't say his name.

"Who married you? What do you mean he married you?"

I put the tray down. My mind flashed through clichéd Bollywood images of instant weddings—bride and groom at a temple, garlands of flowers in hand. But the way my sister thrashed her arms and legs, I didn't think she and Guitar Bobby had played at a wedding in the sight of gods. Her desperation to get her words out, or rather to bottle them in, hinted at other images, far less spiritual. I didn't know why, but I thought of the moment when Guitar Bobby had looked my sister up and down as though she stood inside a store window.

"What do you mean marriage?" I asked her, slowly this time. "As in the films? What the hero and heroine do behind bushes?"

Before she could speak, she was seized by a series of sneezes that caused her whole body to shake.

"He had the fan on high," was all she managed to say.

I stormed toward the annex, my heart pounding. Ugly images throbbed inside my head—my sister, Guitar Bobby, legs, arms, his ugly almost-mustache, his ugly mole against my sister's perfect skin. Who did he think he was? No wonder he had no friends. No wonder they'd expelled him from his previous school. Before I could bang on the door, Ila tugged on my sweater.

"Don't, or he will call the guards and they will shoot you."

"Let them shoot."

Ila collapsed on my feet, held my legs with both her hands. "I want to go home. I want Bebe. Tell her to come back. I want Bebe."

We crept out of the garden hand in hand. This was all Bebe's fault. Why did she keep going to Delhi?

Equally, it was my fault. I should never have brought Ila to Guitar Bobby's. I struck my face once, twice. We held each other and cried.

The rickshaw dropped us outside the train station. The red building with the cream domes glistened angrily in the sun. We'd left the over-grown green of Lal Imli far behind. Inside, the platforms felt warm from all the passengers waiting to leave our untrustworthy town. Ila and I walked through the warmth, her leading the way, me following, with my heels sticking out of her constricting shoes. The Wheeler and Co. peddlers had their beautiful wooden cart out, its polished wood reflecting the blue station lights. With an irony perfected over the past fifty years, they displayed Hitler's *Mein Kampf* next to Gandhi's *My Experiments with Truth*.

While Ila browsed books, I went to get some tea to soothe my throbbing head. At the snacks kiosk, a wide man with a wide mustache filled a small paper cup the size of my palm with steamed milk, shoved in a teabag, and took my five-rupee coin. The tea tasted good. I bought a cup for Ila.

She didn't want it. She was content with her baby apple.

"It tastes like childhood. Like the India of our childhood."

She rolled her eyes. "That's the problem with synecdoches. The tea does not taste like India, stop saying stuff like that. How do you know what India tastes like?" Her eyes went flinty and she leaned meanly toward me as she talked. She must have got into the business of arguing at her university, having to defend her opinions. I took one last sip of the tea, tilting my head to ease the last drop into my mouth.

"I mean it tastes nostalgic. I don't know if they serve tea like this all over India, but I hope they do. What's wrong with having a national drink?"

"What's wrong? About the same as having a national language or a national religion. You should be suspect of a national anything."

"Well, I suppose it does kill biodiversity to keep growing the same kind of tea."

"Exactly. We are not at war anymore. We shouldn't have the same kind of war economy, producing tea for a billion people like we are trying to feed an army, when some of us want to drink coffee or herbs or just plain water."

I didn't have a comeback. I couldn't bring the second cup of tea to my lips, so I gave it to a boy filling water bottles at the public tap. Lal Imli had triggered bad memories. It hurt to have her snap at me like that. She crossed her legs and bent over in a gesture of pain.

"Do you need to use the bathroom?"

She shook her head in annoyance.

I'd forgotten her fear of public restrooms. To distract her, I returned to our earlier conversation: "The tea really did taste the same as our childhood. I don't get tea this good in New York."

"You can enjoy your tea, but don't say stupid stuff like the tea tastes like India, that's the same as saying India smells like shit or India is poor. There is no such thing as India. It only exists in the dreams of foreigners like Columbus or Dickens or whomever."

"Neither Columbus nor Dickens came to India."

"Well, Vasco da Gama, then. The East India Company. Stop looking at India from the vantage point of England or America or Europe."

"You've never been away. You don't understand the value of nostalgia."

"Not everyone wants to leave India like you."

"I thought you said India didn't exist."

Her eyes became two daggers.

"Sometimes you have to distance yourself from a problem or a place or a person to see them clearly."

"No, you have to live in a place and deal with the problem to see it clearly."

"Is that why you decided to go past his house?" I'd said too much.

Ila stood with her arms over her belly, as though I'd punched her, her eyes burning.

I walked to the platform's edge. I'd had enough of my sister. If only I could hop on the train, fly back to New York, retreat into my studies. New York had places for me to hide—libraries, bookstores, cathedrals, the Hudson.

I tried to think of Bebe. The last time I saw her, six years ago, she lay in a hospital. I couldn't shout at her then any more than I already had. If I saw her now, would I be able to get a word out?

The lady on the intercom announced the Shatabdi. Only half an hour late.

At quarter past two, the royal blue train swept in, a river of faces and smells and expectations. Where was my mother in all this? Was she on it, with her heart full of secrets, or had she bailed?

Then I saw her. She was stepping off the train, a suitcase in hand. She'd lost weight, enough that her faded cream blouse fitted loosely over her tan belly. She looked up from over her reading glasses, regarded the platform with mistrust, as though it might turn into quicksand. She'd stopped coloring her hair and a smart lick of white snaked its way from her forehead. Then she saw her children, staring at her with all their eyes. Her breath came out fast. She held onto the door handle, one leg still on the train. The damn stupid rude train jerked.

I ran to her as she lost her balance. "Let go of the train, I have you."

Ila took her bag. We caught our mother as she fell into our arms.

September 1944

1

Nigar Jaan's letter had earned Chhote Nanu monthly beatings from the warden in the torture chamber. He was hung like a towel and whipped, just so he wouldn't forget how he'd breached the rules. His quarters were searched each night, his bedding pounded. His pillow had been confiscated so that he had one less place to hide any missives. At mealtimes, they served him watered lapsy that tasted like feet.

But despite all the hardships thrown at him, Chhote Nanu couldn't stop thinking about Nigar Jaan. If anything, the monthly lashings, the weekly humiliations, and the daily taunts only caused his fervor to grow stronger.

On Sundays and on holidays the superintendent and the warden didn't visit the jail, and the prisoners relaxed. Chhote Nanu enacted the scene of going to see Nigar Jaan in his imagination. He would beg for her forgiveness, gift her little boy his bicycle, shower him with treats and toys. "The war is going in the favor of the British," she would say, and he would find a way to comfort her. "Leave Mutton. Come away with me." He wondered what he could offer her when they were finally alone. He lifted his shirt. The hard labor at the oil press had given his body definition. His once sinewy arms had gained bulk, his chest didn't seem flat, and his legs didn't wobble as before. He thought of Nigar Jaan's body, the particular delight of her skin, and how it had glowed on that afternoon of the wrestling match. The idea of her felt sacred, the act of conjuring her like praying. He gave himself the permission to dream of her, to think kindly of her because she'd been kind, forgiving him for bringing a bomb to her house. How else could he read her letter except as an indication that he'd been forgiven?

One Sunday, Chhote Nanu dared to ask the jailer if he'd send Nigar Jaan's maid a message.

"Come on, Gangadhar," Chhote Nanu tried to persuade him. "You know my days are numbered."

The amicable, amorous jailer needed an excuse to see the maid, and agreed.

"Could you tell her," Chhote Nanu enunciated, almost sang as soon as he saw Shehnaz from across the cell door, "I am very sorry for what I did. I was given the impression that doing so would shake up the English, at the very least bring Mutton to justice." He'd also vainly hoped that the crime would make Nigar Jaan see him differently. He told Shehnaz this too. "I am to be transported to Andaman; who knows how long I have left. I set off the firecracker only once Baby Jaan had left the room." Being marked for transportation released something inside Chhote Nanu. He had to live his life now; in Andaman it would be too late.

Nigar Jaan replied right away, this time in the form of a letter Shehnaz wrote on Gangadhar's arm: "I don't think you understand Mutton's reach, and his importance to the colonial government. I feel I am endangering your life by writing to you . . ."

Chhote Nanu replied, scribbling with a makeshift quill and ink on Shehnaz's arms, even though the writing tickled her and she kept fidgeting: "Don't stop writing to me. I am a candle all but snuffed out. I have nothing to look forward to except your words. What did you do this morning? Did you go to the park? Did your son demand treats?"

Nigar Jaan replied: "My little boy asks about you. He wonders when Cycle Uncle is going to visit. He discovered the little stream behind the poplars. You made quite an impression on him."

Chhote Nanu dared to say: "And what about you? Did I make an impression on you? That stream has fish and frogs. Be sure to show them to your boy."

Nigar Jaan replied: "If you hadn't made an impression on me, would I risk four lives to write to you?"

In the privacy of his room, he fantasized about taking her wheat-skinned hand and strutting together indomitably down Mall Road, in view of the wooden queen, in view of the English *mems*, in view of the marching band. They'd dine at Nedous Hotel, enjoy sandwiches and gin fizz.

Soon his privacy was curtailed. In November 1944, the U.S. army bombed Singapore. Allied troops captured a horde of INA soldiers and shipped them to Indian jails. Chhote Nanu's quarters became crammed. He had to share his cell with six other prisoners, including two INA soldiers and his nemesis, Chiragh.

At first the soldiers admired Chhote Nanu for attempting to assassinate the superintendent. But when he confessed he'd felt ambivalent about the task, they mocked him. They'd planted real bombs and killed real soldiers, many of them Indian, with the sole purpose of liberating India from the British yoke. They couldn't empathize with Chhote Nanu's wishy-washiness. "*Darpokh chuha*," they mocked him, "little ninny." Chiragh added fuel to fire: "He's no revolutionary, no poet, just a confused waste of space."

"If it weren't for you, I would be teaching right now," Chiragh told him. "My sisters would be married. My mother wouldn't have to take up washing the neighbor's clothes."

It killed Chhote Nanu that Chiragh received letters from his family, gifts even. Once, he even feasted on a plate of homemade dinner—roti, *sabzi*, dal, dahi, *papad*, achar. The scent of ghee brought all the prisoners to their knees, tears in their eyes. The INA soldiers hovered around Chiragh for a morsel. Chhote Nanu wept quietly in the corner, the smells releasing fresh memories of Chaiji's cooking.

Sometimes their fights ended in blows. Sometimes Chhote Nanu woke up to find the poet straddling him, pounding fists into his face.

Once, his cup of water tasted like piss. Twice, Chiragh had threatened to slit his throat in his sleep.

"It isn't just my fault you are here," Chhote Nanu would say in his defense. "The superintendent didn't have to arrest you."

The INA soldiers jumped in, instigating Chiragh. "You should slit both their throats, this ninny's and the superintendent's."

"I will. I won't spare anyone. I won't spare this cheat, I won't spare Mutton, I won't even spare his English whore."

"You are a *badtameez badzubaan* foul-mouthed hack," Chhote Nanu said, leaping on him, as the INA rebels cheered them on.

At night, while his cellmates slept, Chhote Nanu stayed awake, fearing Chiragh's fists and subterfuges. He wished he had a sharper tongue, he wished he had a dagger. He turned to face the window, from where he could see the moon.

An INA soldier crouched beside it, scraping something on the windowsill. The way his elbow moved, Chhote Nanu could tell the soldier was etching the symbol he'd drawn in the hallways and at the oil mill.

"What does it mean?" he dared to ask.

The soldier crawled into bed. "The circle is our brotherhood. The quadrants inside represents our four principles: valor, sacrifice, honor, justice. We never let the guilty go unpunished. We always take our revenge."

The INA sounded like Chhote Nanu's cup of tea. If he'd been given the chance, he'd have joined the rebels. Once, Chhote Nanu had belonged to a brotherhood. Some kind of brother Samrat was though—he never wrote, he never visited.

The INA soldier punched his pillow and turned to face the other away. "Don't trust your English *mem*. None of the English can be trusted. All they want from India is to make a profit. All they know how to do is divide and rule, divide and rule. How many of my own Indian brothers I killed in Burma, in Singapore before the INA united us." Then he turned to face him. "Too bad your mission failed. Mutton has serious war crimes on his conscience."

"The bomb needed more ammunition," Chhote Nanu said weakly. "I did what I could." He couldn't help but seek the soldier's approval.

The soldier grunted at Chhote Nanu's excuses, as though he had little tolerance for incompetence. "Someone else will have to finish your job."

"Someone else?"

"Do you really think the INA will let Mutton go unpunished? We are focused on the battles overseas. But soon he will get his comeuppance."

The soldier's words chilled him. Ought he to warn Nigar Jaan to stay away from the superintendent? But what if he frightened her for naught? "So many of the INA soldiers are in jail. What makes you so confident you can hurt Mutton, or liberate India?"

"They might jail thousands of us, but thousands more will take our place. The future is as clear as glass. Just wait and watch." The soldier turned away and soon began to snore.

Could the INA really free India and bring Mutton to justice? The future wasn't clear at all. The future was a murky lake full of algae and sea-green moss. Meanwhile, the question of his transportation, along with India's freedom, hung in the balance.

Soon the news of Gandhi's release from prison reached Lahore Central Jail. The local prisoners became hopeful. Surely this meant independence was nigh, even their independence. The great pacifist would kick the British out and offer a blanket pardon to all prisoners. They talked excitedly about going home, seeing their family, proposing to old loves. But not everyone celebrated. Some reasoned that the British had released the mahatma because of his old age; the British didn't want his death weighing on their conscience. The Raj had taken three hundred years to dig its stronghold into India. It would take three hundred years to dismantle; a quick transition would be messy. The British had found India as a bride brimming with jewels; they'd raped her, stolen all her jewels. They wouldn't leave her just like that.

And if they did, they'd leave her a pauper. What reason could there be to celebrate?

"The British won't leave India in once piece," Chhote Nanu heard a Muslim jailer tell a Hindu one. "My brother says Pakistan is all they talk about at Aligarh Muslim University."

"Pakistan?" Chhote Nanu asked. This was the first time he'd heard the word.

"The nation for all the Muslims," confirmed the Muslim jailer. "The upper-class Muslims want a separate nation. Jinnah Bhai, the Muslim League leader, is convincing all Muslims to move to Pakistan."

"But where will it be, this Pakistan?"

"Who knows! Wherever they draw the lines."

"It's not really going to happen, is it?" Chhote Nanu asked.

"It's already happening. The League has taken millions under their fold. They've been campaigning all this time. In all likelihood, we will be split into two nations. Maybe more."

◆

Sitting in his jeep, patrolling the Shahalmi neighborhood, Superintendent Mutton contemplated the news of Gandhi's release. Now that the news had been made public, it felt more real. It must mean something awful for the administration. How could it not? As of late, his superiors hadn't relayed any opinions, and it was up to him to interpret the new development between the Congress and the British Raj. He drummed his fingers on the steering wheel as he waited for his servants to return with reports from the market. He sent them periodically to spy on the locals. If they saw Gandhi's release as a sign of Britain's weakening power, they'd think *his* power had weakened. He'd had to crack his whip harder after the blow that firecracker boy had inflicted on his reputation. Mutton knew he was hated. A lot of scoundrels wanted him dead, but such was the nature of his job. All he had to do was to stay several steps ahead. Only reason the firecracker scoundrel had got so close was because of Nigar Jaan. Soon he'd ship the boy off to Andaman. Even after a year, Mutton hadn't received the sign-off from his superiors. If the Japanese controlled the island, the British ought to build another cellular jail. There had to be appropriate punishment for crimes, otherwise chaos prevailed, and this was no way to run an empire or win a war.

More than the bomb, Nigar Jaan's letter incensed him. He feared Gordon had hidden the more incriminating parts of it. He'd caught the gist, however: her trying to keep the boy informed of developments outside. Mutton wanted to shake her. *Are you not happy? Have I not given you everything you wanted? You wanted to keep the baby, I let you. You wanted your poetry, I allowed it. What more could I do?* Maybe she'd incited the bomb. Maybe she and the boy had a thing going on long before the gathering. He wouldn't put it past her to entertain boys like him. It was her profession, part of her nature to fool him with a veil of faithfulness. Maybe she was composing a second letter that instant.

2

Nigar Jaan was in fact composing her tenth message to Chhote Nanu. In addition to the missives, she'd asked Shehnaz to keep an eye on Chhote Nanu, find out how the superintendent treated him.

Shehnaz came back with terrible news.

He'd been tortured. When Nigar Jaan didn't follow, Shehnaz demonstrated the towel hanger. She flung open the window, pressed her belly into the ledge. Her upper half dangled out, suspended in the early morning air (causing passersby in the lane to hoot at her), the other half inside. She raised herself and looked at Nigar Jaan with bulging, bloodshot eyes.

"Is it painful?" Nigar Jaan asked, biting her lip, already aware of the answer.

"It's difficult to breathe." She lost her balance, dizzy from the blood rushing away from her head. Chhote Nanu, she reported, had spent several hours in that pose, likely a whole day. His hands and feet had been tied. He'd been beaten numerous times.

To think that Mutton had ordered the torture. The father of her child was a cruel man. She'd known this all along. But the painful fact of the matter was, she had no place in his life to question his ethics or ask him to become a better man.

She wasn't his wife. He'd never invited her to his living quarters in the civil station, not once. If he wanted to spend time with her, he came to her. She couldn't make demands on his time, or on his behavior. He did not like the use of prophylaxis. Having to put it on right before impeded his erection. Still, he was careful with his health, and he paid to have her tested. She didn't know if he had himself tested, even though she was certain he saw other women, because some months he disappeared entirely. He didn't take her anywhere, not to the club (off-limits to women like her), not to the pictures (far too many American GIs). He didn't like being seen with her in public. The wrestling attracted no one of consequence, and he tolerated her presence there, but didn't sit with her. He didn't remember her birthdays, made cruel, rough love to her that left her sore for days.

The child they shared had been an accident.

As soon as he heard the news, he offered to take her to a surgeon in Simla. At first she'd agreed. They drove quietly in his jeep, the roar of the engine building with the thunder that promised a storm. They drove for an hour on the wet, treacherous street until her conviction grew that they'd embarked on an unholy, unforgivable mission. With everything inside her screaming, she told him, as calmly as she could, to stop the car.

They were parked on the side of the road. His breath came out hard, condensing on the window. The scent of his cologne made it difficult for her to breathe.

"Why do you want to bring a bastard into this world?"

She flinched at the word, but didn't shift her newfound resolve. "You may not want it, but I do. I don't feel right parting with it—with her."

He looked at her with a pained expression. He didn't seem angry, only confused, and a little scared. He reached for the keys and switched off the engine. For a long while, they stayed like that, not speaking. It began to drizzle, and the fog penetrated the car. Outside, the deodars disappeared and reappeared. Then it began to rain hard, and the whole world disappeared. The jeep stood on a hill, and if he made a fuss, she could jump off into the white void. But he didn't say a word. The rain stopped, and as soon as it did, Mutton put the car in reverse and turned around.

She felt so giddy with gratitude, she called that feeling love.

Later that night, they made love with a renewed energy.

"You are not an unkind man, Mutton," she told him unabashedly. "And only I know it."

He held her, flashed an uncertain smile, and she knew that moment was bigger than a proposal of marriage, as close to a proposal of marriage as she was going to get from him. She could live like this. This was as close to love as it would get for a woman like her.

Then Henry was born.

Mutton came straight from the station. He held his son all afternoon, wouldn't let the baby go. He stayed the whole day, even as she came in and out of sleep.

But the gift of Henry, all three years of him, couldn't take away from the fact that Mutton had hung a chap upside down for days and thrashed him like a towel. And then there was the ghost of Jallianwala. The men, women, children he'd killed mercilessly, without a second thought.

Three years after Mutton's act of kindness, Nigar Jaan felt not ungrateful, no, but in need of another reminder of his goodness. Lately, she found the ordeal of spending time with him onerous. His hair was thinning, and his small, cruel mouth was never pleasant to look at. She had to drag herself through her toilette. If she sent word she felt sick, he came round, feigning concern for her health. He asked her a dozen uninteresting questions about her day, and after all that, she couldn't ask him about the jail.

✦

After patrolling the markets, Mutton drove to Nigar Jaan's. He was still thinking about her vile letter to the boy.

She had prepared herself for him. The old lace dress looked pretty against her thin, dark arms. The little yellow buttons on her bodice, he wanted to pluck them off one by one. He imagined the face she would make if he did so, full of pleasured pain. He wanted to own that face, the only man who saw it.

He gave her a parcel of sugar candy, and she feigned surprise as she accepted it. He would never guess such a lovely woman could be so devious. But even as he doubted her, he couldn't help but feel a little protective.

"Keep it in a tin jar," he instructed her.

She nodded absently and shouted for the helper girl to bring him a glass of water.

He sat in his usual seat while she saw about the dinner. "Gandhi's been out, did you hear? They finally made the news of his release public."

"Is it because of the mahatma's failing health?"

Their world was about to end, and she took it lightly. She sat opposite him at the other end of the table, not next to him like she usually did.

"Or is this for fear of an INA resurgence? Will the rest of the Congress leaders get released? Maybe it will ease the tensions in the market?"

He'd had enough INA talk. "Since when do you care about the Congress or the tensions in the market or the INA?"

"I live here. Why wouldn't I care?"

For the first time, she baffled him. He thought she'd elevated herself above the market, that she didn't like to think about belonging to it and living there. That's what he'd liked about her, that she didn't reduce herself to the lowest common denominator, kept herself sequestered.

"You don't even like Indians."

She got up to help the girl put the place settings. He wished she'd sit down; he wished things would go back to the way they were.

"My father is Indian. My grandfather also."

"Your grandfather was a criminal."

She froze, the place mat still in her hand. He'd gone too far. He reached for her hand, pulled her closer. But something felt off in their embrace. She didn't run her fingers through his hair.

"Will you take me to England? When you leave?"

It always came down to this—her place in his life. Despite all that he'd given her, it was never enough. "Why am I leaving for England?"

"Everyone knows Britain can't keep India forever." She pulled away.

"Keep India? Darling, India is a part of the British Empire, whether she likes it or not."

Her eyes were two daggers.

"Nothing's been decided. And even if it has, and we leave, why would I?"

"But if you leave, will you take me with you?"

He dropped the napkin onto his lap, ignored her question, and ran his knife through the leg of lamb she'd put before him.

◆

Nigar Jaan watched Mutton leave. She couldn't understand why he found it so surprising that she cared about the future of the city she'd called home all her life. She knew she'd upset him by bringing up his move to England. Why would he wish to stick around in a country that clearly despised him?

Now, she reclined with her mother in the older woman's bed. Her mother had given Nigar Jaan the lovelier, east-facing room. Her own windows faced a back alley.

"Do you regret staying here, Mother?"

She meant Lahore, she meant India, she meant this neighborhood, she meant their lives.

"What has brought this on, pet?" Her mother took her fingers and held them in her long, delicate ones.

"Maa," she rested her head on her mother's shoulder. "Why didn't Grandmama return to England?"

"You know this, pet." She stroked Nigar Jaan's hair. "Your grandfather, Nana Saheb, was a very powerful man. He was very kind to your grandmama. Same with me. My nawab, your father, has been very kind. Our lives, Baby Jaan, have been a series of kindnesses thrown our way." She sat up to plant a kiss on Nigar Jaan's forehead, and the bed squeaked indulgently, as though confirming her mother's hypothesis.

But Nigar Jaan couldn't agree. She looked around her mother's room—a pretty teak dressing table gifted by the nawab, a stack of jewelry, also the nawab's, a vast four-poster bed with lace pillows, photographs of Nigar Jaan's English grandmother and her Indian grandfather. It felt lonely to live so isolated, to be disallowed from the club and cut off from half their community. Didn't she yearn for another life?

"I know what you are thinking. But, Baby Jaan, this isn't the way your father looks at you, full of pity. You know, long ago in India, they prized women like us. I know that is irrelevant, but your grandfather couldn't have treated your grandmama the way the army treats us. It isn't the way Mutton sees you."

Nigar Jaan didn't agree. Mutton may have prevented their disintegration into the common society, but what was so noble in holding herself aloft? "He doesn't see me the way you think he does."

Her mother didn't contradict her. "He is a powerful man, Baby Jaan." She didn't say anything more, but Nigar Jaan was convinced she meant cruel. Mutton was a cruel man.

The next time Mutton came around, Nigar Jaan prepared herself to question him about what went on in his jail. But he wasn't in the mood to talk. He took her straight to bed, where they made painful love. After that, he looked more calm. She offered him a cigarette to keep him there beside her in the state of undress.

"Do you ever think about what happened in Jallianwala?" She meant to say jail, but at the last minute, she changed her mind. Perhaps it was safer to refer to his earlier misdemeanor.

"I shan't discuss it at any other time," he said, leaning back. "But yes. It ought not to have happened."

He took a drag of his cigarette, still keeping stiffly to his side, and when she snuggled next to him, he didn't put his arm around her.

"Frankly, they ought not to have gathered." He leaned forward. "We had declared a curfew."

"But weren't they peaceful? Mostly women and children?" She

didn't walk him through the picture in her head, but she allowed herself to: three hundred women, children, men, all gathered in a park to celebrate the coming of spring, and suddenly Mutton and his men fired at them from a narrow alleyway as they tried to escape. Not escape, no, run to meet their deaths. Blood everywhere. Fathers, mothers, sons, daughters, babies. All dead.

He took a long drag, leaned back, reached over for another cigarette. A cloud of smoke hid his face. "The whole country is feudal. Small landowners commit more crimes than the entire British apparatus. Your grandfather was quite the miscreant too, wasn't he?"

Her grandfather, Nana Saheb, had drowned a hundred or so British men, women, and children into a well during the Mutiny of 1857. How was what he'd done any better?

"I'm not sure I'd condone what he did," she said weakly.

"It sounds to me like you might now." He batted the smoke away from between them, waving his hand left and right, as though she'd conjured the smoke as a curtain. His eyes had something mean in them. "You didn't use to be this way. You didn't even like Indians."

"That's a rather odd assumption, seeing as how I am Indian."

He continued to stare at her. She could tell he was burning to ask her something. Why didn't he go ahead and do it?

"You wrote to him, didn't you? That miscreant who tried to blow up your house."

Her face burned. But she was glad he'd finally confronted her.

"Why did you do it? Why did you write to him?"

"Because I knew you'd put him under the strictest possible punishment."

"He brought a bomb to your house."

He spoke to her like she was a complete idiot.

"He was misguided. I'm sure he was."

"Can you hear yourself? You are defending a criminal."

She couldn't keep her voice down. "It wasn't even a bomb, just a firecracker."

His eyes narrowed. Her rage made him quiet. Perhaps she was

winning. He leaned back with a thud, pulled out another cigarette absently. "It is my job to straighten out these misguided youths."

"You didn't have to hang him upside down and rip off his skin."

He sat up straight, quite close to her, breathing hard. "How do you know what goes on in my jail?"

"You are a cruel man, Mutton." She couldn't help it. They'd circled around it long enough.

He leaned back, tossed his cigarette to one corner of the room. "You don't know what you are saying. You'd better get some rest. You have a fever."

Unused to hysterics, she nearly believed him, and ran her hand over her forehead to be sure.

"I won't let you push me aside." Her voice was flailing. She couldn't keep the thought away. All this time she'd had the distinct feeling that Chhote Nanu was in jail not for what he'd done, but because of her. Mutton had punished him for falling in love with her. All those people at Jallianwala, those women and children, she'd condoned their deaths, kissed the hands who'd engineered the massacre. And the British women and babies inside the well in Cownpore, she'd caused that too. She was connected to their deaths. She'd survived. They hadn't. Her grandfather had let her grandmother live, but not the women in the well. Nigar Jaan couldn't save the women in the well. But she could save Chhote Nanu.

She turned to him, all her love brimming in her eyes. "Don't be so cruel, Daniel. For my sake, for Henry's sake. Don't you want to set a good example for your son?" Bringing up their son, she felt like she'd cleansed the air between them. Surely, he would see what was at stake. Gently, she put a hand on his. Her body leaned into his of its own accord.

For a minute, he let her stay. A smile played on his lips. "You like him, don't you? You were seeing him long before your gathering, weren't you?"

He'd always been possessive, but this paranoia was new. "I have seen him once in my life. The night of the gathering, that is all." It didn't feel like a lie. Before the gathering, she wasn't herself. The boy wasn't himself. They'd come into a new understanding of each other the night of the gathering. This statement she'd given wasn't a lie.

"I don't believe you."

He hopped off the bed, picked up his shirt, put on his pants.

"Where are you going? Won't you stay?"

"I should have done this the minute I got my hands on that little shit. I should have done this to all the jokers who hang about your house. Remind them what a whore you are and slapped some sense into them."

She couldn't believe her ears. "Please don't say such things, for Henry's sake."

"I should have known," he said, buttoning his shirt. He stormed into the attached room. In another minute he was back with Henry asleep in his arms. The boy had on his favorite pajamas, pistachio green with blue stripes, and socks because he got cold at night. A cowlick stuck out from the back of his head. She reached out a hand to flatten it. He swatted her hand away.

"Your sudden interest in sympathizing with criminals makes you unfit to care for my son."

"What do you mean?"

"I'm taking him."

"Daniel, don't do this." She dropped herself on his feet, but he pushed her aside. She sprung upon Henry to pry the boy out of Mutton's hands. But her son stirred only to cling tighter to his Pop-Pop.

"You won't set eyes on him again. Mark my words."

"Daniel, please. He is only three. How can he live without me? How can I? You are right. I shouldn't have questioned your judgment. Don't be so cruel, please."

His mouth curled with unkindness. "I am a cruel man, remember?"

"I beg you, don't. You don't know the first thing about him."

Mutton bared his teeth at her. It was the most hideous smile she'd ever seen. "Aren't you forgetting? He is my son." With that, he stormed out of the door.

She raced behind him, pleading. Shehnaz heard the commotion and came running. They tried to pull the boy out of Mutton's grip, but he smacked them both aside. They thundered down the stairs, Mutton, Nigar Jaan, Shehnaz. He hopped into his jeep, the boy still clinging to his chest.

Nigar Jaan tried to flag down a tonga. But then she remembered: she wasn't allowed in the civil station. Even if she made it past the guards on the streets, his helpers wouldn't let her into the house.

3

Across town, Barre Nanu's little boutique supplied five hundred uniforms to the British army each month. The lights never went off at Ansari-Khatri Tailors. A platoon of weaver-turned-tailors operated the six sewing machines from morning until dusk, and, after an hour's break, from dusk until midnight. Dear, determined Moin Bhai had learned the work in no time; he'd trained his nephews too. Turning a deaf ear to the protests surging in the lanes demanding the freedom of the INA soldiers, the tailors sewed. Moin Bhai controlled them like an army general. At break times, he hovered over their machines, placed a gentle, warm hand on the wheel. Everyone got twenty minutes, no more, no less. No one took liberties. Moin Bhai had that kind of serious, unsmiling face, his eyes keen and focused. The severity of his skeletal frame inspired only dedication. Five times a day he unrolled his prayer mat and bowed toward Mecca, his movements delicate, almost feline. Promptly after, he returned to his own machine, which sat next to Barre Nanu's workbench, who'd mastered cutting if not tailoring.

Their work was neat but slow. Barre Nanu's workers didn't know he was racing against time. In a year, he'd saved eleven hundred rupees. If he had more tailors, he could have turned into a civilian bespoke and made even more money. Perhaps with a bigger bribe he could get Chhote out of prison. His sources had failed to confirm if any prisoners had been shipped off to Andaman from the Lahore jail. If the British were leaving India for good, perhaps his brother's transportation might even be canceled. He needed to slap the corrupt constable with a hefty wad of cash so he could get definitive news.

His employees weren't lost in mad pursuit of a goal like him. In fact, Gandhi's release and the subsequent campaigning by the Congress and the Muslim League had emboldened his employees to talk politics all day.

One day, Moin Bhai's nephew asked Barre Nanu point blank: "What will you do after the war, sahib?" Rustom, the young upstart, had a charming face; it was hard to ignore him. He snipped a thread from a shirt he'd finished sewing.

Barre Nanu stole a glance at Moin Bhai, whose feet slowed on the pedals. Quietly, the weaver bore his eyes into his nephew.

But Rustom remained undeterred. "When the English leave, won't you leave Lahore? Everyone is saying India is to be free. Gandhi is saying so. Jinnah Bhai is saying so. India will be free and she will be divided. You will have to move."

"Rustom!" Moin Bhai warned, slapping a hand on his machine.

The upstart didn't cower. "I am only stating facts, *khalu jaan.* What if our *janaab* leaves, what will happen to the shop? Where will we work? What will we eat?"

"Why am I leaving? Where am I going?" Barre Nanu asked impatiently. He hated these unnecessary interruptions to the work.

"Where all the Hindus go. You must have heard the rumors, sahib. Lahore will go to Pakistan, the country for Muslims."

Barre Nanu felt the skin under his collar grow hot. The cruel, hot winds of politics had invaded his shop, the one place he'd hoped the comfort of friendship and the grind of commerce would keep him safe. He looked to Moin Bhai. What did he think? Would Hindus have no place in Lahore? Didn't he hope they'd continue on like this, working together, growing wealthy, growing old? In time their children would take over the shop. He waited for Moin Bhai to reprimand his nephew, to declare they were all the same. Lahore belonged to Lahoris, Muslims *and* Hindus. But the weaver focused on the needle with the same look of furious concentration he'd frightened Barre Nanu with all year long.

"*Bhaijaan,*" Barre Nanu asked as he rose from his proprietor's seat, "do you think I should move away with all the Hindus? Should I leave Lahore?"

Moin Bhai's feet slowed on the Singer. He lifted his gaze from his needle to Barre Nanu, swallowed hard. "It is not up to me, *bhaijaan*. It's not up to any of us. We are too small to matter. I only want peace. If that is achieved by you staying, you should stay. But if you have to move, who am I to say anything?"

Moin Bhai had as good as tossed a twig to a drowning man. The weaver put a shirt seam under the machine and resumed work, but his nephew took his time.

"We can worry about the future some other day," Barre Nanu said defeatedly. "Right now the British are still here and there is a war going on and uniforms need to be made."

◆

Tijori Uncle hadn't succeeded in persuading the magistrate to reduce Chhote's sentence. Despite the thousands of rupees he'd contributed to the war effort, he couldn't convince the Englishman to take pity on his nephew. The letters of appeal he'd written to the magistrate's Ooty office had received only one response: "While the army applauds your generous donations, it cannot overlook the radical intentions of your nephew's act. The safety of India is too important. We wouldn't want a Japanese resurgence, which would occur if we release INA rebels into the public. We must ride this difficult time together, we must all make sacrifices." The man was retiring. He didn't care about India any longer. He'd returned the second bottle of American rum, unopened.

"I should have funded the INA rebellion instead of the British war," Tijori Uncle said agitatedly, tossing a dart at a beautiful imported Irish dartboard, a recent acquisition. Thankfully (for Barre Nanu), his uncle's newfound rage against the English hadn't deterred him from indulging in their pastimes. Like the rest of the country, he was starting to hate British rule but falling more and more in love with their exports.

Barre Nanu wondered if this would happen to him soon. He too would hate the English while continuing to clothe their army. His hypocrisy would be complete. But no, only the very rich could afford the luxury of hypocrisy. People like Barre Nanu and Babuji could only sustain sincerity. This realization made him fear his uncle a little.

His uncle took off his big topaz ring, dropped it distractedly on the table, from where it rolled onto the floor; he didn't so much as look at it. Barre Nanu picked up the ring, and felt its weight. It would fetch at least a thousand rupees. He returned it to the table.

"If I'd sent money to Bose," Tijori Uncle continued, "if all the wealthy had funded the INA, the British would have long departed India. We could have been independent long ago." Even Tijori Uncle sang the praises of the INA. Next, he'd praise Chhote's misdemeanor, tell Barre Nanu to think of Chhote as a martyr. Barre Nanu had to get out of Tijori Uncle's house before this happened. He was Babuji's son, not his uncle's. He felt a moment of relief knowing which side he belonged to. "Do you think I have a big enough bribe for the constable?" he asked.

"Enough for the constable. Not enough for the officers." Tijori Uncle regarded him. "You know you can always come to me if you need money."

Barre Nanu's sides began to sweat. How easy it would be to ask his uncle for a loan. But no. Barre Nanu would never ask for a cash handout. He wanted to get Chhote out on his own merit. He wanted them to know the cost of things. One day he would tell Chhote, this is what it meant to get a glimpse of you. It took six men a year of working twelve-hour shifts. He would tell him this not to hold it over his brother's head, but to serve as a reminder that love demanded labor. It demanded sweat and tears.

4

Nigar Jaan wondered why she had thrown her life away. At night she dreamed of Chhote Nanu hanging on her window ledge, his wild hair caught in the phone lines. Mutton stood in her room, whipping him. Then little Henry replaced Chhote Nanu. The crack swooshed through the air before it landed on her child's bottom. She tried to intervene, but Mutton had tied her to a chair. She woke up covered in sweat.

Shehnaz tried to keep an eye on little Henry. On days Mutton worked long hours, she went past his bungalow. She tried to bribe his staff, but the threat of a beating from Mutton had tied their tongues. She hung about the quarters after dark. Sometimes she followed the superintendent and the boy to the gardens.

Nigar Jaan kept the hope alive of having her little boy all to herself one day. She would steal him away. They'd live high on a mountain, just the two of them. By then Mutton would have left for England, or been ripped to shreds, avenged by one of the many men he'd tortured.

But for the time being, she had to live without her boy. She lay in bed, refused to see anyone. Once word got out that she and the superintendent had broken off, more and more men called round requesting her company. A local nawab, a widowed army captain, a couple of American GIs. Shehnaz sent them all away.

✦

The unrest in the city kept Mutton busy. Daily they made five–six arrests. Misguided boys protested the war, businessmen refused to contribute to the war fund, some were caught syphoning money to the INA, who continued their guerrilla skirmishes against the British troops. Once, a fleeing bicycle smashed Mutton's jeep window. The culprit vanished into the local market before they could catch him. He ought to fear for his life, he knew; he had two of his best constables keep watch outside his bungalow at all hours. No one would dare touch him, no one would come close now that he'd expelled Nigar Jaan from his life. The hurt in his heart throbbed like a bruise. He loved her more than he'd loved any other woman. He wasn't too proud to admit it, at least not to himself.

He looked forward to coming home. His little boy waited for him at the door, waved his chubby hands to welcome his Pop-Pop.

It had taken an army of caretakers to get the boy's mind off his mother. The driver, the gatekeeper, the gardener, the butler, the cook, and the new ayah had to entertain him, get him to sleep, get him to stop crying. One day, Mutton looked him in the eye and told him: "From now on, you are to do without your mummy." He sounded like he was giving orders to a subordinate, the way he waved his finger at the boy. He had to be firm. "You are to forget that woman. You must learn the truth of things."

Mutton too was trying to learn the truth, and to live with it. He too had determined to sail forth. Lahore would continue to be their home, his and Henry's. The administration, whoever ran it, Indians or the British, would need his experience.

But it wasn't as simple as before. All kinds of people poured in to govern India. They walked willy-nilly into posts, then gave up halfway and sailed back. These nitwits drove him mad. The new magistrate, an Oxford-educated man, sympathized with India's independence. On the one hand, he gave Mutton free rein and condoned the arrests, and on the other, he talked about leaving India. Mutton had orders to crack down on dissent, while at the same time to prepare to leave, in six years at the earliest. But no one could say for sure if they would indeed leave India. And then there were the GIs. The city overflowed with them. He stormed in at Nedous Hotel, where they partied until two-thirty most nights, the owner keeping his guests steeped in his secret stash of imported gin and American jazz. Mutton ordered them all to pack up. The GIs sniggered at his old face, took their time to leave. He followed the GIs to another bar on the Mall and into Heera Mandi at Nigar Jaan's. He heard jazz and sometimes Hindustani music from her windows. He stayed in his jeep until the ruckus grew louder, and then he sent his constables to break up the scene. Of course he never saw the GIs leave. He couldn't order them about. No one could.

The nights he spent under her window, he was especially glad to return home to Henry. So what if she went back to her career. He had their Henry.

✦

Meanwhile, things got worse for Chhote Nanu. The jail overflowed with INA soldiers. The prisoners were packed ten, twelve to a cell. Their meals were downright inedible and insufficient—a solitary ladle of watery rice and dal a day. This was no way to live, and a slow way to die. They decided to stage a hunger strike to protest.

When news of the hunger strike reached him, Mutton became livid. If word got out to the magistrate, the fool, new to India and unfamiliar with Mutton's accomplishments, might transfer him.

He had to think of a way to break up the strike with the least amount of effort and harm. Five days in, the prisoners debilitated by hunger, Mutton ordered a few into his office, offered them release in exchange for quitting the strike and convincing others to do so. One prisoner he decided to threaten with immediate exile to Andaman.

Mutton hadn't laid eyes on Chhote Nanu since the last time he'd whipped him, three weeks ago. Had he bulked even more in that time, despite the meager nourishment? The uncertainty that had been a feature on the boy's face had solidified into a permanent look of doubt. Is this what she fancied? And what was that stench? Mutton had the urge to shoot the bastard and be rid of him.

He assumed a position beside the window and picked up his baton. "When did we bring you here?" He tried to command as much authority into his voice as he could muster.

Chhote Nanu looked at the calendar on the wall. It was January 1945. He'd attended Nigar Jaan's gathering in September 1943. "One year and four months," he counted on his fingers. "Over a year. Sahib."

The "sahib" had been an afterthought.

"That's right. It is January of 1945. We have won Andaman back. The INA have lost. Do you know what that means?"

"No, sahib, I don't." The boy seemed to be having trouble holding himself up. He leaned on the wall for support, his hands on his knees.

"Stand straight," ordered the jailer behind Chhote Nanu. "You are in the presence of an officer of His Majesty's police."

A hacking cough took over the boy's body. When he stood up, he looked disoriented, as if unaware of his surroundings. Had he been snooping about Nigar Jaan? Did he know they had broken up? Even though Mutton was standing fully clothed in his office, having eaten a breakfast of sausages and ham and eggs, he felt like he'd lost to this shabbily dressed, half-starved boy. He'd received her kindness; she'd risked everything to write to him. Mutton couldn't help saying what he said next: "She is going to Yorkshire with me, you know. Did she write to you about that?"

"Who, sahib?"

Mutton nodded, and the jailer whacked the boy on the back.

"I have not heard from anyone, sahib," replied the boy, shuddering.

"Isn't this sort of thing disallowed to you? Consorting with Muslim women? Isn't this the same as crossing the black waters for a Hindu like you?"

"I have not consorted with anyone, sahib."

"Since you have already committed the crime, why don't I give you the punishment for it?"

"Sahib?" the boy looked up, his eyes filled with fear.

"We are going to put you on a boat to Andaman, along with the rest of the INA riffraff. No more freedom for India. India belongs to the Crown."

Chhote Nanu made a racket on his way back to his cell, screaming at the top of his lungs: "Britain, quit India! Down with imperialism! *Inqalaab zindabaad*!" The rest of the prisoners joined him. The jail resounded with echoes of the collective chants. In response, the jailers threatened the prisoners with floggings, banged their batons on the doors.

Chhote Nanu's head throbbed from hunger, and he couldn't help but chew the flesh around his fingers until he bled. The hard skin on the soles of his feet became his dinner, too. He didn't care if his cellmates stared at him. They had their own bad habits. The INA rebels snored with abandon; Chiragh attempted handstands, crashing into them when he failed to hold his balance. Chhote Nanu didn't know when the transportation would happen. He had to wait for the warden to escort him to the jeep, and for the jeep to drive him to the boat.

Was Mutton telling the truth? Gangadhar confirmed it. The Japanese had lost, the INA with them. No more freedom for India. The British had regained control of Andaman. His transportation was really imminent.

"When?" He asked Gangadhar, but the jailer did not know.

"Are you ready to break your fast?" Gangadhar nodded at his fingers raw with blood.

"This is not a fast," replied Chhote Nanu. "This is a strike."

Gangadhar shook his head. "Why do you do this? Why did you fall for the *gori mem*? She belongs to Mutton."

Chhote Nanu shut his eyes. "You've read her missives. Does it sound like she belongs to that boor?"

"You may be right there. But eat something, fasting won't solve anything."

"I'd rather starve than eat the terrible food here."

"Sounds like you're not afraid of anything," Gangadhar said, locking Chhote Nanu's cell.

Was Gangadhar right? Had he become fearless? Only fools didn't fear anything. Perhaps he was a fool through and through.

5

Since the shop opened, Barre Nanu had saved close to fifteen hundred rupees. A handsome amount of money by all accounts. The lucky constable could build his family a nice house with it. Barre Nanu was going to do it, break another of his father's rules and offer a bribe. He packed Chhote Nanu's poetry books. He wished he could take Chaiji with him. His bribe could pave the way for future visits. In the market, he bought a box of *jalebi* and a box of milk sweets.

He bided his time outside the jail to make sure he caught the older constable alone.

The man had grown more portly. He'd had a steady salary all this time. Barre Nanu had to remind him of Chhote's misdemeanor, and why he'd come.

"He still cannot receive visitors," the constable snapped.

Barre Nanu leaned in conspiratorially. "I haven't come empty-handed." He tapped his trouser pocket. He set the boxes of sweets on the desk.

The constable's eyes lingered on the treats. "What gave you the impression—"

"Sahib, did I miscalculate?" Barre Nanu didn't want to give the chap a chance to think. He fumbled through his pockets and purposefully nudged the wad of cash until it fell to the floor. Hundred-rupee notes flopped open, lush and plentiful, with their promise of the luxuries that could be bought.

The constable rolled his eyes as though to say, how clumsy. "It is unlawful of you to offer me a bribe. And in the office too. If you don't leave right this minute, I will arrest you. You can join your brother in jail."

Barre Nanu backed away. The constable leapt at the cash and slipped the money in his pocket.

"Sahib," Barre Nanu urged. "Since you're taking the money, can I see my brother?"

"What money?"

Barre Nanu panicked. "That is over a year of hard work. You must fear God. My brother hasn't heard from his family—"

The constable slammed his baton on Barre Nanu's shoulder.

Fire with fire. "In that case, I will report you to your superior. I will wait for the *gora* sahib." Barre Nanu held his place.

"You can wait behind bars." But the constable made no motion to arrest him.

A few minutes later, the superintendent stormed in. The constable leapt at him.

"Sahib, this is the brother of the boy who tried to blow up your house. And look!" He pulled out the money, half of Barre Nanu's hard-earned money, the other half tucked away in some secret pocket. "Bribe!"

Barre Nanu jumped in. "Sir, my brother has never done anything unlawful until that unfortunate incident. He was set up. All I am asking is to see him. He has a brother, a mother, a father, but he hasn't heard from us in over a year."

The superintendent looked annoyed. The mention of family didn't seem to soften him; in fact, he looked even more incensed.

"Sahib, he comes from a good family," protested Barre Nanu. "He had a momentary lapse of judgment. We are all educated. I myself went to Government College."

"Did you hear that, Ram Singh!" snapped the superintendent. "Their family is educated." Ram Singh chuckled obediently. "You may think your degree has elevated you. But I don't think anything good comes of educating your lot. It's no good expecting Indians to act like Englishmen. Aspiration only leads to confusion; failed aspirations lead to failed revolts."

Barre Nanu felt his resolve fail. All that hard work! Ought he to turn around and leave?

"Do you love your brother?"

Barre Nanu hung his head. "Sahib, I have tried to do my best for him since he was born." What he meant to say was, he'd failed to do his best for Chhote. He'd failed at a crucial moment. He ought to have stopped Chhote from seeing Samrat. His Chhote. His big hair, his wet eyes that always looked up to him for permission. As a little boy, Chhote would take Barre Nanu's hand to go to the bathroom at night. Barre Nanu could almost feel Chhote's little warm fingers inside his palm, hear Chhote's voice begging him not to disappear. "You won't go away when I go inside?" He could picture Chhote, legs crossed, waiting for a promise.

"I could have loved him more, sahib," Barre Nanu hoped his confession might melt the officer's heart.

But the superintendent did not look moved. If anything, he looked bored. He folded the money and handed it to the constable, motioned for the constable to leave them, and took a decisive step toward Barre Nanu. His lips curled in disdain.

"I must tell you your brother was put on a boat to Andaman at 0600 hours this morning. I might have permitted you to see him if you'd come earlier, but you've missed him. By all of six hours. What a shame!"

Barre Nanu's words caught in his throat. Before he could protest, the superintendent put on his cap and left the room.

Barre Nanu came home floating on a bubble of self-pity. He kept seeing the superintendent's face, his mouth curling as he said "You've missed him by all of six hours." He couldn't hold the floodgates of grief.

Chaiji caught him sneaking past her and up the stairs and demanded to know what was wrong.

"He's gone. They took him . . ." But he couldn't finish the sentence. He turned back, flew down the stairs, and out of the house.

Chaiji's words trailed behind him: "What have they done to Chhote? Why won't you tell me?"

Before he knew it, he ended up at a liquor shop. He ordered a bottle of whiskey. He found the two sips he took revolting, but at least he felt he was doing something destructive.

That night, when he returned home, not drunk but delirious from grief, he found his mother putting finishing touches on a magenta trousseau. He collapsed into her lap, the wire flowers digging patterns into his cheek.

"Did they ship him?" Chaiji's fingers on his forehead were a map of scales.

He took her hand and slapped his head with it.

They heard Babuji make a noise upstairs. Chaiji freed herself from Barre Nanu's grip and went up. A minute later, she called for him. His father wanted to see him.

Babuji had guessed the news. He lay in his bed without his pagri, his head like a field in drought, scalp showing in places where the hair had thinned. Barre Nanu couldn't hold back. He grabbed his father's feet and confessed to his latest crime of bribing an officer, an act Babuji had advised against, an act that had come to naught.

"You were right, Babuji," he cried, hoping his father would prop himself up, if only to smack him or offer a gesture of encouragement or abuse.

But Babuji didn't get up. Instead, he pointed to the books on the shelf. Chaiji fetched them for him.

Babuji asked for the Gita to be put on his chest. He grabbed Chaiji's hand. He raised his other hand toward his son, and Barre Nanu took it greedily. Babuji's breath came out shallow, as infrequent as the call of the cuckoo outside, with which it seemed to be keeping time. A wave of pain and emotion rocked his body, and he clutched their hands tighter. His face contorted. His eyes drifted from the holy book to his wife to his son, the three things he prized the most in the world. The fourth, his Chhote, was missing, and his eyes flew to the door in search. He wanted to say his son's name, but he'd forgotten the art of speech, lost the mechanics of it. Barre Nanu tried to help his father to sit up, but Babuji's body felt stiff. He saw the images in Babuji's eyes, his own face and Chaiji's. The images swam for a while, and then they stopped. The world stopped moving. Babuji was no more.

They couldn't cremate Babuji until the third morning. They had to wait their turn, the pundits being overbooked because they still weren't allowed to make fires at night for fear of air raids. Babuji's body had to be kept wrapped in a white sheet, with all the windows open. Chaiji cried and cried.

"It is wrong to keep him waiting."

When his turn came, they carried his body through the lanes. Because he trusted no one else, and wanted no one else, Barre Nanu asked Moin Bhai and his neighbors to lend a shoulder. Three Muslims and a Hindu carried Babuji to his pyre on the river Ravi.

At night, Chaiji awoke covered in cold sweat and shouted random words. Barre Nanu had taken to sleeping in her room on a second cot so he could coax her back to sleep.

Liberated from her labor of sewing (there was no need to sew now that Chhote had been transported), she started roaming the neighborhood. His neighbors would stop by his shop to tell him they'd seen Chaiji by the Ravi. Shopkeepers accused her of shoplifting, demanded he pay for the bar of soap or the hair clip she'd nicked. He began to lock the house when he left for the shop.

Moin Bhai encouraged him to take the time to mourn; he could manage the shop. But Barre Nanu needed to pick up materials and drop off the finished products and do quality control. The army had high standards. He couldn't give up his shop now that the livelihoods of the tailors depended on him.

He began bringing Chaiji to the shop, tried to nudge her back toward the lighter, simpler sewing of buttons and buttonholes.

Chaiji's condition didn't improve. Eid came, and then Ramadan, and then Muharram, the season of mourning. Men in black kurtas marched through the market, chanting "Yah Hussain! Yah Hussain! Yaaaaaaa Hussain!" Every eye cried for the Prophet's martyred son-in-law. They slapped their chests, swung metal chains about their bodies until their backs bled. The chains hung from a circle and ended with small daggers. Young men, even boys, liberally swung these knife-chains to puncture the skin on their backs, such was the fervor that consumed them.

The display of blood upset Chaiji, and her eyes streamed behind her glasses, her wild hair raised in shock. Barre Nanu wondered if he should join the mourners and wail, hide behind the mask of public crying and mourn liberally for Babuji, for Chhote.

Past the mourners, another set of men carried silver-foil replicas of a martyr's tomb, three–four feet high. The shoppers pressed into the shops.

Two ladies in black burkas, their faces visible, entered the boutique, reluctant at first, but as the cymbal players passed, they asked if they could sit on the front benches. Barre Nanu nodded them in. He caught a glimpse. The lady in the far corner was unusually beautiful. She had dark hair and Indian skin, but her features were decidedly English. She had a proud, thin nose and light eyes. He could see her English shoes, scuffed at the heels. He had a feeling about her.

The local girl with her was short and her eyes were outlined in kohl, silver anklets on her feet. She seemed the lady's helper, judging by her worn slippers.

"Heera Mandi?" he whispered to the local girl.

The girl looked annoyed. "We will only stay a minute. Please understand."

She'd taken him for a prude, thought that he disapproved of women of their sort. "Stay as long as you like." He retreated into the gloom of his shop. What did he care? His shop didn't need a pristine reputation while the war went on.

But Chaiji saw them. Thankfully, she had no idea what the women of the market looked like. Their burkas, which they'd no doubt worn for the occasion of Muharram, made them appear respectable, high class, even. She smiled at Nigar Jaan, admiring the gold locket that sat on her chest. Just then, a jeep began to blare its horns at the procession, demanding passage. The soldiers banged the bonnet, ordering the chanters to step aside.

Chaiji's face shook. "Why did they have to destroy my house?"

The English lady regarded Chaiji, her eyes full of concern.

Moin Bhai tried to explain away Chaiji's rage. "The lady has had a terrible shock. Her son was transported. Then Babuji, our master's father, died."

"Did her son fight in Burma?" The helper girl's eyes were full of admiration.

"My brother did not fight with the INA." Barre Nanu's voice leapt out of his body. "It was a small firecracker. He shouldn't have carried it to the gathering. He was misled."

The English lady looked at her helper girl, then dropped her head. She seemed to be wiping her face roughly for no reason, and when she held her head up, her eyes were red. "Has he really been transported," she said, to no one in particular. For many seconds, she seemed to be considering something. Her fingers rolled a piece of stray fabric she'd picked off the shop floor, a ten-inch piece Barre Nanu wanted to bolster a shirt collar with. What did she care what Chhote had done? Why ought he to discuss his private matters with this English girl?

"Did you keep in touch?" the English girl asked Chaiji. "Did you send him your best wishes before he left? Books? Sweets?"

"We haven't laid eyes on him since his arrest," Barre Nanu said. "It's been a year and a half."

"You didn't see him once?"

Her false kindness was unwelcome. Barre Nanu wanted to tell her to go away. But the lady tucked the piece of fabric she'd found on the floor under the side of Moin Bhai's sewing machine, so it didn't fly away. Cloth was scarce; she knew what a scrap meant to a little shop like Barre Nanu's.

She turned her head toward Chaiji, but didn't dare raise her eyes. "Are you his mother?" A change seemed to have come over her, and she grabbed her silk burka in bunches, her knuckles turning white. Outside, the procession had passed, and the street began to clear.

"It was all for nothing," she whispered to herself. "All for nothing." She leaned in the direction of Chaiji, and although she couldn't raise her eyes to meet the older woman's, she said before she flew out of the shop, "I know how you must feel."

August 2002

Our mother nestled in between us on a rickshaw like a fragile work of art. Her starched peach-colored sari fanned over our legs. In the middle of a barely twenty-minute journey, she asked the rickshaw wallah to stop so she could use a bathroom. Ila helped her off. *What?* She stared at me challengingly. Too often women suppressed the urge. This is how Bebe had ended up with a nearly fatal UTI. Ila held our mother protectively, planted several kisses on Bebe's cheek as though stamping her for postage.

Not once did Bebe rest her eyes on me. I nudged Ila. We weren't going to spare her this time. Our mother was going to tell us the full truth about our fathers.

"Are you with me?" I whispered to Ila, but she told me to shush.

As soon as we reached our lane, we remembered we had a new worry. Chhote Nanu wasn't actually ill. Ila had lied to make Bebe come home. Also, pilgrims had taken over the lower part of the house. Ila and Bebe both inched back, hiding behind me as I knocked. A woman in a plain white sari and shorn hair opened the door.

"Did you bring milk?" she asked before letting us in. I shook my head.

Chhote Nanu was pacing his second-floor balcony as we entered. He saw Bebe and he paused, as did she, their eyes acknowledging each other. He leaned over to get a better look, and a tree of worry clouded his brow. He was going to tell her to leave, tell her she was not welcome inside her father's house. But he turned back into his room, and Bebe let go of the free end of her sari she was hiding half her face behind.

As soon as Bebe saw he was well, she dug her eyes into Ila. *I will deal with you later*, her gaze said. She concentrated on the pilgrims next. She saw the men inside the living room eating and chatting, the women in the kitchen chopping vegetables in big vats. Her eye caught a flash of something, and she stormed into the kitchen. A woman was wiping the counter with a piece of cloth with an elaborately embroidered bird. Bebe yanked the tea cozy out of the woman's grip. The woman stared at her open-mouthed. For all her frailty, Bebe marched away, dusting the tea cozy against her sari.

She moved about the courtyard with an agitated energy, pushing the wicker chairs into place, picking up a stray packet of tobacco and tossing it into the trash pile. She caught the priest on his way to the kitchen carrying a small silver tumbler full of ghee with an elaborately carved silver spoon.

"That tumbler and spoon are not for *puja*. I have fed my son so much goat curry with them."

The priest tossed both the tumbler and the spoon on the floor. "*Bhrasht naalaayak* woman!"

Bebe picked up the utensils and handed them to me. These were my first birthday gifts from my grandfather. The tumbler had his name engraved around the lip.

Upstairs, in our room that was once hers, Bebe opened her suitcase, hung her saris in the green cupboard. She saw my clothes lying in a pile inside, and she began folding these. I sat on Barre Nanu's rattan chair, falling into an old pattern of watching her arrange the room. I hadn't seen her in six years, but our bodies remembered their familiar routines around each other. It was easy to act like a child around Bebe. Even Ila dragged her to bed and put her head in our mother's lap. Our questions burned on our tongues, but we couldn't help savor these first moments with our mother.

"You are getting gray hairs." Bebe stroked Ila's head. "I've pulled the two that I saw. Don't go out in the sun so much."

"If she doesn't go out and rally, Delhi's moral compass will break," I teased.

Both Ila and Bebe swatted at me, and I pulled away. Finally, I felt

I had come home. She might not have been at the station to greet me like I wanted, but Bebe was here now, and we had her with us inside our childhood room. It was possible to turn back time.

I was contently swimming inside my nostalgia when Ila shook me out. As casually as she'd dragged Bebe to bed, she titled her head and said: "Have you heard from my father?"

Bebe shoved her head off, smacked her shoulder. "Don't ask me about him, I have told you how many times?"

"I don't even know his address."

"Why do you need his address?"

"To write to him."

Bebe's face crumpled. "Your father is not a good man. You of all people should understand."

"No." Ila shook her head with the incipient gray hairs. "I don't understand. Why have you kept this secret for so long? Why did you marry my father if you knew he was bad? Why isn't he a part of my life? Why don't I have a single memory of him? Any memory, even a bad memory, is better than no memory. You have to tell me. You have to tell Karan about his father, too. You hid behind Barre Nanu for too long. Now you have nowhere to hide. Not even Chhote Nanu will take your side."

I couldn't believe Ila could be so determined. For a minute, I felt sorry for Bebe. Her children had turned on her.

Bebe shut her eyes. "His family is not so good. What if they took you away from me? I couldn't even trust them that much." She turned to me, pleading. "Yours too. What if they took you away from me?"

I looked at my sister's cold, hard face, her lips a straight line. "I am with Ila on this one. You have kept your secrets for far too long."

"I want to hear the truth," demanded Ila. "What made my father so bad? Why did you tell me he died?"

Bebe decided to come clean.

"After your father left me brokenhearted," she began, her eyes on me accusatory, as though I was responsible for my father's commitment phobia, "I went to Delhi to live at my cousin's house, at your aunt Sulochana's on the Delhi University campus. I kept having these fainting spells, so Sulochana dragged me to the doctor's one morning. That is how I discovered I was pregnant. I was twenty-five. Your father hadn't proposed marriage, he wouldn't have proposed marriage, and even if he did, our parents wouldn't have approved.

"But as soon as I confided in Sulochana, your aunt forbade the idea of abortion."

I had my caustic aunt, Tijori Uncle's daughter, to thank for my life. Not Bebe.

"Please don't look at me like that, Karan. I was young. As young as you are now. I didn't know the first thing about looking after a baby. But yes, I suffered a moment of madness, and I'm grateful Sulochana had been there to talk sense.

"Poor Sulochana. At that time, she'd been married for fifteen years, but didn't have any children. When I landed on her doorstep like that, she saw an opportunity. She offered to assume all responsibility of the baby and of me for as long as we needed. She also promised to keep my pregnancy a secret.

"For the next six months, Sulochana did exactly that. She told me to apply to the art history PhD program so I had a valid reason to stay on in Delhi long-term. When the time came, she sewed us both A-line gowns that were popular back in the 1960s. The gowns kept my pregnancy a secret. We linked arms and took walks around the campus together. The faculty and students called us the seersucker sisters. That is how I passed the first seven months of my pregnancy. For my last two, we went away to Dehradun, where Sulochana's husband knew a doctor.

"That's where you were born, in Dehradun's Alexander Clinic, overlooking the foothills of the Himalayas. You came out quick, straight into Sulochana's waiting arms, as though you couldn't wait to meet her. I had to feed you, I wanted to hold you, but I don't remember them giving you to me. You spent your first days spitting all over Sulochana's green tops.

"A month later, we returned to Delhi, Sulochana a little plumper from all the sitting around and bottle feeding, and me a lot svelter from all the early-morning jogs Sulochana forced me to go for. The Delhi University community completely bought our story that you were her child. Her husband knew, of course, and felt ever so grateful for the gift, but no one questioned our disappearance for the three summer months.

"In return for my gift, Sulochana offered to give me my life back.

"'What life is that?' I asked. I could hear my baby crying in Sulochana's room, the ayah trying to soothe him and failing. But no, I couldn't see you. I don't know who had imposed this rule. Was it Sulochana? Was it me? I can't remember.

"'Don't let this mishap derail you,' she said. It stung to hear you referred to as my mishap. But Sulochana can be very authoritative. She had her hair cut in this pretty bob, and she wore the smartest sunglasses. She might have been thirty-five, but she looked posh if not young; she had her husband's generous income and a lively intellectual community at her disposal. She was never bored, not once in her life. Always on the go, with her handbag swinging from her shoulder. She took my chin in her perfectly painted fingers and told me I was still beautiful. Still young. 'All those years of running and high-jumping in school. Really, you have the figure of an athlete,' she said. 'And you just happen to be surrounded by India's most eligible bachelors. You couldn't do better. Chetan and I can fix you up in no time.'

"She kept her promise. In the evenings, I came home from swimming laps in the university pool to find Sulochana's beautiful faculty bungalow brimming with the best and the brightest students, all male, and drinks and catered food from Narula's. Civil engineers, physicists, mathematicians, all crowded the mini bar drinking scotch. She caught me at the front door and rushed me into the guest room, forced me into bright bell-bottoms and peplum tops, saris with sleeveless blouses, spritzed my wet hair reeking of chlorine with her expensive perfumes. She pushed me toward the men, talking me up: 'Here, meet my beautiful, athletic cousin from Kanpur. She's here working on a degree in art history.' Deeper and deeper into the horde of men she pushed me.

"I tiptoed around her living room feeling like a deer entering a forest teeming with skilled marksmen. I don't know what I was doing there. I felt tainted. They'd all call me tainted if they knew. It seemed like I had to make it my life's mission to find a place to hide that taint. I had other options: I could bury myself in my art studio, or, I could return to Kanpur to my father's business; every month he wrote to me asking when I'd send him new designs. But I couldn't face my father. I couldn't face Chhote Nanu. I suppose I drifted toward the idea of marriage that Sulochana was trying to sell so hard. I allowed myself to imagine my head resting on someone's sympathetic shoulder. I allowed myself to hope for love. I circulated among the men, tolerated their stares, their incessant questions about my likes and dislikes.

"'What do you like to cook?' they asked. 'Nothing,' I said with a straight face. 'I've never set foot in the kitchen.' They laughed in disbelief, and Sulochana pinched my arm and blurted out a list of dishes her cook had made that week. 'Chop suey, veg Manchurian, *idli patakha*, butter chicken, Spanish omelette.' The lies always worked. When it came time for me to ask them questions, I doddered. I didn't want to know their potential salaries, their ambitions. Money or the pursuit of it cannot reveal a person's character. I wanted to know about their mothers. All of them were mama's boys, they had to be to reach the age of twenty-seven–thirty and not know how to boil an egg (their own proud admission). I asked them if their mothers had studied, and how far, and if they liked to read books, and which ones. While the men aimed for my heart, I hunted for a mother-in-law kind enough to forgive me; my baby wasn't a secret I intended to keep forever. Yes, I had every intention of getting you back, of having you know your real mother."

At this point in her story, Bebe glanced at me, her eyes full of guilt, beseeching mine. I offered her what she sought, allowed my head to rest on her shoulder. But it must've weighed her down too much because she pushed herself away. Her face filled with a new kind of resolve, recalling a different time in her life, one that did not have any place for me.

"At one of Aunty Sulochana's parties, I met a man named Keshav.

I'd seen him before riding motorcycles around campus, a pair of aviators hiding his eyes. Often, he had a woman with him, riding sideways, their denim outfits coordinated. Always a different woman. I knew he was trouble. After introductions, I took my glass of pineapple juice and turned toward Sulochana's room, where I could hear my baby crying. But Keshav took me by the waist and danced a two-step to the Bee Gees' "Stayin' Alive" as he pulled me to a window.

"'I don't want to be seen with the terror of DU,' I said, hoping my rudeness would make him disappear.

"'Is that why you can't take your eyes off me every time I ride by?' he asked.

"'I just want to see if the women ever fall off your bike, that's all.'

"But Keshav had caught me out. I did in fact stare at him every time I saw him riding up the main campus path, and every time I caught him in the lunch hall. He had a way with women; I couldn't understand how he managed to surround himself with so many of them. All of them seemed to be having a good time, tipping their heads back and laughing at everything he said. I had to admit he was handsome; he had a broad jaw, a beautiful smile, perfectly straight, even white teeth, flinty eyes, and a high forehead. He dressed in the fashion of the times, in faded jeans, smart leather boots, and jean jackets. He boxed for the college team.

"I suppose you could say I was infatuated. I intended to steer clear of the charming disaster named Keshav, but Sulochana stepped in and wove her beautiful web.

"'We are like sisters, aren't we?' she asked me one day, entering the room with my baby swaddled in her arms. If only for that rare sight of you, I stayed and listened. 'Keshav was asking about you. Will you see him again?'

"'I don't know,' I said distractedly, taking you in my arms. Oh, what it was to touch you.

"Sulochana continued her advocacy of Keshav: 'As I am older, it falls on me to tell you that Keshav is a good man.' Her husband had taught Keshav in his first year. He came from a good family who lived comfortably in Bombay. His mother had left Rawalpindi, escaping the violence of Partition on her own.

"I felt cornered. On the one hand, I had a feeling Keshav was trouble. On the other, if his mother knew what it was to suffer, I could finally empty my heart of its guilt.

"'I don't know. I will think about it,' I told her.

"'Don't take too long,' warned Sulochana. 'He might lose interest.'

"I hoped his interest was fleeting. If he flew away, so much the better. But after two months of seeing him every day—he relaxed on the benches while I dipped into the swimming pool, he waved when I finished my laps, he waved at the canteen, offering to buy me coffee and samosas—I gave in. I wanted to know if Keshav was my second chance at romance. I decided to take a gamble and tell Keshav about the baby.

"I invited him out one night. He sounded intrigued by my boldness. 'See you soon, babe,' he said on the phone.

"We walked along Connaught Circle. He bought me a knot of purple cotton candy. His eyes were glued to the striped peplum shirt Sulochana had forced on me.

"I told him I wanted to disclose something sensitive, and it was up to him to do what he wanted with the information; I wouldn't hold his reaction against him. I told him I'd been in love once, trusted a man too much. I told him about you, my baby, about having to give you up. My heart felt hollow. I hid my face behind the cotton candy.

"Keshav's eyes remained steady. How long can he go without blinking, I wondered. We paused outside the wooden doors of Madras Café. Inside, couples drank filter coffee and shared ice cream sundaes.

"Keshav pinched the cotton candy, the sugar melting between his fingers, coloring them a deep purple, the name of a band he said he loved. 'None of us are without sin.' He put his fingers in his mouth, still staring at me.

"I flinched at the word 'sin,' but gave him a shaky smile.

"'I myself am not free of sin.' He took my hand with the cotton candy and kissed it. 'Your honesty is special. It makes me love you even more.'

"'Love?' I pulled my hand away from his grip.

"'Yes, love, what else.' I was the most special woman he had ever laid eyes on, he confessed. What with the swimming and the art and the graduate school, and now with this scandalous past that only seemed to elevate my experience in the world over his. How much more mature I was than him. He couldn't believe how lucky he felt to have met me, for me giving him this chance. Could I make him the happiest man in the world and marry him?"

Bebe's cheeks colored like a bride's. She'd been young once, someone wanted her once, she wasn't a dejected, discarded piece, like one of her unfinished paintings.

"At the wedding, we all danced: me, Keshav, Sulochana, even you, little baby Karan, in my arms no less.

"I locked all my fears inside a trunk, just like my pregnancy gowns. I looked the other way when Keshav found his old college crowd, especially when he put a hand on the shiny shoulders of a girl in a halter top and pulled her toward him (was she even wearing a bra?), hinting at an intimacy a long time in the making.

"My fears came tumbling out the first night of our honeymoon and all over the houseboat stuck in the backwaters of Kerala. Tired from the train ride, I'd fallen asleep and woke to find my husband gone. I went up a beaten path toward the main building of the hotel. At the bar, I caught him having a drink with a local singer, their knees touching. I didn't have it in me to interrupt them, so I circled around the garden, lay on the hammock by the water watching the fireflies, imagined the lotuses in the water were little bombs about to explode. When the mosquitos had eaten me raw, I returned to our room. Keshav sat there, alone, but I knew by the state of the bed and the rumpled sheets that the thing he'd intended had in fact happened. I had it on the tip of my tongue to ask him, but I didn't want to degrade myself by putting it into words. I pushed open the windows to let out the smells, stood frozen by my side of the bed, unable to touch the polluted sheets. I went to get the radiator from the closet. Keshav watched me walk across the room.

"Maybe it was the way I walked, faint with the knowledge that my world was collapsing, but he caught hold of my hand.

"'I told you I have flaws. You are on your period, so . . .'

"I reached for his leather boot and smacked his head with it.

"After that, I went to the front desk and requested a separate room.

"We returned to Bombay, to the flat he shared with his mother, our marriage in the doldrums. But Rampyari's caustic presence and her dagger words, which Keshav was as much a victim of as I was, fused us into some sort of a solidarity. We decided on an unhappy medium: if I ignored his philandering, he would let me take classes at the prestigious Sir J. J. School of Art, even take my side when his mother and I fought.

"But the pact did not last long. For Rampyari, a daughter-in-law a year older than her son, and one that couldn't cook but could name all the art movements of Europe, was as useful as rainboots made of straw. Daily, she criticized my cooking, my inability to roll perfect, round chapatis. 'What am I eating today?' she complained. 'The map of Africa?' 'You wouldn't know Africa if you saw a world map, Maaji,' I muttered to myself. Overburdened with the studio, the unsavory house chores, and looking the other way when my husband turned in late reeking of other women's perfumes, I burned breads, undersalted curries, curdled milk. I couldn't help but think that I was just a free maid to these people. For two years I let them use me.

"Rampyari hated a mutterer even more than a bad cook, and she told me to say whatever I had to say out loud. Those days I was always on edge. I stirred a pot of chicken curry, the steam clouding my face, sweat trickling down my sides. I set the ladle on the counter and turned to acknowledge my mother-in-law, but the ladle flipped over the counter's edge. The curry splattered all over Rampyari's small wooden temple. Lacerations of curry and spatters of chicken flecked the benign, blinded smiles of her idols.

"'*Hai*!' Rampyari screamed. 'You have destroyed my religion! *Hai*! *Hai*!'

"Keshav came running into the kitchen. Trying to broker truce, he rushed his mother's idols to the sink to give them an emergency bath.

"I was fed up. 'If you don't want chicken curry all over your idols, why do you keep the temple in the kitchen?'

"Rampyari didn't like my tone. 'You will allow this stupid girl to talk to me like this?'

"'I am more educated than your whole family put together,' I snapped.

"Keshav gestured to me, *don't escalate things.*

"But I wasn't having it. I was tired of being told I couldn't cook, as if cooking constituted my sole mission in life. I hated this life with a family of uncultured narcissists. 'Your stupid son doesn't scare me, neither of you scare me.' I wasn't in the mood to defer to Keshav any longer. 'Why don't you tell your mother what keeps you out so late.'

"'What is she talking about?' Rampyari asked. 'I have raised my son to be a gentleman.'

"I let out the most derisive laugh I could manage. 'Gentleman, my foot.'

"Rampyari dug her rheumatoid eyes into her son. She beat her chest, the same chest that carried the scars of Partition. Rumor had it, Rampyari had been captured by a gang of men as she tried to cross the border on foot. The men had dragged her to a shack tucked in a field of maize, and there they had raped her for days. As a parting gift, they'd carved a curse on her breasts. Growing up, Keshav had learned one thing: mother had suffered. Mother must never be made to suffer again.

"The suffering mother demanded of her son: 'What is this woman accusing you of?'

"'Nothing,' Keshav said faltering. He turned on me to deflect his mother's rage. 'Don't listen to her, Maa. She isn't so pure herself.' He looked pleadingly at his mother. 'Her family claims she has never married, but she had a child with another man.'

"Rampyari held her son like he was about to jump off a cliff. 'You brought this kind of a woman into my house?' She grabbed me by the hair and hit my head against the window grill. 'You were never fit for my son. Get out.'

"'Gladly!' I flung her arms off my body. I could feel tears streaming down my face. But I wouldn't wipe them away, wouldn't straighten my hair, wouldn't give Rampyari the satisfaction of having caused me pain. I went into the bedroom and started packing, but halfway through I remembered something and stopped.

"Keshav came into the room. I could see his muscular arms as he flicked his wrists, as though getting ready for a fight. But he collapsed into a chair. Quietly, he offered to call an auto, offered me money to rent a hotel room while I waited for the next train. He would do nothing more. Our marriage was over.

"'Keshav,' I said, not repentant, not angry, only concerned. 'I am expecting.'

"He took in a breath and rose. 'I can't be sure if it is mine. You have the freedom to do what you like. Keep it, give it up, let it out.' He pushed me aside, shut the clasps on my suitcase, and walked away with it. I had to shove my grandmother's jewels into my handbag, slip on my shoes and run after him, only, he wouldn't let me walk beside him. I had to walk two paces back."

We gave Bebe our hands, but she didn't want them. She shut her eyes before continuing on with her story.

"I came home to Kanpur saddled with grief. Another pregnancy I'd found myself emotionally too far along into to give up on, but if I took the father out of the picture, which I already had, I wouldn't think of giving up. This time I had no regrets, nothing to hide. I had been married, the child was legitimate, and no one in the world could tell me I'd done anything wrong.

"My only bit of good fortune—a phone call from Sulochana. She'd had a miracle. At a routine visit to her doctor, she'd been diagnosed with hypothyroidism, and after only six months of treatment, she'd finally got pregnant. So while she would be happy to keep my boy, she would understand if I had managed to convince my husband to adopt my first child. In which case, Sulochana could be convinced to part with Karan. 'Keshav is a good man,' Sulochana said again. 'I'm sure he will adopt Karan.'

"*You just don't do this,* I thought, *take a child and give it back.*

"'I can keep him on, really, I can. As it is, I will hire a nanny,' Sulochana offered.

"'No,' I said. I felt emboldened by my righteous anger, strengthened by my pregnancy hormones. 'I'll fetch him. I'll hop on a train next week.'

"As soon as I hung up the phone and climbed the stairs to my room, I felt as though I had been released from a private hell. I had missed you, Karan, every day of your life, regretted your loss more than the PhD I'd given up, more than the ending of my marriage. I didn't care if people talked, I could tell them whatever came to my head. That Karan was adopted. That Karan belonged to Sulochana. That Karan was Keshav's. Or, better still, Karan's father was dead. That would be justice served. Both fathers were dead. I would be a widow. I would play to people's sympathy. I would tell my children this so they clung to me even more."

Her story over, Bebe collapsed, her body flat and narrow against the wall like a local Kanpur lane. Ila lay against her, in tears. She didn't have it in her to ask any more questions of our mother, at least none about her father, and for a while, neither did I.

June 1945

The big war in Europe had ended. The papers teemed with news about the fall of Berlin and the Allied victory. On the front page of the *Times,* Churchill waved to a sea of faces in Whitehall. On the same page, near the bottom, a cluster of emaciated women with matted hair smiled uncertainly after their release from the concentration camps at Bergen-Belsen. In the *Times of India,* a headline shouted: "Hitler and Wife Commit Suicide." Why hadn't Hitler taken Gandhi's advice six years ago, the reporter demanded, and spared the world a whole lot of atrocity? At least the dark days were over in Europe, the reporter said. People were ringing each other all across the continent, yelling, "It's over, it's really over!"

While Europe celebrated, India mourned. British officials from top to bottom—the magistrates, the governor generals, the viceroy— returned to an old conundrum. What to do with their beloved colony, their finest jewel in the crown? Of late, India had become more a liability than a resource, with its leaders refusing to shut up about self-rule and inclusion in the governance. The nuisance of having half-dressed but fully turbaned men showing up to the parliament and demanding all sorts of leeway! Tossing the entire Congress Working Committee behind bars had achieved nothing. New rebel outfits such as the INA kept cropping up and demanding Britain leave India. What a shock the INA had been! Betraying, backstabbing bastards, conniving with the Japanese, conniving with Hitler, killing their own brothers in Burma. Even though they languished in jails and POW camps the general Indian public loved them, despite the way the war turned out. The war had exhausted Great Britain's resources and her patience.

The Labour Party had come into power, and Attlee, the new prime minister, favored independence for India. What now, they wondered. Was it time to let India go?

Daily, Mutton received a litany of messages. Yes, they were leaving India, his superiors confirmed. No, this did not mean they were to pack up right away, or that the leave he'd requested to take Henry on a holiday in Ireland was sanctioned. He was needed here and desperately, because tensions in the neighborhoods continued to rise.

The disturbances were no longer caused by the INA rebels, nor were they aimed at the British. Now the Indians were busy fighting among themselves. The old boy gangs had returned. Skirmishes broke out between the Congress and the Muslim League goons. Soon enough, Hindu merchants began turning away Muslim customers, and Muslim workers refused to cooperate with their Hindu bosses.

◆

Similar fights broke out in Barre Nanu's shop. His tailors, all of them Muslim, threatened to run away with the equipment if he did not continue to employ them. But Barre Nanu hadn't received any new orders from Tijori Uncle, who hadn't received any from the army.

Still, Rustom, Moin Bhai's nephew, who'd elected himself spokesperson of the tailors, kept coming around and demanding work. "Our children don't get enough to eat. I've been wearing the same pajama for the past six years. Look." He lifted his shirt and turned around to demonstrate. If it hadn't been for the patch on his bottom done with leftover fabric from the army jackets, he would have felt too humiliated to walk around in public. "All of us are dirt-poor, and you are bribing police."

"Take them!" Barre Nanu shouted. "Take the machines, take the fabric, take the door off the hinges." He grabbed Chaiji's arm and stormed out of the shop.

A few hours later, when he returned, he found all the spare cloth gone. If he went to the tailors' houses, he'd find them mending their clothes. Either that or they'd sell it on the black market for a good price.

Barre Nanu knew he had only himself to blame. Rustom was right. Their shop could have been making civilian clothing if he hadn't emptied his pockets before the corrupt, unprincipled cheat of a constable. What now, he wondered.

◆

The police remained the least-informed arm of the administration. Things were developing too slowly, the magistrate told Mutton. Then, a week later, things were developing too quickly. "We leave sooner than expected," Mutton was told.

His spies knew more. In the markets, the locals predicted the British would clear out within the next few months.

On August 6, America dropped an atomic bomb on Hiroshima. Three days later, a second bomb on Nagasaki. By August 15, Japan declared its intention to surrender. The same day, on their way back from a round of the markets, Gordon broke the news that he was leaving India. He was heading back to Somerset. He had already asked for his release.

Mutton couldn't suppress the contempt he felt for Gordon's confidence in his decision, for having a place to go back to. "Funny," he said, swallowing air. "I rather saw you staying on."

"Not me, sir." Gordon turned off the engine.

They were parked outside the station. Gordon made as if to step out of the jeep, but Mutton made no motion. He wasn't ready to release his subordinate. After five years together, the chap couldn't ask what Mutton intended to do, not even out of curiosity. Fine, then. He would volunteer his feelings on the matter.

"I might stay on," he said adamantly.

"Really, sir?" Gordon maintained an impassive face, but the forced surprise in his voice was perceptible. What did he mean? That Mutton ought not to stay?

Mutton waited for further questions. Nothing. "They are bound to need people like me," he continued. "If the Muslims and the Hindus cannot see eye to eye, which they won't, they are going to need a neutral party."

"And you are a neutral party, sir?" What did he mean? Mutton had involved himself too much? Was he hinting at his affair with Nigar Jaan? Or was he referring to that ancient debacle of Jallianwala?

Mutton couldn't keep the rage from leaking into his words. "Of course I am neutral. I am neither bloody Hindu nor Muslim, am I? I think they will find me invaluable. You can't throw out the baby with the bathwater."

"And you are the baby, sir?"

The bloody cheek! How did he manage to be so insulting without saying anything outrightly offensive? Mutton pounded his fists on the steering wheel. "I can't be the bloody bathwater, can I? I can be useful. In various capacities. I could consult. They're going to have their hands full, aren't they? They're going to find me irreplaceable."

"Right, sir."

The bastard.

"Will that be all, sir?"

Mutton nodded vaguely.

Gordon swung out of the jeep, turned around, saluted him as primly as he'd always done, and left.

◆

As he marched into the station to collect his things, Gordon felt a tinge of sadness. The colonial apparatus would be dismantled, but Mutton would hold on, pretend he was still on top and necessary. What did the fool think? He'd stay on as superintendent? Fat chance. And that son of his, the poor boy. How completely wretched the child would grow up to be, with Mutton for a father, who thought they still mattered, that Indians would give him the time of day, come knocking on his door for consultations on how to police themselves. Likely Lahore's next deputy superintendent of police, an Indian, would buy Mutton a ticket home, tell him never to come back. That is, if one of the many people who hated Mutton didn't kill him off first. At least Mutton was no longer Gordon's problem! From now on, he was free to openly hate the sorry chap. He couldn't wait to get back to England and bury the ghost of Geraldine. Find a decent position and a decent girl, and then fly off to the States!

From the station, he went straight to Montgomery Hall for a party. They were getting repetitive and boring, attendance dropping every day. Everyone was leaving. This victory was lusterless. Gandhi called it an empty victory. Gandhi, the moral curmudgeon. Even his own people did not like him anymore. Not Nehru, the leader of the Congress, and certainly not Jinnah, the leader of the Muslim League. Gordon had to stop thinking about India. He would, as soon as he boarded the plane home.

✦

With Gordon gone, Mutton felt as though he worked inside an echo chamber of sorts. His Indian subordinates never once disagreed with him, certainly didn't mock him to his face. But they were starting to get lax, taking a second too long to salute him, rising at a glacial pace when he entered the room. He knew the Indian subordinates accepted bribes behind his back. Was it just his imagination, or were they mocking him, hinting that his time in India had come to an end?

The jails were still full of INA rebels.

"What are we to do with them?" he asked the magistrate. He got no reply.

A few months later, he read in the papers. The rebels were being tried in Delhi, Lucknow, and Bombay. Soon after the Delhi verdict, in January 1946, Mutton received a mandate. The magistrate told him exactly what to do with the INA soldiers in the jail.

February 1946

Chhote Nanu still awaited the boat to Andaman. It had been a year since Mutton had announced his transportation. The hunger strike had petered out, like embers in the rain. The Indian jailers kept prisoners updated on the war—the fall of Berlin, the Axis retreat, Hitler's suicide, the Congress leaders' release, the Japanese surrender, and finally, the INA trials. In Delhi, three prominent INA soldiers had appeared before a judge, who'd found them guilty of high treason. But the public protested night and day, blocking roads, striking at factories, demanding release for the INA soldiers. The judge was forced to grant them pardon. The news didn't give Chhote Nanu much hope. He'd spent two years and five months in Mutton's prison. He had been condemned to transportation to an island far away from everyone he knew. How could Chhote Nanu hope for a different outcome?

One day Gangadhar knocked on his door. "*Chalo*! Your time has come. Get out!"

Chhote Nanu assumed the jailer meant the island. He bid his cellmates adieu, followed Gangadhar meekly out of the cell.

"I beg you, let me see my mother. God will grant you a long life in exchange."

But the jailer ignored him and moved on to another cell. "Out, everyone out."

More prisoners joined Chhote Nanu, begging Gangadhar for mercy. Andaman was final. Could they see their loved ones before sailing off to the dreaded island?

Gangadhar went through the corridor until he'd unlocked all the cells, told the prisoners to get out. "War is over," the jailer declared;

the chain of keys clanged against his hip as he ambled past. "You are no longer the concern of the government. Get out."

The prisoners followed the jailer, pleading. Even the INA rebels joined. They'd expected to appear before a judge like their comrades in other cities.

"We are not going to set foot on a boat without a trial."

Gangadhar pushed the crowd down the hall. Other jailers joined him. They herded the prisoners out of the jail. The men reached the courtyard, but the jeeps were missing. At the jail gate, there were no trucks to take them anywhere.

"Get out," shouted Gangadhar. "You are free to go."

"Free to go where?" someone asked.

"Hell, heaven, your choice."

"I want to hear a *gora* officer tell me I am free to go," an INA soldier challenged Gangadhar.

The jailer rolled his eyes and walked back into the prison.

It made no sense. Why would the authorities let them go? Hundreds of prisoners stood about wondering what to do next. Gangadhar came back a few minutes later with more prisoners, found them stalling in the prison courtyard, and shouted: "You want me to lock you up again or what? Go, I said, clear out! You have been released."

Released! The euphoria of freedom carried the prisoners out of the jail and into the open air. The collective marched together like a Trojan horse, shouting and jumping, hand in hand. Chhote Nanu was dragged left, right, forward, backward. He saw tear-streaked faces, mouths contorting with laughter, fists pumping in the air. They'd been released. They really had been released, no foul play. From now on, no more oil pressing! No more bad food! No more hanging upside down like a towel! No more whips! No more walls! An abundance of sky, flowers, fields, grain, food, so much food, such good food! They could sit wherever they want, talk to whomever they want. Sit in a chair, lie in the middle of the road, jump into the river! From the collective, individual faces and prayers percolated and popped like bubbles. A fifteen-year-old boy, jailed at thirteen for singing anti-war songs, would sleep in his mother's field under the stars. His sixty-year-old friend would reopen his barber's shop. Someone asked Chhote Nanu about his plans.

"Me?" He hadn't really thought. "See my father, my mother, my brother." Ask them why they had kept away all this time.

"What about you, Chiragh?" an INA soldier asked.

"Slit this bastard's throat," he said, grabbing Chhote Nanu's neck. Before Chhote Nanu could shake him off, Chiragh let him go. "But first I will touch my mother's feet and beg for her forgiveness for causing her grief." Everyone nodded in agreement and patted the chameleon's back.

The Trojan horse paused under the peepul tree outside the jail. Where had the tea stall on the opposite corner gone? The *paan* wallah had gone too. Where had these people moved? The prisoners had missed things. Births, deaths, marriages. A prisoner wondered if his secret sweetheart still awaited him. Another wondered if he'd find his elderly parents living.

"I have to go this way." A prisoner pointed to the north and went away. Another went south. Person by person, the collective disbanded.

Chhote Nanu ambled through the streets like a cloud. Workers at a flour press mounted weights on a scale, their limbs white with flour. At a tea stall, college students leaned into heated political discussions. There had been changes—all the army recruitment posters had been removed, the INA posters too. The new signs belonged to the Muslim League and the Sikh Akali Dal and the Congress; each claimed Lahore for themselves in the new India. Who would get Lahore? Pakistan or India? He walked past Anarkali Market. He turned a corner and ran into a League rally. The protesters chanted slogans. "Long live Pakistan! We want Pakistan!"

He ducked into another lane, entered Shahalmi Market. Did anyone recognize him? He had his old clothes on—a white kurta and his big brother's achkan, which finally fit him. What would his mother say when she saw him? And his father? Why hadn't they come to visit him? Why didn't they write? Why hadn't Barre Nanu found a way to extricate him? He was going to storm into the courtyard and demand an answer.

A ration shop owner waved his red *gamchha* in the air, beckoned him over.

"Is that you, Chhote *mian*? I knew this bad time would be over soon! You must be proud of fighting in Burma? My, how you have grown! What can I get you? Anything for you! Free of charge!" But then he saw Chhote Nanu's unkempt hair, smelled the awful stench rising from his unwashed body, and the corners of his mouth dropped.

Chhote Nanu wanted to rush home and see his family. "Excuse me, I have to—"

"Yes, yes, another time."

When he got home, the lock on the door confused him. Never in all his life had he ever seen his house locked. He didn't know the panes could shut all the way. Where had they all gone? He kicked a stone. The sky felt heavy; it looked like it might rain. He circled the block. No washing hung on the house's balconies. He couldn't see all three floors because the banyan in the courtyard had grown. He knocked at the neighbor's.

Ahmed Bhai looked as though he'd seen a ghost. The tall, strapping wrestler was older than Barre Nanu. They'd lived next to each other for as long as they could remember. Still, Ahmed Bhai didn't pull Chhote Nanu close and hug him. In fact, the man didn't say a word, and Chhote Nanu had to introduce himself, point to the house next door.

"Is that you Chhote?" Ahmed Bhai finally said. There was something strained in his smile. "How long have you been away? You have grown!" Ahmed Bhai smiled, but his eyes did not linger.

"I'm the same." Chhote Nanu didn't know if he believed his words. The two years had gone into a dark cave and stayed there. He wasn't sure if he had changed. "I have to find Chai. Do you know where they have gone? The house is locked."

Ahmed Bhai clasped his hands together. He opened his mouth, but no words came out.

"What is it?" Chhote Nanu's heart began to beat faster. Maybe he ought to ask for the spare key and wait at home. He was thinking of excuses when Ahmed Bhai gave him the news. His neighbor had to repeat himself.

"Are you listening? Babuji went to heaven. This time last year. They received bad news from the jail. I don't know what." His hands still rested on Chhote Nanu's shoulders, his face close, waiting for a re-action, and when Chhote Nanu shook his head, more out of confusion than grief, Ahmed Bhai pulled him to his chest and held him there.

The last thing Chhote Nanu remembered was stumbling out of Ahmed Bhai's home. The streets passed by in a blur—the waves and the shoulder pats from people who knew him, shoves from people who didn't, the army and the GIs storming past and honking, one even knocking him out of the street and onto the steps of a corner shop, where he sat.

Babuji, the well of silence, inside which he'd swum like a frog and felt safe. Half his life, the well of silence had ignored him, as wells do. For a horrible minute, Chhote Nanu felt he himself had died. He tried to stand, and his knees remembered the yoke of the oil press and buckled. He felt unhooked from the universe, set aside for all kinds of tragedies. The desperate need to see his big brother consumed him, but he didn't know where Barre Nanu or his widowed mother had gone. He'd left Ahmed Bhai's in such a haste.

He wandered toward the Ravi, slept on the steps by the river.

When he awoke, the flower sellers were opening their stalls. Bathers waded into the water in their white saris and lungis and prayed to the rising sun. A man with a shorn head tipped a brass lota full of ash, the flecks landing on the bathers' bodies. A fleck of ash landed on Chhote Nanu's cheek, and he touched it, watched it disintegrate into the skin on his fingers. Chaiji and Barre Nanu had mourned Babuji without him. From a flower stall, he ordered a garland of marigolds and a flour lamp. He had no money, however. He offered the man his jacket. The flower seller examined the fine material.

"Cloth is like gold, sahib," the little man said frankly, perhaps to give Chhote Nanu a chance to reconsider. But Chhote Nanu had nothing else to offer.

He set Babuji's lamp to sail on the water, sat on the river steps to see how long it would go on, but already his eyes confused it with the dancing lamps of other people's loved ones.

The sun rose higher. Day turned into afternoon. His stomach growled. He couldn't remember the last time he'd eaten. A meal of porridge yesterday. More pebbles than porridge. He watched the lunch stalls. Cream lassi. Onion fritters. Bread *pakora*. He dug into his pajama pockets. Nothing but the disappointing, empty comfort of cloth. The clock tower struck one. He looked at his wrist to confirm the time. The watch! Babuji's gift from when he had passed his tenth standard exams. It was missing!

The flower seller swore up and down that he hadn't found a watch in the jacket. The frankness of the stitches on his shirt caused Chhote Nanu to believe him. He walked away dejected, but the flower seller called him back.

"Take it back, sahib. It is more use to you than me."

"I don't deserve your kindness," he said, walking away.

Chhote Nanu sat on the river steps, trying to keep his body from collapsing into itself. He couldn't believe he'd lost Babuji's watch. His father had fastened it on his wrist back when Chhote Nanu was still in his graces. He felt his wrist, but the skin no longer carried its impression. He dug his hands into the dirt and flung it upon himself. He caught two college boys staring at him. They turned back to their lunch boxes open before them on the river steps. Chhote Nanu remembered. He'd taken off the watch and placed it on the blighted tin box the night of the poetry recital. He couldn't remember if he'd put it back on. Was it still at the jail? Had one of the jailers taken it? Or perhaps it was still at Nigar Jaan's. Had she already sailed to England?

The reception he received at her house was one of outright contempt. Once the doorman recognized him, he refused Chhote entry.

"You come to bomb the place again?" The man stood blocking the stairwell from which Chhote Nanu had tumbled out handcuffed over two years ago.

"I left something valuable here. Baby Jaan wrote to me. Is she still here?"

The doorman pushed him into the street.

Chhote Nanu began to shout. "Shehnazji! Memsahib!"

The girl from upstairs raced down. "Move aside," Shehnaz told the doorman. "Baby Jaan wants to see him."

"She is mad if she will allow him into her house again."

Shehnaz pushed the doorman aside and escorted Chhote Nanu up.

Halfway up the stairs, he remembered that night.

He entered the big room where it had all begun. The once-opulent room, studded with crystals and shimmering curtains, was now sparse. The Persian rug had been replaced with smaller, brighter squares of busier patterns. The chandelier was gone. Table lamps stood sentry in the four corners, their lights low. He saw the tail end of a black mark on the floor partway under the carpet, where the bomb had gone off. He'd done that, he'd scorched the floor. He thought of the things he hadn't seen—the bruises, the cuts, the head-aches, the temporary losses of hearing, the permanent fear of loud noises—these had been his contributions to the cause of India's in-dependence. He'd been jailed rightly, he'd deserved those two years and five months.

"I am sorry," he said to the room as it swirled around him, hunger causing him to swoon. "It's terrible."

"Yes, terrible." Shehnaz looked coldly on. "Baby Jaan is mad to let you in."

He stared at the girl guiltily, then let his gaze drop. "I've come for my watch. That's all. My pockets are empty this time."

"You should frisk him nicely," someone said, the voice full of sarcasm. Nigar Jaan stood uncertainly in the doorway, as though afraid to come near him. She may be mad to let him into her house, but she hadn't left for England with the superintendent.

◆

Nigar Jaan watched Shehnaz leave with a huff. The girl felt protective of her. Nigar Jaan couldn't fault her for that. She pointed Chhote Nanu to a seat, but he wasn't looking at her. She couldn't believe he stood before her. He was taller now, and his body had filled up with muscle and resolve. And guilt too, from the way he slouched, as though wanting to disappear into himself. His beard gave him a gloomy aspect. He bent to examine a speck on the carpet, and she had a vision of him stretched on Mutton's torture device. At least he hadn't been transported. All this time she'd blamed herself for his transportation, and he'd been in Lahore all along.

"I can't tell you how relieved I am to see you," she blurted. "I thought you'd been sent to Andaman. Will you have some water?"

He hung his head, or maybe he shook it. "I left something valuable here. My father's watch. Please, if you still have it." His manner was distant. She tried to recall his face from that night as they dragged him down the stairs, handcuffed. That hopeful, naive boy had gone, and an aloof, closed-off man had taken his place.

"I left my father's watch here," he said again.

"Won't you sit?"

He shook his head, and his locks shook with it. "I shouldn't have done it. I didn't mean for it to happen."

She wanted to tell him she believed he'd been set up. So much had happened since then. They'd both lost so much. What were some glasses and a floor and a chandelier? What were they compared to her little Henry? If he'd damaged her house, the jail had damaged his psyche. If he'd precipitated the loss of Henry, the jail time had likely caused his father's death. Her grief came like a wave so strong, she couldn't listen. He was saying something about a watch.

"My watch, I left it here. Please, if you still have it. My father gave it to me."

"Have you heard, then," she said softly. "Your father passed away."

"Please, my watch . . ."

"Please, listen." She took a step toward him.

But he turned on his heels and bolted out the door. He thundered down the stairs. Then she heard him fall.

✦

Chhote Nanu sat in the stairwell at Nigar Jaan's house, a few feet away from the room he'd bombed. He shouldn't have returned to the crime scene. More painful than the memory was the forgiveness she offered. More painful than that—the realization that time had passed and yet some things hadn't changed. He still found her wildly beautiful. Even after all this time and all that had happened. He couldn't help it. Her gaze had lingered on him, scanning his body, searching his face. The audience he'd once sought with her was finally here.

"I know about the jail," she called to him from upstairs. "He is a cruel man, the superintendent."

Did he hear her right?

"You were probably set up, it wasn't your fault."

She was inviting him back inside, but all he wanted was to curl into a ball and burst into a million little pieces.

"If you hadn't made an impression on me, would I risk four lives to write to you?" Her words. But no, so much had happened since then. Slowly, he turned around and said: "The superintendent told me you had left for England."

"Where would I go in England?"

"Anywhere. The whole country is yours."

"I have never left India. I wouldn't know the first thing about where to go."

He got up from the stairs and crept into the room, standing near the stain he'd caused, surprised Nigar Jaan hadn't thrown him out, surprised just how much he wanted her. But all she felt for him was pity, pity for his suffering in the jail, pity for the loss of his father.

"I cannot remember the last time I saw my father," he blurted. He didn't want her gaze to leave him now that she'd directed her magnificent gray-blue-green-brown eyes at him.

He squatted on the floor, curling into himself, remembering he smelled from the jail. He hadn't washed properly in two years, hadn't had a proper haircut or a shave. He sat in abject apology, brushing his arms, wishing he could shed the layer of his boyhood that had caused the blast.

What she did next was not to fill the silence and cover his apology with words or gestures, but to put before him the object he sought— the watch, the very one Babuji had given him. The glass had a little crack, and when he put the strap on his wrist, he had to use a new notch. But the watch worked, it still worked.

"Shehnaz found it the morning after the gathering."

The watch fastened around his wrist, he turned around to excuse himself from her presence forever.

"Won't you stay for a little while?"

The maid came in, bearing a plate of food. "Look what Baby Jaan does for the person who bombed us," she mocked, nodding to a seat. "Come, eat. God knows when you had a decent meal."

The scent of the clarified butter, too powerful to resist, brought tears to his eyes. What a display. Fresh roti, three curries, a cold salad. He wept as he ate, dipped some bread in curry, delighted in the chewy softness of the meat. The jail had taken his appetite away. Equally, it could be Nigar Jaan's presence. He couldn't understand her kindness, nor could he bring himself to thank her for it.

The lady sat facing him, as though he was a guest of honor. Two years ago, she wouldn't have given him the time of day. Perhaps more than just the furnishings had altered in the room. Gone was the oppressive splendor, gone was the scepter of the superintendent's hold.

"He doesn't come here anymore, in case you were wondering." Nigar Jaan shuddered slightly. "For a long time, I convinced myself I belonged with him." Her eyes were distant. "I told him he is a cruel man. It was foolish of me." She buried her pretty face in her hands. "He took my little boy away. He took Henry away."

Chhote Nanu got up so quickly, his chair fell backward. "We must go at once and get him."

She shook her head. "I can't defy the superintendent any further."

Chhote Nanu felt as though his heart was going to burst. The little boy! He'd carried the child in his arms, put him on his bicycle, fed him milk sweets and breakfast. The cruelty of it! He didn't know the woman seated before him, not until now. Her true aspect revealed itself to him only now. She wasn't the fainthearted lady hiding under a man's hat, but this bold creature who'd suffered consequences for her boldness.

His heart came pouring out: "How could this have happened? That Mutton!" He felt too angry to speak. "To do this to you. A woman like you! Women like you are rare . . . this is why I fancied you. It is hard to imagine."

His words touched her. She sat up, wire straight. "Why is that hard to imagine?"

Coyness suited her. He would indulge her in any way he could. "You were, you remain, out of reach."

"We both walk on God's green earth."

She said it so simply. "Hardly," he responded.

"If you weren't so determined to etch lines, you'd see there isn't much difference between us."

The meaning of her words caused him to feel as though he were tumbling from the sky. Do you really see me?—this is what she was asking, with her body leaning toward him, fingers extended on the dining table, inching the plate of food toward him, encouraging him to eat. To want her again like he did before, a return to his innocence, to those days of summer under the tent at the wrestling match, before the bomb, before Babuji's death, before Barre Nanu's lack of visits, before the jail, before the lashings. He could have some of it back. She could be the road to his past, also the road to the future.

"You are right," he said. "You are no different. You are thoroughly Indian. And brave. Like Tipu Sultan and the revolutionary queen Rani Laxmi Bai. You have more in common with me than with Mutton."

Yes, her body said, as she reached for his hands, then, becoming shy, retreated them. In his words she found acceptance.

Gently, with shaking fingers, he took her perfect hand, its rings and roughness and fears and all. "Have you been to Multan? They call it the City of Saints for good reason. You can do whatever you like there. Read poetry, write poetry, teach Farsi." The effect of his words caused her to turn a rose-red. She didn't pull her hand away, didn't turn away when his knees touched hers.

He wandered the city that night, thoughts of her consuming him. His body ached from fighting the urge to dash back to her house and hold her. Overcome with exhaustion, he collapsed on the steps of the tomb of Saint Ganj Baksh, a view of the green marble dome in his eyes.

The next day, she came to offer prayers. She asked her maid to fetch him a blanket.

"You won't stop taking care of me."

She shook her head.

Chhote Nanu regarded the pigeons cooing on the marble roof of the shrine. The birds here seemed nobler than the city birds, as though they aspired to a higher reality.

In the street, another procession passed, demanding Lahore for Pakistan.

"Have you thought about Multan?" he asked her, and she nodded yes.

Local men pointed and stared at the oddity of an English *mem* talking to someone who slept at the shrine. They didn't know her history, didn't know her grandfather's story, how she lived reading poetry. She'd known no other place but India.

More processions passed, bringing more strange men into the shrine from far away. More people who wouldn't understand Nigar Jaan's heart. They'd take India away from her, wrench it away if they could. They'd put her on a ship with her mother, send her back to a place she didn't know. Only Chhote Nanu. Only he knew her, understood what she needed.

In this manner, they saw each other for a month, trying to avoid one another, but running into each other nonetheless. This is how Chhote Nanu knew *she* was his future, his everything, and not his own family: not once did the urge to run to his house consume him. He was still upset at Barre Nanu for not writing, not visiting. He wanted to punish his brother a little longer, exactly as long as he'd been punished. He thought only of Nigar, wanted only Nigar. Twice more he asked her about Multan. Every time she said she was eager. They made up their minds.

They acknowledged they were running away from Lahore, from Henry's ghost and Mutton's and Babuji's. The questions of what they would do and how they would survive didn't scare them. Nigar Jaan had some jewelry she would be happy to part with, and Chhote Nanu couldn't wait to see what might come his way with his English-school education and nearly three years of hard knocks.

"Why did you forgive me?" he asked her on the train heading southwest. Her answer was as surprising as the gift of the watch. He'd seen her Indian side; he'd been the only one to do so. He wanted to fight with her, for her. He wasn't so much a reminder of the loss, but the hook in the chain of cause and effect that grounded her to her life.

August 2002

I didn't want my mother or my sister to venture downstairs and face the demands of the pilgrims. So I offered to bring them dinner. Only, out of habit, I went to the *keema* shack near the public garden. When I returned home with the brown-paper packet releasing the aroma of roasted meats, I realized my blunder. I crept to the stairs as soundlessly as I could, but the priest, supervising the dinner preparations, emerged from the kitchen and caught me red-handed.

"Is that *maas-machhi* I am smelling?" His puffed face was the color of beets. "You bring meat into a 100 percent pure-veg guesthouse?" He stormed up to the second floor and banged on Chhote Nanu's door.

I slipped upstairs. We ate our shameful dinner with the doors and windows shut. We spread newspapers on the floor, ate directly from the tin can and aluminum foils, taking turns to rip the bread. It was only a matter of time before Chhote Nanu thundered upstairs and kicked us out. I'd violated the sanctity of his temple.

We told Bebe not to worry, let her sleep. Ila and I retreated onto the balcony.

"What if I find a job," I said. "Here, in India?"

"You are not going back to New York? What about your degree? What about Omar?"

Her words conjured the sunshine on Mott Street. It was always sunny on Mott Street. Sunny inside the 7 train with its multitude of tongues, rails screeching in crescendo as all eyes turned to see the magnificence of Manhattan before it disappeared behind the ramshackle of Queens. The unjust depression of Jackson Heights, subdued aunties hauling groceries on Seventy-Fourth Street up rickety stairs, refusing help, trusting no one, not even clean-shaven South Asian men without a clue about their fathers' identities. My room overlooking Delhi Durbar and Kabul Kababs awaited me. But the thought of the now quiet, odorless stretch of Seventy-Fourth Street, the bloodred pages of the hateful website, the imam's patchy, closed face, and the charred walls of the Flushing mosque made me want to keep away. I hadn't heard from Omar since the SMSes. Why hadn't we exchanged emails yet? New York didn't feel like home. But then, neither did this house. It wasn't possible to return, and neither was it possible to leave.

"Maybe it's time to leave Chhote Nanu," I ventured. "He has new friends." This muddled house wasn't ours anymore. The pilgrims had claimed it. We had to give it up.

To my surprise, Ila nodded. "Extended family is an outdated concept. That's what I am writing about."

"That's your dissertation?" I asked half-jokingly. "Family planning to shrug off uncles and aunties and cousins?"

"More like, how to cut ties with your co-caste people to nip the power enclaves in the bud. All marriages should defy caste and religious divides. No more same-caste and same-religion alliances."

"And no more same-gender alliances, am I right?" I tried, probing my sister gently.

"Exactly!"

"Brava!" I patted her on the back. "That's as radical an idea as any."

"The idea isn't radical at all. Ambedkar wrote about it long ago."

"Well, it is radical if we put it into practice." I raised my hand and Ila returned my high five.

Losing our childhood home was fusing us together. We had nowhere to go, together. We could rotate our visits to each other's rooms like bees pollinating flowers. We had to let go of our beehive.

"As long as we can take Bebe with us, we can build our beehive anywhere."

"Maybe she wants to stay in her *barsati* in Delhi." Ila was still angry at Bebe. She went inside her room, rummaged through Bebe's bag, produced a stack of papers, returned to the balcony.

"Look at this." She handed me a greeting card, its hinges yellow with age. Still, the purple flowers on the three-panel card held glitter inside their hearts.

It was a birthday greeting from Ila's father. On the left panel, he'd written a letter. Soon after he'd learned of her birth via a surreptitious letter from Chhote Nanu, exhorting him to acknowledge his child, Keshav had bought toys, packed a bag, bought a ticket. But on the day of his journey, his mother found out. She ripped the ticket into two, forbade him to visit Bebe. In the greeting card, he explained his helplessness, appealed to his daughter to forgive him. On the right panel, he'd crossed out certain words and replaced them with his own, instructing Ila to "~~enjoy~~ bravely suffer your birthday and be ~~ready~~ strong-willed for all the ~~fun times in store~~ questions you will ask your mother about your father. Only one kiss."

The card was dated May 20, 1979, the date of Ila's birth. The ink had faded with age.

She handed me more cards, more letters he'd mailed her that Bebe had intercepted, refused to pass on until now.

I browsed through fifteen-years-too-late proofs of her father's love, words crossed out, old flowers and hearts expressing his frustration with his mother's prejudice and Bebe's recalcitrance, and his failure to show Bebe how much he would continue to love her, regard her as the strongest woman he'd ever met. I felt a tinge of jealousy. Ila had concrete proof of her father, even though it was twenty-three years too late.

"It's not fair to you," I said, fingering the embossed details on the cards.

"It's not fair to Bebe. To have refused love. To not have fallen in love."

In the morning, Chhote Nanu came to give us an earful about our offensive dinner. He trudged up the stairs shouting for Bebe. His breath couldn't keep up with his rage, and he stopped, holding his walking stick in his fist like a gun. He pointed it at us as though he were firing shots.

"Just when I think you can't sink any further. I cannot provide *shuddh shakahari* pure-veg place with you three about. You have violated my house for the last time. If you don't leave by tomorrow, I will change the locks."

"Won't you come up, Nanu?" Ila asked, slipping down the stairs.

He flicked his wrist and turned away. He thought of something, turned, and said, "If you want to be useful, make me some tea. No sugar."

After the tea, Ila and I packed what little we had left in the room. I folded all my clothes and put them in my suitcase. Ila's pile of books disappeared from the desk. She left her laptop and a stack of reading out. This and our three toothbrushes, one tube of herbal toothpaste from the Gandhi ashram on Mall Road, three towels. This is what's left when you're done clearing your childhood: your toothbrush. There's no good way to pack a toothbrush.

"Are we ready to leave?" We all sat in separate corners, as though waiting for Chhote Nanu to physically evict us, like he'd done in the past.

"I heard you two talking last night," Bebe said, rubbing her feet together.

Ila and I exchanged glances. Our silly plans must have frustrated her. But little else frightened her except husbands.

"You are wrong, Ila." She pulled her feet up on the bed, leaned against the wall. "I did fall in love. Twice. The second love, your father, you have heard about. Yes, that was love; it might have been as brief as a week. You haven't heard about my first love. I want to tell you about Karan's father. You should know."

"Our romance was doomed from the start, your father's and mine." Again, her accusing eyes dug into mine, as though I was the reason why my parents' relationship hadn't worked out. Perhaps I was.

"We'd grown up together, Irshad Siddiqui and I. We came in and out of each other's homes like the wind. Our houses faced each other;

in fact, the Siddiquis occupied the pink house opposite, its walls and windows and people separated only by a hot, narrow lane from ours. His sensitivity was miles long."

She looked at me pointedly, as though she were seeing someone else.

"But even before I loved Irshad, I loved his mother. Ammi Jaan, from her perch on her terrace, kept an eye on me as I grew up, witnessed every scrape, every burn, every tear. Her heart ached for me, the little girl growing up without a mother with two men who meant well but had no skills for parenting. Little by little, Ammi Jaan began to interfere. 'Eh larki!' she would call, and I would run over to her house. She gave me rotis that weren't burned or store-bought, and kheer and sweets, and, in time, lessons in sewing buttons and making tea and boiling an egg. Ammi Jaan bought me my first bra, taught me how to make sanitary pads out of old sheets. I did well in most lessons, only my cooking could not be helped. Still, Ammi Jaan, who'd wanted a daughter but was blessed instead with a son, continued to give me lessons, prided herself over how well I was turning out under her tutelage.

"Quite possibly Irshad inherited Ammi Jaan's love for me. At the time, Ammi Jaan didn't separate neighborly love from motherly love. She let the lines cross.

"We rode to school together, Irshad and I, sitting side by side on the same rickshaw. In the evenings, we ran to the same chaat wallah for papari chaat, steel cauldrons in hand, room enough for the fried brinjal base and the chutneys and the garnish.

"Under Ammi Jaan's watchful eye and with Irshad's constant belligerence and companionship, I grew up full of confidence. I was the high jump champion of my batch at the S. N. Sen School for Girls. All the schoolgirls teased me for my strong legs—'What beautiful calves you have'—they couldn't stop complimenting my athletic form. Because Irshad wouldn't believe I was any good, I demonstrated one of my jumps one morning inside the buffalo shed, the animals out on their stroll. I took off running from one end of the shed, launched myself in the air, landed a good distance away near the shed door and straight into a pile of dung. Irshad held his stomach and laughed, snorting through the nose. He was thin as a reed and tall, his skin stretching taut over his smile; he wore his father's white kurtas that gave him a studious, cultured aspect, and that caused everyone, even adults, to take him seriously. I hated when he laughed at me. I was so cross with him, I leapt to smack him, slipped on the wet cobblestones.

"Our camaraderie continued into college, even after I gave up sports and picked up art for my master's degree and Irshad picked up cricket. I spent hours bent over miniatures, coloring a 0.5-inch elephant or a 0.2-inch prince wielding a sword. It fascinated me how you could represent the abundance of nature, the intricacies of trees, the idiosyncrasies of character in such a small space. While I painted, Irshad issued taunts from his window across our hot little lane. He echoed Ammi Jaan's words, who worried that the hours I spent ruining my eyes over the paintings would render me spectacled and unfit for marriage.

"'Ammi is right,' he mocked. 'Learn to cook instead. Your husband is going to expect a little more than just a cup of tea.'

"Then Barre Nanu launched his sari workshop, and for the next year I lost myself in stacks of tracing paper and yards of fabric, adapting ancient patterns for sari borders, while still going to graduate school. My eyes grew weaker, my back developed a slight hunch, but Irshad remained on the window opposite, every bit as persistent, convivial, flirtatious even.

"'I am serious,' he shouted at me from time to time. 'You are a confirmed spinster now.' I was twenty-five, which put me three, possibly four years past my marry-by date.

"'Worry about your own prospects,' I shouted back. 'You haven't married either.'

"'I have my father's publishing company to run.'

"'I have my father's sari business.'

"'We are both very dutiful children.'

"Why did he taunt me so much about marriage? Was that the only way he could express his interest? Was he interested? One afternoon I found out.

"The day had been a difficult one for me. My art teacher, Mr. MacCaulay, had come by looking for some pieces for an exhibition he was putting together in Delhi. He'd always believed in my talent, believed he could see my work displayed in solo shows in the national museums, maybe even in London, Madrid, Paris. But the pieces I showed him, the old miniatures I'd copied from books on Islamic art, were no good. He rejected these outright. They were nothing but pretty patterns, like the ones I drew on the saris for my father's business. These weren't art, Mr. MacCaulay pronounced decisively. If I wanted to make a name for myself in the art world, I had to draw like the European masters—Renoir, Botticelli, Da Vinci. His words cut me to the core. I raced up the stairs to my room, and threw my easel out the window.

"When Irshad saw me moping from across the lane, he rolled up his sleeves, revealing thin, cultured arms and a Casio wristwatch, and leaned over the windowsill. 'Is that your old art teacher I saw? Forget him. He's Scottish. What does he know about Indian art? I bet he calls it "Oriental."'

"I didn't agree. I shut my art books, stacked them in the wall shelf. 'Actually, he calls it "the art of the Orient."' I didn't mind my teacher's labels. He was an artist himself, and my master's thesis committee chair. He'd considered me significant enough to solicit pieces from.

"'We can't keep taking directions from Europeans,' Irshad pointed out. 'We are an independent nation. We have to forge our own paths.'

"'Says the ex-captain of Christ Church College's cricket team. You are the biggest rule follower I know.'

"'Cricket is a gentleman's game. But art is different. Art has to represent subjectivity. You can't paint like Botticelli or Velázquez. You have to get there by way of Persia. Figure out a way.'

"I slipped off my bangles, watched them cascade down my arms and onto the bed. 'I am tired of trying. I am a commercial sari designer. That is all.'

"'Stop complaining. Here,' he tossed me a brown parcel. 'Abboo's latest publication. Some poetry to take your mind off.'

"The book landed on my bed. It was a collection of poetry by the famous Mir Taqi Mir. I lay down to browse. The words were in Urdu, a script I did not know (but Chhote Nanu did), but the pictures were familiar—Persian miniatures of war scenes with elephants and riders and horses and princes, paintings I loved getting lost inside, but an aesthetic my teacher had condemned, a path I had to leave behind. I lay in bed, admiring the vibrant colors, the orange background and the bright blue shirts, the silver wine goblets and the violet grapes. So what if Picasso didn't paint miniatures? Why did the whole world have to follow Europe's path? I raised the book closer to my eyes, and a paper slipped out. A miniature, Turkic from the looks of it. A woman stood on one end of a room and pointed accusingly to a man standing a few feet away. Between them, a judge sat at a podium, contemplating the object in his hand, a replica of the man's organ. I had goosebumps on my arms. What kind of a pornographic drawing was this? What was going on? Was the woman accusing the man, her husband, of infertility? Or had he caught her pleasing herself? The scandalous painting made me laugh. The couple looked traditional in dress, but so bold and modern in thought. Something clicked inside my head. The painting presented an unconventional story with drama, characters, and a situation that felt decidedly modern. A common married couple with common problems. I could learn from this, achieve subjectivity and still work within the format of miniatures. I ran out of the house, retrieved my easel from the lane, set it up, and began to draw.

"In the window facing mine, Irshad snored in his bed, a pile of books beside his head, another pile by his feet. I thought about him and his life, a publisher and an editor with a pile of manuscripts, books to read, poetry resting on his lips, a cricketer with dust on his shoes, tension in his strong muscles, grime on his neck. I began to draw him. First I drew his house, the pale-pink paint, the blue trimming on the windows, then the lane outside the house, a gulmohur tree shielding the front door, the goat tethered to the tree, a bicycle resting against it as well. Inside the house, a man slept in a pose that suggested fatigue, an arm covering his eyes, a leg hanging off the bed. Beside him, a pile of books lay collapsed, as though they had been kicked by the editor's frustrated foot. That foot became the focus of the painting, and I drew it delicately, down to the fine hairs on the toes. I added a surreal element, a ghost escaping up and away from the man's window, a spirit, which I painted in white.

"My teachers received the painting well. Mrs. Baghchi, who had studied with the great A. K. Coomaraswamy, found my work groundbreaking, a new way of representing Indian reality. Even Mr. MacCaulay conceded he'd never expected me to come up with something as 'contemporary' as that. 'Isn't it positively Gulammuhammadian?' said the perky old lady in a sleeveless blouse, and Mr. MacCaulay nodded his head of gray hair. 'But her color palette is entirely her own, as are her figures, more sturdy and present, less frail.'

"I felt overjoyed. I hadn't expected such a reception. Even more unexpected, the fact that I had, for once, Irshad to thank.

"The next day, I invited him for coffee, an offer he readily accepted.

"We sat alone in the courtyard, cups cradled in both hands, feeling awkward and formal.

"'Can I see the painting?' he asked, and I took him upstairs.

"He peered at this representation of himself; he could see it was him, and my heart beat like a drum, waiting for him to comment. A devilish smile played on his lips. I felt as though I was going to burst.

"'Well? What do you think?'

"'I don't look that wispy, do I?' he asked, laughing, pointing to the faint brush trails.

"'You want to be a romance hero?'

"'I thought you were Botticelli. Paint me with a bigger brush. I've got biceps! Fine, I know very little about art, but I am tickled you used me.'

"I rolled my eyes. 'You were the only subject I could find at short notice.'

"Another devilish smile played on his lips, and his hair fell into his eyes as he sipped his coffee (it tasted bland, but he didn't complain). He stared into it as he asked his next question: 'Where did you get the inspiration?'

"I felt my cheeks color. I'd completely forgotten about the little pornographic painting inside his book. For the first time in my life, I felt shy; I didn't know what to do with my hands, my face, whether to smile (would he think it too forward?) or to frown (would he think I was upset?). I kept fidgeting with my hair and my shirt just to keep my hands occupied.

"Just then the power went out, the entire mohalla uttered a collective sigh, and in the sanctity of the pitch-darkness, Irshad took hold of my hand, pulled me close, and kissed me. Youthful hormones, youthful insolence, but I didn't protest, and in fact I kissed him back. I hadn't been raised to be bashful."

Bebe's face took on a new color. The telling of her love story made her younger somehow. She sat up, smiling, revealing her new teeth, even the crooked one she felt conscious of. "Some lovers promise you a beautiful future," she said. "Other lovers link you to the past. You always prefer the latter. Always."

I looked over to see Ila's reaction, hoping to see her seething with jealousy, but at that moment, I didn't care what she thought.

"After our first kiss, Irshad and I began to meet in secret in the *barsati* on the terrace, a room I equipped with a full-size woven charpoy, my easel, and my paints, my own private artist retreat from the world. I began spending all my time there, painting and waiting for Irshad to hop over his terrace, make his way across the little obstacle course of the lane, and announce himself at my door. He came full of ideas and critiques, his understanding of my art coming across as love, channeling other kinds of acceptances and needs, especially the physical. His touch, the way he dug into my flesh with his strong bones, I felt as though I were a wisp of his imagination and might disappear if he didn't hold me down. How well we knew each other! With him there, I saw the little *barsati* bathed in a golden glow, the oil lamps glittering as though set on a river, and already it felt like a marriage of sorts. We'd stayed single for each other, hadn't we? We forgot everyone around us, and that felt like the biggest, weightiest truth.

"But soon I was shaken awake from my dream. I'd forgotten one of the most important people in my life—Ammi Jaan. One day, Ammi Jaan caught me dancing to Vicki Robinson singing "Turn the Beat Around." Across the room, her son was staring at me, his eyes full of lust, and she knew the nature of our friendship had changed. She gave such a shout, she scared the crows off the trees.

"I saw the fire in Ammi Jaan's eyes. Only then did I realize the blunder I'd committed. I'd not only violated Ammi Jaan's trust, I'd completely ignored her. I might have gained a lover, but I lost a mother.

"Barre Nanu overheard Ammi Jaan berating her son for locking eyes with the girl next door, and he came up to see me. He offered his own failed marriage as warning.

"'You don't want to repeat your father's mistake, *beta*.'

"When Chhote Nanu heard, he lost his temper.

"'You think you can do Hindu-Muslim romance better than your uncle?'

"I fought back. 'This is not the same. It's not like what happened with you and Nigar Jaan—'

"'*Bas!*' He raised a hand. 'Do you know what could happen to you? You will face prejudice every step of the way. One riot and the neighbors will drag you out of your house and murder you two together.'

"I couldn't hold back my tears at his lack of support. 'Times are changing.'

"'Are they changing for the better? Tell me, do you know of a single successful middle-class Hindu-Muslim union in our town?'

"I had no comeback. I'm sure I knew of interfaith marriages, but I couldn't remember any names.

"Chhote Nanu kicked my easel and stormed out. He felt helpless and disrespected. That evening, before I could call him to dinner, he left the house."

Bebe had twirled Ila's hair around her finger so tight, my sister winced, pulled our mother's hand out of her hair. But Bebe was in greater pain.

"The next time Irshad came to see me, he brought more bad news.

"'Ammi Jaan doesn't approve. I can't think why. There isn't anyone she loves more than you.'

"'She doesn't love me. She doesn't think I'm good enough for you.'

"'It's not that. It's religion.'

"'What can I do about that?'

"'I will talk to her.'

"But he couldn't get through. Ammi Jaan saw the world a certain way. Hindus and Muslims shouldn't commingle. The splitting of the Indian subcontinent was proof. Abboo Jaan having to constantly consider shutting down his publishing firm because the bank wouldn't approve his loan was proof. Why was everything reserved for the Hindus? None of this was my fault, and Ammi Jaan loved me, but not as a daughter-in-law. I would never understand the suffering inflicted upon the Muslims in India. If I wanted to make amends, I would have to stop my foolish pursuit of her son.

"But Irshad and I continued to meet, our meetings taking on the hue of forbidden love. The impending doom made it even harder for us to pull away.

"Ammi Jaan knew Irshad well. She'd brought him up with so much coddling. She blamed herself for his disobedience. She felt that she ought to have drawn clearer lines between neighbor, friend, family, love. She was prepared to play dirty. She didn't care if we hated her; she knew we'd thank her later. One day at breakfast, she slipped Irshad a photo of his cousin.

"'Look how pretty Sara has become!'

"Irshad tipped his head and looked.

"That same afternoon, Ammi Jaan invited a local busybody lady friend to tea and babbled on about arranging a match for her son. Irshad was going to have a beautiful bride. He couldn't take his eyes off the girl's photo. The busybody came straight over and babbled to me.

"The next time we met, I threw a book at Irshad's head. 'I hear you are marrying your cousin.'

"Irshad tried to deflect my anger. 'I have to shut down Abboo's publishing house. The bank won't extend another loan. The new management is prejudiced.'

"But I couldn't empathize, not when something even more dire hung over my head. Irshad was that dire to me, more dire than bread. He couldn't see it then, nor could I convey it. All I wanted to know was if Irshad wanted to accept his cousin's hand in marriage, if my world was going to come crashing down.

"Irshad lost his patience. 'Can't you see I have bigger issues to deal with? Maybe I should marry my cousin. At least she will understand. At least she will care for something more than herself.'

"I couldn't believe the words coming out of his mouth. 'If that's how you feel,' I said, 'you shouldn't come here again.'

"Irshad, as recalcitrant as me, tucked his book under his arm and stormed out. I heard him hop down to the parapet of the neighbor's terrace. Just like that, he was gone.

"His house, that pretty pink house that had also been mine for all my life, prepared for a wedding. Daily, Ammi Jaan invited jewelers, flower sellers, caterers. I could hear her negotiating with the shopkeepers, telling them she wanted to spare no expense. I had to leave the house and the city. I couldn't bear the thought of sitting in the same small room, working on the same paintings. Art had connected me to Irshad. I had to sever that connection. I wrote to my cousin in Delhi, asked if I could visit for a while. When Sulochana said yes, I hopped on a train. At the time, I didn't know I was pregnant.

"Three months later, when I discovered the truth at a doctor's office in Delhi, the news didn't so much frighten me as give me a silent energy. The doctor suggested a way out. Briefly, I considered it, but after Sulochana's offer of help, I dismissed the thought. I knew in my bones I'd made the right decision. I had loved Irshad, loved him from the beginning, when he'd first smiled at me from behind Ammi Jaan's skirts, offering me not only his love but his mother's as well. By the time

Sulochana offered to take the baby, I didn't care what came next. A sort of insanity had prevailed. 'You are Muslim,' I whispered into the pillow. 'I am Hindu, we aren't meant to be.' I swam against the current until my lungs ached. Irshad and I had exhausted one another. After spending our whole lives together in such close quarters, we needed a break. I didn't know if we would be together again, but I no longer felt afraid or sad. For the first time I felt bold, and aware of a new mechanism inside my body, like the opening up of a new chamber in my heart."

Bebe relinquished her hold on Ila's hair. She rested her head on a pillow. Neither Ila nor I had it in us to comfort her.

August 1946

1

In Multan, a town three hundred kilometers southwest of Lahore, they rented a terrace room in the main market square in a house that belonged to a tomb caretaker. With his salary as editor of the local newspaper, Chhote Nanu could afford little else. He wouldn't let Nigar Jaan part with her family jewels. She had grown up with extravagance, with caretakers and access to a royal purse. He didn't want her life to become bleak, lest she hold a grudge and leave him.

But Nigar Jaan wasn't the sort to complain. She kept busy with her collection of poetry journals and with drafts of his articles, helping him with edits. She'd studied at St. Andrew's in Kalimpong, her command of Urdu, basic Farsi, and English impeccable. She could have joined an office as a typist, worked alongside him at the press, or run a factory making aircrafts like Rosie the Riveter, and the other American women he read about. He worried that she'd take the move to a small town as a step backward. But Multan was a kinder city than Lahore, full of the tombs of saints. No one knew them here. It was their time to repent and return to God.

"Not that you have anything to repent for," he told her at night in bed, the lamp snuffed, the lights from the bazaar dancing on their walls. They didn't resemble the lights of Heera Mandi, salacious and loud and stigmatizing, and he hoped she could see that even though they lived in the market, they had their little private life, untouched and secluded, and it belonged only to them.

"Do you like it here?" he asked her, inching closer. "Do you miss home?"

"You ask me the same questions every night," she said.

He was the one to choose Multan. The City of Saints, drinking from a wholly different river than Lahore. While it thrilled him to no end that she surpassed him in every field, his having made the choice for them made him feel her equal, her protector even. Oftentimes he felt like a child and she the adult, leading him, guiding him. He hoped that one day she wouldn't realize this and leave him.

"I want you to be perfectly happy." He kissed her good night. "Tomorrow we can go to the shrine," he whispered. He liked to end the day with a promise, so they had something to look forward to.

Soon, they had something else to look forward to—a new addition to their family. Nigar Jaan was expecting. Chhote Nanu nearly fell over when she told him. Every morning since he heard the news, he rested a hand on her tummy, introduced himself to his child, claimed his child. The gods had forgiven them for their individual misdemeanors and given them this gift. Their world was going to change for the better, for the very best.

Because they were still getting to know each other, Nigar Jaan didn't tell him that she had been to the shrine every day for the last four months to pray for the good health of their child. Her second one, she would never let out of her sight; it would grow up with her until her old age. She would make certain. She had trained her inner eye on this child. She felt aware of its existence from the moment of its conception, when an ache traveled down her belly and into her lower back and stayed there for days. Two weeks later, she gave up her morning tea, the eggs smelled foul, and she knew she'd been granted a second chance.

Chhote Nanu wasn't simply malleable, he had a gentle temperament. He never once raised his voice, not at the editors that rejected his stories, not at the milkman, who always came late in the mornings and made Chhote Nanu late to work, not at the cock that crowed before the crack of dawn and clucked about importantly amid their washed clothes hanging on the clothesline. He never once accused her of incompetence at housework. She'd never had to wash clothes or boil an egg, and he didn't expect her to start now.

"You must think I'm a real *mem*," she said to him, trying to get a reaction. "I'm afraid I have failed as an Indian housewife."

"You are a very good *mem*," he mocked her playfully. "I should call you memsahib."

He teased her, but he didn't complain. He washed their clothes, even cleaned the house. The jail had taught him to be self-reliant. And hungry for company. Every morning, he woke up before her, made himself tea, prepared her chair with her Kashmiri shawl laid out for her, and waited. He came home for lunch, bounding up the stairs calling her name, didn't leave her out of his sight the whole evening.

Their marriage ceremonies had been quiet. They walked around a fire in a small temple, after which they sat separated by a white sheet and said "*qubul hai*" three times at the shrine. Their landlords, the tomb caretakers, a man named Firoz and his wife, Khadijah, witnessed the ceremonies, and afterward hosted a little party for them on the terrace with a meal Khadijah prepared. Firoz and Khadijah didn't have children of their own, but the whole town knew them and came to bless the newlyweds, to eat Khadijah's biryani, and to listen to Firoz play the flute.

They were going to be both Hindus and Muslims together. Chhote Nanu tried to grow a beard to look the part, and Nigar Jaan installed a small brass idol of Krishna on the mantlepiece.

They'd managed to make a little life far away from the ghosts of Lahore, both surprised that they could each conjure up the determination to stay away. It was easier for Chhote Nanu: he continued to nurse his anger and disappointment in Barre Nanu for not visiting him in jail. Nigar Jaan had a far more pressing concern tying her to her present. She'd committed body, heart, and soul. Her perpetually swollen ankles and the ink on his fingers were proof they could thrive, they wouldn't fall through a hole in the universe.

Only, they couldn't hide from the specter of their former lives for too long. Multan might have escaped the chaos of Lahore, but one day trouble came to the town of saints. A goods train arrived at the station, its walls marked with the message: "Goodbye wogs! We quit India!" written in white paint. The departing tommies didn't look back with forlorn eyes at the receding country vistas, not the mountains, not the streams, not the milky falls. Their numbers began to dwindle rapidly, and the only place to spot a British face was at the train station. The week after, the viceroy announced Britain's plan to quit India. He had invited the Congress to form an interim government. Only problem was, the Muslim League didn't wish to participate. The Simla talks between the League and the Congress had failed.

A few days later, in Calcutta, in the far east of the country, League leaders made fiery speeches in favor of Pakistan to be carved out of the northwest and the east of India, in states where the Muslim population far exceeded the Hindu one. Things turned violent at the rally. Hindu and Muslim militias clashed, brandishing daggers, homemade country bombs, guns, and army grenades. Within hours, thousands of men and women lay dead on the streets. The scenes were such that even the reporter on the radio choked up. Whole trucks, he said haltingly, were packed with dead bodies, three, four feet high. Blood flowed on the streets like a river.

Chhote Nanu worried the violence would move north to their City of Saints. Here too, Muslims and Hindus might clash over the question of Pakistan. "I should have picked someplace remote. Kalimpong, Simla, Pondicherry."

Nigar Jaan continued on with her knitting. "You couldn't have predicted this, *jaan*."

He watched her ensconced in the wicker chair, a picture of health, their future in her hands. All he wanted was to keep her safe.

"Why can't the Congress and the League agree?" Chhote Nanu couldn't understand it. Their leaders had sat down countless times with the English serving as negotiators. But the greatest talking heads of India and Britain couldn't find a compromise on the question of Pakistan or no Pakistan.

"They want two different things," Nigar Jaan said simply. "The Congress wants an undivided India, and the League wants Pakistan."

He took her hands. "What do you want? That is all that matters."

She released her hands from his, tucked them under the base of her belly. "I want this."

"But what about after? We could move to Kalimpong. Or Nepal. I want *her* to turn out just like you. Wherever you want to move, I will agree to it. What does it matter if the country is called India or Pakistan or something else?"

She rested her head on his chest. "*He* can go to school here too, turn out like *you*."

He planted a firm kiss on her forehead. They would stay in Multan until the baby came. The little life they'd created would decide everything. In the meantime, they would ignore the outer world.

But the outer world refused to remain quiet. After the Calcutta riots, as Chhote Nanu had feared, the violence did indeed spread north and west like an infection, decimating communities heretofore peaceful in central India, in the north, and finally northwest in Lahore. At a public fair, Hindu attendees argued with Muslim shopkeepers; the argument turned bloody. A Hindu mob torched the Muslim part of town. In response, Muslim mobs destroyed Hindu businesses. Neighbors resorted to the "eye for an eye" policy, forgetting Gandhi's adage that this sort of behavior would leave the world blind. "Better blindness than cowardice," gang leaders opined in Lahore newspapers and on radio shows.

Chhote Nanu came home one day, and Nigar Jaan could see his distress.

"What is it? What's happened?"

"There was a fire in my mohalla in Shahalmi. Where we live. In Lahore."

"I should have encouraged you to make peace with your family. Go before it is too late."

"But how can I leave you now?" She was due in three months. While Firoz and Khadijah were helpful, they were old, and couldn't be relied upon for everything. Nigar Jaan had stopped going to the markets alone. What with her swollen ankles, she avoided tasks that required her to stand or squat for too long, such as making herself porridge or a cup of soup. Chhote Nanu had been taking care of the house. How would she manage without him?

"You are only going for a few days," she said. "I promise I won't soil all the clothes."

"I won't be gone for more than three days, or even two. I only need to see them once." He volunteered to check on her mother. He would ask her to come back to Multan with him. Nigar Jaan needed her mother. They could ask Khadijah to let them have a second room downstairs. As long as no one knew their past, their present and their future would be secure. Once their child came, they could rent the house next to Khadijah's. They'd visit the *dargah* as a family, offer prayers to the saint buried there, gather the white flowers from the mulberry tree that grew at their doorstep. Its fruit would continue to fall until winter; Nigar Jaan could make a jam or pickle it with Khadijah's help.

As they ate the *khichri* Khadijah had brought over, Chhote Nanu kept looking at Nigar Jaan. "Maybe you should come too," he suggested weakly. He had no idea if things were safe in Lahore. He didn't want her to face the rough streets, her neighborhood full of vile.

"I don't want to travel." She took a morsel of rice. "I prefer my peace and quiet."

"I will come running back, I promise. I won't listen to Chai or my brother to stay back. Even if they promise the world, I won't listen."

The next morning, he held her hand as she stood at the threshold, bidding him goodbye. He knew he had touched her with the sincerity of his love. He hoped he had restored her faith in the world, undone the horrible thing the superintendent had done to her. He stood taking her in, her honey skin, her black hair left loose, and her face that had become even more tender, a reminder of her acceptance of him.

2

The train reached Lahore at midday. As soon as he stepped off, Chhote Nanu regretted leaving Multan, his blanket of quietness. Lahore station had turned into a raucous chorus of mechanical sounds. People pushed and jostled, the departing tommies yelled at him to get out of the way. A huge troop marched toward the first-class compartments, their faces set, an army of resigned brown-skinned red-shirted coolies behind them, carrying their impressive luggage. English ladies, the few left, looked peeved, and a little spooked. One madam in a stiff white jacket counted her seven-piece safari luggage repeatedly and shouted at the Indian coolie, accusing him of theft, while the fellow swore on his life he hadn't taken anything. Where would he get the energy to haul off one of her elephant-sized suitcases, he reasoned. Chhote Nanu wondered if he might see the warden or even the superintendent departing, but there were far too many unfamiliar faces.

A new kind of meanness had taken over the markets. Ration shops displayed crude handwritten signs that announced not the price of lentils and rice, but the kinds of customers they would serve: "Hindus Only," "Muslims Only." He entered a lane and read one kind of sign, entered another, read the other. One section of the market looked abandoned, the old shops shuttered, street dogs strutting up and down the lane freely. Another lane boasted a whole new set of shops. New families had moved in. The newcomers regarded him with suspicion. Only frowns greeted him.

Chhote Nanu went past Anarkali Market, looking for Tabrez's ration shop. Tabrez was the one who'd greeted him when he got out of jail. He walked the whole length of the street but couldn't find the shop. He turned around, passed the same businesses, and then he saw it. The room had been emptied like a cave, its shelves vacant. He stepped over charred wood, smashed glass, and a metal sign with Tabrez's name painted on. Tabrez was crouching in the back. He gathered fistfuls of rice from the floor, returned them into a jute bag. He saw Chhote Nanu enter, but he was in no mood for a chat.

"Who did this to you?"

The shopkeeper emptied the jute bag of rice into a ceramic canister. "The war stopped in Europe and moved here," he said, his voice laced with regret. "I should have posted a sign long ago: 'No Hindus.'" He rested his head on his palm. Grains of rice fell from his hair. "You can keep shouting 'Hindu-Muslim Bhai-Bhai' until you're blue in the face. It won't do you any good. They want you to pick a side. If you don't, they come and smash your shop."

Chhote Nanu's heart sank. "Which side did you pick?"

"It's been picked for me, hasn't it? Pakistan. Lahore will go to Pakistan."

"What about Multan? Will Multan go to India or Pakistan?"

"Everything west of Lahore will be Pakistan."

Chhote Nanu and Nigar Jaan would become citizens of Pakistan. He sank onto his haunches, tucked his chin between his knees. Would Pakistan accept Hindus? Ex-convicts and women previously in the trade? He'd heard that Jinnah Bhai was very modern. "Jinnah Bhai will let Hindus stay in Pakistan, won't he?"

"I don't know what to tell you, except, now I see the need for Pakistan." Tabrez's heavy eyes surveyed the floor; half his merchandise lay spoiled. A smashed pot of gooseberry preserves had already attracted a determined line of ants.

Looking at things from his perspective, Chhote Nanu saw the need for Pakistan too. Who'd watch for Muslim interests otherwise? A worry snaked into his heart. What if Barre Nanu and Chaiji moved to India? If he stayed back in Multan, a permanent border would separate them.

"You better leave, Chhote." Tabrez nodded to the door. His face shook with an empty resolve. "If a mob sees you in my shop, there's no telling what they might do. Also, I'm no longer serving Hindus." He thrust a small lump of jaggery into Chhote's fist as a parting gift. A shaft of sunlight bore through the window and revealed the wasted flour lingering in the air, flour that would only be served to people on the right side of the divide.

Chhote Nanu went west. The city had changed. The scent of burned wood permeated the air. On the other side of Mori Gate, where he expected to see a neighborhood behind the wool mills, he saw a clear sky, an open road, as though a monster had swallowed a chunk of the lane. He asked a passerby what had happened to the houses behind the mill.

The man looked at him perplexed. "They burned the houses down last week. Where have you been?" Chhote Nanu couldn't believe his eyes. An entire neighborhood had vanished, erased like it were an etching in pencil. A hundred homes and even more people had disappeared, their houses dismantled into rubble. He stood on the remains of which friend's house, he couldn't be sure. "I used to come here to eat bhatura. I used to fly kites on a terrace . . ." But which terrace? How to imagine a terrace, a set of stairs, walls, windows, vistas, out of a pile of rubble?

Chhote Nanu walked through the markets, the loss of fellow feeling evident all over the city. He was pushed, shoved, not greeted, not recognized in the city he'd spent all his life in. At the civil station, outside Lawrence Gardens, all the signage had turned green and white, the colors of the Muslim League. Everywhere he looked, the posters screamed "Pakistan! Pakistan! Pakistan!" The Hindu RSS and Congress factions had all but disappeared, having shifted their operations to Delhi and Amritsar. Europeans had dwindled to one in a hundred. No more army jeeps buzzed by. He wasn't knocked off the street once.

He turned into the old nawab's mohalla. His feet stopped. He stood outside Samrat's old mansion. He'd spent the better part of his childhood here, chasing his friend through the vast corridors, lying on Samrat's bed practicing English, then cursing the English.

The bottom floor of the once-stately, four-story house had been converted into a shoe factory. A sign outside announced the headquarters of Qaumi Leathers. The door was open, and he walked through. Piles of rawhide lay in the courtyard. A blue tarpaulin ceiling had been stretched under the open sky to protect the merchandise from rain. The air smelled of decay. In one room, craftsmen sat on the floor, hammering nails into soles. Once, Chhote Nanu had derived his sense of grandeur from this mansion and the various ramparts of the East Wing, where Samrat's father lived, and the West Wing, where his mother lived. The wind would whoosh through the colonnades in the courtyard. Now the air felt stifling. Workers went past him without paying him any mind. A slightly better-dressed man in a black overcoat and a child on his hip locked a far room and came toward him. The child had helpless kohl-rimmed eyes. When the father's eyes landed on Chhote Nanu, his feet stopped.

Samrat's first reaction was to cover his face with his hand, as though he expected Chhote Nanu to punch him. He angled his body to shield his boy from Chhote Nanu's gaze.

"What are you doing here?" he asked urgently.

Chhote Nanu could see that he was no longer welcome in his old friend's house. Some friend, who'd made no attempt to ascertain his life or death, left him to rot in jail.

"I'm afraid I can't invite you in. We don't live here anymore." Samrat said uncomfortably. "Amma and Abboo sold the house to a shoe factory. We are moving to India." Samrat and his wife would leave as soon as their funds had transferred. He continued to shield his baby, so that Chhote Nanu saw only half its face.

While Chhote Nanu rotted in jail, Samrat had enjoyed a normal life, acquired a family, planned a future, made an informed decision as to which side of the border to live on.

"Aren't you going to introduce me to your son?" Chhote Nanu said savagely.

Samrat's grip on his child tightened. He appeared resigned, his combed-back hair topped with the velvet boat-shaped Gandhi cap, an acceptance of his fate and that of the nation.

"This is an old friend of your baba's," he said to his son. The child dug a chubby hand into his mouth. Chhote Nanu's bitterness shifted inside his throat.

"I'm in a bit of a rush." Samrat's breath came out heavy, as though he'd been running.

His old friend was asking Chhote Nanu to leave, to let bygones be bygones. A year ago, Chhote Nanu wouldn't have allowed that to happen, but now he had a family of his own. Now more than ever, he understood the value of moving on. Soon, he would have a child like Samrat's. Soon, he too would know the primordial urge to slice the head off any man who dared look at his offspring.

Chhote Nanu swallowed his anger. "I didn't come here to bother you. I'm here to see my brother. I return to Multan tonight. To my wife." To Nigar Jaan the beautiful, he wanted to say. The details of her face, a vision he could conjure easily, he wished to flaunt like a treasured jewel. But his old friend had disapproved of the dalliance. He might still consider her a market woman.

A shadow lifted from Samrat's expression. "You married? That's the best news." A smile dissolved the sanguine craters on his face. He swung his child, who giggled with delight. "You are living a normal life."

No thanks to you, Chhote Nanu thought bitterly.

"Why did you move to Multan?" Samrat asked.

"Multan, Lahore, what does it matter where I live?" Chhote Nanu said, feeling foolish. Even old Tabrez had made a choice. Informed ex-gang leader Samrat had as well. "You don't think Multan is a good choice?" he said suddenly, falling back into an old pattern. "Where is it safest? Lahore? India? You always know more: more about the riots, more about bombs—"

Samrat covered his son's ears, pressing the boy into his bosom. "Don't bring all that up. We were silly boys playing with fireworks. That time has gone."

"Silly boys?" Chhote Nanu felt incensed. That's not how the old Samrat had preached the idea of revolution. He'd sung about liberating India, about Bose and the INA. Chhote Nanu had gone to jail for Samrat's principles. Had Samrat tossed his principles away? What about the old newspaper cutout of Bhagat Singh? Had he burned the revolutionary's face? Tossed out the books about the Bolsheviks? His old ancestral haveli had turned into a smelly shoe factory. A bloody shoe factory! Didn't he care?

"The time to do anything revolutionary is long gone," Samrat said, his head hanging low, his lips grazing his child's head. "Thugs are running the show, the goons of all these political parties. All our old idealism amounted to nothing, Chhote." He raised his eyes, and for a moment, Chhote Nanu caught a glimpse of the old fire lurking behind them. But just like that, the spark was gone. "Maybe the INA changed the tide against the English. Or maybe they didn't. Who knows really why the English are leaving. But now that they are, there is no need for Indians to come together. Now all everyone cares about is getting a share of the spoils. All these parties and their goons are ready to carve up the subcontinent. Our bomb, yours and mine, it had a purpose—driving out the British, bringing Mutton to justice. What are these new rogues in the street fighting for? They're only killing each other."

A great change had come over Samrat. The old bomb maker had washed his hands clean of his days of misdemeanor, rolled up his posters of revolutionaries, sold his books on the Bolsheviks, or likely burned them. He had a point, though. Ordinary life was the best kind of life.

"Go back to your wife. The time when boys like you and I could dabble in politics is over. We dreamed of an India once. This is not that India."

Chhote Nanu reached a finger to touch Samrat's child, and this time his old gang mate didn't shrink back.

Chhote Nanu considered returning to Multan straight away. But he would regret coming all this way and not seeing his family. He persevered through Shahalmi Market. But, as he'd feared, his old childhood house was locked, Barre Nanu and Chaiji nowhere in sight. His neighbor told him he'd find his family at their old cloth shop. He continued to the market.

The family boutique had a new sign. It was now called Ansari-Khatri Tailors. There, inside the shop, in the gloom, sat Barre Nanu, mending a trouser seam.

Chhote Nanu leaned on a handcart parked outside to steady himself. His brother was alive!

A second person sat beside him, tucking a shirtsleeve under the needle of a sewing machine. He had to look again to recognize her. His mother's hair was gray and wild, her kurta mourning white. Chhote Nanu leaned further into the handcart, tipping it down.

◆

Barre Nanu looked up and saw him.

In another minute, Barre Nanu stepped into the street, trying to make out the face of the man who'd been watching them.

"Praji! It's me."

Barre Nanu recognized the voice. He threw himself on his brother, squeezing him so tight, he heard him cry in pain. How much Chhote had grown, nearly as tall as him, hair wilder, face hiding behind a beard. He dragged him into the shop.

Chhote Nanu fell onto his mother's feet. She had no idea who he was. Barre Nanu had to force her hands onto Chhote's head, dig her fingers into his hair. "Yes, this is your son come back from jail, from Andaman, from hell." She began to cry, began to whip him with the tape measure.

"You naughty *shaitan-ki-aulaad!* You ill-timed miscalculation. Where did you go? Where have you been all this time?"

Barre Nanu too gave way to his rage, shaking Chhote Nanu, then pulling him in for a hug. "You were released last year. Why didn't you come home right away?"

Chhote Nanu sat in his brother's shop, hugged, coddled, kissed, feeling as though missing limbs had been returned to him. But then his old indignation returned. If he'd kept away for a year, they'd kept away for longer. In all the twenty-nine months he'd spent in prison, his brother hadn't visited him once, nor written a word. While he pressed oil, suffered the superintendent's cane, Barre Nanu had launched a business. Chaiji had likely wiled away countless afternoons in gleeful hymn singing with her friends. He resented them their twenty-nine months of freedom, their three years without him.

"You didn't visit me once, think about me even once." His voice filled with bile. "You've been busy at your shop."

"Once?" said Barre Nanu. "You little rascal. I did little else except think of you." He waved his hands about the room. "The only reason this shop exists is so that I could get one glimpse of you."

"Nonsense. You have been making all this money while I was suffering in jail."

"All this money?! You don't know the half of it." Since the war ended, Barre Nanu's business had come to a standstill. The tailors had abandoned him, and all his efforts to make civilian clothes had come to naught. The rationing from the war had continued. The yarn shortage made it impossible to buy cloth. And no one would lend him an anna. The moneylenders were moving to India by the truckloads. The boutique, if it could even be called that, Barre Nanu explained, was only a facade, a place to take Chaiji to so the empty house wouldn't torment her. They'd been mending clothes for Muslim families who were kind enough to employ them despite the segregation.

Chhote Nanu regarded his mother. She'd stopped dyeing her hair. In her widow's white kurta and white shawl wrapped about her face, she'd acquired a pronounced air of austerity. Babuji had been her scaffolding, her reason to look presentable. Even her affection had dried up. She turned away from him and focused on threading the needle. The concentration on her face made her look much older than she was.

Chhote Nanu turned away from their mother's deterioration. This would never happen to him; it would never happen to Nigar Jaan. They would take precautions to never need each other so much. He took a breath. No, he would need her. If she left him, he would break apart like Chaiji. Nigar Jaan constituted his whole world.

"Praji," Chhote Nanu whispered to his brother, taking another breath. "I married the woman from Heera Mandi."

Barre Nanu's eyes dilated like a bullfrog's. He dragged Chhote Nanu to the door. "Are you out of your mind? She is not our sort of person. She isn't even . . . she isn't even Indian."

Chhote Nanu turned to his mother. "I married her, Chaiji," he blurted. "I married the woman from Heera Mandi."

"What is he saying?" she asked Barre Nanu.

"Your *bevakoof* son married the superintendent's mistress."

Chaiji slapped her forehead. "Wasn't it enough she sent you to jail?"

"She did not send me to jail."

Barre Nanu slapped him. "Don't raise your voice at Chai. You have lost all sense of right and wrong."

Chhote Nanu's face was smarting. His brother hadn't come to see him once in prison and yet he felt as though he could dictate Chhote Nanu's life. Chhote Nanu had faced the superintendent's blows. Faced starvation. "I can marry whomever I want," he repeated himself. "I don't have to listen to you."

Barre Nanu tossed his head in displeasure. "Don't listen, then. Go and live your life. Why did you come back?"

"Why did I come back?" His brother had cast him out of his heart. "I heard our old mohalla caught fire." He fought back tears. "I was afraid you or Chai—"

"Our lane was spared. If you cared about our well-being you'd have come straight home from prison instead of chasing that market woman."

"I came! I came straight home. But the house was locked. The neighbor told me about Babuji's passing. Why isn't Chaiji at home?

Why have you put her to work? Are you so desperate for money, Praji?" Chhote Nanu looked around the shop. The six sewing machines whirring all at once certainly ought to produce a decent revenue.

Barre Nanu slapped his brother once more. "Yes, I am desperate for money. I gave every anna I made to the constable, so I could see you. He had me believe he would take a bribe. You are the reason I started this shop. Six workers worked very hard for years. Chaiji is nearly blind from all the trousseaus she mended. All for nothing."

The news hit Chhote Nanu harder than Chaiji's curses. "But why didn't you write? The other prisoners got letters."

"Chaiji wrote every month. I made so many trips, I lost count. But every time they threw me out. The wardens intercepted our letters. I took sweets, I took clothes, I took money. Nothing softened their wicked hearts."

Chhote Nanu felt as though he was going to faint. His brother had written, revived the old shop for him. Chaiji had written. She'd cried, prayed, fought with her gods, tucked her head low and sewed by a lamplight. Babuji had died hoping. In return, he'd cursed them, run away, denied them his love. The knowledge made him sick. He wanted to plunge into the Ravi and never emerge.

"Is that why you married her? To spite us?"

Chhote Nanu couldn't speak. His mouth felt stuffed with cotton.

"She was involved with the superintendent. She is the reason he didn't let us see you."

"Praji!" Chhote Nanu covered his ears. He couldn't hear his brother speak ill of Nigar Jaan. She wasn't a jewel sitting in the market. She was a jewel no matter where she sat. And what she had given him, and was about to give him, far surpassed anything he could ever deserve. He had to return to her.

"Praji, I am going to be a father. My wife is expecting my child." He inched closer to Barre Nanu, heart full of remorse. "Talk to Chai. I want her blessing."

The news caused Barre Nanu to take a step back. A new kind of coldness possessed him. "Saving you once ruined me. I cannot save you a second time." He turned away and returned to their mother. He took the mended shirt out of her hands and added it to a pile of finished clothes.

Chhote Nanu dove toward his mother's feet. "I am to be a father. If you love me, come see us in Multan. Ask for the Bahauddin Shrine. We live with the caretakers." He waited for the cloud of worry to lift off his mother's face. He waited for her to place her hand on his brow. But she buried her face in her palm and kept it there until Barre Nanu handed her another shirt for mending, nudged her to resume work. Chhote Nanu gathered himself off the floor. With a broken heart, he turned away from his mother and he left his brother's shop.

3

Back in Multan, Nigar Jaan heard a knock on the door downstairs. She wondered how Chhote Nanu could have come back so soon. Oh, but how she would love him if he had! She had just made herself a breakfast of sweet porridge and dried fruit. Their kitchen was small, but Chhote Nanu had bought her the electric toaster she wanted. He'd put a table and two chairs near the stove so she could sit near him while he cooked. Their little room had all the comforts she wanted—a reading nook and rattan chairs. She dogeared the page she was reading in *Majlis-e-Ravani*, a magazine published out of Lucknow. Chhote Nanu would fill up the silence with news from home. She hoped he'd seen her mother. She needed her here. She put the water to boil. Her husband would want tea. Her husband. She felt a warmth spread through her body at the thought. She heard footsteps on the stairwell, and her heart beat. But when she opened the door, she found not Chhote Nanu but Superintendent Mutton staring at her.

From across the terrace, he strode toward her. Every bone in Nigar Jaan's body told her to hide. But her legs felt rooted into the ground. How had he found her? It had to have been the doorman. Her mother would never. Nor Shehnaz. Maybe something had happened to Henry. It had been a month since Shehnaz had sent news of her son.

Mutton parted the clothes on the clothesline and stood before Nigar Jaan. He wasn't wearing his uniform. Still, in his tweed jacket and cravat, he looked official. Had his post ended? He was gazing at her hard, his button eyes small and mean, his mouth smaller. She wanted to retreat inside her room and shut the door.

"There you are," he said in his familiar way. "I thought you would like to know. Henry came down with a stomach flu." He took a step closer.

How could she not speak to him now? The sun hit her eyes, but she couldn't lift her arm to block the light.

He hovered above her so that his shadow fell upon her face. His proximity confused her; he hadn't changed since she'd last seen him, the same pink complexion, the lines on his hands hard and dry. She turned away and walked into the room, hoping he'd magically disappear. But of course he didn't. He followed her inside.

In his usual proprietorial way, he surveyed her new house, curious about her current life. He paused by the bed that hadn't been made, took in the books that lay around, a pile by the rocking chair, several by the window, where she'd thrown cushions to sit and read. He circled around her and came to stand facing her.

"Did you not hear me? I came to tell you your son is not well."

She had to look at him. His eyes had seen her boy more recently, his hands had touched him.

"How is he now," she asked.

"It looks like you no longer care."

His gaze came to rest on her stomach. Her arms shot up to protect it. But then he stared at her through Henry's eyes. How much he looked like Henry right now, the side parting in his hair, and the cowlick at the back, exactly like Henry's. She told herself he wasn't Henry, he was Mutton.

"Are you headed back?" she managed to ask. "To England?"

"You would like me to go far, far away, won't you? So you can live your sin in peace."

She shut her eyes at the accusation.

"The Raj is packing up, you may have heard."

She had heard.

"I don't know if you know, but it is no longer safe for us to be here. Just the other day, someone threw a brick at my jeep. I know I am hated, I don't care about that, but last year I could have made arrests. I am quite powerless now."

Maybe it was one of the many people you tortured, she wanted to say. But she no longer cared for his safety. He mattered only as far as his connection to Henry.

"Well. That is why I am here. To take you."

She was certain she'd misheard. "Where? To Lahore?" She swallowed a hiccup.

"To England. If you like. Or we could make a home in Dublin."

After all this time! After all that had happened? She caressed her stomach.

"About that—I know a doctor."

"It's too late for that."

"In that case, have it. Leave it here. You will have your hands full with Henry. He will start school in a few weeks."

She knew that. Which institute had Mutton picked? The one in Dehradun? Or the one in Kalimpong for Anglo-Indians? She'd always pictured Henry going to St. Andrew's, like her, wearing the gray trousers and white shirt with the school emblem on the blazer.

"I got him his uniform."

Her heart swelled with so much pain, she felt it would burst. What if her little Henry had forgotten her? What if he saw her in the street and turned away? She couldn't help but ask: "Does he ask about me?"

Mutton didn't answer. He pursed his lips and smiled. He was enjoying himself.

"Why do you want me to come with you?"

He took a step toward her, but his gaze wasn't threatening. In fact, he lifted one of her fingers, brought it to his lips, and kissed it. "It's been very hard." He looked at her the way he used to, scanning her head to toe, and suddenly she was transported back to their first days together.

She understood what he was trying to say. It had been hard not just for Henry, but for Mutton. She knew his life. He had no friends. The only company he kept were his servants, whom he paid. Her too, in a way, he'd paid, but they had love between them once.

"This is no place for us. Even for you. They won't stop to consider the nuances of your skin. They will make one rash judgment based on your hat, your clothes, your shoes, and that will be that. In England, we can give Henry a good life. We can start fresh. Let India go to the dogs. Or gods. It's all the same, anyway."

Only he could wish India to the dogs, not her. She was Indian. She was! India no longer had a place for Mutton, who was hated and English and cruel. But there was plenty of space for her. She had more in common with Chhote Nanu than with Mutton. That's what they'd decided, hadn't they? She dug her fingers into her hair, it was spinning so, and the room with it. She tried to bring the objects in the room into focus—the bed with the blue sheets, the cushions in their silk teal covers, the table in the kitchen with its azure tile top.

Mutton looked about the room. "Your lover boy has nothing to his name, no prospects. You've known him all of two days. Let me make it easier for you to decide. They won't spare you. You're not all that Indian, you know. You can't stay on. It's simply not safe. This new Pakistan, as they call it, well, you know what the name stands for. It's going to be run by clerics. There won't be a place for you here."

She looked at him. His little kiss on her finger still burned. This man she'd once loved. And Henry, her dearest one. How had she gone for so long without seeing her dear boy. He had been waiting for her all this time.

"The time apart has taught me things. I am not the same man as before."

Nigar Jaan sank on the bed. To choose a life of comfort and safety with Mutton and Henry, or to give up on Henry and risk it all with Chhote Nanu? She turned to the window. Outside, on the dome of the shrine, pigeons came to roost in the early evening hour. She saw Firoz and Khadijah sweeping the terrace, their brooms swinging in long arcs. After the sweeping, their evening would be filled with prayer and food, their community swirling around them, and before long, they would go to bed. They saw her from across the distance and waved. All well? Khadijah pointed to her guest, and Nigar Jaan nodded vaguely. She wanted to shut the window and hide, so she could extricate herself from this scene, their view. But she was part of the sky here. Extricating herself would mean breaking off from a constellation, like a star falling from the sky. It would mean death. But then, living away from Henry had been a kind of death.

◆

The train was packed, the journey slow, with more and more people getting on at every station. In the distance, he saw fires in the passing villages. Were they Hindu homes that burned, the passengers asked, or Muslim? He couldn't tell. In the dark, militias rode on horses across the expanse. Chhote Nanu prayed they wouldn't stop the train. Young men borrowed walking sticks from the elderly in case they needed a weapon, the women pulled out prayer beads and amulets. No one slept. When the train finally pulled into Multan, Chhote Nanu felt as though he'd escaped within an inch of his life.

He raced up the stairs to the terrace. The door to their room was ajar. Nigar Jaan must have risen early, anticipating him. He took off his sandals and washed his feet at the tap outside, calling out to her to see what he'd brought for her—dates from Anarkali Market, a kilo each of almonds and cashews and figs, foods to aid in her delivery, milk sweets from her favorite shop in Heera Mandi. When she did not respond, he crept inside, wondering if she was asleep.

What he saw as soon as he entered his home knocked the wind out of him.

A man lay on his bed, in a state of sudden collapse, one leg flung to the wall, the other on the floor. His arms were spreadeagled, his eyes open. A discreet hole on his chest was marked with blood. Chhote Nanu had to take a step closer, turn the man's head to see his face. The superintendent of police, Mr. Mutton, lay dead in Chhote Nanu's bed.

He backed away, delirious, stepped on a foot. She was sitting in her favorite rattan chair. She bore in her body a similar hole in the same place, only her hands were folded, her head hanging, as though she may have been taking a nap, waiting for him to come home.

He'd woken up inside a dream, but slapping his cheeks, shaking her body, kissing her awake, banging his hands on the floor did not shift the scene. Neither did running into the terrace like a madman, or screaming for help. Khadijah and Firoz came running, and they too beat their heads with their hands.

More people joined the scene and expressed the same kind of bewilderment.

Who had done this? The superintendent had many enemies, yes, but he was plain clothed. His belt had a holster, but no gun. In fact, Mutton's gun was nowhere to be found, and the police took note of this.

The only clue—a chalk drawing of the circle-and-cross symbol, which the police recognized as the INA rebels' calling card. Had one of the INA soldiers Chhote Nanu spent two years with in Mutton's prison done the deed? Oh, why hadn't he murdered them all right then and there?

"Mutton had it coming, didn't he," said the lanky Indian policeman, who knew the orchestrator of the Jallianwala massacre by reputation. "I'd have shot the bastard if I had the chance."

His constables, both Indian, sniggered at their superior's declaration as they moved about the scene. They seemed uninterested in solving the case. They picked up books at random as though they were in a bookshop. They did not express any sympathy. As far as they were concerned, justice had been served at long last.

"But why did they have to kill Nigar sahiba?" the landlady asked, fighting back tears.

"Nigar sahiba!" the policeman sniggered. "She was his whore, that's why."

Chhote Nanu leapt at the officer, but the constables held him back.

"Oye! What is it to you?" The policeman turned to the landlords. "Why does he care if Mutton and his whore are dead?"

They didn't answer. And neither did Chhote Nanu. A few years ago, he had tried to assassinate Mutton. His life had come full circle. Mutton had been killed, but a part of Chhote Nanu had died alongside him. Steeped in shock, his body on fire, he began to tell himself a story: he had come to the wrong address, intruded on someone else's happiness. A man lay in bed, the man's wife sat beside him, a picture of domestic bliss. What greater sign of true love could there be than to die together? Nigar Jaan belonged to Mutton in life and in death.

He took his grief outside the room and pounded his fists on the terrace floor. She didn't belong to him. She had left Chhote Nanu nothing except her body to bury, with the dead child inside her.

August 2002

I asked my mother if she'd kept any of my father's letters. She hung her head. "No." My father hadn't written to me once.

In the courtyard, Chhote Nanu sat under the banyan tree, listening to the pilgrims as they chanted hymns. His eyes were closed. He had lost so much. We oughtn't to begrudge him the opium of religion, let him find his peace any which way he could. He'd been my guardian once.

"Nanu," I dared to disturb him. "Do you know my father?"

He opened his eyes. His expression soured, as though he'd swallowed a lemon. "I never approved of your father. I told your mother not to see him. And look what happened. You were born. Your mother ruined her life and yours."

I felt the gut punch of his words. Still, I persisted: "Do you know where my father lives?"

Chhote Nanu shut his eyes. "He lives in this neighborhood. Two lanes down. Damn stupid of your mother to keep such a thing from you."

That close?

I had to find my father. Ila had a whole stack of cards and letters from hers; in all my life, my father hadn't written to me once.

Where could he be now? The pink-white haveli next door had been locked up and boarded for as long as I could remember.

An old phone book revealed the address of an Irshad Siddiqui as 56/81 Mall Road. Searching a house by a number in this neighborhood was like looking for a needle in a haystack; the divisions and subdivisions didn't follow any order. In a mohalla like ours, buildings sprouted additional floors like grafting; sometimes an entire house came up where no empty plot had existed. If people acquired money, they gave their house a lofty, poetic name, like Dreams or Heaven or Blessing, but the numbers remained random.

I circled the block and entered the lane parallel to ours. So much had changed since the last time I'd walked past. All the nameplates, posters, even graffiti were written in Urdu. Sadly, Urdu wasn't an option for me at school. I'd studied French and Sanskrit instead. It seemed like a calculated move by the government to leave Urdu out of the school curriculum.

The lane seemed to belong to another country, another time. The houses had their own color schemes—more greens and whites and pinks, red roses sprouting from yellow butter cans. The residents sounded more polite, calling each other "darling" and "*jaan*" and "*jaa-nam*." I smelled cardamom, *kewra*, hing, cloves. The young men wore skullcaps, the old sported beards. More and more Muslims from all over the city had concentrated here, where they felt safe in numbers.

I asked for Irshad Siddiqui at a corner shop selling *paan* and cigarettes and Coca-Cola. My neutral outfit of black jeans and a T-shirt set off alarms on the proprietor's face. But then he saw the logo of the Islamic Center of Flushing on my chest, a blue dome flanked by two minarets, and his frown disappeared. He raised his betel-red finger to a house in the distance.

I stood before a modest two-story haveli of gray stone, hiding behind a lush laburnum tree, its yellow flowers in bloom. A yellow curtain on the door blew listlessly in the breeze, beckoning to me. My father hadn't written to me once in all my life. I couldn't be sure if he knew of my existence. I held the yellow curtain between my fingers. I had to go through.

There was no one in the courtyard. A jute charpoy stood under a palm full of sunlight and dancing shadows, and below it a stack of books. A stone fountain hummed in the other corner. Bright orange fish skimmed the water's surface. "Hello," I said softly, but no one appeared. I crept to the charpoy. Most of the books were written in Urdu, poetry collections and novels, and an Urdu primer, a picture book with the Urdu alphabet. If only I knew the language.

A moment later, as though someone had turned the dial on a radio, I heard shouting outside the house. A march was passing by my father's lane. I heard stray slogans—"Vote progress, vote for the Trident. Make your country like foreign, go to the ballot and vote for the Trident."

A man emerged from one of the inner rooms. He saw me kneeling by his books and froze, as though in panic.

"I am sorry, I didn't mean to intrude . . ."

His eyes of light green and amber flashed in recognition, his long, brown, cultured arms flicked as he rolled up his white sleeves. The man from Bebe's last story. The unmistakable light in his eyes was proof.

"I had a feeling you would appear like this one day—unannounced." He drew closer.

"Baba? Is that you?"

Bebe had been sending him photos all these years. He knew about me since I turned two, right around the time Bebe's marriage broke. They'd kept in touch. They didn't meet here in Kanpur, not with so many people watching and disapproving. They met in Delhi, when Bebe's work took her there. They met out in the open, at Khan Market, at Nizamuddin. At the *dargah*, they sat close together on the marble floor, listening to the *qawwali* performers singing and clapping. Sometimes they pretended to be a couple, shared a smile or an anecdote about me. Most times they sat as friends, parted as friends.

"All these years we lived in the same city, in the same neighborhood. You didn't see me once."

"I did see you, *beta*, only, from afar. I saw you at your school shows. On some birthdays, I sent small cakes through the neighbors . . ."

The sound of shattering glass cut our conversation short. Someone shrieked, and the neighborhood was plunged in silence. A second later, we heard drums. The procession marched along the lane. The marchers urged people to vote for the Hindu Party. "Muslim friends, you belong in Pakistan," someone shouted through a microphone. "Vote for Trident if you want to live in Hindustan." My ears tried to piece apart their cries, even though all I wanted was to not look away from my father's face. But the commotion had answered my question. This was what had kept us apart—people and their prejudices.

Then I remembered I'd left Ila and Bebe in a house where our presence had become contentious.

"Your shirt . . ." my father pointed to the ICF logo, the dome in the center, flanked by two minarets. A question formed on his lips.

It was one of Meelad's T-shirts. I must have taken it by accident, but I didn't want the sparkle in my father's eyes to die. "I used to go there."

"To an Islamic center?" A frown clouded his brow. "It isn't safe for Muslims in New York, I heard." So easily he slid into the role of my father, without ever being a presence in my life. He put a hand on my head and kept it there, and the warmth spread through my body as though the touch were liquid. "You will be careful there, yes?"

I smiled back, grateful for his benediction; I hadn't asked for it, it was unsolicited.

Another spot of yelling distracted us, and I grew eager to return home. Suddenly, I had a favor to ask of my father. "Would you like to see Bebe?" It was a frivolous request, but I wanted to see my parents together, even just once.

"That wouldn't be a good idea," he said resolutely. "I haven't been that way in years."

"But our house is only two lanes away."

"It's another world."

I hung my head. The segregation of Hindus and Muslims in our neighborhood had been so complete, they could avoid each other for decades.

"It's hard to believe," said my father, watching my hesitation. "But I have never needed to pass through your mother's lane since I left. Our lives don't intersect."

"But your lives are intersecting now." I placed my plea before him and turned to leave. Why should my father break his principles for me?

"Wait!" he called after me. He reached for a sleeveless half-achkan hanging on a peg in the wall. "This is why I don't have children—" he looked at me and colored. "I mean, any more children. What's the worst that can happen, *haan?*"

We walked through the neighborhood. The march had forced everyone indoors, but I could feel eyes behind the windows. Irshad walked tall until we reached the end of his lane, but as soon as we turned the corner and entered mine, he grew nervous. He was clean-shaven, but he began to stroke his chin, as though a ghost beard had magically appeared to single him out.

"Most of our neighbors are good people," I said. This was true, or had been for the better part of my childhood. But Irshad had lived here longer, seen families move in and out, governments form and dismantle.

"Yes," he agreed. "It was in this lane where I fell in love with your mother. You must have heard the story."

I felt myself blushing, as though he'd declared his love for me. People passed us as though we were two ordinary men, father and son. The corner shop had its shutters pulled low, and beyond it, the proprietor read a newspaper. The buffalo herder herded his buffalos. The composition of our neighborhood, as I saw it through my father's eyes, was a million little decisions to coexist. To carry the weight of a smile, to negotiate small spaces and tight corners. No one here paused to ask or look if your head was covered and how and with what material and what size cloth. The bad element asked you your religion, a force cultivated and transported, its purpose limited. Not boundless, not limitless, not infinite. Only love operated that way. Hate shot like a spear, but love spread as a cloud.

March 1947

1

The riots came to Barre Nanu's neighborhood. Daily, a house in their lane burned to the ground, its inhabitants barely escaping with their skins intact. Families were seen with all their belongings piled high on handcarts or stuffed inside a car, and headed to the train station.

Barre Nanu had a decision to make. Ought he to move to India or stay back? He hadn't heard from Chhote Nanu in over six months. Sooner or later, Chaiji would ask about her grandchild. What if Chhote needed them and came looking? Where would he go, what would he do if he found his big brother gone?

Tijori Uncle packed his Gowal Mandi house reluctantly. He had already sold off two other houses. His funds had been transferred to a bank in Delhi. But Barre Nanu could tell his uncle did not want to part with his favorite haveli.

Tijori Uncle took mournful steps around his living room, putting one foot in front of the other, his jeweled hand scraping the empty wall. He wore a black pinstriped suit, as though he'd arrived at an English funeral. For the first time, he looked small, unfunny in the empty room that had once brimmed with French furniture.

"This move is probably temporary," he said uncertainly. He sipped from a can of condensed milk punctured at the top. His cutlery had been packed, the tea, the teacups. "I should keep this house, one foot in this country. If I miss anything, I can drive to Lahore."

"Or take a bus," suggested Barre Nanu. Surely all modes of

transportation would connect the cities across the border. Everyone, both rich and poor, would want to make the journey. Saying so would lessen the pain of his once-cheerful uncle.

"There is still room in my trunk if you want to send things to India. You are my responsibility, now that Babuji is no more. Although, you've always been a self-starter." He passed the condensed milk to Barre Nanu.

I am not your responsibility, Barre Nanu wanted to tell his uncle. But at that moment, subdued about his move, Tijori Uncle resembled Babuji a little. Barre Nanu took a sip of the cloyingly sweet syrup. What did he wish to take to India? How about his shop, or the lane where it stood, with its unique variety of neem and mulberry and deodar trees. Or how about the Ravi River, where he and Moin Bhai had once swum laps as boys. Or his childhood home. He couldn't believe he had to say goodbye to the room where he'd studied and slept for the past twenty-five years, or the corner in the courtyard where he'd peed as a child and discovered a plant had erupted the next day and believed his urine possessed magical properties. Chaiji too, she had to vacate the room where Babuji had breathed his last breath. It was Barre Nanu's life's failing that he couldn't save his father's house, keep it for Chaiji until her dying day. But they had nothing left, no cash after they'd cremated Babuji and paid a useless bribe. They had to sell their house and move into the bottom floor of another haveli in a different mohalla, by Lohari Gate. Their new landlord, a Hindu, was moving to India. Barre Nanu would have to find yet another accommodation for himself and Chai.

Perhaps they ought to move to Multan, rent a *barsati*, a room on someone's terrace with an attached kitchen and a bathroom. They ought to get used to living narrowly, forgetting they had wingspans, evolve from birds into rodents. Having to do this to Chai, reducing her from three floors and balconies to one floor, and now to one room. He and Chhote had both failed as sons.

"Do you want to send your things to India?" Tijori Uncle asked again.

"Don't you think I should wait for Chhote? He might turn up any day."

"There isn't time," Tijori Uncle said. "The viceroy claims they won't leave until '48–'49 but they might throw in the towel and leave tomorrow. Sell everything and move to India as soon as possible."

But everything belonged to them together, to him and to Chhote. What if Chhote needed money for the baby?

Tijori Uncle sensed Barre Nanu's indecision. "Look, nephew, you are going to regret waiting. It is my duty to warn you." He grabbed his lapels, not possessively, not importantly, but in a gesture of helplessness. He'd failed to mold Barre Nanu in his image. His nephew remained a follower of Babuji's principles. It pained Barre Nanu to refuse his uncle. But all Khatri men were stubborn, bound by their principles. If only they could come together, what couldn't they accomplish.

His uncle caressed Barre Nanu's shoulder. "Don't think too badly of your corrupt uncle. I know you will prosper wherever you go. What with Babuji's blessings and his good moral judgment with you."

Would he? Barre Nanu had his doubts. His shop had tanked. He'd failed to rescue Chhote, failed also to follow Babuji's scruples. Nothing he'd undertaken in the past four years had come to fruition.

Within a month, Tijori Uncle shipped all his possessions to Delhi. He locked up the haveli and gave the keys to his neighbor, just in case the creation of Pakistan turned out to be a hoax, in which case he would return to Lahore. In April 1947, as the hot winds coursed through the plains of Punjab, he boarded a plane to Delhi. He promised to write as soon as he landed. He would help his nephews in whatever way he could, only, he suspected it would take him a while to get back on his feet.

Another month went by. Barre Nanu still hadn't heard from Chhote. It had now been eight months since he'd appeared at the shop. The boutique was the only way Chhote would find him. He couldn't sell it, even though he wanted to hurry up and move to India. Still, he decided to part with some family heirlooms—old furniture, Babuji's clothes. He was prepared to be cheated; he knew he'd waited too long. What hurt more than losing money was parting with the memories haunting their beautiful things—Babuji's rattan chair, where he'd sat to read the papers, the brass lion-head handle on the sandalwood cane that still bore the scent of their father's hand.

Then one day, as if to add insult to injury, Chaiji dropped a bag full of her jewels into the pile growing in the courtyard. Seeing her bare wrists, which had always clanged with two solid gold bangles, hurt him even more. He told her she needn't part with her jewelry.

"Who am I saving these for?" His emotionless, unmaterialistic mother did not turn around. She walked away from her jewels softly. Built only for work, not to reap the joys of her labor.

Barre Nanu hoped to meet a beautiful woman one day, make a family. He felt too shy to tell his mother this, so he said, "Save them for Nigar." He didn't know what to call his sister-in-law. Nigar Jaan wouldn't do—the suffix highlighted her market days. She'd made a home with his brother; they couldn't put her out of their minds forever.

Surprisingly, Chaiji didn't contradict him. She turned back to face him. "Have you heard from him?"

He shook his head. He'd posted several letters, but hadn't received a single reply. "Let's give him two more months." After that time, he would himself go to Multan.

Chaiji squatted by the pile, both her knees creaking. Her elbows poked through the fabric of her kurta. How she had thinned. Still, her long, brooding nose was her nose and his and Chhote's, and possibly Chhote's child's. He knew she ached to meet her first grandchild. She unknotted her bag, opened a red velvet box, revealing a necklace studded with semiprecious green stones. "Give this to Chhote's wife when you see her."

Nathhuram came to appraise the pile. The old pawn wallah had turned into a big merchant. He'd taken out an ad in the newspaper that read: "Departing Refugees!!! Take Notice! Best prices offered for family heirlooms! We buy all!"

"Nathhuram, take mercy on me for old times' sake," Barre Nanu asked.

Nathhuram smiled. "I go by Nadeem now." He shouted for his associates, who cataloged everything in small brown notebooks.

Barre Nanu couldn't look. The old pawnbroker was making a killing, profiting from the exodus. The leather shoes on his feet were proof.

Nadeem offered to pay Barre Nanu six hundred rupees and sixty paise for the whole lot.

Barre Nanu's eyes burned. He wanted to slap the man. Hurt to the core, he kicked a chair. "Take it, take it all!"

2

In Multan, Chhote Nanu had spent several months on the marble floor of the Bahauddin Shrine, half of those months in a state of delirium. People offered him food, dogs licked his feet, and holy men, confounded by his behavior, saw him as a competitor and challenged his knowledge of Sufism. "Go home," they told him. "You have suffered a temporary setback." But night after night, he lay on the floor and gazed at the sky or wept at the sight of a family in the worship hall. The holy men saw him as a harbinger of ill luck and resented him.

Chhote Nanu ignored their taunts. If he could, he'd ignore the kindness of strangers, too, turning away from the plate of fried bread and potatoes the worshippers offered him. Then hunger gnawed at his sides, and he dug through the pile of trash and retrieved a respectable, half-eaten apple.

His old landlords checked on him each night, Khadijah making sure Chhote Nanu had a blanket on his body, a cup of water by his side. She tried to lure him back to his old life, brought him an old copy of the newspaper, but he didn't touch it, and in fact shifted to the opposite end of the courtyard to get as far enough away from them as he could. His old colleagues at the newspaper couldn't get him to return to work, either. He seemed to have lost the urge to do anything, go anywhere.

One day, a young mother walked across the shrine's courtyard, carrying a little boy in her arms. Chhote Nanu's eyes followed the child as he ran from his mother to the man who emerged from the prayer room, his father. The child, flanked by his parents, distributed fruit to the destitute. Chhote Nanu's turn came. The boy held a perfect pear in his small, bright hands. He looked as old as Nigar Jaan's boy. Chhote Nanu had last seen him at the poetry gathering, seeking his mother's arms.

Nigar Jaan hadn't felt the need to share her firstborn with him. She'd hid so much from him, including the fact that she'd kept in touch with the superintendent. She'd mentioned her child only once after their move to Multan. One afternoon, as she sat knitting a hat, she revealed she had great expectations for their baby. "I want our child to be a teacher. He is going to be someone respectable. Though not in the civil service."

"How do you know it is a he?"

"Because *he* is in exchange for something I lost."

"The superintendent's boy?" Instantly, he regretted his words, regretted also that Nigar Jaan didn't wish to talk about the child. She'd made it clear she didn't want him involved. She'd instructed Shehnaz to keep an eye on the boy; any more, and the superintendent might suspect.

"I wish we could bring him here, raise him with his brother."

She put a hand on her belly and caressed it in a way that made Chhote Nanu feel at once proud and helpless and vulnerable.

Chhote Nanu bit into the pear the boy offered. It tasted sweet and overripe. He thanked the boy for the fruit, and the child ran to the next pauper, his parents following him. Nigar Jaan's son had lost both his parents. Chhote Nanu felt a dull ache in his heart. He hadn't tried very hard to get to know little Henry. If only he had insisted they snatch the boy away from Mutton, she could've cut off all ties with the superintendent, and none of this would have happened. He tossed the core to a dog. After a minute, he rose and hobbled in the direction of the train station. He had to see about Nigar Jaan's boy, the one who'd survived.

Nigar Jaan's mohalla had all but disappeared from the map. The three vast havelis where most of the women lived had been burned and gutted. Their bare brick structures were charred, their stairs smashed. Some doors had ugly signs: "This is Paak-istan, not Paap-istan, Sinners not Welcome in the Pure Land of God."

Nigar Jaan's house was locked, a wooden plank nailed across the doorframe. After a lot of inquiries to the peddlers in the market, he learned that Mrs. Jamal, Nigar Jaan's mother, had moved to the other side of the walled city, into a mohalla near the Akbari Gate.

Mrs. Jamal opened the door. She wore a black *salwar-kurta* and a black scarf over her head. Despite her mourning, she looked staid, calm, still beautiful. Her skin was alabaster, lighter than Nigar Jaan's, her eyes bright with emotion. If Nigar Jaan had lived a full life, she would look like her mother one day.

Chhote Nanu was worried she'd kick him out, refuse to speak to him. But she pointed him to the sofa, took a seat opposite him.

"The coroner said that it was a boy," she said.

Chhote Nanu felt a stabbing in his heart. He wanted to turn into a rock, so he could feel dead inside; he wanted to both run away and bury his head in her feet. "I shouldn't have left her, not even for a minute." He broke down. He could feel her shifting closer to him, pressing a hand against his back. After a minute, he said, "I came about little Henry."

Mrs. Jamal's eyes shone like two lamps. "It must not have been easy for my daughter to talk to you about him." She looked at him meaningfully, as though she understood something pivotal about his and Nigar Jaan's relationship.

She called for the boy, and a six-year-old child came running from one of the rooms, a stuffed bear tucked under his arm, the same one Chhote Nanu had rescued at the wrestling match. He had Nigar's face and Mutton's blue eyes. No other part of him looked Indian except the size of his eyes. He stared at Chhote Nanu for a minute. Then, growing shy, forced himself between his granny's knees.

"Where are your manners, young man? Say hello to your new friend." She pushed him toward Chhote Nanu.

"Actually, we have already met, haven't we," said Chhote Nanu. "Remember your cycle uncle?"

The boy nodded, put a delicate hand into Chhote Nanu's and mumbled a "How do you do."

Chhote Nanu pulled a sweet from out of his pocket, a slab of Karachi halva, and the boy's eyes glowed at the neon-green treat studded with nuts. *Could I?* His eyes asked his granny for permission. He inserted himself between Chhote Nanu's legs.

"There!" Mrs. Jamal looked pleased. "You have bought his affections."

Chhote Nanu put his arms on his knees, encircling the creature, afraid to touch him. His urge to hold the boy must've become clear, because the child rested a sticky hand on Chhote Nanu's knee and kept it there. He wanted to show Chhote Nanu his room. Mrs. Jamal nodded her consent.

The house looked comfortable: sparsely furnished, with a generous, bright kitchen. Upstairs, several rooms looked unoccupied. Henry's room contained a child's bed, a cheerful blue Persian carpet on which were spread a few picture books. On the wall above his bed hung portraits of his parents. Did he know what had happened to them?

Later, Mrs. Jamal asked him what he thought of Henry.

"You must wonder what kind of a life I could give him," she said.

"Your house is wonderful." He did not know how to reassure her.

"It's the nawab's generosity." Her old benefactor had passed away last year. He'd left her the house in his will.

Mrs. Jamal was well-mannered and gentle, like Nigar Jaan. The world knew her as a "market woman." But in private, she carried the title of "Mrs." Nigar Jaan had told him that her mother didn't want to be called *jaan* after she turned forty. "Jamal" wasn't the nawab's first or last name, just a part of it. How tightly the institutions of marriage and prostitution held hands, Nigar Jaan had once remarked.

"You seem to have everything," Chhote Nanu told Mrs. Jamal. But as soon as he'd said it, he wondered. How long could she keep Henry? Lahore got more and more violent with each passing day. The big markets were shut, the main streets deserted, no police in sight.

At every boom or bang, people ran for their lives. It wasn't safe to leave the house, it wasn't safe to stay inside, either. Armed militias went about targeting certain families and individuals, burning houses and businesses. Would they target Mrs. Jamal for her market days? For her European blood? For Henry? No one looked out for her and the boy. He had to wonder.

"I want you to have him." Mrs. Jamal's face was determined. "I want you to have Henry."

Chhote Nanu felt dizzy. "But he barely knows me."

Mrs. Jamal sank into a chair. "I don't have it in me to raise another child. I am getting on."

He could see her perspective. Setting up a new house, cleansing herself of her old reputation, having to look after a little boy might expose her to new hurts and humiliations. But what made her think he could do the job? Then he thought of Nigar Jaan. Henry was hers. Her body, her flesh. He had no doubt in his mind that he could and he would love Henry as his own.

"Do you really think I can look after him?"

Mrs. Jamal gave him a little smile. "You loved my daughter. You were about to raise a child with her."

Because the tensions in the neighborhood made it dangerous for people of one mohalla to visit another, and because she wanted him to get acquainted with Henry, Mrs. Jamal offered Chhote Nanu a room in her cottage. She cleared a chamber for him next to Henry's. Not that Chhote Nanu had any use for the space. He wrote to Khadijah to send over Nigar Jaan's books, but the postal system in Multan must've collapsed because he never heard back.

Chhote Nanu began to prepare Henry for first grade. They had to hope for the return to normalcy. In the mornings, they read nursery rhymes and storybooks recommended on the syllabus at St. Andrew's, the same school his mother had attended in Kalimpong. Would conditions become safe enough for schools to reopen? No one knew, but everyone hoped. Chhote Nanu wrote to the matron there, to register the boy under the name of Henry Daniel Nigar Nana Saheb Jamal Khatri. The child would carry in his name the constellations that had come together to create him—his mother, his father, his grandmother, his grandfather, his great-grandfather. Chhote Nanu had inserted himself into the mix, reluctantly at first, then with gusto, knowing that he would be the last one left to love the boy. The Hindu last name would make the boy Hindu in the public eye, but in private, Henry would be free to practice whatever he liked. They would move to Bengal. He could find work at a newspaper there. The child's life had been full of setbacks. Chhote Nanu would make sure on his next move he would set down roots.

"You will like Kalimpong," Chhote Nanu told him. "That is where your mother spent her childhood. There will be lots of boys your age."

Henry only had two questions: "Will Granny be there? And you?"

Chhote Nanu couldn't understand how quickly he and Henry had become so friendly. The boy had accepted his parents' deaths as well as a six-year-old could, carrying it inside his body like knowledge of a cut or a bruise, holding himself back from too much joy.

One day, Henry asked him: "Were you close to my mother?"

"Very close."

"As close as we are?"

"Exactly as close as we are."

"Did you love her?" His blue eyes were two shining lakes.

"With all my heart. I would have done anything to protect her." This had turned out to be a lie. He'd failed miserably to keep her safe. Henry hopped out of bed and came to give Chhote Nanu a hug.

Chhote Nanu's heart felt full. "Now we can be friends, you and I," he said.

Henry shook his head. "Friends leave on summer break. Can you be my Baba?"

Chhote Nanu's heart felt constricted. "Do you want me to be your Baba?"

A head full of golden hair bobbed up, down.

Chhote Nanu set Henry down. Could he take Mutton's place in

the boy's life? The man he'd wanted to kill once, could he become father to his boy? "Do you remember your Pop-Pop?"

The head bobbed up, down.

"He loved you very much, didn't he?"

The head didn't move, but Henry's eyes teared up. He couldn't stop himself from crying.

"There, I have you." Chhote Nanu held the boy. "I will love you the same. More, even. I will try to love you more."

Henry was his family now.

But guilt over ignoring his birth family gnawed at him. It had been nine months since he had seen Barre Nanu and Chaiji. What if they went to Multan looking for him? What if they'd moved to India?

One day, he left the house full of compunction, but he got only as far as the end of the lane. A barricade of corrugated iron and sacks of cement prevented people from entering and exiting. A self-appointed vigilante, Nigar Jaan's old doorman, sat behind the barricade and frisked a queue of peddlers, who had to uncover their baskets, over- turn fruits and vegetables, so they could pass through. From some the doorman extracted a nominal fee for passage; to others he denied pas- sage entirely.

Chhote Nanu looked at the rifle on the doorman's shoulder. He pulled out the letter he had written to Chaiji. "I only want to mail this letter to my family."

The doorman laughed. "You think the postmen are working? Everything is shut! You can't pass from one lane to the next just like that. Every lane is demarcated: Hindu, Muslim. Go back home if you want to live."

The peddlers confirmed the veracity of doorman's words. The postal system had collapsed. Dejected, Chhote Nanu returned to Mrs. Jamal's, to his new family, to Henry and to the memory of Nigar Jaan. He ought to embrace his new life. Barre Nanu and Chaiji might live and breathe only a few kilometers away, but an impenetrable wall had been erected between them. If he wanted to live, he had to forget them.

He tried his best to forget them. One night, while tucking Henry in bed, he saw a great mass of fire in the distance. He could hear people screaming, flames roaring. He said a little prayer for his family. God, keep them safe. Protect them from harm. They are kind people. He stayed awake, unable to fall asleep. The next day, he went to look for news of their deaths in the papers, but the doorman confirmed: even the presses had shut down.

3

Minutes before the fire, Barre Nanu consulted the timetable for the train to Multan. He would see Chhote, welcome his nephew or niece into the family, and together the brothers would decide whether to move to India or stay back. Barre Nanu was checking the train schedule when the roof collapsed on him.

The racket sounded like a thunderstorm. He felt insanely hot, as if someone had turned up a tandoor nearby. Beads of sweat collected on his forehead. Before he knew what was happening, a wood beam crashed into a sewing machine. The ceiling fan fell down next, as though hammered through. Then the bric-a-brac of the carpet store above came tumbling onto his floor. The glass display cases crashed into the machines, and the treated fibers singed and crackled in the hot air.

Barre Nanu tried to bat down the flames with the discarded army uniforms, only they outsmarted him and leapt on the worktables. His six sewing machines sat in a pool of fire. He cursed himself for not selling the shop when he could. It had become a second home. He and Chaiji ate their meals here. Chaiji prayed to her gods. Her incense sticks burned, releasing the scent of jasmine. All his merchandise was burning before his eyes. Barre Nanu had to watch it burn.

He couldn't settle for this. He threw his own coat over a sewing machine and put the machine under his arm. The bundle nearly burned off his skin, but he told himself the pain was temporary. He stepped over the rubble to the exit. He pulled the handle, but the door was stuck. Someone had latched the door from the outside. They wanted him dead.

Who would want such a thing? No one who knew him, certainly not his old employees, certainly not his old friend, Moin Bhai. In fact, that afternoon, the weaver had overheard his neighbors talking about the fire in Shahalmi. In retaliation for all the Muslim shops burning in Amritsar, a despicable lot of thugs had doused the Hindu mohalla with kerosene and lit a match.

"You worked there, didn't you, Moin-eya?" asked his neighbor.

Moin Bhai thought of the day Barre Nanu had appeared at his house, sweets in hand, with an offer of a partnership. The money he had earned had provided Jamal with proper medical care. They'd eaten two square meals for four years. He had acquired a new skill: he could make export-quality shirts and trousers. All because of Barre Nanu. What if his friend was inside the burning mohalla? Knowing Barre Nanu, he would be at his shop mending something, unable to let it go. Moin Bhai knew his friend's reluctance to leave Lahore. He was hit with a bad feeling. He ran into his house and shouted for his wife to bring him a spare burka.

Moin Bhai ran through his neighborhood like a madman. In the lanes, men wearing cloth masks carted cans of diesel on bicycles. In other lanes, peacemakers doused the fire with water, telling him not to go any further. He ignored them and slipped past.

The Shahalmi mohalla resembled an orange blaze. A few men hauled junk out of the rooms, whether to save it or to steal it, he couldn't tell. Barre Nanu's shop was on fire, the Ansari-Khatri Tailors sign blackened and illegible. The latch was notched shut. He yanked it open, terrified of what he would find inside.

Barre Nanu knelt in the middle of the room, clutching a sewing machine, a hacking cough shaking his body. A wall of fire raged behind him.

"What are you waiting for?" Moin Bhai shouted. Any minute, the fire would leap onto them and consume them both.

"My machines . . ."

"They weigh as much as anvils. Do you want to die with your machines?"

"It's over. It's all over," Barre Nanu mourned, looking at his shop. "Where is Chaiji?"

"At home."

"Thank god for that. What are you waiting for? Come on!"

Barre Nanu pulled him back. "They will see I'm not Muslim."

Moin Bhai forced the burka he had borrowed from his wife over Barre Nanu's head. "Pretend you are a lady."

The weaver dragged his old employer through the burning lane. The fire hadn't spared anyone. Beeju Boot House, Kamlesh Carpets, Tiwari Sweets, all burned equally with their leather, fabrics, milk, the odor of burning clarified butter from Tiwari Sweets scenting the air outrageously delicious. Only after he reached the end of the lane, looked back, and saw his shop from the outside did Barre Nanu realize. He'd lost every inch of floor, the four walls, every needle, every thread, the little cash in the register, all the names and addresses written in the ledger in his neat handwriting, all the hours he'd toiled.

"What was it all for?" he cried.

Moin Bhai wanted to tell Barre Nanu that his shop had given him a new life, a new skill, but there wasn't time. They had to get out of the burning neighborhood.

◆

Moin Bhai's mohalla hadn't been set on fire. Barre Nanu could see cooking fumes emerge from the windows. A group of men were repairing an automobile, a trade he had never before encountered in the neighborhood of weavers. They'd recently moved into the lane from across the new border. Barre Nanu could see distrust in their eyes. They saw Moin Bhai bringing a woman home and whispered conspiratorially to each other.

The weaver's house hadn't changed. The same small courtyard with its locked-in scent of correction fluid and fabric welcomed him back. The leaky tap on the stone tank dripped water onto the floor in a tap-tip-tap-tip rhythm.

Moin Bhai forced Barre Nanu up the stairs. "Hide in the zenana. They won't check the women's quarters."

"They?" Barre Nanu asked. Then he remembered the cold stares of the men in the lane.

"It happened two houses down," Moin Bhai revealed. "A neighbor invited a Hindu *baniya*. The men saw him from the window, drinking tea, yanked him out and dragged him away."

Barre Nanu climbed the stairs.

Upstairs, they turned the bedroom upside down trying to find a place to hide him. Moin Bhai's wife, shy but cooperative, noted that all those places—under the bed, behind the *almirah*, inside a large trunk—were too obvious, the first the men would check when they came looking.

Barre Nanu returned downstairs. If he was to die tonight, he ought to accept his fate.

"You have done enough," he told his friend. "I cannot put your life at risk or your children's." He collapsed on his haunches beside the pit that had once contained Moin Bhai's old loom.

The pit looked different. He'd never seen it empty before. The handloom on which his friend and his friend's father had woven cloth was gone. Not a trace of it remained. "What happened to your loom?"

Moin Bhai looked shaken. "Remember the day I came to ask you for a job? Just after my beloved Jamal lost his arm. I couldn't help myself. I sold my loom as firewood, like you had recommended."

Barre Nanu felt ashamed. How he had hated the loom for keeping his friend locked inside the past. He stepped into the pit gingerly, as though to beg the machine's ghost for forgiveness.

Moin Bhai watched his friend surveying the six-foot-long, three-foot-deep pit. "I have an idea." He instructed Barre Nanu to lay supine against the hot earth, while he threw a blanket over him.

"What's this? Am I to play dead?"

"No." Moin Bhai shouted for his wife to bring all the clothes she could spare. The couple filled the pit with all their pajamas and shirts and shawls.

"What's the point of all this?" Barre Nanu shouted through the fabric.

Moin Bhai put a hand on Barre Nanu's forehead. "Lie down. And don't make a sound." He threw more clothes into the pit, drowning his friend in fabric. Once he'd filled the pit to the brim, Moin Bhai dragged and unfurled a carpet on top, to make it seem like the floor never had a hole.

Around midnight, a group of men knocked on Moin Bhai's door, demanded to search his house. Moin Bhai welcomed them inside as calmly as he could. There were five of them and they carried sticks, an axe, and possibly one of them had a gun, but Moin Bhai couldn't be sure, because the man never pulled his hand out of his khaki drill-trouser pocket. He did not recognize any of them. They likely belonged to nearby villages and were hired by local parties. They didn't look angry or aggressive, only mildly curious, as though doing a routine job. Still, he ought not to be fooled by their ordinariness, Moin Bhai told himself.

They said that they'd seen Moin Bhai bring a woman home.

"It was me," his wife shouted from upstairs. She sat at the top of the stairs, listening to every word. "I went to visit a sick friend a few days ago. He brought me back."

"So you say, sister," replied the tall man in the khaki drill. He consulted the rest and shouted a warning: "We are coming upstairs, sister, you can take purdah." They waited a few seconds, then raced up the stairs. They peered under the bed, opened the *almirah*, gaped at the emptiness inside. They opened the trunk, pulled out a lone shawl. They peeped inside the bathroom. One young upstart lifted a pajama leg and squatted on the latrine without warning. In the kitchen, they overturned pots, ignoring Moin Bhai's wife, who hid in the corner, her *dupatta* pulled down over her face. They scrambled to the terrace and banged the clump of coal with their sticks. The children slept on a charpoy; the men raised their lamps to their faces.

"This family doesn't even have spare clothes," observed the oldest among them.

The fanatic in the khaki drill smacked his friend. "Next time don't wake me unless you have proof." The men looked bored, disappointed. They'd wanted a chance to flex their muscles, beat someone within an inch of his life. They put out their biris and returned downstairs. They turned to leave, but remembered they hadn't checked the first-floor rooms.

The room where Moin Bhai had kept his loom was sparse, containing only a chair and some baskets of bobbins. But then an old fanatic tapped his *lathi* on the carpet. The stick pushed through where the ground wasn't solid.

Moin Bhai's heart stopped. The man in the khaki drill bent to lift the edge of the carpet, and Moin Bhai shouted: "Don't! That is my father's grave."

"A grave? Inside the house?"

Moin Bhai collapsed on his haunches as abjectly as he could. "I must have been ten years old, but I remember the day as if it were yesterday. My father's boss had come for a visit. My mother seated him on that chair, served him tea and snacks on a silver platter. But the boss refused the treats. He had come with bad news—he could no longer afford to buy our cloth. My father was sitting before him on the floor, just like I am. He folded his hands and pleaded. He'd spent all his savings and woven hundreds of yards of expensive muslin. How could he pay off his creditors? How could he feed his family? But the boss didn't budge. The British had raised tariffs on Indian cloth once again. The boss couldn't sell my father's muslin, nobody in the market would buy it. 'Take my advice,' Babuji said, unblinking. 'Stop weaving, pick up some other trade. A lot of weavers are joining the English mills.' Abboo *jaan* couldn't stomach the shock. He couldn't believe that after decades of working together, Babuji would abandon him like that. 'Take me with you,' my father pleaded. 'Whatever you do, I will do it too.' But Khatri Babu's heart was broken, set. 'I don't know what I am going to do, *bhaijaan*.' That day, my father lost the will to live. A few months later, he died in this very room. All I had of him—the muslin he'd woven. I couldn't sell it, but I couldn't part with it either. You may call it storage, I call it burial. One day I might sell it. If God is willing, I might weave again."

The old man with the stick looked chastised. "This is why we need our own country, free of these Hindu *baniyas*, all untrustworthy."

The fanatic in the khaki drill tossed his biri into the corner. "You are not lying, are you?"

"If you think I am lying, you can kill me."

"The carpet looks new. The edges are still curled."

"I stole it from a carpet store in Shahalmi."

The fanatic nodded at Moin Bhai. "Once we have our own country, you will weave again."

Once the men had left and the front door was locked, Moin Bhai peeled back the carpet. After what felt like an eternity, Barre Nanu saw the light, breathed free air. He'd heard everything. Cloth, an excellent conductor of grief, had transmitted Moin Bhai's father's pain of losing his livelihood. He had heard about Babuji's cruel, sad heart too. He felt responsible for his friend's distress. He remembered Babuji's guilt. He finally understood what Babuji meant by taking everyone along, leaving no one behind.

"I cursed your loom once. But now I hope you replace it soon so you can weave again."

Moin Bhai pulled Barre Nanu out of the pit. "It will be easier to continue on as a tailor. Your shop wasn't a waste. It gave me a new skill. It fed my family."

Barre Nanu held his friend's hand. "Once this madness is over, please go back to my shop. See if you can salvage the machines. Keep whatever you want." Barre Nanu regarded the keen eyes of the weaver-turned-tailor. His unbending conscientiousness, his skeletal, elemental purity would prevail. Barre Nanu hoped Moin Bhai would continue running the shop, continue the Ansari-Khatri name.

Moin Bhai promised. He offered the upstairs room to Barre Nanu for the night. The husband and wife would sleep downstairs, in case the fanatics returned.

4

From across a distance of two kilometers, Chhote Nanu watched the Shahalmi mohalla burn. He heard a loud crash, then another. He buried his head next to Henry's, cursing himself for not going to see Barre Nanu sooner. Later in the night, once everyone had gone to sleep, Chhote Nanu went out into the street. He snuck past the sleeping guard. He reached Shahalmi Market, but the shops had been reduced to rubble. He couldn't find his brother's shop. The door must have burned down, the signboard with it. He could see the ceilings of several shops collapsed, all merchandise turned to char. His throat constricted with regret. Needlessly, he shouted for his brother, his mother, but got no answer.

He saw men picking through the rubble; he couldn't tell if they were looting or salvaging. A wave of nausea took over, and he threw up. Reluctantly, he made his way back to Mrs. Jamal's. At the mouth of her lane, he saw the barricade breached, the cement sacks punctured, the guard nowhere to be found.

His heart raced as he entered the house.

Mrs. Jamal, Shehnaz, and little Henry stood before him, all dressed, their shoes on. He detected a strong smell of something burning. Outside the window, a house had been set on fire.

"We have to leave the city." Mrs. Jamal put Henry in Chhote Nanu's arms.

He hadn't time to ask if Henry wanted to take his favorite books.

Mrs. Jamal brushed Henry's hair. "The boy is your responsibility now."

They ran through the lanes toward the railway station to catch a train going they knew not where. Chhote Nanu raced in front, Henry fastened around his torso like a frog clinging to a stem. From time to time, Chhote Nanu looked back to make sure the ladies followed. Mrs. Jamal, lagging behind, waved frantically for him to keep going.

The station overflowed with refugees. Villagers, farmers, day laborers and their families jostled toward the trains. Elbows and knees knocked into Chhote Nanu, pushing him this way and that. He held onto Henry with all his might. He turned back for Mrs. Jamal, but before he could locate her, he was pushed forward toward the platform's edge.

When the train arrived, and the crowd pulsed, Chhote Nanu felt relieved he would get on first. "Amritsar," he screamed over the din, "Get off at Amritsar, Mrs. Jamal." He hoped his voice would reach her, because his body couldn't.

He grasped the door handle and hopped on the train even before it came to a stop. But what he saw inside chilled his bones. He covered Henry's eyes to shield him from the view. Only, the boy had seen what he'd seen—all the passengers lay dead, chests cut open, bellies distended, heads smashed. Men, old and young, women, even children. They all lay dead.

Chhote Nanu pushed back, staggered onto the platform, and smashed his way through the crowd. Already people were scattering. He joined them as they ran out of the station, trying not to get killed in the stampede.

Chhote Nanu carried Henry like a bundle. The men before him were running toward the Badshahi Mosque. He diverged from the crowd, hopped onto the steps of a shuttered shop, but even after an hour's wait, he didn't see Mrs. Jamal. The market nearby, Nigar Jaan's old neighborhood, had long been gutted, but the domes of the mosque glowed untouched, pristine. He raced up the mosque steps.

The mosque's courtyard teemed with people. Families hid in the shadows, with babies and women and the elderly and goats. He hopped over them as he raced to the inner chamber. He found space in the prayer hall and sat there, settled Henry near him.

"Don't speak in English," he warned the child. "If anyone sees you, speak Urdu. Tell them your name is Jamal. Or no, tell them your name is Punnu. Nicknames don't reveal religion." Ought they to pretend to be Hindus or Muslims? He couldn't decide. He pushed back the boy's hair and wrapped the shawl tight around his body. From a spot on the marble floor, a black mark left by someone's boot, he scraped off dirt, spat on it, and smeared it over Henry's cheeks.

"If my name is Punnu, what is your name?"

"Also Punnu." He put the child on his lap and held him.

From the vantage point of the mosque, the city resembled a forest on fire. What wild emotions had gripped his fellow men! He'd felt such emotions once, but for only one man who needed to be brought to justice. Samrat was right. The whole nation had gone mad, everyone killing each other. He wondered if the fire would come for them. Or an axe. Or a bullet. He hoped the Badshahi Mosque would be spared, spared for all eternity.

A low hum enveloped them, and then a series of echoes, as more people joined them in the prayer hall. Someone began to pray. He heard babies crying; a goat bleated. He overheard conversations. People were planning to go to the refugee camp. From there, they would find transport to India.

"Aren't we in India?" Henry asked.

Chhote Nanu held the boy tighter. "We don't know, pet, we don't know anymore."

♦

The next morning, Moin Bhai escorted Barre Nanu home. Chaiji had gone missing. Barre Nanu knew exactly where she'd slipped off to. He ran to his old neighborhood and found his mother in her room, sitting on her old bed.

She bent forward and retrieved a jute *punkha*, rotated the fan in her hand. For as long as he could remember, she'd sat like this on her and Babuji's bed. A deep sense of contentment flushed over her face.

Barre Nanu took his mother's soft hand in his. She paid him no mind. He told her about the shop, but she looked on blankly. Her fingers felt like wet clay inside his.

"Chai," he spoke to her soothingly. "We can't live in this house any longer. We sold it, remember? Besides, I don't think they will spare this lane much longer. Tomorrow they might decimate us too."

Chaiji stopped whirling her fan and looked at him as though he were a stranger. "I am not going anywhere. This is my home. My husband is resting here."

"We have to move to India."

"I am going to die in this house."

Barre Nanu couldn't make a dent in Chaiji's resolve. She lay on the four-poster bed clutching one of the columns. If he so much as approached her with a "but" or a "Chai," she screamed at the top of her lungs.

He dug his fingers into his forehead. He had no one to ask for help. Not Tijori Uncle, not Babuji, not Chhote. Everyone had left. He sat beside her and caressed her hair to get her to calm down.

"No one is taking you anywhere, Chai. Let them come and do their worst." This was their end. They were going to die together.

"Water," she cried, "water."

With a heavy heart, he descended the stairs.

Chaiji wasn't mad. The world had gone mad. How could his house stop being his house? He ran his hand down the white stone balustrade; the grainy limestone marked his arm. Their tulsi plant looked parched. Who would take care of their little garden?

In the kitchen, he filled a tumbler with water. He'd reached halfway up the stairs when he heard a crash. Part of the wall they shared with Ahmed Bhai came tumbling down. More bricks fell out. Ahmed Bhai stepped over the rubble and into the courtyard, carrying a bundle of clothes.

His neighbor looked surprised to see him. "I thought you had vacated," he said, averting his eyes.

It looked as though his neighbor had seen fit to usurp his house. Barre Nanu couldn't help but feel bitter.

"You must think I am doing something wrong," Ahmed Bhai began, dropping his clothes on the floor. He scrunched his shoulders trying to appear small, but there was no hiding the wrestler's powerful build, his neck a small hillock.

Barre Nanu crept down the stairs, unafraid, indignant. "Is there another way to look at it?"

"You must think me an opportunist. But, the same thing is happening in Bengal. My sister is on her way. If I tell you what they did to her . . ."

Barre Nanu's heart skipped a beat. Bilqis had lived next door until she married a man in Calcutta and moved across the country. "What's happened to Bilqis?"

"She won't have anything when she arrives. Not a square of spare fabric, not even a fistful of wheat." Ahmed Bhai squatted by his bundle of clothes. "I want to prepare your house for her. If we leave it empty, they will destroy the lane. If more Muslims move in, they might spare it . . ."

Barre Nanu squatted beside his powerful neighbor. He'd caught Ahmed Bhai in the act of taking over his house. But no urge to push him back through the wall he'd breached consumed Barre Nanu. Instead, he remembered the crush he'd harbored for Bilqis all his life. "She will come! You'll see. She'll come," Barre Nanu said. For every bad element in the world, there breathed a Moin Bhai. He held on to the memory of the weaver's face. As long as this held true, the world would survive. "Have faith in God," he told his old neighbor.

Ahmed Bhai nodded. They sat observing the wild courtyard. Over the years, Chaiji had planted tomatoes, chilies, brinjals, even. The vegetation had been left to its devices; creepers creeping, tomatoes ripening and dying. "What was the shouting I heard earlier?" Ahmed Bhai wiped his eyes.

"Chaiji believes Babuji's soul is resting in the house. I can't convince her to leave. But we must. I should take the next train out—"

"Don't take the train. The trains are not safe. They are butchering everyone on the trains. I told my sister to find an army truck. I will tell you the same thing."

"But Chai doesn't want to leave."

"So let her be."

"But how can I move to a new country and leave my mother behind?"

"Leave her with me. I will take care of her." Ahmed Bhai's face was composed. "Let me do this, in exchange for the house. As long as there is strength in my arms, Chaiji will always have a room here."

"But what about the man I sold the house to?"

"I have squatter's rights. My sister will have rights. You were smart in selling. Use the money for your journey. Leave tomorrow. But whatever you do, don't take the train. Find an army truck. And don't worry about Chaiji. I have her. I promise."

Barre Nanu didn't know if he could part with Chai. But he could, indeed, trust Ahmed Bhai. The wrestler would protect Chai, protect the neighborhood. Barre Nanu felt a sense of safety sitting next to Ahmed Bhai and his powerful body. He pulled out a wad of cash and put it between them, but Ahmed Bhai pushed it away, shaking his head. Barre Nanu's heart hung heavy with gratitude. Ahmed Bhai was taking over his house, but all he felt at that moment was gratitude. His head throbbed with fear of tragedies yet to come.

Barre Nanu slept badly the last night in his childhood home. Down the balcony, he could hear Chaiji's soft snores. By midnight, the crescent moon appeared in the left corner of his window. It looked paper-thin, as though afraid to manifest itself in the city of sin. He sat up to see if there had been more fires, if one was heading his way. But he believed Ahmed Bhai. If Muslims occupied the vacant houses, the lane might be spared.

He slipped out of bed. From the top of the stairs, the courtyard looked small, in need of guarding. Chaiji's vegetable garden needed tending, someone to water the plants, resoil the roses. With Bilqis's care, the vegetation might revive. He hugged himself to keep out the cold. Perhaps he too might survive. And Chhote. "Where are you, my brother?" he asked the night chill. "*Khuda hafiz, Allah hafiz,*" he prayed.

In the morning, he packed a trunk with a few clothes, an army uniform, the first one Moin Bhai had completed at their tailoring shop, and a handful of Chaiji's jewelry. He woke her up. She'd slept well, she said. She'd dreamed of Babuji.

"You don't have to leave the house," he told her, taking her hand. "Ahmed will take care of you."

He couldn't tell if she understood. She waved him away and went into the kitchen.

Ahmed Bhai had left a pot of milk. Chaiji began to make tea, as though commencing an ordinary morning. Mother and son sat on the kitchen floor and drank their morning tea.

"I am going, Chai," Barre Nanu whispered to her feet. He held them tightly. It was best to leave now, when she had no cognizance that she was likely seeing her son for the last time.

"You want some money, my little boy?" She held his ear like she used to when he was a child. She thrust a hand in her bosom and pulled out a coin.

Barre Nanu held the coin, still warm from sitting close to his mother's heart. Without looking back, he picked up his trunk, walked out of the kitchen, out of the courtyard, out of his house.

Ahmed Bhai was right. The railway station resembled a war zone. On the platforms, rows and rows of corpses lay under white sheets. More emerged from waiting rooms on stretchers carried by a devoted group of volunteers. Barre Nanu had never seen so much death. He felt as though he would collapse. He staggered out of the station, at his wits' end. Ahmed Bhai had given him the address of the refugee camp. Barre Nanu ran in that direction, dragging his trunk behind.

In the refugee camp, tents grew like weeds, as far as the eye could see. Families from nearby villages had gathered with as much of their belongings as they could carry: beddings, grain, utensils, furniture. India lay two hundred kilometers to the southeast. Everyone had to make the journey somehow.

A stench rose from the grounds. Villagers had come with cattle. A farmer with a handsome pair of bulls patted their backs. How could he part with his animals? A camel wallah had the same problem. The animals were family. The beasts would have to brave the long journey with their owners.

Past the tents, in the distance, Barre Nanu saw the army trucks. A queue of men and women snaked around the campgrounds, waiting to get a seat. He heard the drivers were charging exorbitant prices. Those who couldn't afford them turned away; they would make the journey on foot.

Others in the camp had better options. A small group of business-men sat sequestered in a large white tent on wicker chairs. Barre Nanu saw someone that looked like his uncle. But of course, Tijori Uncle had crossed safely on the other side. A man haggled with a pilot for seats on a plane. He wanted a seat for all ten of his family members. But then a competitor offered a higher price. The bidding war ended at two thousand rupees per seat.

"As soon as we touch down in Delhi, I will have the plane refueled and sent back," promised the winner.

"Yes, if we are still alive, we will board it," said the other bidder, then turned to another hustler and thrust a wad of cash in his hands.

Barre Nanu joined the queue to the trucks.

"I hear a seat is twenty rupees now," the man in the front informed him. "Money doesn't guarantee you a spot. You might have to wait hours, days."

Another man in the queue chided him. "Why did you say twenty? It's only ten."

The liar shrugged. "You want all of Punjab to compete for a seat?"

Misery made men devious. Barre Nanu wanted to get far away from the cruelty of the people in the back of the queue. He gave up his position and marched all the way to the front. Men shouted, pulled at his sleeves, but he brushed them off. He opened his trunk and put on another layer of clothing.

A horde of refugees crowded near the front. An ex-army wallah with a pistol in his holster collected the fare. Barre Nanu tapped the ex-soldier's arm. The man glanced at Barre Nanu's army uniform approvingly. Ahmed Bhai had told him to dress as a soldier so the army trucks would offer him free passage.

"It will cost you to break the queue," the army man said. "Fifty rupees for a passage."

"I have the money." Barre Nanu dug his hand in his pocket.

The ex-soldier accepted the cash and directed Barre Nanu toward the roof. Barre Nanu climbed the rickety rope steps.

"Baggage will cost you another fifty," the driver said, and Barre Nanu dug his hand inside his pocket once more. "Brothers and sisters, you have to help your fellow passengers," shouted the driver.

Barre Nanu took the hands of strangers and pulled them up.

"Which regiment?" The army man asked distractedly.

Barre Nanu gulped. "Malta. I was posted in Malta."

5

Refugees packed the truck to the brim. The women stuffed themselves inside, the men squeezed together on the roof. Barre Nanu surveyed the camp; he shut his eyes to take the memory of Lahore with him. When he opened them again, he saw an odd sight in the distance—a madman with wild hair and a jaunty gait, running toward the trucks. He nearly leapt off the roof. His Chhote!

"Stop!" he called to the driver, stomping his feet on the roof of the truck. "My brother is alive. Let him on! Let him on!"

Chhote fought his way through the crowd. His clothes looked disheveled. He was alone, without his wife or the baby. He appeared to be carrying a bundle on his back. Barre Nanu pulled him up.

"Where have you been all this time? Where is Nigar?"

Chhote didn't answer. He pulled the bundle forward and unwrapped the blanket. Inside was a boy—six or seven years old with a full head of golden hair. For a wild moment, Barre Nanu wondered if Chhote had fathered a son long ago and neglected to tell them.

On the truck, the refugees hurtled toward the new country. They resented the Khatri brothers for taking up so much space, resented Chhote Nanu for appearing Muslim when he was really Hindu. Barre Nanu had to stuff ten rupees in the unibrowed man's pocket to shut him up.

"Who is this child?" Barre Nanu pressed his brother, but Chhote stared shamelessly back.

"Child, where is your mother? Father? What is your name?"

"*Meraa naam Punnu hai,*" the boy responded. Apart from his name, he did not reveal anything.

That the child belonged to Nigar Jaan was obvious. But why wasn't she accompanying them? What if the couple had had a disagreement and Chhote had taken off with the child? Barre Nanu tried to spot similarities in the two faces, but the boy's golden hair, his blue eyes, his thin pink lips hinted at a wholly un-Indian lineage. Could he belong to the superintendent?

Their truck jostled over the Grand Trunk Road, the fields of Punjab passing them by. Through the woods, they caught sight of the traffic on foot—an endless stream of men, women, and children. Whole towns and villages had emptied. The refugees carried everything they possessed—their cattle, their grain, their utensils, their jewels, their sick, their unborn, their dead, their gods, their ghosts.

An hour later, the truck stopped. They stood at the new India-Pakistan border. A group of soldiers milled about, waving at them, but no wooden or metal fence or barbed wire divided the landscape.

"Everyone off," shouted the driver. "Another truck is going to take you to the next refugee camp."

The hundred-odd refugees stared at each other openmouthed. They had paid for safe passage to a new life, but now they stood in the middle of nowhere. They couldn't even see the foot caravans. Reluctantly, they hopped off the truck and watched the vehicle drive back to Pakistan. The families dispersed to nearby shrubs for shade. When the sun began to inch toward the horizon, people began to panic.

"We are halfway between Lahore and Amritsar," Barre Nanu said to his brother. "If we keep walking along the Grand Trunk Road, we will reach Amritsar by nighttime."

A handful of young men rose off the ground. Their wives and their elders sighed quietly; they had no choice but to follow.

En masse, they walked east, following the Grand Trunk Road, not so grand in places, a mere patch of dust in others. Their caravan consisted of families who'd managed to keep together: single men who'd lost everything, widows, an orphaned child of thirteen. They walked in groups of twos and threes. They had to walk slowly for the sake of the old. The distance of fifty kilometers, which only took two hours by train, was taking much longer. Every ten minutes, someone asked to stop to relieve the burden of their cases.

Chhote Nanu had brought nothing with him, nothing at all except Henry, but carrying the child slowed him down.

"Give me the boy," Barre Nanu offered, but Chhote refused to part with the child.

Henry tugged at Chhote Nanu's sleeve. "Why do we have to walk? Why can't we ride in Pop-Pop's jeep?"

"Pop-Pop's jeep is far away." Chhote Nanu lifted the boy in his arms.

"Why didn't we take it with us? We could have helped so many people." The boy wasn't taught to hate Indians. Chhote Nanu gave him a peck on the cheek.

"You are right. We should have taken Pop-Pop's jeep. I forgot all about it! When we get to India, we will buy a new jeep."

"Who is Pop-Pop?" Barre Nanu asked. "Son, who is your pop? His name is Mr. Mutton, isn't it?"

Neither the boy nor Chhote answered him.

Night began to descend. The road ahead disappeared. Someone lit a kerosene lamp. The caravan could see little specks of light in the distance—a train crawling toward the new country. Had they filled this one with the dead, too? Better to crawl along the road. They kept to their resolve, bearing their burdens stoically, even the families with heavy aluminum cases. They had strength in numbers. They had each other.

The caravan decided to seek shelter deep into a thicket, a safe distance away from the main road. They ought to have had guns, the young men reasoned. The Great War had flooded Punjab with weapons. They ought to have obtained ammunition. But they were simple-minded middle-class folk. Accountants, teachers, lawyers, doctors. No one had held a gun in their lives.

They spent the night in the woods, elected a group of ten to watch over the fifty.

Chhote Nanu chose to stay awake. He tucked Henry next to him, covered the lad with Barre Nanu's army jacket, and reclined on a eucalyptus tree. He hummed to himself to stay awake. The night was bright and starry. A quiet wind rustled through the leaves. His thoughts returned to Nigar Jaan. "I failed you," he muttered. "I shouldn't have left you for a second." He linked his arm with sleeping Henry's and cried for the woman he'd lost.

When he awoke, the sun was peeking through the poplars. Bright beams of light shone through the thicket and poked him in the eye. People chatted, brushed their teeth with twigs of neem. He patted the bundle next to him. Henry must have curled up into a ball. He kissed the bundle and fell asleep again.

Barre Nanu was shaking him. "Wake up! The boy is missing."

"Henry is here," Chhote Nanu grumbled. But no, the bundle next to him was just a bundle—a blanket, some clothes. "Why didn't you wake me?"

"I tried. You wouldn't move."

Chhote Nanu ran through the woods. "Henry! Henry! Beta! Where are you!"

He ran until he reached the road, ran back. He shimmied up a tree to get a better view of the plains.

The caravan tried to help. They dispersed, calling for Henry and Jamal and Punnu. They met nearby villagers and demanded if anyone had seen a golden-haired child. But after four hours of searching, they couldn't find him, not a trace of him, not a scrap of his cloth, not a hair.

The refugees grew restless. They'd spent half the day looking for the boy.

"We have to get going." They had their own lives to get back to.

"Heartless," Chhote Nanu mumbled. A few of them had lobbied to throw him off the truck for his Muslim prayer. Maybe the same men had harmed Henry.

"My brother and I will stay back," Barre Nanu declared. "Everyone else can go on ahead."

"You have no food, no water," someone reasoned.

"Maybe a jackal took the child."

"It must be dacoits." A bold woman held Chhote's hand, trying to comfort him. "Such a beautiful boy, how could they not! They took him means, he is alive. They will keep him alive."

Dacoits was of course a misnomer the British had slapped on the illustrious tribe of nomadic men who lived isolated in the Chamba Valley, high in the impassable mountains by the Ravi River. For generations, they practiced hunting and gathering, eschewing the agricultural phase of human history. They had only one motto: a man must not hoard any more than his stomach or his hands can carry. But then the British descended onto the subcontinent, morphing mountains into roads, making passable that which ought to remain impassable. The new roads cut off the tribe's sacred routes, desecrated the remains of their dead. The elders decided to teach the civilized a lesson. The tribe began attacking British goods trains, stealing coal and selling it at higher prices to the independent princely states. The British responded with guns and laws, criminalized the dacoits and their unfashionable ways.

The tribe lived as outlaws, with their own system of justice. Rumor had it that, due to Partition, their usual sources of income lost, the tribe attacked affluent caravans, anyone who looked like they were traveling with a little too much gold and wouldn't miss it if some were taken away. If this band of Robin Hoods had found Henry, the boy might indeed be alive and well looked after.

"The lady is right." Barre Nanu did not know for certain what Henry meant to Chhote. But he could see his brother loved the boy. "We will go to Delhi and ask Tijori Uncle to help. We can come back with a vehicle, search properly. We can get the police to search."

"How can I leave Henry behind? He's only six. How can I leave behind the only memory I have of—" Chhote Nanu rushed toward his big brother, shoved him with all his might. Dodging the hands trying to catch him, he raced away from the crowd like a madman, spewing curses.

Barre Nanu chased him through the woods and down the Grand Trunk Road. Chhote wasn't simply running, he was sprinting, lifting his knees, kicking back the earth with full force. Barre Nanu couldn't understand how Chhote had got so strong. The jail sentence hadn't weakened him.

Three hundred meters in, Barre Nanu's heart bursting, he heard a honk. He slowed to catch his breath as the promised second army truck pulled beside him. The driver waved.

"Get on," he yelled.

The caravan had hopped on; the men and the women waved to him with desperate hands. Barre Nanu, eager for the collective embrace, could think only of his aching groin, his pounding head. He was bathed in sweat. He accepted the hand of a fellow refugee and climbed on the roof. In a minute, they would pass Chhote and force him on.

But Chhote had vanished off the hot road like vapor. He must have scampered into the woods, because even as Barre Nanu begged for the driver to let him off, a request the fellow declined, he could see the road was empty. Empty for as far as they could see. The refugee women rubbed his back as Barre Nanu broke into a hacking cough, trying to keep the tears away.

"Your brother will find you," assured the wise woman. "Have faith in God."

Barre Nanu had no other option.

◆

Miles away from his brother, Chhote Nanu was losing faith. As he hopped over brambles, his limbs scraped and sore, he knew the tribe of dacoits who'd taken Henry hated the British. They wouldn't keep him alive. But if they did, they'd turn Henry into one of them. One day the boy would appear at Chhote Nanu's doorstep, dressed in a dhoti and kurta, a rifle slung on his back. "Why did you let me go?" the boy would want to know. He had loved Nigar Jaan with all his heart, and little Henry Jamal with what was left of it. He had to find the boy.

August 2002

My father stepped under my mother's front-door awning, his eyes registering a beloved space. He traced a finger on the door hinge, rubbed the dust on his hands and brought the fist close to his heart. How long had it been since he'd been to our house?

"Bebe," I called as soon as we entered the courtyard, my voice full of longing. "Bebe, come down! Look who's here!"

My shouting brought Chhote Nanu out of the prayer room. As soon as he recognized my father, the tree of worry reappeared over his brow.

"What are you doing here?" Chhote Nanu demanded. His face shook, his eyes clouded.

How long had it been since they'd seen each other? Judging from the way my father took in the changes to the house—the pilgrims, the chanting, the food smells—he hadn't looked our way in decades.

"If my father is not welcome here, I can take him up to our quarters," I suggested.

"Wait, wait just a minute!" Chhote Nanu balked. The annoyance drained from his face. He pointed to my father. "Your latest book. I read it. You didn't include all the history of the Bahauddin Shrine." His face didn't contort in pain for once; he looked only a little disappointed.

"What book is this?"

"*A Survey of Punjab's Sufi Shrines*," Chhote Nanu and my father said in unison.

"I have your previous titles too," Chhote Nanu said with a distinct note of pride. "Let me get them." He ambled up the stairs with a newfound energy.

"He would know the Bahauddin Shrine best." My father nudged me meaningfully. "Having lived near it."

So much my mother had kept from me. My father was a writer. He'd been a chronicler too. He'd written about the shrine where Chhote Nanu had built a little life and lost it. My granduncle returned with books—smart pocket-size volumes with beautiful color pictures, shiny pages and pullout maps. They seemed to be scholarly guidebooks on Muslim historical monuments in South Asia. They smelled of the incense in Chhote Nanu's room—jasmine and sandalwood. They'd been published by one Siddiqui Press.

"I am writing about the shrines in Kanpur and Allahabad next," my father volunteered. "I wonder if I can interview you—"

"No," my granduncle said. "I don't know anything on the subject. I haven't been anywhere in India. This country still feels new to me."

"But you read about them," my father pointed out, encouragingly.

Chhote Nanu looked away. Had seeing my father released new recollections of old memories? Partition had chopped his heart into two. My father's books may have helped him to put it back together, even as they reminded him of old aches.

My mother and sister came down the stairs. Bebe saw my father and froze. The way my parents exchanged glances, I could tell they had seen each other recently. She tucked her hair behind her ear, made a concerted effort to smile. I'd never seen my mother act coy. Her youth had returned.

By now the pilgrims had emerged from the prayer room and were staring at our awkward family gathering by the front door. We had no place to go, no living rooms, no parks, no restaurants where we wouldn't be stared at or admonished, not in our town.

My father sensed the discomfort and took it upon himself to defend our case. He led us to the wicker chairs sitting in the far corner of the courtyard, away from the pilgrims. He placed a hand on my shoulder and said, "I hear my child is no longer welcome in this house. It is his grandmother's house, as you know, sahib."

My hairs stood on end. Until a few hours ago, I didn't know my father's name. And now here he was, pleading on my behalf, participating in the family squabble. I looked to Bebe, but she immersed herself in my father, taking in his appearance, reaching a hand to pluck a hair off his kurta. He'd always been part of our family, an invisible, unspoken presence. He was the wound Bebe had inflicted on Chhote Nanu. He came as the bearer of our family history.

Chhote Nanu looked cross. "His grandmother left us long ago."

"Think of your brother, sahib," my father insisted. "Think of the troubles he went through to get this house, the years he spent missing his wife here, the year he spent missing you. He wanted to share this house with you. Why kick his daughter and his grandchildren out?"

I felt a catch in my throat. If grief were a currency, Barre Nanu would have paid for the house several times over.

September 1947

1

After a third army truck deposited him to the refugee camp in Delhi, India, Barre Nanu spent days waiting in queues to receive his life assignment. A disgruntled rehabilitation committee volunteer assigned him an accounting job at the Reserve Bank in Kanpur. Barre Nanu had heard unpleasant things about Kanpur. The town had earned a reputation for its leather, its wool mills, and the 1857 revolt. But then he remembered Nigar Jaan's grandfather had participated in the Kanpur mutiny. He gave up his dreams of settling in Delhi and hopped on the train, hoping that Chhote Nanu would come running.

From the custodian of evacuee property, Barre Nanu obtained keys to 17/81 Mall Road, roughly the same size as the family haveli he'd had to leave behind in Lahore.

He arrived into the new neighborhood in a horse carriage, bursting with hope. The street with his future house ran perpendicular to Mall Road, the main artery, and began behind the telegraph office. The dome of a mosque signaled the presence of Muslims, and Barre Nanu wondered if they outnumbered Hindus. Or, perhaps the Muslims of the lane had departed. Or worse, been forced out. He feared blood, remnants of brutal fights lingering in the streets. His heart drummed as he entered the lane.

But the gray cobblestones looked clean. The street smelled of soap and rain. The interconnected lanes, as narrow as eardrums, recalled his old mohalla of Shahalmi. A similar sky hung on the neighborhood, cut up by a thousand electrical wires. A feeling of tightness clutched his lungs. An old woman swept the steps before her house with a loud bamboo broom. A mosque cleric with a set of books tucked under his arm went past importantly.

The row of houses looked less grand than the one he'd left behind in Lahore; no elaborately carved bannisters or bay windows jutted out. The houses looked basic—brick walls, white paint, cotton curtains. Most rose to two stories, some just one. The only extravagance: a plethora of potted plants on the windows—rubber and roses and hibiscuses. The numbers on the doors did not follow an order—House No. 202 led to House No. 50/56, which led to House No. 20/81. The neighborhood, he would later learn, wasn't preplanned, had cropped up without ordinance or overseers after the mutiny, when a sizable group of Muslims were thrown out of their original homes. Halfway up the lane, he ran into a gang of buffaloes. Their shiny butts ambled solemnly in the late evening air, some plopping fresh dung onto the cobblestones. He maneuvered around the pats.

"*Arré bhai*," Barre Nanu called to the milkman sauntering ahead. "Which one is 17/81?"

The boy pointed to the building behind Barre Nanu. "You are standing before it."

The haveli at 17/81 Mall Road had a name—Tilat Villa—carved in a flourishing English script under the stone lattice that stretched the height of the building. The house had not one, not two, but three floors, unlike the rest around it. Three identical balconies jutted out into the lane, their corners rounded in the art deco style. A Farsi verse under the main-door awning welcomed all guests as part of the family of God. A young banyan growing in the lane threw its leaves over the verse, as though guarding it.

The rosewood front door felt solid, and required all of Barre Nanu's strength to push open. In the courtyard, a gust of wind swooped down on him from the open sky like the breath of God. He felt dwarfed by the three floors and the high, hot flush of pink bougainvillea on the white wall beside the front door. On the other three sides of the courtyard, rooms were arranged around the open space, containing all the mystery of a stranger's house. And yet, the geography, the air, the light, all felt eerily familiar, an echo of the old house in Lahore. Looking at the gloom of the faraway rooms, Barre Nanu half expected Chaiji to emerge from one of them and inquire about his journey, offer tea and solace.

He took a survey of the house. There were living rooms on the bottom floor, a kitchen facing the bougainvillea wall, and two bathrooms with functioning commodes. A white staircase without a balustrade led to the second and the third floors. These contained the bedrooms, with a bed each. Further up, a long terrace stretched out before him, ending in a high wall, on which a delicate trumpet vine snaked all the way across. Potted plants of white frangipani and jasmine crowded the floor. To his right, the high brick wall of the adjacent house shielded half the view, but to the left, the neighborhood buildings ascended and descended as though the notes of a song—the buffalo shed with its thatched roof, the neighbors with their terraces, and in the distance, the dome of a white mosque. The scent of spices roasting in the sun wafted through the air. "*Yah Allah*," cried a woman's voice in a luxurious tone. If he closed his eyes, Barre Nanu could almost believe he was breathing in Lahore.

All this and no Chhote to share it with.

He went back downstairs.

A strange thing Barre Nanu noticed about the house was that the rooms weren't empty at all. In fact, the walls were covered with family photos and frames containing painted verses from the Qur'an. In the bedrooms, the beds were made, sheets and pillows rumpled as though recently slept in. A wardrobe contained a man's coats. Inside a coat pocket, Barre Nanu found a train ticket with a departure date of October 1, 1947. The wall shelves in that room were full of law books in bounded red leather, *Black's Law Dictionary*, second edition, reports from the House of Lords, 1889–1947. Barre Nanu opened a book. The name stamped upon the first page read Barrister R. K. Rehman.

In the other bedrooms, he found the wardrobes full of women's clothes—*shararas, ghararas*, saris, and kurtas in fuchsias and lavenders and ambers. A doll made in Germany sat in a chair, staring at him. A photo on the wall caught his eye—three girls in matching kurta pajamas sat cardboard stiff on a lime-green settee (the one he'd seen in the living room downstairs). The girl in the center clutched her sisters' arms, holding them like shields. She was the tallest, also the prettiest. Her painted lips and sharp eyes hinted at a quick temper. Barre Nanu had to force himself to peel his eyes away.

In the kitchen, the pantry was stocked with steel cauldrons of rice and wheat flour; potatoes spilled from a sack, and inside a copper cage, a parakeet chirped hungrily.

Barre Nanu filled the bird's bowl with water. The previous occupants must have left in a hurry. He knew he had. Maybe this unfortunate family, the Rehmans, hadn't had the time to sell anything, or pack.

Even though the house smelled of someone else's ambition, Barre Nanu prepared the lawyer's bedroom for the night. He hung his military jacket in the teak wardrobe. The bundle with Chaiji's jewels he put inside a drawer behind the clothes. The photographs of Chaiji and Babuji he hung on the pegs on the wall, taking down identical family portraits of the barrister's.

He couldn't sleep. A warm breeze blew through the window, and the jade-colored curtain tickled his ears. He heard the crickets chirping, and then the buffaloes in the shed began to grate their horns against their troughs.

The next day, he moved a jute charpoy into the courtyard. He'd angered the house's spirits. He would sleep under the stars. But even on the second night, he could hear commotion, a picture crashing, a book falling, the house rejecting his things.

He begged the house for forgiveness, returned the barrister's clothes to the cupboard, hung the original photos back on the walls. They ought not to have given him the house. Barrister Rehman was holding on tight. Wherever he'd gone to, he'd left his spirit here until he returned. What if one day he materialized and asked Barre Nanu to leave?

It happened as Barre Nanu predicted. Two months later, early in the morning, he heard a knock on the front door and found a young woman standing before him. She carried two black leather cases. A set of keys hung from a loop on her finger, and the way she knit her eyebrows assertively, Barre Nanu felt as though he'd wronged her in a bad way, even though he'd never seen her before in his life.

She pushed him out of the way, dropped her cases, slipped off her canvas shoes. Written on notebook paper pasted on the sides of the luggage, he saw her name written in English—Attiya Rehman. Below it, the address: 17/81 Mall Road, Kanpur.

"Who are you?" she demanded. "Where are Abboo and Ammi?"

He'd seen her somewhere. Her big eyes bore into him. She'd painted her mouth recently, although the color had worn off. He recognized her as the girl in the photo hanging in a room upstairs, the sister in the middle. She wore a tight pale-pink silk kurta that ended above her knees, a bold choice of fashion.

Barre Nanu realized what was happening. The girl had come back to claim her father's house.

His heart burst with shame. Despite homelessness staring him in the face, he told the girl the whole story. He had arrived from Lahore two months ago. The custodian of evacuee property had assigned him the house, title and all, thinking it was empty.

"He is wrong." The girl pounded bangled fists into her thighs. "The house isn't his to assign. I have the key." She stormed to the door, picked up the lock resting in an alcove, tried to force a key inside. But the key didn't fit. "They changed the locks!"

Someone had come to the house, broken the old lock, peeped inside, decided the place had been evacuated, and slapped on a new lock.

"Whoever did this, they had no right." The girl was breathing hard.

"I can see that now." Barre Nanu felt every bit like a convict.

The girl went about the house, looking for clues to her parents' disappearance.

"When did you see your parents last?"

The girl told him. Two months before Partition was announced, she'd gone on a summer-long college field trip to Shimla to collect specimens of the local flora. They rode up the winding tea-estate roads on mules, took in the majestic mountain views. But one day news reached the peaceful hill station that talks between the Congress and the Muslim League had failed. Rioting broke out in the streets. Then the trains began arriving with the bodies of the dead, and the police shut down the railway station. Stuck there without transport or phone service, Attiya Rehman couldn't contact her parents. After weeks of trying, when she finally reached them, her father instructed her to stay in Simla until the killings stopped. In October he would leave for Lahore, where he would assume the post of attorney general. He promised to wait for Attiya; they would leave for Pakistan together.

But now it seemed the family had left in a hurry. Judging by the state of the frangipani plant on the terrace, her parents and two sisters had left the house a little over eight weeks ago.

"Is that why the government thinks his house was evacuated? Because your parents left?"

Attiya Rehman slipped on her shoes. She sat on her cases, as though waiting for an answer. The two bangles on her forearm tinkled. Barre Nanu thought of his mother. At that time of day, Chaiji would be saying her prayers. He hoped that Ahmed Bhai's sister had made it to Lahore and his house was still standing. Bilqis would never turn Chaiji out. Ahmed Bhai had promised. Bilqis would treat the old rooms with care, forgive the old flush system. She wouldn't reorient the sun, the moon, the winds to fit her beliefs and preferences. If he could benefit from their kindness, how could he not extend it to this girl?

"It seems the custodian made a mistake," he said to Attiya. "Your claim to the house is greater than mine."

The girl burst into tears, a flower shedding its petals. To be helpful, he picked up her cases, put them at the foot of the stairs. She lingered at the staircase, stared at Barre Nanu's feet. "Do you have someplace to go?" she asked.

He took a jagged breath; it felt as though it would rip him into two. "I am new to the city," he said with some difficulty. "Could I stay until I make alternate arrangements? I won't be in your way."

He'd crossed a line. How could a man and a woman, not related and not married, live under the same roof? The neighbors would talk.

"There are so many hotels," Attiya said uncomfortably, "on Mall Road."

Barre Nanu remembered the run-down buildings with leaky pipes, tuberculosis breeding in their curtains. He'd seen a man hacking away on the steps of one. And what if Chhote came looking? How would his brother find him? He'd given the address of this house to the Office of the Missing Persons. Besides, Barre Nanu wasn't ready to say goodbye to this house. It resembled so much the one he'd lost in Lahore. He felt silly to hope, but he wanted Chhote to see this place once, just once. The nostalgia he'd felt, the sense that Lahore had been restored, he wanted to share that feeling with his brother.

"I could pay rent." Guilt laced his voice. Greed also. "I have a job at the bank."

Attiya Rehman passed a hand over her brow. He'd presented her with a dilemma.

"Soon you might make your way to Pakistan. Your family may send for you. Or, my bank might give me housing. The arrangement will last only a few days." Without knowing what he was doing, he took a step toward her, grasped her hand.

Attiya Rehman pulled away. Her eyes were two black nights.

"Please don't talk to the neighbors," she said tentatively. "Don't tell anyone where you live. My father is broad-minded. But he would never approve of this." She picked up her cases and fled up the stairs, her feet leaving wet marks on the steps.

Barre Nanu returned to the custodian of evacuee property, but the custodian refused to empathize. The number of refugees bleeding from the gash of the India-Pakistan border had tripled, quadrupled in the last two months. He couldn't offer Barre Nanu alternate housing.

Attiya Rehman felt similarly stumped. All her friends had moved out of the city. She couldn't decide whether to kick Barre Nanu out, or make her way to Pakistan to join her family. She couldn't reach her family over the phone. Her defenses began to shut down. She entered a deep period of mourning. All she did day and night was to write copious letters to her father and mother and sisters.

"Why did you leave without me, Abboo?"

She tried to imagine her family in their new Lahore home, an old colonial bungalow, her two sisters sitting on a bed in a big room, Barqat reading magazines and Parizaad painting her toes, their mother in the kitchen, their father in the study. They'd been named alphabetically: Attiya, the eldest, Barqat the middle one, Parizaad the youngest. How could they have forgotten the eldest?

Other times she didn't blame them at all. It wasn't their fault they'd forgotten her. They were trying desperately to reach her, sending her messages, calling her on everyone's phones, only the lines were cut.

But what if something awful had happened to them? She imagined her father's intelligent brows stained with blood, her mother's almond eyes bulbous, the color of shallots, her sisters' faces frozen with fear.

✦

The silence upstairs had begun to bother Barre Nanu. He hadn't seen Attiya Rehman in three days. He ought to vacate her house. But the bank had rejected his plea for accommodation. He made inquiries at the telegraph office for both his sake and Attiya's. But the communication lines were still overwhelmed.

On the last day of the month, when it had been a week since he'd seen Attiya, Barre Nanu decided he had to intervene. He went up to see her, protocol be damned.

Dust gathered in swirls on her balcony. He noticed a pile of orange peels, dried and crisp. He took another step, trying to peek inside her room.

"Miss Rehman?" He knocked lightly on the door left ajar.

She slept in her bed, her hair lush and draping off the white pillow. He watched her for a minute, feeling tender, protective.

"Miss Rehman," he said, a little louder.

She woke up with a start.

She wiped her mouth, tucked her hair behind her ear. She didn't ask him to leave.

He noticed the book on her pillow. Salim Ali's *The Book of Indian Birds*. Two storks graced the cover.

"Is that what you studied in college? Ornithology?"

"Cell biology." She shut the book.

He looked about her room, at her life before the chaos. She read books on wildlife and science. He saw her canvas shoes lying near the door, the laces frayed at the end, a block of French chalk next to it. Emboldened by this rare view into her world, he said:

"I know why you are hiding in your room. I wanted to do the same in Lahore, when the time came to leave."

She stared at him with her bright, cold eyes like two distant stars. "You want me to leave so you can have my house."

"That is not what I mean."

She tucked her chin between her knees, pulling the covers about her indulgently. She wanted her childhood to swallow her whole. But this could only be a temporary solution.

"I had a difficult time leaving my childhood haveli. But they burned the other houses around it. I had no choice."

She raised her eyes, sobered by his admission.

"My mother didn't want to leave. She would rather die in her old house than live anywhere else. I understand what you must be feeling."

She breathed deeply. Her former rage had left her eyes. "The house belongs to me as much as it belongs to my father."

"So does the rest of the city." He would drag her out, even if it made him look like a villain, made it seem like he was usurping her house. "The colleges have reopened. Why don't you resume your studies?"

She buried her head in her knees again. "I can't. I have no money."

"Then it is good I am paying you rent."

That week, they shared a tonga for the first time, Attiya Rehman and Barre Nanu. He got off at the bank, she continued on to Christ Church College. When he came home in the evenings, he invited her down to the kitchen, asked about her studies, her day, made sure she ate some dinner before turning in.

After a few months of cohabiting and looking after her well-being, Barre Nanu dared to buy his landlady a present.

One evening, he found her watering the plants on her balcony. She wore a chestnut silk kurta with big white marigolds all over. She looked happy. Her studies were going well, she'd told him about her viva exams, chatting with abandon one afternoon on their shared ride. That same boldness colored her cheeks now.

He extended a small brown parcel toward her. "I went to the market. I thought you might like this."

She pulled the little pink-and-white packet out of the paper bag and sniffed the soap once, twice. "It's a new scent." The pink tulips on the soap wrapper looked pretty. She would keep the paper, she told him, inside a notebook so the scent followed her to class. Or, Barre Nanu hoped, so she thought of him.

◆

Attiya Rehman was tickled by the gift. She wondered where Barre Nanu had bought the soap, if he'd made a special trip to one of those ancient stores in the four-foot-wide lanes of Shivala that sold women's hosiery and makeup. She realized she didn't know if he had sisters; she knew hardly anything about him.

"Is this a brand your sister liked?" she ventured trepidatiously.

He shook his head, didn't say more.

She realized he might not want to relive bad memories. He had secrets to keep, fears and losses that he'd rather not divulge.

"It's my brother's favorite soap," he confessed. "My younger brother."

"Where is he now?"

"Somewhere in between India and Pakistan. We left Lahore on the same truck, but didn't manage to reach India together." Barre Nanu fingered the petals of the frangipani.

She and her parents couldn't even manage to leave town together. Still, the end result was the same: separation. Attiya Rehman raised the soap to her nose, inhaled the intoxicating, flowery scent. Was there hope for the two of them? She didn't know. She was only beginning to realize how much Barre Nanu had lost—a city, a home, a brother, a mother. How similar they were. How much stronger he'd been, pulling himself up and out, pulling her out, too.

Her eyes lingered on his shoes. He dressed well, sent his clothes for ironing. Even his sleepwear of white kurta pajamas was ironed. The fit of his suits was snug, even though he had a svelte figure. His arms, she could tell, were strong. He'd played a sport in college. In the morning, he prepared butter toasts, the scent bringing her down into the kitchen. She liked to watch him move about the courtyard, his hair wet and wavy from the wash. His warmth felt inviting. It recalled the way the house smelled and sounded when Abboo got ready for work.

He stepped back. "Please tell me if I can be of use to you. Nothing would please me more."

Everything about their situation was awkward. But she no longer thought it his fault. He'd tried to look for alternatives, just as she'd tried to contact her family. "Any word from your brother?"

Barre Nanu shook his head. "Every week I go to the telephone exchange to see if they've restored the phone lines to Pakistan so you can call your father. Not because I want you gone. I also applied for a loan to buy land. Who knows when my permit will clear. You might have to face me until we are old."

She smiled at his hope of them living together.

"I want to see you happy," he went on. "Will that be in Lahore? Or here? Perhaps you are the happiest here? In this house? With me?" There. He'd said it.

How many girls had he said some version of this to, she wondered, and then wondered why she wondered about that. There was something unabashed about the way he leaned forward, as though released from a cage or a protocol. A mischievous light played in his eyes.

The watering can had run out of water, and she set it down. He reached for it, offering to refill it, surprising her with his closeness. She didn't step back.

Silence engulfed her when he left. He'd rescued her, she was sure of it; but he'd been calculating. This advance was a calculated move toward resolving the house issue. To her surprise, she felt intrigued that a man with such pluck had taken an interest in her. He'd usurped her parents' house, while at the same time making sure she didn't go without food, fresh air, and scented soap.

✦

In March 1949, when Barre Nanu proposed, Attiya accepted. A common ruin united them. They'd chugged through life blindfolded, with only each other as guides. His forward-thinking outlook, his job at the bank, and her own unequivocal acceptance of him would carry them. A few months later, on a warm August morning, they exchanged marigold garlands at the snake temple with their neighbors Mr. and Mrs. Siddiqui and a few bank colleagues as witnesses. Then they went to the mosque to offer prayers.

2

For weeks after he lost Henry in the woods, Chhote Nanu wandered up
and down the Grand Trunk Road, memorizing every square inch of the
woods near Amritsar. He even camped under the tree where he'd seen
Henry last, hoping the dacoits would return, if only to finish him off. But
after three months of sleepless nights, he'd had no such luck. The refugees
he met on the Grand Trunk Road told him about the organizations that
could help find Henry, so he registered the boy's name at the Office for
the Restoration of Missing Persons, and reluctantly, at the Office for the
Persons Presumed Dead in Amritsar. In the evenings, he offered prayers
at the Golden Temple. The ascetics preached on the eventuality of death.
"It's inevitable," they told him. "It happens to all of us."

"Why didn't it happen to me? Why the little boy?"

The know-it-alls didn't answer.

He enlisted the police, hoping they had a warrant for the dacoits,
but no one reported having seen the criminal outfit. It made sense;
half the locals worshipped the dacoits as Robin Hoods, the other half
felt too afraid.

"Maybe the boy made his way back to Lahore," the police ventured. "Did he have family in Pakistan?"

Could Henry have found his way back on a truck heading to
Lahore? He had only one way to find out.

At the refugee camp in Amritsar, where Muslims waited to make
their way into Pakistan, the officials issued Chhote Nanu an Indian
passport. He had family in India, not in Pakistan. He belonged to the
Indian state; he had no business in Pakistan.

He made rounds to the Office for the Restoration of Missing Persons each day, annoying the clerk at first, then easing the chap into friendship. Chhote Nanu told him about the bomb, the jail, the happy few months he'd spent in Multan. Revealing his losses to a stranger felt easier than revealing them to his brother. The clerk must've heard many such stories, because he reacted with the same clear-eyed concern each time. His upper lip sweated and he dabbed his mouth with a white handkerchief, his eyes pinned to Chhote Nanu's face. Empathy dripped from those eyes, and while no words of comfort escaped his lips, and Chhote Nanu told himself he didn't need to hear them, the telling of his stories was the healing he sought. With a light heart, he returned to the Golden Temple, where he'd been offered the post of roti maker in the kitchen. He'd rented a room near the temple. The hope of seeing Henry kept him going. In this manner, he passed a year and a half in Amritsar.

In reality, however, the clerk, overwhelmed with the incessant inquiries about missing family members from not one but hundreds of refugees, did not welcome Chhote Nanu's visits.

Fed up, one day, the clerk called the Delhi office and asked if someone had reported Chhote Nanu as missing. He supplied them with Chhote Nanu's name, approximate age, and description. He called the Lucknow office next, then Agra, and finally Kanpur.

The Kanpur clerk confirmed that such a man sporting long hair and a military jacket had indeed gone missing near the Grand Trunk Road.

The next time Chhote Nanu came to inquire about Henry, the clerk had the policemen waiting. An inspector and two constables clamped their hands on Chhote Nanu.

"You can't arrest me," he shouted. "I haven't done anything wrong."

"This is the law," the inspector barked. "The work of restoration necessitates your arrest."

"Can't you people understand," Chhote Nanu pleaded as he struggled. "I have to find my son. I cannot go home yet."

The clerk dabbed his upper lip like he'd done so many times, only that expression of empathy was now tinged with impatience. He took his job very seriously. Restoring lost people had become a matter of national pride: ministers of both India and Pakistan had taken vows in the parliament to return each other's lost people. If he could mark Chhote as restored, there'd be one less person the machinery would have to worry about.

"Go home, Chhote," he advised. "Don't you miss your family? We will contact you as soon as we've located your boy."

"Henry *is* my family," Chhote Nanu protested as the policemen dragged him away. They escorted him to the railway station. One of the constables would accompany him all the way to Kanpur.

At the Amritsar railway station, as he waited for the train to arrive, the constable watching him from the corner of his eye, Chhote Nanu's body gave in to fatigue, the fatigue of prison, the fatigue of missing Nigar Jaan, the fatigue of looking for Henry. He felt tired of running in circles. He missed Barre Nanu. His older brother might be harsh, but at least he cared. He missed the normalcy of a friendly face.

He took a seat on the crowded train, the constable's warm skin next to his. The passengers stared at the pair, raised eyebrows at Chhote Nanu's delinquency. He thought of Henry. The memory of the child would grow like a cactus inside his heart. Henry had been given to him in exchange for the baby he had lost. But Henry had gone. Just like Nigar Jaan, just like his baby, the boy had evaporated into to the clouds.

Inside his brother's new house, under the newlyweds' room, Chhote Nanu contemplated the reality of his new life. Barre Nanu had furnished the room with a four-poster bed, a long table, two chairs, and a bookshelf with books on Urdu poetry. Chhote Nanu opened a collection, read a verse, gave up. On the table, he found forms for enrollment into Christ Church College. Barre Nanu wouldn't let him slip through the cracks.

But Chhote Nanu had learned something about himself—he wasn't built for academic rigor. Any interest he'd had in learning had gone. He wanted to do absolutely nothing. Nigar Jaan had left a giant hole. He wanted the world to give up on him.

He couldn't tell Barre Nanu about Henry or Nigar Jaan. He hadn't the words to describe what he'd been through. Not describe, no, retell. Not retell, no, transmit. Convey. Confer. Yes, confer, Chhote Nanu decided. The incidents would have to be conferred, like the conferring of a degree. Barre Nanu would have to study the scenes, relive every painful minute, demonstrate his grasp of them on a test for Chhote Nanu to believe his brother understood what had transpired to Nigar Jaan and him. A mere retelling would not suffice.

The newlyweds dragged him to college one morning, insisted he ought to sit in a class before giving up on college.

Chhote Nanu only lasted an hour into Poets of the Progressive Movement. After lunch, he wandered the city. The park on Mall Road beckoned, with its chirping birds and dancing trees, and he followed the garden path to an opening. He lay on the grass, observing the sunshine. In the distance, the eucalyptus trees rose tall and indomitable. Then they shook with an invisible force, and broke into a thousand screeches. Bats! The trees reminded him of the woods where he'd seen Henry last. He left the park. On Mall Road, he noticed the Office for the Restoration of Missing Persons. He couldn't help himself.

The harried clerks moved about like shadows in the tiny one-room office.

"I am looking for a boy," Chhote Nanu said quickly.

One of the men picked up a pen and opened a register. "Name? Age? Last seen?"

"Eight years old. This tall. Although, maybe this tall now. Hair is golden. Eyes blue-green."

"Name?"

"Henry?"

"Last name?"

"Jamal Mutton Khatri."

"Sounds like the menu of some Delhi restaurant. When and where did you lose him?"

"Two years ago on the Grand Trunk Road between Lahore and Amritsar."

"Did you go back and look for him there?"

Chhote Nanu wanted to smack the clerk. "Yes."

"What relation is the boy to you?"

"Son. He is my son."

The clerk smirked. "You have a *gora* child? You married an English *mem* or what?"

Chhote Nanu turned to leave.

"Wait," the clerk called, intrigued. "I will alert our Amritsar office."

"Don't bother."

The clerk took offense. "I'll have you know, our offices have managed to restore thousands of people. Our network of volunteers is spread all over the country." The clerk pushed a stack of papers across the desk. "Before you go, take a look at this list. See if you see anyone you might know. You help your fellow citizens, and they help you in return."

"I don't know anyone in town yet."

"No matter. Look at the list. Just like you are missing your son, others are missing sons, daughters, wives. You do a good deed, and it will come back to you."

Chhote Nanu's eyes glazed over the names, mostly women and children reported lost or abducted from Kanpur. Fifteen pages long. The names blended into one—they weren't even arranged in alphabetical order. But then his eyes paused. Maybe he even said her name out loud, or perhaps he mouthed it: Attiya Rehman. Chhote Nanu set the papers down. His sides burned. He hoped the clerk hadn't noticed.

"What is it? You stopped. You didn't even look at the rest."

Chhote Nanu felt his throat constricting. "Please let me know when you find Henry."

"Wait!" The clerk called. "Where do you live? We need your address so we can let you know when we find your lost person."

Chhote Nanu scribbled his brother's office address next to his name on the register. "You can write to me here, care of Balraj Khatri."

"We need your home address, young man."

But Chhote Nanu bolted out the door.

He walked briskly down the road. Twice, he looked behind his shoulder to make sure he wasn't being followed. Ought he to tell Barre Nanu? Tell Attiya? The best thing to do was to bury the story, erase the memory of her name on the list.

At home, the walls spun. He sat outside the bathroom to catch his breath.

An hour later, his sister-in-law came home, found him sitting dejectedly.

"You don't have a fever." She felt his forehead. She sat him on a wicker chair, offered to make tea.

"Your old family," he asked as she walked to the kitchen. "Don't you miss them?"

Attiya gave him a coy nod. "My family is here now, no?"

Chhote Nanu waited for his sister-in-law's tea. He tried to shut out the bad memory of the office, tried to think of the dinner Attiya would cook. He forced himself to look forward to a future. Henry wasn't in it. He wasn't in it.

Four years passed.

Then, in the summer of 1953, the Office for the Restoration of Missing Persons wrote to Barre Nanu. They'd located Henry. They needed Chhote Nanu to come by their office for some paperwork.

The old clerk had grown plumper, more confident. "We have a letter for you about your Henry." He waved a slim yellow envelope covered with postage stamps. "But first we need your home address," he demanded, pushing a register in front of Chhote Nanu.

Chhote Nanu had no choice. He scribbled his address in the worst handwriting he could manage.

The clerk squinted at what he'd written. "Is this 17/81 or 17/61? Is that the same haveli where Barrister Rehman lived?"

"How do I know?"

"Find out or I will rip this letter into shreds."

"All right, all right," snapped Chhote Nanu. "The plaque outside the house says Rehman's."

The clerk licked his lips. He adjusted his glasses. "You live in that big mansion alone?"

If only Chhote Nanu had lied. If only he'd nodded yes, how the Khatri fortunes would have changed. But Chhote Nanu, the old fool, couldn't calculate the full design behind the clerk's curiosity. He gave them Attiya, in exchange for news of Henry. "I live with my brother and his wife," foolish Chhote Nanu said.

"Your brother brought his wife from across the border?"

"No, they met here."

"What's her name?"

"I don't know her name, I call her sister-in-law."

"Tell me her name or you'll never read this letter."

"It's Attiya, Attiya Rehman," said Chhote Nanu.

"Aha!" The clerk perked up. He scribbled something on a notepad. "It seems we will have to give you and your family a visit. Have some tea and snacks ready for us, yes?"

Chhote Nanu curled his lip at the insult. "Give me my letter, please."

"Yes," the clerk snorted. "Here's your Henry Jubble-Bubble," he mocked. He rubbed his hands in delight. Finally, after years, he had a lead for the elusive Attiya Rehman. No doubt a great career advancement, a medal, a pat on the back from Prime Minister Nehru awaited him.

Chhote Nanu tore open the envelope as soon as he left the office. He read the contents hungrily as he walked down Mall Road.

Just as the wise woman from the caravan had predicted, Henry had been kidnapped by dacoits, who'd found him wandering the forest, crying for his Pop-Pop.

For weeks Henry rode with them along train tracks as they oversaw the redistribution of goods among the village tribes. One day, the leader asked the boy his name. Little Henry declared the full appellation Chhote Nanu had bequeathed him—Henry Daniel Nigar Nana Saheb Jamal Khatri. The men laughed and wondered why such a small boy had such a long name. But when the leader learned the boy was a descendent of the great Nana Saheb of Kanpur, the rebel who'd fired the first shots in the mutiny against the British, he sobered. They didn't have wealth, he told his compatriots, but they had principles.

The next week, little Henry Jamal rode back to Lahore with the Chamba tribe. The boy remembered the sleepless night he'd spent at the Badshahi Mosque, cloaked under a blanket with Chhote Nanu. The tribe took him to the mosque, which, for the past several months, had been converted into a refugee camp. Tents had been pitched across its vast inner courtyard, spilling into the sacred inner chamber. After making inquiries with the officials, they found Mrs. Jamal. The old lady had been living in the camp with hundreds of other refugees for the past two months.

The tribe felt profoundly proud for escorting the great-grandchild of the famous Kanpur daredevil. They offered Mrs. Jamal a generous amount of money, so the old lady could set up a house.

Mrs. Jamal thanked them, but she had her own jewels she could sell. She asked instead for a safe passage to Bombay. The next day, the tribe hijacked a car, forced the owner to drive the grandmother and grandson and their caretaker all the way to Bombay. The coastal metropolis had been Mrs. Jamal's mother's first stop in India. It seemed an appropriate place to bring up Henry.

In Bombay, she bought a one-bedroom flat, enrolled Henry in a nearby Catholic school.

Mrs. Jamal wrote all this to Chhote Nanu. But on the matter of restoring Henry to him, she disagreed.

She couldn't deny her disappointment that Chhote Nanu had lost her grandson in all of two days. Her separation from the boy had made her realize she wanted to raise him after all. The Office for the Restoration of Missing Persons might be duty bound to return Henry to Chhote Nanu because he'd reported the boy missing, but seeing as how he had no biological connection with the child, and Mrs. Jamal did, she had the greater claim. If he wanted to fight her for the child, she was willing to go to court. But she hoped it wouldn't come to that. She hoped Chhote Nanu remained the same sensitive man who'd once loved her daughter. She wished them to resolve the issue amicably. She would be happy to send him regular updates on Henry, to keep him informed about the boy's life. She wanted Chhote Nanu to know he was growing into a well-mannered child, if shy and reserved. As a memento, she'd enclosed a recent photo of Henry.

Chhote Nanu pulled out the black-and-white studio proof. It took him a minute to recognize the boy. In six years' time, Henry's face had grown gaunt, settling into what he might look like as a man. He had a crew cut, his sides shaved close, his beautiful hair gone. The photographer had seen fit to highlight the blue eyes, as though they were the main feature on the boy, but to Chhote Nanu, who'd known him, Henry's main features had always been his hair and smile. If he hadn't spent a summer with the boy, if he hadn't known Henry the way he had, Chhote Nanu would have concluded that the child staring at him from the photo looked every bit the carbon copy of the late Superintendent Mutton.

Chhote Nanu felt hopelessly inept. As soon as he reached home, he slipped Mrs. Jamal's letter inside a book of poetry. He did not look at the letter again. Nor did he dare to write her back.

That day, he made a resolve never to marry, never to love again. He would be tempted over the years; people would tug at his heartstrings. But he wouldn't let anyone in. He would live his life alone, trusting no one, wanting no one.

3

A year into Barre Nanu and Attiya's marriage, in August of 1950, Attiya suffered a miscarriage. Then in August 1952, three years into their marriage, ten days before their wedding anniversary, she gave birth to a girl. Attiya named her Rehana. Rehana Rehman Khatri. Baby Rehana had Attiya's mother's hazel eyes, and Chaiji's strong Punjabi arms. While her parents celebrated these endowments, they mourned the fact that she would never meet either of these women in her life.

Then, in January 1953, a black Buick Super forced its way into the Khatri lane. From its velvet interior emerged two women, one Pakistani, one Indian, both heads of their respective organizations. Three policemen and a haggardly clerk from the Kanpur branch of the Abducted Persons' Office accompanied them. The policemen knocked on the heavy rosewood door, and, finding it ajar, came inside. They gave a shout for Miss Rehman.

Attiya came down the steps, a five-month-old baby on her hip, surprised to see so many people inside her house.

The officials took in the courtyard, craned their necks to observe the reach of the three floors, looked approvingly at the pink bougainvillea. They pointed to the living room, inviting themselves in.

"Do you know what brings us here?" The Indian lady, the national head of the Abducted Persons Rehabilitation Committee, had her thin hair pulled up into a severe, tight bun. She stared at Attiya threateningly.

Attiya sat facing them on the lime-green sofa, bounced the baby on her knee. Did their visit constitute the new government's plan to reward couples who'd made the best of the worst times? Would they photograph her and Barre Nanu for the cover of *India Today* as Nehru's prime example of a secular India? If so, she felt ready. She smiled coyly, and brushed her hair back with her free hand.

"We are here because of your father."

"Abboo?" The mention of her father reminded her of that morning long ago when she'd appeared at her house, luggage in hand. For a minute, she saw herself standing in the courtyard, shoes on, feet wet, waiting for Barre Nanu or God to intervene. Just then the baby bit her cheek, and Attiya yelped. She put a finger inside the little mouth to feel the little ridge, almost bursting with teeth, almost. She was no longer that girl in the courtyard. She'd become a mother and a wife.

"How is Abboo Jaan?" she asked the officials.

The Pakistani woman took over. Her manner was less severe, more perfunctory. She wore thick glasses that gave her a studious profile. "The attorney general is well. He has been looking for you for a long time."

Attiya felt the sting of the words. "But I was here, in our family home, all this time."

The Pakistani woman rolled her eyes at Attiya's ignorance. "Miss Rehman, over two lakh women and children have been reported missing. A lot of chaos has ensued. Your father had to leave for Lahore in a hurry. He'd hoped to send for you as soon as he could provide a safe passage. But after the riots in Simla, officials initially misreported you as among the dead. When he learned you were still alive, he put an ad in the newspaper. That is how we were alerted."

"Is that all he did? Put an ad in a newspaper?"

"He wrote letters, called every politician he could think of, bribed officials. He came to know that his house had been awarded to a Hindu family. He thought you'd moved in with friends in Delhi or Bombay. He told us to look there. We wasted five years scouring every Missing Persons' Office in the big cities. Then last year the local paper in Kanpur published your law school entrance test results with your full name. Our volunteers saw that. Last week your brother-in-law confirmed you were indeed living in your family house."

It made her feel a little better he'd looked, he'd suffered for her just as she'd suffered for him. "When is he coming?"

"Actually, you have to come with us."

Attiya, overjoyed, jumped up. "Of course! When do we leave? My husband and I—"

"You have to come alone." Miss Pakistan bore into Attiya with her cold eyes. Attiya had been reported missing, and only she could be restored, no one else. Her husband did not count. He hadn't been abducted. In fact, Attiya's marriage to Barre Nanu did not count. In the eyes of the law, she was the abducted daughter of a citizen of Pakistan. She belonged to her father, like a mule belongs to its owner. She had no legal right to marry. Just like a mule or a stool cannot marry.

Miss Pakistan clamped a hand on Attiya's elbow. "Come, Miss Rehman, it's time to go."

"What do you mean? *Arré, suniye!*" Attiya shouted for Barre Nanu. She begged the women. "My daughter is still a baby, how can she live without her father? Please understand."

Miss India pulled Rehana out of Attiya's arms and put her on the floor. If her marriage was illegal, then so was this child.

"What do you mean my baby is illegal?"

"Miss Rehman, in the eyes of the law, an abducted person has no right to bear children."

Miss Pakistan motioned for the policeman to handcuff Attiya. Both countries judged her. How could she marry without the blessing of her father? How could she procreate?

Attiya begged, but to no avail. She shouted for Barre Nanu.

He came down the stairs, saw his wife in handcuffs, and lost his mind. He pulled out his wallet, offered as big a bribe as the two misses wanted. He offered his mother's jewelry. But the women refused to be bought. They belonged to well-off families, they didn't need his trinkets. Besides, they each had a quota to fulfill. The ministers had signed oaths in the parliament: Pakistan and India had promised each other their respective abducted women.

The policemen held him back as the women forced Attiya out of her house and into the Buick. Barre Nanu tried to break free of the constables, but they beat him with their batons until he lost the will to move. They left him in the lane and hopped into the car.

Barre Nanu hobbled after the Buick as it bounced on the cobblestones. Attiya's eyes, her face leaning out of the window was full of panic. She disappeared behind a black burka Miss Pakistan forced on her. She leaned out as far as she could. But she didn't say, "I will be back, I will see you soon." She didn't say, "Take care of my child, take care, bye, *alvida, khuda hafiz, phir milenge*," no, nothing, she said nothing, and she didn't wave.

4

For years, Chhote Nanu resolved never to love.

But Bebe melted his resolve with her constant need for a mother, and Chhote Nanu kept stepping up. He kept coddling her and rescuing her from Barre Nanu's negligence. He took her out for treats of Manchurian dinners and *kulfi* and ice cream snacks. He shared his Urdu books until she took red markers and colored around the calligraphy on every last one of them. He'd purchased his books from old shops that became defunct because everyone who spoke Urdu had vanished. He couldn't say no to Bebe. He nurtured her love for Persian miniatures, bought her her first watercolors.

Her affair with Irshad touched a nerve, and even though he detested that she'd endured the same tragic ending, he gave her his shoulder, nudged her back toward her art and a semblance of love for a second time. Then, her marriage ended, and he busied himself with both her children as the resident grandmother replacement with his cracked feet and poetic temperament. He sang her children songs, Urdu ghazals by Ghalib and Momin and Faiz, so that Karan's first word was "*jannat*" (or so they thought), and Ila's was "*huur*" (or so they hoped).

Then, in 1987, Chhote Nanu came across Henry. In *Women's Era*, a magazine he intercepted from Bebe for the recipes, he encountered an article on the salt marshes of the Rann of Kutch. Stunning photographs graced the pages—white sky uniting with the white earth, a sand-colored camel in the distance with its red-turbaned keeper. The photographer had taken the trouble to include night shots of the

Kutchi tribes, their glistening fireside meals, their mirror-bedecked women dancing in the light. The accomplished photographer Henry Jamal Mouton. The accompanying square-inch photo revealed a handsome blue-turbaned Anglo man whose blue eyes couldn't be subdued, a veritable Lawrence of India. He must've turned forty-six that year. A man now, with a whole life separate from Chhote Nanu; someone who knew about salt marshes and deserts and their topographies. Not a man Chhote Nanu might ever meet or ever have a reason to meet, certainly no one whose life might intersect with his.

Chhote Nanu's hands sweated, the world around him vanished. He sat on the floor with a thud, magazine in hand. With feverish fingers, he plucked a paper from the writing pad, scribbled a desperate note, tore it, rewrote it, and before he could decide against sending it, mailed it to the offices of the magazine. For weeks he waited. Desperately, impatiently, bribing the postman twice just in case the fellow might have any reason to misplace Henry's reply.

Eight weeks later, he received a response, a brief note signed, "The Editor." It read: "Mr. Jamal is in receipt of your letter of inquiry. He wishes not to pursue this correspondence further. Any inquiries on this matter might be discarded without being read." That was all.

Chhote Nanu's disappointment solidified into a rock that no one could shift. He didn't leave his room for days, the days turning into weeks. He ignored Bebe and her children's cries. They tried to draw him out of his sarcophagus of a room. He told them to get lost. He contemplated leaving the house and never coming back. But he feared the ghost of the Office for the Restoration of Missing Persons. The ministry had long disbanded it, but he feared Barre Nanu would go to the police, who'd handcuff him and drag him back home. He begged Barre Nanu to kill him, and when his brother told him to live with the consequences of his actions, he directed his fury at Bebe and her children. Bebe had repeated his mistakes. Karan and Ila would too. They'd give their hearts away to Henrys and Nigar Jaans who'd consume them. He'd been a bad influence. He'd taught everyone to fall in love with the wrong people. He had to get them far away from him. He had to show them how bad he could truly be. One day he tossed their belongings out the window. "Get out, get out of my life," he shouted. "Don't come back here. There's nothing for you here. Go to Bombay. Go to Delhi. There are bigger, better places. Don't depend on two old fogies to take care of you. You have to take care of yourselves. Go live in the future. There is nothing in the past but pain." He shouted at them because he couldn't shout at the dead, or the ones who'd left him and gone.

The neighbors came to their windows to watch. "*Yeh dekho, batwara ho raha hai.* Division of the big house. Partition in the same family. Poor Khatris."

August 2002

My father reminded Chhote Nanu that the house belonged to Attiya.

Chhote Nanu shifted uncomfortably from foot to foot. "I know all this," he said gruffly to my father. "Why are we reliving these memories? Why are we talking about a mother who left and never looked back?" His knees wobbled; he clung to his walking stick with both hands, knuckles white, as though it were a life raft.

I knew why my granduncle had paused my father's narrative. But without a reconnaissance of the past, there could be no forgiveness. He would keep holding on to his grudges. He wouldn't see the history of our distress, nor the origins of Ila's and my rootlessness.

Bebe dabbed her eyes. Her head bowed, she mourned quietly for the memories she didn't have of her mother. She didn't remember Attiya leaving, she didn't remember Attiya staying. All her cruelness and carelessness and bad cooking and her love for Persian miniatures stemmed from this: her not having her mother.

"*Janaab*, you keep forgetting whose house this is," my father interjected. "I had to remind you."

Chhote Nanu's chin wobbled. He wrung his hands on his walking stick. "As if I could forget her. How can I forget Attiya? It's because of me she was taken. I am to blame. If it weren't for me, Bebe would have had a mother. If I hadn't opened my mouth. Your father should have tossed me out."

Bebe wiped her nose on her sari. "The authorities would have found Attiya eventually," she said. "They saw her name in the newspapers, remember? How long could she have hidden from her father?"

"Poor motherless girl," Chhote Nanu's pent up love for Bebe came pouring out. He inched over to her and stroked her head.

Bebe wasn't going to torture him any further. "If it weren't for you, my father might not have learned to love. You set the crazy, impossible example."

Barre Nanu without Attiya, Chhote Nanu without Nigar Jaan and Henry. The brothers had only each other. And baby Rehana and a house full of memories. They had to coax a future out of these, if not for their sakes, then for the sake of Bebe. Bebe stroked Chhote Nanu's hand, traced the veins and the knuckles as though drawing them into existence.

"You did what you had to," she said to Chhote Nanu. "You couldn't look at me and not think of Lahore."

Chhote Nanu nodded at his niece's words, then disagreed with her. "You weren't just a reminder of loss, *beti*. I had you. I had my poetry. But what did your father have? He had only grief."

"My father had his looms."

We looked at the doors to the left of the courtyard, locked for the past year, home to Barre Nanu's six handlooms he'd bought after retiring from the bank. My grandfather had made a promise to Moin Bhai to undo the division precipitated by the British economic policies. He couldn't bring his friend across the border, so he employed the Muslim weavers of Kanpur. Moin Bhai had once said, "Muslims are the warp and Hindus are the weft, that is the fabric of India." Barre Nanu had opened a sari workshop to keep the memories of his friend alive. He'd named the shop Rehman Saris.

"I wish I had the knack for business like your father," mourned Chhote Nanu. "I was completely useless to him. And a whole lot of trouble. He wasted his life on me."

"I wish we could reopen Rehman Saris," I tried. It would take a whole lot of investment.

"Finish your PhD." Ila knocked a fist into my back. "Don't go off starting new ventures without finishing old ones." Ila the wise.

"I have summers and winters off, I could look into it during my breaks."

"Weren't you going to Pakistan in the winter? To Lahore?"

"You're going to Lahore?" Chhote Nanu asked. The pain on his face was palpable.

Was it Lahore I wanted to see? I couldn't say for sure. If I could, I would take a train to the summer of 1985. On one of those afternoons, Barre Nanu sat supervising his sari workshop, Bebe beside him. His weavers swung the beams on the handlooms, his printers stamped woodblocks, and Ila and I ran past the workers. Our game of chase took us upstairs. We flopped on our granduncle's bed. Chhote Nanu, more in love with Urdu poetry than religion, opened a book, and began to fill our heads with the image of the Qutub Minar in Delhi, describing the calligraphy on the pillar, all those elegant, long strokes of the letter *l*. The same minute, the ladies at the temple down the street began chanting, and Ila and I raced to the balcony to chant with them: "*maa daato, maa daato.*" Our childhood felt harmonious at that moment, the picture of perfect peace. Our childhood memories had a season—it was always summer inside them.

"I think I may have met Attiya Rehman's grandson," I announced. "Our cousin."

Ila pinched my arm. "Karan, don't be cruel. Think of Bebe."

"I *am* thinking of Bebe."

Despite my dismissal from the Flushing mosque, Omar, Meelad, and I had remained friends. One evening, Omar revealed that his great-grandfather had been the first attorney general of Pakistan. That is why he'd decided to study law in America.

"That is definitely your grandfather, *janum*," my father told my mother. "A country doesn't have two first attorney generals."

"Maybe you misheard," Bebe said, shifting uncomfortably. "Maybe your friend said second attorney general. Or third."

Chhote Nanu pulled Bebe by her arm. "What does it matter if you meet Attiya or not? Go to Lahore. Look for our old house in Shahalmi. Find your father's weaver friends. Find their families. Bring me back the soil of my old home, and some Karachi halva. Kanpurites don't know how to make it."

We sat in the courtyard, a fractured family. A drop caused us to scan the sky, parse the wrinkles and the folds of clouds for signs of impending rain. This monsoon, like the one in 1947, had been slow in coming.

I opened my father's book, stared at a map of India on the first page. Maps were simply fractures of earth. Maps had cruel hearts. They'd been cruel to our family. If only we could make our home in a season, point to a season instead of an address and say, this is where we live.

Maybe that summer when things went right existed in Lahore. The soil there ought to remember; the trees might sprout memories of my grandfather, my great-grandmother. We had to look to find out. Our visas might be slow in coming, or they might be denied entirely, but we had to try. We had to make the first move.

Bibliography

A truncated list of scholarly books consulted:

Bayly, C. A. *Indian Society and the Making of the British Empire.* Cambridge, UK: Cambridge University Press, 1988.

Bhasin, Kamala, and Ritu Menon. *Borders & Boundaries: Women in India's Partition.* New Brunswick, NJ: Rutgers University Press, 1998.

Bose, Sugata, and Ayesha Jalal. *Modern South Asia: History, Culture, Political Economy.* London: Routledge, 2004.

Butalia, Urvashi. *The Other Side of Silence: Voices from the Partition of India.* Durham, NC: Duke University Press, 2000.

Daiya, Kavita. *Violent Belongings: Partition, Gender, and National Culture in Postcolonial India.* Philadelphia, PA: Temple University Press, 2011.

Glover, William. *Making Lahore Modern: Constructing and Imagining a Colonial City.* Minneapolis, MN: University of Minnesota Press, 2007.

Gooptu, Nandini. *The Politics of the Urban Poor in Early Twentieth-Century India.* Cambridge, UK: Cambridge University Press, 2001.

Jaffrelot, Christophe, ed. *Hindu Nationalism: A Reader.* Princeton, NJ: Princeton University Press, 2007.

Khan, Yasmin. *The Great Partition: The Making of Modern India and Pakistan.* New Haven, CT: Yale University Press, 2017.

————. *India at War: The Subcontinent and the Second World War.* New York: Oxford University Press, 2015.

Pandey, Gyanendra. *Remembering Partition: Violence, Nationalism and History in India.* Cambridge, UK: Cambridge University Press, 2002.

Riello, Giorgio and Tirthankar Roy, eds. *How India Clothed the World: The World of South Asian Textiles, 1500–1850.* Leiden, The Netherlands: Brill, 2009.

Zamindar, Vazira Fazila-Yacoobali. *The Long Partition and the Making of Modern South Asia: Refugees, Boundaries, Histories.* New York: Columbia University Press, 2010.

Acknowledgments

My endless thanks to—

The entire team at Milkweed Editions, especially Daniel Slager, Bailey Hutchinson, and Adriana Cloud for whipping this book into shape, and Mary Austin Speaker for the beautiful cover(s), and Morgan LaRocca for sending this book out into the world.

Sorche Fairbank for never losing faith and for being tireless.

My teachers: Leslie Epstein, Ha Jin, Allegra Goodman, Daphne Kalotay, Fanny Howe, Askold Melyczuk, and Michelle Hoover. Especially to Fanny, who read the many initial drafts. Especially to Daphne, who's been more friend than teacher. Especially to Michelle, whose nurturing I benefit from to this day.

Prof. Sana Haroon for restoring Lahore into my pages and my heart. Sana, I'm so grateful for your scholarship and friendship! This book wouldn't exist without you!

The National Endowment for the Arts and the Massachusetts Cultural Council for their generous and timely gifts.

Jack Jones Literary Arts and Kima Jones for giving me a room with a desk and a view at a critical stage of the writing.

My friends and early readers: D. M. Aderibigbe, Rowena Alegria, Chekwube Danladi, Andrea Gregory, Nazila Hafezi, Adriana Rambay, Jen Soriano, Constance Sherese, and Shubha Sunder, and my Grubbie friends: Colwill-Brown, Kathleen Gibson, Deborah Good, Sharissa Jones, Kim Libby, Alison Murphy, Bonnie Waltch, and Cara Wood.

My early guidepost, Amit Basole, for supplying the initial sparks and to Nandini Basole for being my home away from home for so long.

Hardeep Mann and Jaspal Singh for their Wednesday dals, discussions, friendship, and love over all these years.

Karen Larsen for her jams and jellies and generous heart and Elizabeth Simmons for her creativity and friendship. I love you both!

My bff and habibi Fawzi Nicolas. The day *you* were born was my lucky day. I can't wait to celebrate your novel soon.

Roger Dunn for providing sunsets and surfing lessons at a critical stage of the writing.

Bahar for choosing to come into my life and promising new stories, new springs.

And most importantly, my mother, Neena Wahi, who taught me everything, who continues to remove all my roadblocks, and who like Shahrazad tells me only one family story at a time. I love you so much.

Matt Eames

SHILPI SUNEJA was born in India. Her work has been nominated for a Pushcart Prize and published in *Guernica, McSweeney's, Cognoscenti, Teachers & Writers Magazine,* and the *Michigan Quarterly Review*. Her writing has been supported by a National Endowment for the Arts literature fellowship, a Massachusetts Cultural Council fellowship, a Grub Street Novel Incubator Scholarship, and she was the Desai fellow at the Jack Jones Literary Arts Retreat. She holds an MA in English from New York University and an MFA in Creative Writing from Boston University, where she was awarded the Saul Bellow Prize. She lives in Cambridge.

milkweed
EDITIONS

Founded as a nonprofit organization in 1980, Milkweed Editions is an independent publisher. Our mission is to identify, nurture, and publish transformative literature, and build an engaged community around it.

Milkweed Editions is based in Bdé Óta Othúŋwe (Minneapolis) within Mní Sota Makhóčhe, the traditional homeland of the Dakhóta people. Residing here since time immemorial, Dakhóta people still call Mní Sota Makhóčhe home, with four federally recognized Dakhóta nations and many more Dakhóta people residing in what is now the state of Minnesota. Due to continued legacies of colonization, genocide, and forced removal, generations of Dakhóta people remain disenfranchised from their traditional homeland. Presently, Mní Sota Makhóčhe has become a refuge and home for many Indigenous nations and peoples, including seven federally recognized Ojibwe nations. We humbly encourage our readers to reflect upon the historical legacies held in the lands they occupy.

milkweed.org

Milkweed Editions, an independent nonprofit publisher, gratefully acknowledges sustaining support from our Board of Directors; the Alan B. Slifka Foundation and its president, Riva Ariella Ritvo-Slifka; the Amazon Literary Partnership; the Ballard Spahr Foundation; *Copper Nickel*; the McKnight Foundation; the National Endowment for the Arts; the National Poetry Series; and other generous contributions from foundations, corporations, and individuals. Also, this activity is made possible by the voters of Minnesota through a Minnesota State Arts Board Operating Support grant, thanks to a legislative appropriation from the arts and cultural heritage fund. For a full listing of Milkweed Editions supporters, please visit milkweed.org.

Interior design by Tijqua Daiker & Mary Austin Speaker
Typeset in Baskerville

Baskerville is the most well-known of the typefaces designed
in the 18th century by British printer, type designer and papermaker
John Baskerville, who was also known to cut gravestones. The
typeface was used to print an edition of John Milton's *Paradise
Lost* in 1758, the *Holy Bible* in 1763, and the 1776 translation
of *The Works of Virgil* into English.